THE COWS

THE COWS

DAWN O'PORTER

HarperCollins*Publishers*

2

A catalogue record for this book is available from the British Library

ISBN: 978-0-00-812603-2

This novel is entirely a work of fiction. The names, characters and incidents portrayed in it are the work of the author's imagination. Any resemblance to actual persons, living or dead, events or localities is entirely coincidental.

Typeset in Berling LT Std by Palimpsest Book Production Ltd, Falkirk, Stirlingshire

Printed and bound in Great Britain by Clays Ltd, St Ives plc

MIX
Paper from responsible sources
FSC C007454

FSC™ is a non-profit international organisation established to promote the responsible management of the world's forests. Products carrying the FSC label are independently certified to assure consumers that they come from forests that are managed to meet the social, economic and ecological needs of present and future generations, and other controlled sources.

Find out more about HarperCollins and the environment at
www.harpercollins.co.uk/green

For Chris and Art.

COW [n] /kaʊ/:

A fully grown female animal of a domesticated breed of cattle, used as a source of milk or beef.

A cow is officially the name given to a heifer when it has had a calf.

If you want a good piece of meat, you need to go for the heifer because cows, having been destroyed by childbearing, do not a good steak make. Cows are incredibly complex animals; they form friendships and even fall in love, they experience fear, anger and can bear grudges.

Cows are destined to be in a constant hormonal state, either pregnant or producing milk. A heifer is a piece of meat, merely a potential source of produce. Beyond that, they don't offer much . . . apparently.

Some might say this is reflected in human society and the way that it regards women.

Some might not.

There are many types of women and every effort is needed for a woman not to be seen just as a heifer or a cow. Women don't have to fall into a stereotype.

Cows don't *need* to follow the herd.

1

A Late Friday Night in April

Tara

I see a bead of sweat pop out of his forehead and flop down his face like a melting slinky. He's nearly there, I can tell. Just a few more gentle pushes from me and this guy will explode with everything I need. He sniffs and hits his nose with the side of a clenched fist. I think it was an attempt to wipe it, but ends up being more of a punch in his own face. The sweat runs over his chin, down his neck and settles on his white collar. It rapidly spreads, forming a little wet patch then, as if on a factory line, another pops out and follows its exact journey. He's going to break any minute, I know it.

We've been alone in a small bedroom in a Holiday Inn just off the M4 for over three hours. I deliberately requested a room facing the road so that I could insist the windows had to be closed because of the noise of the traffic. It's boiling in here; the hottest day of the year, and I had to shut down the aircon because the camera picked up the noise. He won't be able to take it much longer. Me? I'll endure anything to get the soundbite I need.

He agreed to do the interview purely on the basis that it was just me and my camera in the room with him. The sleazy creep seems to have forgotten that the basic function of recording equipment is to capture a moment that could potentially be broadcast to millions.

I've been making a documentary about sexual harassment in the workplace for months. Shane Bower is the MD of Bower Beds, and I have interviewed multiple female members of his staff who have all told me about his wandering hands. Yesterday, I door-stepped him at nine a.m. as he left the house for work. I told him about the accusations and asked him what he had to say. He denied it, of course, and got into his car. I threw a business card in and instinct told me he'd be in touch. I was right; two hours later my phone rang. He asked me what my programme was about and what I wanted. I told him I was making a short film about sexual harassment for a new digital channel, and that I wanted to know if the allegations were true. He denied it on the phone, but I told him I had mounting evidence against him, and that he would be wise to try to convince the viewers of his innocence, because the footage would be broadcast with or without his contribution. Hearing that, he agreed to an interview. With only me. In a bedroom. I made sure the camera was recording the second he walked into the room.

'I don't doubt that you're telling the truth, Shane,' I say

from behind my camera. I'm lying. He's so guilty you can smell it on him.

'I just think the audience will be confused as to why so many of your staff seem to tell the same story. The one about you asking them to jump on the beds, then asking them to jump on your—'

'OK, OK, please, stop saying it,' he says, spitting and spluttering from all of his orifices, the wet patch on his collar now creeping down onto his shoulder. 'I love my wife,' Bower continues, and I see genuine fear in his eyes. He is stunned, like a spider in the middle of the night that freezes when you turn the lights on. But if you leave the lights on long enough, the spider will move. It has to.

I keep the camera rolling, he doesn't ask me to stop. I am always amazed by how people resist the truth to this point but then explode with it, almost like it's a relief to just get it out. He could shut this down and storm out, giving me no concrete proof and leaving himself open to wriggle his way out of all of this, but guilty people so rarely do. I hand them a rope, and they always hang themselves.

'My kids, they are everything to me,' he says, fluid pouring out of his face at such a speed I wish I had a dribble bib to offer him.

'If you're honest, then maybe it will all be OK,' I say, knowing I'll cut almost everything I have said and edit this to look like he built himself up to his own demise. And then he gives it to me, the most glorious line I could imagine.

'Those silly sluts acted like they were gagging for it. How is a guy supposed to know they didn't want it?'

Ahhhhhhh, beautiful!

I lower my camera, leaving it to record just in case he offers me any more nuggets of TV gold, but it really doesn't matter what happens now. I've got what I need. A confession. An end to my scene. The police can take it from here; I'll follow it up with them.

And I'm wrapped in time for lunch. Damn, I'm good at my job!

'Nailed it,' I say, throwing the camera cards down on my boss' desk.

'What, he confessed?' says Adam in his usual grating way – thrilled about the footage, worried he might have to praise me.

'Yup. The perfect confession. I got him, I told you I would.'

'OK Tara, stop acting like you're in an ITV cop drama. He was an easy target.'

'An "easy target"? I had to lock myself alone in a small room with him for hours to get that. There was nothing easy about it.'

Adam gets up from his desk and, taking the camera cards with him, walks into the main office, where he waves them and says, 'We got him.' There is a round of applause, as everyone realises that the show we have been plugging away at for months has a good ending. I stand behind Adam, watching him take the praise, wishing I had the guts to scream, 'THERE IS NO FUCKING "WE". I GOT THIS ALL BY MYSELF.' But of course, there is no 'I' in team.

'OK, Tara, Andrew, Samuel – can we have a quick meeting

in the snug, please?' Adam says, urging the three of us to follow him into a little room with multicoloured walls, bean bags, magazines, a TV and a big circular IKEA rug. It was designed to motivate creativity and it's where the development team come and pretend to work. They sit and watch hours of TV, read books, magazines and study the MailOnline to come up with ideas for TV shows. There are three of them, led by Samuel, and in the last two years only one of their ideas has actually made it to the screen. Not that it matters, but I'm on my fifth.

I dread these meetings, as I have to deal with three very strong male egos who all know I am amazing at my job but can't bring themselves to admit it. There is Andrew – Head of Production, Samuel – Head of Development, and Adam – the boss. People say TV is a male-dominated industry, and the reality of that is certainly true. It's odd though, because there are actually loads of women in television and a lot of them have high-ranking jobs. The problem is that when it comes to viewing figures, the general consensus is that women will watch male-centric programming, but men won't watch anything too female. So if everything is more male than female, then broadcasters won't lose the 'football' audience. Already, before a single programme has been made, they are saying that what women want to watch is less important than what men want to watch. This sexism filters up through the industry to the people who make the shows, and you can find it in all its glory right here in the offices of Great Big Productions.

As we sit down on the brightly coloured plastic bean bags, my faux-leather trousers make an enormous fart sound.

Everyone, of course, knows what caused the noise, but I can sense an element of doubt, and possibly hope, that I did just humiliate myself with a real guff. There is a pause for aroma, and when the air is confirmed clear, Adam starts the meeting.

'OK, so . . . oh no, wait, we need coffee,' he says, calling in his PA, Bev. I knew he would do this; he takes any opportunity he can to show me he is the boss, and this is a classic move of his. 'Can we get three coffees please, and some water?' he says as Bev enters the snug. She's wearing a skirt that's a little too short for work, and a white shirt that you can see her pink bra through. 'Chop chop,' he adds, hurrying her along so he can get on with his plan, which is to stare at her arse and make weird grunting noises as she walks away. There is a 'Phwoar' and a quiet, 'How's a guy supposed to get any work done?', a few other snorty sounds and of course, the glance at me, to make sure I am watching it all. I look directly at him, leaving no doubt that I have acknowledged his fake sexual intentions.

This is how Adam has tried to mask his homosexuality from me, since a moment two years ago when I walked in on him watching a men only three-way on the Internet. He panicked when he realised I could see his screen reflecting on the window behind him, and told me it was research for a show he was developing.

'About gay orgies by swimming pools?' I asked.

'Yes,' he answered, closing his computer but not getting up.

We never mentioned it again, and of course, I never saw a treatment for a show about gay orgies.

Since then, Adam has taken every opportunity he can to show me that he fancies women. Objectifying his assistant, Bev, is his signature move. I don't know why he isn't just honest about it, but he's more interested in being the big guy than the gay guy. I actually feel quite sorry for him, that level of denial must be exhausting.

'Shall we talk about work?' I suggest, wanting to move things along.

To cut a long story short, we are a TV production company who has realised that the future is online. Therefore, we are working to create digital content and multiple web series to build our online presence so that when TV becomes irrelevant, *we* are still relevant. We will make shows predominantly about real people in real situations, and I have been pulled in to head this up because I have a history of making brilliant TV shows about all echelons of society that my boss thinks would work excellently in fifteen-minute webisodes. He's right, because he's very clever, despite being incredibly rude and annoying. It's a massive deal for me as I've worked tirelessly for years on long-running and low-budget productions and now finally have this opportunity to make much 'edgier' (horrible TV word) programmes, with less Ofcom and more swearing. We're launching with my sexual harassment doc. It's going to be brilliant, and kind of my dream job. The downside is I have to spend a lot of time with these three.

'Just because we're now working on online content doesn't mean we can be more relaxed about money. The budgets are small. You realise that, don't you?' says Andrew, looking at me patronisingly, as if I have no concept of being thrifty. He's not particularly good at his job, and knows it. He uses rudeness to mask his fear of getting fired.

'Don't worry, Andrew. I won't use the budget to buy tampons and shoes. I think I can control myself.' I use rudeness to stick up for myself.

'And the hours will be long. Low budgets mean long days,' he continues, knowingly.

Oh, here we go! This is where I have to re-explain my situation, even though they already know it very well.

'I have to leave at five p.m. to pick Annie up from childcare,' I say. I am careful to say 'childcare', instead of 'my mum's'. They take it more seriously when they think I pay for it.

Queue the eye rolls from Adam, the stroppy huffing from Andrew, the switch of crossed legs from Samuel as I admit to being, as Andrew once put it, 'uncommitted'. They know exactly what they're doing, and they also know it will be fine.

'I can't get childcare beyond five thirty on weekdays,' I continue. 'You know this.'

'Can't you get your mum to have her when we get busy?' says Adam, pushing his luck.

'No, I can't,' I say, defiantly. Of course Mum could have her, but that isn't the point. I want some time with my daughter. I leave at five, that was the deal I signed when I started at Great Big Productions four years ago, and Adam has been trying to back out of it ever since.

'Fine,' says Andrew, huffing and crossing his arms like a petulant child. Samuel also tuts and crosses his legs in the other direction. The irony of the time they are wasting on this is beyond them.

'It's just not really fair though, is it? On the others?' Adam says. I know he doesn't actually have a problem with me leaving at five because it never affects my work. He's just found an opportunity to assert himself and he's taking it.

'I'm a single mother, Adam. Please don't "fair" me. I work full-time and all I ask is that I get out at five p.m. to pick my daughter up from childcare. I'm here two hours before anyone else in the morning and I haven't taken a sick day in three years. I do my job.'

He takes a few minutes to let the tension give me a headache before saying, 'Being "on the job" is what got you into this mess.' Cue dirty laugh, cackle, snort. Etc.

'Good one,' I say, sitting back on my bean bag, making another huge fart noise. 'Sorry, big lunch.'

That moves them on.

Cam

www.HowItIs.com
Camilla Stacey

I'm six foot one, an un-natural blonde and if I don't pay any attention to my eyebrows, they meet in the middle. I should also mention that I have quite freakishly large hands and feet and exceptionally long limbs. I appreciate I sound a bit like Mr Tickle and Cousin It's love child but actually, I'm kind of nice looking.

I look like I'm from the Amazon, but the truth is, I'm straight out of North London – my dad is from Woking and my mum's from Barnet. I'm just long with big hands, what can you do?

I've never had an issue with the way I look, despite my imperfections. I don't know about the fear of putting on a bikini, or taking my top off in front of a guy. I don't worry about my weight because I never gain any, no matter what I eat. I wear size ten clothes even though I'm probably a size eight, but need to go bigger because of my sprawling appendages.

My face is nice too, I like it. I look a bit like Emma Stone but with a stronger nose and more olive skin. My eyes are big and brown, I have freakishly long eyelashes and my cheeks are naturally blushed. My teeth are not straight, but I never considered getting a brace after Kate Moss made being a bit wonky really beautiful. I've taken a lot of time to absorb the way I look, not in a vain way, more in a scientific way. I've stared at myself naked many times, because it's my body and I should know it better than anyone else. I've squatted over mirrors to see what men see, and inspected my face with a magnifying mirror and counted my wrinkles. I know myself really well, because I've taken the time to do so. At thirty-six years old, I'm happy with who I am.

I suspect some people will read this and be angry

with me for being positive about my own image, because we're not supposed to do that, are we? We live in a world that celebrates being thin, or having big boobs or a nicely toned arse. Society encourages us all to get, and feel, beautiful. But the minute someone admits to enjoying their own appearance, we think they've taken it all a bit too far. But don't be angry with me for saying I like the way I look. I'm not saying I think I'm perfect, better than anyone else or desirable to all mankind, I'm just saying that body image isn't something that gets me down. I've got plenty of issues, but the way I look isn't one of them.

I can't be the only one who feels this way. So come on, what do you see when you look in the mirror?

Cam x

Stella

What do I see when I look in the mirror? I think to myself, as I eat the last mouthful of an all-butter croissant and finish reading Camilla Stacey's blog. I love Cam; Alice and I used to quote her best bits to each other. It's like she's always thinking what we haven't thought of yet. *What do I see in the mirror, Cam?* Well, my description of myself wouldn't be as positive as yours, that's for sure. It isn't that I don't think

I'm attractive; I have no issue with what I actually look like. It's just that looking in the mirror makes me either sad for my past or scared of my future. If all I could see was the way that I look, I probably wouldn't hate doing it so much. Instead I see the ghosts of my mum and sister staring back at me.

I scroll down my Facebook feed. As expected, it's flooded with messages.

Thinking of you x x

Hope you manage to smile today, I know that wherever she is Alice will be having a few glasses of Champagne x

Can't imagine how today must feel for you. I always remember the two of you and your wild birthday parties. Miss her so much. Lots of love x

Still doesn't feel real. Hope today isn't too painful. I'll be wearing my pink ribbon with pride x x

There must be twenty-five messages, saying anything but the words 'Happy Birthday'. I haven't seen most of these people since Alice's funeral five years ago but they still, every year, write these vacant messages all over my page. They probably wouldn't even remember if Facebook didn't remind them.

Looking through my feed, there are countless status updates about Alice, people claiming their relationships with her, outpouring their sadness. Hoping for sympathy and attention by writing pained messages about how much they miss her.

It's all so transparent. I've never even mentioned her on here; I hate attention-seeking posts. The ones where people write boldly or cryptically about the bad things in their lives, all with the hope their 'friends' post sympathetic messages. One, written by Melissa Tucker, a girl who went to school with us and who played netball with Alice, says,

Today is the birthday of one of the best friends I ever had. She was fun, and beautiful, and kind and generous. I've never known anyone else like her. RIP Alice Davies, the world is a darker place without you in it.

'Never known anyone else like her?' She was my *identical* twin sister. I don't know if Melissa is cruel or stupid, but I have to fight with myself not to write abusive words all over her page. Who says that?

I look at the little green dot to the bottom left of the screen, 'Alice Davies – online', and imagine her lying on her bed in our flat, posting silly things on her Facebook page like she used to.

I told everyone I shut her page down when she died, but I didn't. Instead I unfriended everyone and set her account to private. I am her only 'friend'. To everyone else it isn't there, but I can look whenever I like, and read all of her old posts. Like the one where she said she couldn't cook the sausage dish she wanted to do because the local Sainsbury's had run out of cherry tomatoes. It's the really mundane day-to-day ones that I love the most. Just her, plodding along, living life.

Every morning when I arrive at work, I log in to her account on my phone, so that when I am at my computer it says she is online. The little green dot makes me feel like she's right there, sitting on her bed, able to say hi at any moment.

'Hi,' says Jason, coming out of his office and making me jump. 'Sorry, didn't mean to startle you.'

I quickly shut down my Facebook page and open the company website, even though it would be weird if I was just sitting here looking at that. Jason probably won't look anyway, he's not that kind of boss.

'I have to go. Dreading this!' he says, standing in front of me with his arms crossed. This is Jason's default position; it's not defensive, or rude. It's just how his hands fall when he isn't holding his camera.

'Don't dread it. She just wants to hear how you're doing, right? You don't have to show her anything?' I say, reassuringly.

'Well I was supposed to hand the first draft in last week, so I'm going to have to explain why I didn't.'

'Just tell her it's coming along fine, and you're all set to meet your deadline. Can I make a suggestion? You need to go on shutdown – no TV or Internet until you've finished.'

'That sounds hideous. But maybe,' he says, uncrossing one of his arms to rub his face. He looks harassed, but it suits him. Jason is rugged, he never looks like he slept well, even if he says he did. He wears loose-fitting shirts with jeans as standard. He's tall and slim with an energy that means he finds it hard to sit still. His brain jumps from thought to thought, not giving him time to worry about what he says, so he often speaks out of turn – but the sparkle in his eye means he gets away with it. Part of his charm is how open and easy to be around he is. It's why he is so good at his job. Well, the photography part anyway; he's proving to be useless at writing books.

'I found an app that's basically a massive child lock for your computer, you won't be able to do anything until you've written a certain amount of words, wanna give it a go? I can also delete your social apps and create blocks for your phone?' I say, thinking it might be his only hope.

Jason takes his computer out of his bag and puts it in front of me.

'Go for it. I need to do something dramatic. Leave my laptop on my desk, I'll come in tomorrow to work. You can do my phone on Monday?'

'No problem.'

He stands for a moment too long looking at me. I raise my head, as if to urge him on.

'You're lucky you know, Stella. That your life doesn't grind to a halt if you can't think of anything to say, or write or take a picture of. You just come to work, then go home to your boyfriend in the house that you own, and tomorrow you know that everything will be the same, it will all be perfect. I envy you.'

Jason envies me? What? I have to stop myself standing up and screaming with such force that he'd fall backwards and hit the floor. He's jealous of *my* life? Has he any idea what it's really like? No, he doesn't. I've never told Jason anything about me. Not about Mum, Alice, my health. He just knows the basics – I live in London, in a flat I own, with my boyfriend

Phil. That's all my boss has ever needed to know. But it's odd, I think, that we come to this studio five days a week, eight hours at a time, talk almost constantly . . . well, *he* does. I'm not even sure how it's possible to skim over the depths of real life in this way and still get along so well, but it is, and we do. A successful working relationship has all the qualities of a bad relationship. If only spending this much time with a boyfriend was this simple.

'I'm not sure I'd call it perfect,' I say, playing down the massively imperfect situation that is my existence.

'Well it seems pretty good to me. You have a boyfriend, security. You'll get married, have kids. A proper family. I'll probably die alone in my studio after being knocked over the head by a falling tripod, or something equally as pathetic.'

He looks aimlessly across the studio, blue eyes still sparkling, despite his ageing, weathered face. Normally, we skirt around the personal details of our lives but there's something about writing this book that is making him relook at everything around him, including me.

'Actually, I'm jealous of *you*,' I say, gently, finding a little voice in the back of my head that feels the need to be heard. 'You get to create, and people are excited by that. You take photographs that change the way people think. Look at them,' I say, gesturing to the studio walls, where huge prints of his work keep me entertained every day. Portraits so detailed, it's as though the subjects' thoughts are written across their faces. 'You capture moments that we'd all miss if it wasn't for you showing them to us. And now you're writing a book. Something that will live even longer than you. A physical piece of evidence that proves you existed. Maybe fifty years from now, someone will be sitting in a hotel, or waiting at an airport, or going through bookshelves at a friend's house, and they will see a copy of your book. And they'll see your pictures and read your words and they'll wonder who the brilliant person was, who captured such stories. And they'll turn back to the front cover, where they'll see your name. And they will read aloud "Jason Scott" and they'll think about how clever you were, and how grateful they are for you inspiring them, and helping them pass that time. And then they'll put the book down and someone else will come along and they will love it too. That's your legacy. The great work, that you produced. You're the lucky one.'

There is a long pause as Jason looks at me quite intensely. He's so sexy, sometimes I have to imagine him on the toilet to get that out of my head.

'That sounded like a speech you've been rehearsing for weeks,' he says, having never heard anything so profound come out of my mouth. I'm quite militant, usually, I suppose. It's what he employed me for. He's a scatty artist who needs organising, and I like organising other people's things because it distracts me from the chaos in my own mind.

'I just think you should be proud of what you've achieved, even though it's hard work sometimes,' I continue, opening his computer as if to close the conversation.

'You're right. I should,' he says, watching me for a moment as I search for the Internet-blocking software and start to download it.

'You're good with words. Maybe you should write my

book?' he winks, playfully. He's only half joking. 'Up to anything tonight?'

'Actually, it's my birthday. So just a small dinner with Phil and some friends,' I say, as unexcited by the prospect as I sound.

'Bloody hell, Stella, you should have said, I'd have got you something. Where are you going?'

'Oh, nowhere glamorous. A nice tapas place on Bermondsey Street, Pizarro. Very chilled.'

'Is it a big one? Your sixtieth or something?' he says, finding himself pretty funny.

'Oi, watch it. No, I'm just plain old twenty-nine. Nothing special, no big deal.'

'OK, well, have fun. Get really drunk and do crazy stuff. I'll see you Monday.'

'See you Monday,' I repeat, watching him leave.

When the door closes, I push his computer aside and get back on mine. For a few moments I stare at the little green dot, willing it to do anything that shows me Alice is really there. Of course, it never will. I click onto her page and write,

Happy Birthday, sis. I miss you x

I pack up my things, and leave.

Tara

I rarely get to pick Annie up from school, so on Fridays, when she has dance class and comes out at four p.m., I always make sure I'm there. It means leaving work even earlier, but I grin and bear the guilt trips from my colleagues, because they're no contest for the mothers' guilt I suffer if I don't do it. Being a single working mum usually means that someone somewhere isn't happy with me. Whether it's work or my daughter, I'm usually having to apologise to one of them for not giving them enough of my time. This feeling of never being fully enough for anyone worries me a lot. Would I earn more and be better at my job if I didn't leave at five? Would my daughter be happier if I always left at four? Who knows what the answer is to getting all of this right; I don't, but I can't help but think the other mums at the school gate think I'm awful.

I've convinced myself they all judge me for my situation and therefore I make no effort to connect with them. This means they make little effort to connect with me either. They all stand around chatting like old friends, and I wait for Annie while answering emails on my phone, barely looking up to say hi. I'm sure they think I'm really full of myself or rude. I suppose I *am* rude; my lack of interest is deliberate, but if they made more effort with me I'd make more effort with them. Don't they think, 'Hey, she's alone. Raising a child by herself. Let's go over, make her feel part of the gang?' No, they don't. They just crack on talking among themselves, casually judging me because Annie doesn't have a dad and my mother does most of the childcare. Mum says I'm paranoid and they chat to her just fine, so it's obviously just that they have an issue with me. Well, who are they to judge? Is being a stay-at-home mum any better than working as much as I do? Are they happier than me? Who knows, and who cares. I was never able to just bond with other women purely on the basis that we both had kids. All of those classes for mums and babies where we were supposed to be open and share our feelings, offer advice, take help; I hated it. I felt like a beacon of controversy glowing in a room full of what everyone else considered normal. I quit the classes within weeks of starting them. Annie and my mum were all I needed. When you go at life alone you learn quickly to rely on as few people as possible. My village was small but indestructible. I was so happy in the comfort of my own decisions.

Five years later, here at the school gate, I still can't slot into this world. It's hard to know how to connect when you've spent the day squeezing information out of a sex pest and they've probably spent the day freezing individual portions of lasagna into zip-lock bags. I find it hard to stand around talking about parenting with people who do nothing but parent, they're a different breed. *Come on Annie, hurry up and come outside!*

'Tara!' shouts a friendly voice that throws me off guard. As I turn around I realise it's Vicky Thomson. Her daughter Hannah is in Annie's class. She's a bored housewife who is desperate to go back to work and thinks she could get a job in TV, despite having no experience. She relentlessly pitches show ideas to me like I'm Simon Cowell and have the power to change her life. Annoyingly, some of her ideas are quite good.

'I've been hoping to see you,' she says, hurrying up to me. 'I've been working on the idea I told you about,' she says, presuming I remember. 'I thought maybe you could take it further by trying to matchmake the gay people at the end?'

'OK, sorry, what?' I say, a little short. She's one of those people where if I give her too much feedback she won't leave me alone. She does nothing for my trying to be inconspicuous.

'My idea, "Take My Gay Away". The TV show idea about gay people whose parents won't allow it so they send them to a camp in America to get "un-gayed". You said you liked it, so I've been working on it more. Maybe we can pitch it to your company? I'm so ready to get back into work, three kids in six years, whoa. I need to think about something else now they're all in school, you know?'

'It's a great idea,' I say, politely.

'So what do you think, shall we pitch it to your company?' she pushes.

'I think it's interesting but we have something very similar in development, so I'm not sure it will work for us right now,' I say, giving the standard answer that I give when people pitch me ideas I kind of like. It covers my back, if I ever get around to stealing it.

'Oh, OK. Well, what about my one about the women who want penises but don't want society to see them as men?' she says, hanging off me like a puppy that can smell lamb in my pocket.

'Wait, that's a thing?' I say, the TV shark in me needing to know more.

'Yup, I found it on the Internet.'

'Jesus, what were you searching for?'

'Chicks with dicks,' she says, as if that's normal.

'Why?'

'I don't know really; I just wanted to know what it would be like to be a chick with a dick, I suppose.'

'Do you want a dick?'

'No.'

'Cool.'

The school doors bounce open and the kids flood out like spilt oil, slowing as they reach their parents. Annie is one of the last, slower than usual. I can tell she is sad.

'Annie, what's wrong?' I say, kneeling down and putting my face close to hers. 'Do you feel sick?'

She shakes her head slowly, and looks down.

'Did something happen at school? Was someone mean?'

'They weren't mean. But Trudy is having a party on Saturday and said I can't go because her mum said there wasn't room for me.'

'Why would she say that?' I ask her, not surprised. Trudy's mum seems like such a cow. She tutted at me for walking into the Nativity play late last Christmas. An actual tut. I'd had to leave a shoot early to get there; Adam gave me so much shit about it but I did it, I left so I didn't let Annie down, only to be tutted at for opening the door just as the Virgin Mary (Trudy) was trying to find a room for the night. It was hardly like bursting into the middle of a performance of *Macbeth* at the National Theatre, was it? I stood at the back and waved at Annie, who was on stage being the greatest donkey I'd ever seen. She waved back at me and one of her ears fell off. Trudy's mum tutted again. I didn't care that time; I knew I'd made Annie's night by being there whether I was late or not.

'OK,' I say, rubbing Annie's arms. 'Let's see about this, shall we?'

I take her hand, and march over to Trudy and her mum, who is giving someone else the details for Saturday's party.

'The theme is Disney,' she says, 'And bring your husband, the more the merrier.' As she finishes her sentence, she sees me storming up to her and coughs, as if that will drown out the words that she has just said.

'Hello,' I say, boldly.

'Hello. Come on Trudy, time to go.' She takes Trudy's hand and forcedly drags her away.

'Hang on,' I continue, with more welly in my tone. She stops, making the kind of strained face that suggests she doesn't want a scene. 'Annie tells me there is no room for her at the party, but I thought there might be a misunderstanding as Annie is such a special friend?'

'Um, well,' says Trudy's mum, looking around, hoping someone will rescue her, 'The house isn't big enough to accommodate everyone. The kids, their parents . . . ' she says. I am racking my brains to remember her name. Verity, maybe?

'I think maybe you thought she was busy?' I say, convincingly. I'm not letting her do this to Annie, it's really cruel.

'Trudy, would you like Annie at your party?' I ask, reaching for the big guns.

'Yay!' Trudy shouts, with pure joy on her face. Annie also lights up. I look at Trudy's mum with persuasive eyes that leave her no choice but to cave. She leans in to me, while Trudy and Annie try to hear what she says.

'I think you need to know that Annie has been saying inappropriate things to Trudy. I don't know what goes on in your home but I do not like it when my daughter comes home and asks me what a pervert is because her friend has told her that her mummy knows one.'

A lump forms in my throat. *Annie's being pushed out of her social group because of me?* That's a nice big mother's guilt pill for me to choke on.

'Look, she's obviously heard me on the phone talking about a programme I'm making about sexual harassment. I can assure you there is nothing untoward happening in our house. There are no perverts. In fact, I couldn't even tell you the last time a man came round. So, there you go, now you know about my job *and* my sex life. Now, Verity, can Annie come to the party or not?'

My job has trained me to ask for what I want. You don't get much from someone you are interviewing if you don't ask them questions.

Verity makes a strained 'for God's sake' face as she covers Trudy's ears in case I say anything else appalling. She then lets out a big, over-the-top huff. Annie, Trudy and I all stare at her, waiting for an answer.

'Come on, Verity,' I say. 'I'll speak to Annie about what she heard and I'll be more careful with my work calls. Please, don't take this out on her.'

'Oh, OK,' she says, buckling. 'Disney. One till three.' She snatches Trudy's hand and pulls her away. 'And my name is Amanda, not Verity.'

Wow, I was way off. God, not even close.

'There you go,' I say, kneeling back down to Annie. 'It's all fine, she just didn't realise how much you wanted to go. Happy now?'

'Yes. I need a costume,' she says, sweetly, and a little piece of me dies as I realise I now have to work out what she's going to wear. 'Can I be a princess?'

I stand up and take her hand as we walk back to the car.

'What did I say about girls being princesses? Remember?'

'You said that little girls don't have to be princesses.'

'That's right. That's what all the other little girls will do, so we should do something different, right?'

'Right!'

'That's my girl!'

'Mummy,' she says as I strap her into the car, 'what's a sex life?'

OK, I really need to watch my mouth.

Cam

'OK, love, that's all the shelves up,' says Cam's dad, coming out of her bedroom. She's sitting in the window seat of her gorgeous new flat, wondering where to put the chaise longue she found on eBay that just got delivered. 'Need anything else before I go?'

'No thanks, Dad. That's it.' She looks at him lovingly. 'It doesn't matter how grown up I am, I'll always need my dad to come and put my shelves up for me, won't I?'

'I hope so. Even if you don't, you always have to pretend you still need me, OK?' he says, going over to her for a cuddle. They both know Cam is as good at DIY as he is. Her asking him to help is always for his benefit, not hers.

'I'm so proud of you, Camilla. I worked all my life and I'm not sure I ever achieved as much as you have.'

'You kept four daughters alive, Dad. I'd say that was a pretty big achievement.'

'Yup, my life certainly became about you guys, that's for sure.'

Cam looks at him sympathetically. She's always been so tuned-in with her dad, much more than her siblings were. Before Tanya was born, the oldest of Cam's three sisters, he worked as a comedy promoter all over the country. It wasn't stable work, and involved lots of late nights that didn't work well with a baby, so he quit. Not really being qualified in anything, he got a job in a local school as a caretaker, and was there until he retired four years ago. He never enjoyed it; it was uncreative, hard and demanding. But he stuck with it, because he's a great dad, and that's the kind of sacrifice people make when they have kids.

'I always told you that success is just being happy, didn't I?' he says. 'People put too much emphasis on it being about money. I was never rich, but you guys were all healthy and happy and no matter what I ended up having to do during the day, coming home to that made me feel like the wealthiest man alive.'

'Yup, you always said that,' Cam says. She knows he doesn't really mean it. If it had been down to him, he'd have carried on promoting comedy and they'd all have made do. But Cam's mum wanted stability, and her dad is a good enough guy not to argue with that. 'But I fucking love being rich,' she says, giving him a gentle dig in the ribs.

They both laugh.

'Don't let your mum hear you use that language,' he says, and of course she never would. Cam and her dad have always shared the same sense of humour and a mutual understanding. He's the only person in her family who doesn't question her choices, and she's desperately in love with him because of that.

'You were always different from the others, Camilla. You stuck to your guns, never tried to be what people expected of you. I'm proud of you, kid.'

'Jesus, Dad! Will you stop. I've just moved in, no tears are allowed in this flat, even happy ones.' They hug again. Before she pulls away she whispers in his ear, 'Thank you.'

'What are you thanking me for? You did this all by yourself.'

'I did, yes. But because you always encouraged me to be myself. I'm not like the other girls, and you let me work out how to be happy my own way.'

'I had no choice. There was no other way you could be,' he says, as he leaves their embrace and heads for the door. 'Call me if you need anything else doing, OK?'

'I will.'

'And don't have any boys round.'

'Oh, Dad! OK, go. Mum will shout at you for being late for dinner. I love you. Bye.'

Cam pushes him out of the door. 'Careful on the stairs,' she says as she closes it, and leans back against it when it's shut. Looking around her flat, she lets a huge smile creep across her face. A 1.2 million, two-bedroom, Victorian flat in Highgate, with views across London. She's sourced furniture from the period the house was built, and she's mixing that with huge pieces of bold, modern art. It's bright, beautiful and all hers. It's in an area of London people only dream of living in. She can't believe it.

Falling back onto the pea green, Victorian-style chaise longue, she reaches for her laptop and rests it on her thighs. Opening *HowItIs.com*, she gloats at what it has become. It not only earns her in the region of £20,000 a month in advertising revenue, but it also earns her notoriety, an audience. It gives her a voice. Cam was never great with people, but she always had a lot to say. This unfortunate mix made school tough going; someone with a head full of thoughts but no outlet for them tends to think too much and say too little. In her case, this personified itself as social awkwardness that other kids saw no fun in, so she inevitably became bit of a loner. Until the Internet burst onto the scene in her early twenties and she finally had a way to show the world who she really was, a chance to express herself without the pressure of social interaction. It completely changed her life.

There are boxes stacked up along the walls, and the TV is still in the box on the floor. Her Internet won't be connected for a few days, so she's using a dongle, meaning she'll never be anywhere she can't blog from. This commitment to her output is what's made her what she is.

As one of the first successful lifestyle bloggers, she has held her place as the 'go-to destination for straight-talking women'. Or so said *The Times* in their list of 'what's hot for the year ahead'. 'The Cam Stacey seal of approval is what every woman wants . . . ' (*Guardian*, Jan 2016). With nearly two million subscribers and eight major advertisers signed up, she is raking in the pennies and clawing in the love. But that isn't to say she doesn't have to be careful. Blogging is a dangerous game, especially if you're talking about women and being as outspoken as Cam so often is. Women want role models; they get behind high-profile females who pave the way for forward thinkers and they hail them as heroes, but if they drop the ball, say the wrong thing or talk a little *too* controversially, they get thrown to the lions.

It happened to a friend of hers last year. A lovely woman, Kate Squires. She wrote about being a working mum, with a high-powered job in a PR firm, and became a real inspiration, with nearly 50,000 Twitter followers. Working mums everywhere looked to Kate for positive inspiration on how to 'juggle' the work–life balance, but then one day she fucked it all up with one little tweet. One silly little tweet that changed the course of her life.

Women without kids, u just don't understand how hard it is to get home & have to look after something other than yourself. #NeedMeTime

The infertile population of the planet came out in their droves. Kate had personally offended every woman with reproductive issues on Twitter and beyond. What she had said was so hurtful that *The Times* covered a story of one woman who, after three miscarriages, tried to commit suicide after reading Kate's tweet. 'It just struck me when I was so, so down,' she'd said. 'I felt like society was telling me I have no value as a woman because I can't have kids.'

People were right to be offended – it was an insensitive

thing to say, but did she deserve an online hate campaign and the succession of terrible things that happened next? Cam followed the case with sympathy but a sharper eye on what she could learn. That tightrope between leading the social commentary and following it is hard to walk. It takes focus, planning and careful attention to detail not to fall off when you live in a world where 140 characters could ruin your life.

Kate wrote the customary, 'I didn't mean to hurt anyone, I just had a really hard day,' tweet, but it didn't do any good. She went on *Loose Women* and made some heartfelt but slightly pathetic apology wearing a floral dress and batting her best Princess Diana eyes. On leaving the studio, she was confronted by campaigners with placards saying 'NON-MOTHERS HAVE FEELINGS TOO'. This was televised on almost every news channel and Kate's image was branded as the face of society's issues with childless women. She appealed to be forgiven, but social media just couldn't do it. Within weeks, she was offline and out of sight. Her PR firm sacked her, saying it was impossible to have someone with a public image like Kate's representing them. She's now out of work and struggling to get a job, her husband left her because she went so nuts, and she lives in a small flat in south London as opposed to her big house in Penge. Kate barely answers the phone; Cam hasn't spoken to her for months. Her whole life turned upside down because of one sleepy little tweet.

Cam watched and learned.

She's managed to find that careful balance of pushing boundaries, being brave, but not offending. Of course she gets the occasional knob who hates her, but she's generally strong enough to ignore those. She's often the target of more conservative feminists who seem to think her attitude to sex is why so many men sexually abuse women, but Cam's aim is to promote the many facets of modern feminism, and pissing off 'The Traditionalists' is just a part of that. Even the rape threats she got after writing quite a punchy piece about Bill Cosby didn't knock her down. It would take a lot more for someone to turn up at her door and physically assault her than it does for them to tweet, 'I'd bend you over a car and make you sorry for saying that.'

Most people online are full of shit. Part of survival in the digital age is to fully appreciate that, and Cam's down with it. But women's rights are a delicate subject. There is one fight – feminism – but there are many different types of woman, and pleasing them all is impossible.

Just as her eyes are falling closed, she gets a text.

This must be yours, it's got your name on it. Want it back?

Attached is a picture of her twenty-eight-year-old lover's erect penis; he has written CAM around the base in felt-tip pen. She thinks of her 600-count cotton sheets and hopes that it is washable . . .

bring pizza and penis x

Suddenly, she's not so tired.

Stella

'I'll get the cod fritters and the lamb,' I tell the waiter taking our order. He's been standing there for ages, waiting for me to decide what to have. It's my birthday, I'm allowed to be annoying. I'm also trying to kill some time; Phil is being weird and Jessica is being excitable, and I'm not really in the mood for either of them.

'Sooooo, Mike and I have some news,' says Jessica, my oldest friend, the only one who made any particular effort with me after Alice died, and didn't make it all about her. She's one of those rare and extraordinary people who genuinely likes herself, and doesn't rely on affirmation from pretend friends. She's sweet, but her energy levels are challenging. Phil doesn't understand why I haven't told her what I'm going through, why he alone is shouldering the knowledge of my family legacy. But it's not straightforward with Jessica; she's never experienced trauma. She's a good friend because she's loyal, but trying to talk to her about my life makes me feel like the most fucked-up person of all time. What is the point in sharing your pain with someone who can't empathise anyway? One of the reasons I got together with Phil was because his dad died when he was fourteen. Something in his tragedy allowed me to open up about mine. And anyway, he's my boyfriend, it's his job to take the burden of my problems. The only thing Jessica and I really have in common is history, but as Phil so often says, I should have at least one female friend, so here I am, about to hear her announcement.

Phil stiffens and goes to leave the table, but I put my hand on his knee and make him stay. I need him to stay. Whether we are falling apart or not, he is my partner, and I need a partner. One person by my side. I'm not enough on my own.

'I'm pregnant,' Jessica bursts, as if we didn't know what it means when a newlywed says she 'has some news'. She's so happy, it's oozing out of her. I know I can be a real bitch in situations where people around me express joy, so I try not to do that to Jessica; she doesn't deserve it.

'Congratulations,' I say, leaning across the table and taking her hand in some weird, regal way. 'When are you due?' I ask, doing my best not to look jealous.

'January 1st. I bet it comes New Year's Eve, the party animal,' she says, snuggling up to Mike, who is also incredibly nice if quite boring. He is smiling, looking happy as anything with his new wife and embryo. In contrast, Phil is playing with his fork like a six-year-old staring at an iPad. I feel the need to overcompensate for both of us, so I get up, walk around the table and give Jessica a proper hug. 'So happy for you,' I say, reaching over to Mike and hugging him too. 'You'll be the best parents.'

'Thanks, we are so happy. Now hurry up you two, this little one is going to need a playmate,' she says, beaming.

'Yup, we're on it,' I say, a little too enthusiastically. Phil drops the fork and starts reading the menu, even though we have already ordered. He used to be so sociable, so upbeat. It's what attracted me to him. I need that person by me, someone more flamboyant, more attractive to others, more sociable. It's how Alice was. Her social skills made us the most popular girls in school. Everyone wanted to hang out with the

Davies Twins. But in truth, they liked the novelty of twins but only one of the set. I wasn't a good friend to people like Alice was. My spiky nature didn't draw them in like her warmth did. Without her, I would never have been popular. When she died, it didn't take long for it to be screamingly obvious that without a more likable counterpart, no one was bothered about keeping me as a friend. Apart from Jessica, whom I keep sweet to stop Phil trying to set me up with other potential girl mates, because he thinks that is what I need.

'OK, who is the birthday girl?' says the waiter, coming back to the table. He's carrying a bottle of champagne and four glasses.

'That'll be that one,' says Mike, pointing at me. Jessica grins at him.

'Wow, champagne? Thanks,' I say, rubbing Phil's leg. He hasn't done anything like this in a while. Romantic gestures used to be quite normal.

'No, what?' he says, looking concerned. 'We didn't order this?'

'No you did not! A "Jason Scott" called the bar and asked us to bring this over,' the waiter says, clarifying. I feel myself blush a little, I'm not sure why.

'Ooooooh, that's so sweet,' says Jessica. 'Maybe I'm allowed a tiny glass?' she says, looking to Mike for approval. He nods, and the waiter starts to pour. 'So, is Jason still as dreamy as ever?' Jessica asks.

'Ha!' I say, genuinely touched by the gesture; a little gobsmacked, if I'm honest. 'Yeah, he's still pretty dreamy. But no, weird, he's my boss. And I've only got eyes for Phil. Cheers.'

I hold up my glass, but only two join it in the air. A huge screech fills the restaurant as Phil scrapes his chair back and stands up.

'Sorry,' he says, realising he caused a scene. 'I'll be back in a minute.' He walks off quickly towards the toilets, and I sit alone with Jessica and Mike, trying to pretend like everything is normal.

Tara

'I'll come pick you up by noon tomorrow,' I say to Annie, kissing her goodbye.

'Come any time, we'll take the dog out in the morning and have bacon and eggs,' says Mum. She's so brilliant, despite finding my choices and lifestyle almost impossible to think about. She's so desperate for me to find a father figure for Annie that she has agreed to have her every Friday night so that I can go on dates. 'Just don't tell your father about this,' she tells me every week as I leave the house. 'You know he can't bear to think of you with boys. The fact you got pregnant as you did, well, it nearly killed him. You proved all fathers right!'

She's funny, my mother. Somewhere between liberal and conservative and I never really know which way she'll go.

'I know, Mum. If you could remind him that I'm forty-two, that would be great. Anyway, look at what we got out of it?' We both peek through the hall door and into the living room. Annie is taking selfies on Mum's iPhone.

'She needs a father figure,' Mum says.

'She doesn't *need* one, Mum, we're fine. But it would be nice for her to have one. And it would also be nice for me not to die alone.'

'Do you have a date set up for tonight?' she asks.

'I do. He looks OK, works in media, cute. Hopefully not a murderer.'

'Tara, please. Don't joke. I read about a girl getting murdered on a date. It's not funny.'

'Mum, people have been dating a long time. But OK, I'll try not to get murdered.' I open the front door. 'Give my love to Dad.' I shut the door, then quickly open it again. 'By the way, what does he think I do on Friday nights?'

I'm curious to know what Mum came up with, because she's right, the idea of me being with men makes my dad convulse.

'I told him you've started a knitting group.'

'What? Mum, that's pathetic.'

'You might have to buy something on eBay and pretend you made it for his birthday. Sorry, I panicked. It was the first thing that came to my head.'

I hug her, and leave. She opens the door a few seconds later and shouts, 'You don't have to sleep with them all, Tara!' down the street.

Was that liberal or conservative? I can't quite be sure.

Back at home I have a quick shower, slip on a cute silk shirt with my faux-leather trousers, a bit of make-up, bouff my hair and I'm ready. I gave up making too much effort on dates ages ago. I always wonder what it must look like to guys, who just wear whatever they wore to work that day, when a woman arrives dressed to the nines in something fancy, with loads of make-up. It sets a precedent at the start that I really can't be bothered to maintain, so I wear a mildly more uptempo version of my usual clothes. I think that's right. Although I'm still single, so I guess that says something.

Being single when you have a kid is weird. Not just because everyone you meet either judges or sympathises with you, but because you have to think about so much more than just fancying someone. It's called being responsible, I suppose. I can't allow fuck buddies into my home to meet my daughter, it would be too confusing for her, so I generally don't have them at all. That's good for Annie but it sucks for me.

Annie has never known me to be in a relationship, so I need to handle the situation carefully. I introduced one guy to her last year because he was so completely awesome. I seemed to abandon all elements of fear when it came to Annie and invited him into our lives. Turns out he was so awesome that he was married. Because obviously, excellent men in their forties are never single. Why would they be? Fuckers.

He spent a Saturday afternoon in my house making Annie laugh so hard she went to bed giddy with joy. When she was asleep he and I started having sex and halfway through, his phone wouldn't stop ringing. Eventually, because it was really killing the mood, he answered it, then burst out crying. It was his wife letting him know that his dad had just had a heart attack and died. He was literally inside me as he took the call. I mean, it was possibly the worst thing to happen during sex since those two people in China were doing it up against a floor-to-ceiling window in their apartment and the window fell out. He was so devastated, I couldn't even have a go at him about not telling me he was married. I had to comfort him, when what I really wanted to do was cut his penis off with some nail scissors and throw it in the road. I was also just really, really gutted.

He left minutes later and I never heard from him again. Annie still asks for him; she refers to him as 'Mr Giggles'. One day I'll tell her that Mr Giggles ended up being about as funny as a dose of the clap. Which, along with the terrible memory of a horrible evening, he also left me with.

Taking treatment for an STD when you have a little girl feels grim. I felt ridden and contagious and begged the bottle of antibiotics to be finished. When they were gone, I vowed never to introduce her to anyone ever again unless a) I was certain they didn't have a wife and b) I hadn't needed an STD test after sleeping with them.

I now hold a lot of hope for my Friday night dates. I want someone good. Someone honest, safe and fun. You never know; tonight's guy, Al, looks OK in his picture. But first, a quick drink with my best friend Sophie.

'Sorry I'm late,' says Sophie, walking slowly up to me at the bar. 'I was getting my hair done, she was taking ages then I decided I didn't like the colour so got her to go back to . . . anyway, heyyyy.'

Sophie is always late, which is why I brought my Kindle.

Sophie and I are both only children. This means that we

have a relationship a lot like sisters and claimed each other around the age of ten, as the people who would play that role in each other's lives. I questioned it loads, because she drove me so crazy half the time. Then another friend at school said that if her sister wasn't family, they would never be friends, but she loved her anyway, because that is what sisters do. That really resonated with me because I realised that if Sophie was to be the sister I never had, it was OK and normal for us to not always see eye to eye. I just had to love her, which I did and still do, because we have history – and you can't erase that, no matter how many times someone prioritises a blow dry over spending time with you.

'Hair looks nice,' I say, because it does. It always does, she's gorgeous. Skinny, blonde, perfect skin. It's annoying, but mostly natural. Other than the hair colour.

'Thanks. OK, can we drink champagne? I feel like I need something fizzy.'

I order two glasses but she shouts for a bottle. So there we are, sitting at a bar at 6.40 p.m. on a Friday, drinking champagne for no real reason.

'I only have twenty minutes. I have a date with a guy called Al at seven.' I smile a little, I have that pre-date hopeful buzz . . . maybe it will be a good one. But probably not.

'God, I can't believe you're still dating, I can't even imagine,' she says. 'Mind you, I never really dated like you do. Carl was my only ever formal date and I ended up marrying him, so it clearly works. Cheers to that!'

I still can't accept that Sophie is married; she was so wild, almost feral. I don't think I have ever met anyone with such a hungry attitude towards sex and partying. Her stamina for both was always fascinating to me.

'So how is Carl?'

'He's good, yeah. You know, same old. Marriage is fine most of the time, as long as I don't mention my past.'

'Still, really?'

'Yup, it's the big sexy elephant in the room. I mean he doesn't know anything of course, I'd never tell him. But he's made all these assumptions about me, and the kinds of things I used to get up to. Annoyingly, they're all pretty accurate.'

'But where's he getting it all from?' I ask.

'He says he can't understand how someone who looks like me didn't get loads of sex when I was single.'

'OK, you know that is actually quite insulting, right?' I say, as I realise it is insulting, but that Carl is absolutely right. Sophie got a *lot* of sex.

'Yesterday, Beth Taylor, remember her from school? She tagged me in an old photo on Facebook. It's a picture of a load of us, we were about seventeen, and in the background I'm snogging some guy. She tagged me and wrote, "This is how I remember you, Sophie. Hope you're well." What a fucking idiot, why would she do that?'

'Yeah, I saw that. I thought it was funny. And I suppose most people in their forties aren't married to people who would give them a hard time for snogging someone when they were seventeen?'

'True. Maybe, but still. I have to be so careful. He's just so old fashioned and I need this to work. It's just easier if I edit my past a little. The fucking Internet means I have to be on guard all the time. Anyone could tweet me, or post a picture of me from back then. Do you remember that time we went to Ibiza, the foam party? Thank God it was just before camera phones, but what if someone had one of those disposable cameras we all used to have and stumbles across me on Facebook? There's probably pictures of me up to all bloody sorts. Jesus, I told Carl I'd never done drugs. He'd lose his shit if he knew the kind of stuff we used to do. As it is, every time a Facebook memory comes up I break into a cold sweat!'

I drink some champagne. 'Hey, we had fun though, didn't we?' I say, giving her a wink.

'I'll drink to that!'

I don't know how Sophie does it, being married to someone who won't accept her for who she is. Playing a new role, with a new past. Watching Sophie coordinate her life around hiding who she was – is? – from her husband has been such a lesson to me, in terms of what I want. There is no way I want to find someone who won't take me for what I am. I don't want to have to lie, or hide, or deny anything. Sophie would never admit it, but she married Carl because she partied her entire life and isn't qualified for anything she would enjoy, so a rich city guy was the only way she'd end up in a nice house and money to buy bottles of champagne when you only have twenty minutes to drink it in, and absolutely nothing to celebrate. I'd rather be poor and lonely.

'OK, I better go, don't want to be late for my hot date,' I say, stepping down off the barstool. 'Here's some money for the champagne.'

'Oh, don't worry, that's what this is for,' she says, flashing

Carl's credit card. 'Oh, and if he asks can you tell him we were with a bunch of people? It would make things easier.'

'Sophie, we've been best friends since we were at primary school, does he still not like us going out together?'

'Nope. When it's only us he presumes we get up to bad stuff, that you're a bad influence. Don't look at me like that! Please, just say it was a few old faces from school. The more eyes he thinks are on me, the better he'll think I behaved, OK?'

I sit back down.

'It's quite controlling, Sophie. It worries me,' I say, forcing her to look me in the eye. She offers a little smile, then breaks away.

'Maybe I need a bit of controlling?' she says, sipping the champagne. 'I can't be left to my own devices, who knows what would happen.' She shoots me a critical look, and I know what she means. We partied hard for most of our lives, but after I had Annie I had to stop. It became immediately clear that despite being wild myself, I was nothing compared to Sophie. Somehow, over the years I had stopped her from spiralling too far out of control. I hadn't even realised I did it, but I took her home when she'd had too much, I dragged her out of bedrooms she shouldn't have been in, I stopped her snorting more lines of coke than she should, prised shot glasses out of her hand. When I got pregnant, there was no one around to do that for her and we saw the danger of that instantly. I was six months gone when I found myself in A&E one Friday night. The hospital called me at two a.m., saying she'd been found in an alley with her skirt around her waist, so out of it she could barely say her name. I'd gone in immediately and found her crying in the hospital bed. She'd been roofied by a barman in a club. There were no signs that he'd done anything sexual to her, but judging by the bump on her forehead and the state of her clothes, he had obviously tried.

'I can't look after myself,' she'd said, pathetically, looking up at me from the bed. 'And you can't look after me any more, so I don't know what I'm going to do.'

I took her home and I did look after her, for a whole week. But then she went back to her place, to 'start afresh'. She was determined to change, to grow up. There were a few more 'incidents', but then she met Carl. They were married within a year, and now she is being looked after as she wished, and as uncomfortable as it makes me feel, I know she is probably better off for it. And she does love him, because he's rich.

'He's good to me in other ways,' she says, flashing the card again. 'I'm happy, I promise. I love you.'

'I love you too,' I say, loyally. 'I have to go.'

She pours herself another drink, and I remind myself it's not my problem any more.

I walk into the Sanderson Hotel on Berners Street and look around the bar. This place is way more fancy than anywhere I would choose; I'm more a pub girl than a bar girl but hey, I'm not going to say no to posh drinks in a nice place if that is what the gentleman so wishes. I'm here to meet Al; his picture was nice, he works in the media, and he was free tonight. Those are three great reasons to go on a date, as far as I'm concerned. Mostly the bit about his picture being nice, of course.

I scan the bar and see him. He's cute, but the photo was obviously an old one. His hair is much longer now, and his face much older. But that's OK. I don't judge people for using the most flattering photo of themselves for online dating, of course they do. Therefore, I always expect to be a little bit disappointed in real life, and hope their personality makes up for it. Al certainly looks older than his photo, but as I get closer to him, I realise he's really, really gorgeous.

'Hi,' I say, sitting on the stool next to him. 'This is so fancy, do you come here often?'

I'm joking. Obviously. No one ever actually says, 'Do you come here often?' He looks a little surprised that I take a seat. Was I supposed to ask his permission?

'No, I haven't been here before actually. I'm not the kind of guy who comes to places like this, if I'm honest.'

'OK,' I say, thinking it odd that he suggested it then. I'd never come to a posh hotel bar like this either, they reek of affairs.

'What are you drinking?' I ask, presuming he's just a little nervous.

'A Pisco Sour.'

'Great, I'll have the same.' I gesture to the barman to bring me one over.

'Just a drink though, OK? I'm not up for anything else,' he says, sternly.

I am so stunned, the best response I can give him is my jaw falling open.

'Sorry,' he says. 'I don't mean to be rude. But I don't like leading people on.'

'I literally just walked in the door. Maybe I don't fancy you either, thought of that?' I say, stepping down off the stool.

'Well, I suppose if you're doing well and in a position to be picky, then that would make sense.'

'Doing well? What? Just because I swiped right on your weird photo doesn't mean I was gagging for you, it's just dinner.' I should walk away, but after dealing with Shane Bower and my boss, I'm done with not arguing back to misogynistic arrogant men who think it's their God-given right to belittle women. Screw him.

'I bet you're married with kids and looking for some young piece of ass to fuck before you go home to them, aren't you?' I continue, a little surprised by my own vitriol.

'Woah. Firstly, no, I'm not married and I don't have kids. Secondly, what the hell does swiping right mean?'

'What do you mean, "what the hell does swiping right mean"? Tinder. You know what I mean.'

'Tinder? I've never been on Tinder in my life,' he says, looking genuinely baffled.

I look properly at his face.

'You're not Al, are you?'

'No, I'm not Al. And I take it you're not a hooker?'

'No! No, I am certainly not a hooker.'

He follows my eyes to the other end of the bar, where a guy with shorter brown hair in a grey shirt is angrily tapping away on his phone and simultaneously looking towards the door. I get my phone out of my bag. I have five messages from Al, each describing himself in more detail and asking 'Which one are you?'

'I'm Jason,' he says, reaching a hand towards me.

'Tara,' I say, realising I am wildly attracted to him.

The barman brings over my drink.

An hour later, Jason and I have drunk three Pisco Sours, eaten two bowls of crisps, a bowl of olives and torn up three swanky bar mats. We've talked about politics, how much we miss our childhood dogs, and even had a heated but jovial altercation about the correct way to make a good Bolognese.

As we appear to be having an unexpected but sensational connection that feels like a date, I notice the real Al leave with a woman in a very tight dress.

'There you go,' Jason says, 'Al did alright in the end. In one hundred pounds' time it'll be like it never happened.'

'I made a lucky escape,' I say, sipping the last of my drink, allowing my eyes to flirt for me. 'So you're single, you don't have kids, you don't sleep with hookers and you don't use Tinder. You were also just sitting in a bar alone on a Friday and not waiting for someone. Now tell me, what is wrong with you?' I ask, cheekily.

'Hey, I love hookers. I just didn't fancy you.'

I affectionately thump him on the leg.

'I'm old fashioned, I guess. And hopeful. I don't use Tinder because the idea of it doesn't sit right with me. I think I'm single because I'm picky and I pick the wrong women. And I'm sitting here alone because my publisher summoned a meeting to assure her that my book was coming along, and after a right royal rollicking I have been sitting here and pretending it's all fine for the last two hours.'

'Your publisher? You write?' I ask, finding that painfully sexy.

'Actually no, I'm a photographer. But I'm doing my first book and I stupidly agreed for there to be a lot of words as well as pictures. My deadline is in three weeks. My assistant has locked me out of the Internet and I'm about to crawl into a cave to get it finished.'

'What's the book about?'

'Well my work is usually centred around people, and mostly people not being who they seem. I did a big story for *The Times Magazine* about multi-millionaires who live like they're on the dole, and it got picked up as a book. It's great, but the article was a thousand words and this will be around forty thousand words and I seem to write approximately ten words every seventeen hours.'

'Wow. I read that article, it was fascinating. Your work is amazing. Why would anyone not spend all that money? It's bizarre,' I say. 'I have so many questions I don't know where to start.'

'Good. Then don't. I don't mean to be rude, but until tomorrow morning I would like to pretend it isn't happening. Can we talk about anything but work?'

'Sure. I don't mind,' I say, really enjoying the idea of that. My life consists of only work and Annie, and as much as I love them both, a night off would be nice.

'But sorry. I should ask you what you do, shouldn't I?' he says, realising it might be rude not to.

'Yup, you probably should. I work in TV. Documentaries. I love what I do, it's challenging and diverse but the details can wait. You're right, it's Friday night and we have other things we should be talking about, don't we?'

'We do?'

'Yes, we do. You said you date the wrong women, so who are these "wrong women"?' I ask, hoping he doesn't describe me.

'Just that. Wrong for me. I'm extremely turned on by ambition and success, so go for women who have achieved a lot, but the downside of that is that they never seem to want kids. And I'm one of those guys who is desperate for a family. I want to fall in love and have babies. But I'm starting to think that's the unsexiest thing a man can say, because whenever I say it I get dumped.'

'Oh,' I say, feeling like a piece of old meat that's well past its sell-by date.

'See? That's what happens. I tell women I want kids and they make that face. The perils of being an old-fashioned man in a modern woman's world.'

'No, I think it's nice you want kids, and you want to do it properly. And that you think it's a woman's world,' I say, pushing my empty glass gently towards the other side of the bar. 'I actually have a kid. A girl, Annie, she's six. I mean, there's no way on earth I'm having another, no way, but she's my world.'

'Who's her dad?' he asks, bluntly.

'Wow, you went straight there, didn't you?' I say, stunned by his nerve, but also relieved by the idea of getting it out the way. I think of Sophie, in that hideous marriage where her entire life is a lie. I'm not doing that. If this goes anywhere, he's going to have to take me for who I am.

'A guy called Nick. I never caught his surname.' I open my eyes wide and raise my eyebrows, as if to say, 'Go on, bring on the judgement.'

'OK, that's . . . was it a one-night stand, or something more sinister?'

'Oh no, nothing sinister. A one-night stand. A very quick, very nice one-night stand where one of my eggs got jiggy with one of his sperms. And before you ask how he reacted, he doesn't know. I never told him.'

I don't look up. Fuck it. I'm forty-two. I'm a mother. I'm very specifically looking for someone to be a part of mine and Annie's life and if he can't take the truth about me, then what's the point in us having another drink? I prepare myself to be rejected.

He calls the waiter over.

'Can I get a bottle of champagne, please?'

'What's that for?' I ask, a little confused.

'If this works out, I just got a free kid.' He thumps my leg back and laughs.

This guy is fucking brilliant.

Stella

I stare at my reflection in the bathroom mirror and force myself not to look away. There is a reason I don't do this very often. It's impossible to forget someone whose face you see every time you see your own. At times it seems cruel, at other times I've felt so lucky that when I need to see Alice, I can.

I scrunch my nose up and widen my mouth, but I can't quite manage it the way she used to. It was the only way people could really tell us apart, by her smile. It was her own, even I couldn't do it so sweetly.

Our mum used to say that she was the rose and I was the thorn. Part of the same flower, but with a totally different effect on the world. My spiky nature was hidden by her softness. Now I'm exposed, without the petals of her personality to hide behind. It's a daily struggle not to prick anyone who comes near me.

'Why are you wearing that?' says Phil, coming into the bathroom.

'You made me jump, I didn't hear you get home,' I say, snapping myself out of Alice mode. He puts a tube of toothpaste into the little cup by the sink, and starts unwrapping a new razor.

'Did you get dinner? I was going to make tuna bake?' I say, realising he's been to the shop and wanting to distract him from his question.

'I got chicken. Why are you wearing that, Stella?'

He is referring to the skirt I have on. A purple and blue vintage circle skirt with a bird print on it. It was Alice's. Her favourite item of clothing. I can't bring myself to chuck it out and I wear it all the time, even though it makes Phil really angry when I do.

'It's just a skirt, Phil,' I say, walking huffily into the bedroom.

Come on, Stella, don't snap, I think to myself. *What would Alice say?* I try to be more like her. More reasonable, more kind, more happy. Even though I want to bite him, make him sting. There is a bomb inside me that is ready to explode. But if it goes off, I'm not sure anyone would survive the destruction. So I swallow hard, channel Alice, and try to put out the lit fuse.

'Maybe it's time to get rid of her clothes?' he says, knowing he is on dangerous ground.

'Sure,' I say calmly. 'And why don't I just shave off my face while I'm at it?'

'OK, Stella, don't be like that. You need to let Alice go. It's time.'

I walk calmly into the kitchen.

'How would you like the chicken done?' I ask him. He follows me in.

'I don't think it's healthy for you to wear Alice's clothes any more, OK?'

'I could breadcrumb it? Or do a stir fry?' I get the wok out of a cupboard.

'Stella, for fuck's sake, will you listen to me. Take that skirt off!'

'Fine,' I shout, slamming the wok on the work surface. I pull the waistband open and push the skirt to the ground. Stepping out of it, I pick it up and I screw it into a ball, then smash it into the bin. 'There, OK? Happy now?'

Phil looks at me pitifully, and shakes his head.

'Now, would you like breaded chicken, or a stir fry?' I ask him, very calmly, standing in my knickers, holding a spatula.

'You need help, Stella. You seriously need help.'

With that, he storms out of the flat, and slams the door. When I know he's gone, I get the skirt out of the bin and put it back on.

I think I'll do the stir fry.

Cam

Lying on her bed, Cam watches Mark sleeping, his hairless body glistening with post-sex sweat, his muscles like a mountainous desert of smooth, sweeping vales, orange from the glow of streetlights flooding the room. He is the perfect lover. The kind of lover authors give to rejected housewives in filthy novels. He's perfect for what Cam needs right now.

She wonders if she should kiss him gently as he sleeps, but reminds herself of the boundaries of such relationships. Sex should be tackled with abandon; affection should be handled with care.

Instead, she reaches for her computer. Having a younger lover is the kind of blog fodder she can't deny herself.

The mid-to-late twenties, it's such a prime age for a guy, don't you think? Post-teenage disaster, pre-any desire to sow their seed and have children. Often at the peak of fitness, finding their way in the professional world and working their way through women like a snow plough with a penis.

I love them. For women like me, dare I tell you

again – thirty-six, single, happy – they really are quite the gift. I recently found myself one whilst queuing in Whole Foods. I was buying organic frozen pizza and he was buying protein shakes. Our eyes met, we made general chit chat and an hour and a half later we were in bed. It wasn't our stilted conversation that pulled us together, it was lust. Just lust. If you judge me for that, then I don't think you understand how mutual adult relationships work. It's healthy and consensual; there really is nothing to have an opinion about.

But we love it, don't we? Judging other people's sexual choices, especially if they have an air of controversy. We laugh, we question, we put on our halos and tell anyone doing anything we don't do ourselves that they're wrong or weird. But really, if it feels good and everyone is happy (and legal), then who is anyone to say it isn't right?

How is it that such a private and intimate act, like sex, gains so much social traction? It excites people in the physical sense, but it excites them even more when they can gossip about someone else's deviances. It makes no sense when society is as diverse as it is, that some still feel uncomfortable when others don't behave in a way that is considered 'normal'.

But we were just told what was normal, weren't we? It was written in the books before we were born, that monogamy was the way to go, that we are supposed to find 'the one', get married, have kids. But maybe monogamy isn't for everyone. Maybe some people, like me, really don't have any fear of being alone. In fact, it's the end goal.

I'm so happy not to be normal. At thirty-six, I have no intentions to settle down. There are some people in my life that find that unbearable. I can't be any other way.

There are more single women in their thirties and forties than any other point in history; we are the fastest-growing demographic, but being single doesn't mean you want, or deserve less sex. My choice is to have a younger lover, to give me the physical attention that I crave, but the emotional freedom that I rely on. That's my choice, and as I sit here looking at a beautiful creature, asleep in my bed, here when I need him, gone when I don't, I feel proud not to be normal. In fact, I recommend it.

Sweet dreams,
Cam x

Tara

At 11.36 p.m. we're outside the Sanderson, getting off with each other like we are very much not on a London street in full view of anyone walking past. 'Come back to my place,'

Jason says gently. 'We can watch TV together. I'll lend you some pyjamas. We can talk about feelings?' He pushes even closer into me and puts his hands on my face. 'Or we can just fuck in this doorway and deal with how much I fancy you that way.'

He kisses me. Our mouths taste exactly the same and go together like jigsaw pieces. Like when you've been trying to open a door with the wrong key for ages and when you finally use the right one it just slots in so easily that you realise how wrong you've been getting it for so long. My sexual desire powers down into my pants like the lights and music on the set of a TV gameshow. My crotch is pulling me towards this guy with a force that feels as good as sex itself. This is the connection I've been pining for every Saturday night that I've spent alone after Annie has gone to bed. Feeling cold, empty and rejected by my own choices after yet another shit date the night before. All I've wanted is to at least feel genuinely turned on. An actual, full body, one hundred per cent real impulse to shag someone senseless, rather than just because of a distant hope that sex might give us the connection I'm looking for.

I pull away. 'Old fashioned', 'wife and family', 'a free kid'. His words ring in my head. *If this is really happening, then it can wait.*

'Stop,' I say, stepping out onto the street and away from him. 'Let's stop. Let's not do this tonight. Let's wait.'

'Oh God, you're crazy?' he says, his mouth glistening under the street lights.

'I'm not being crazy. Let's not do this tonight. Let's go out again, next Friday? Date. The "old-fashioned" way?'

Even if I never see him again, I can at least walk away from this amazing night with no sexual shame.

'I want to see you again,' I say. 'I just think it's OK to be sensible sometimes.'

'You know they still had sex in the old-fashioned days?' he says, adjusting his crotch but giving me a smile that shows he understands. 'At least let me get you a cab?'

'No, I'll get the train, honestly a cab will take ages, I don't live far from the station.'

'Where do you live anyway?' he asks.

'Walthamstow,' I tell him.

'Walthamstow, I've never been. Maybe next Friday will be the night I take the Victoria Line all the way?'

'Maybe you will,' I say. 'It's a pretty sexy train.'

I loop my arm through his, and we walk to the station.

'Take my number,' I say, when we get to Tottenham Court Road tube. 'I promise I am not trying to make a polite excuse, I really want to see you again. I want to do this again.' I kiss him, showing him that without any doubt I really do fancy him. After a few seconds, he pulls away and takes his phone out of his pocket. He taps in my number as I tell it to him.

'Is text sex allowed?' he says. To which I laugh and nod my head.

'Any text is allowed. Just text me.'

'I will,' he says. 'Answer the text.'

'I will.'

He kisses me again and doubt nearly makes me say, 'I'LL COME BACK TO YOURS AND RIDE YOU ALL NIGHT.' But I think of my feelings, I think of Annie, and I manage to control my urges somehow. As I walk away, I feel so good about myself – wildly turned on and like I could turn back, rip his clothes off and shag his brains out in the middle of Oxford Street – but also, so good about myself.

Just as I get to the bottom of the escalator, I get a text.

Tonight was perfect. Can't wait to do it again. Jx

I stop. I have one bar of signal and want to send a reply before I go further underground. I've made my point, there isn't really any need to hold back any more, I don't want to leave him with any doubt about how I feel, so I just go for it.

I'll not be so polite next time. I'll want more of what happened in that doorway. I wonder if you'll have any special requests?

I press send and a speech bubble pops up right away but my signal goes. It'll be something nice to read when I get back above ground.

Jason

Jason is still standing at the entrance to the train station, hoping that maybe she changes her mind and comes back out. But seeing as this isn't a Richard Curtis movie, he soon realises she really has gone. He's disappointed, until he gets Tara's text.

'Any special requests?'

How incredibly hot. Jason can't believe his luck. She's clever, funny and sexy as hell. He fancies her more than he's fancied anyone in ages, but he wants to play this right too.

'Any special requests?' Hmmmmm. Maybe it's a little too soon to tell her that he loves the idea of her whipping her hair all over his body? It's just his thing, he can't explain it. It's nothing seedy, or weird. He just loves women with long hair. Of which she had plenty. Long, thick brown hair. It was the first thing he noticed but luckily sense got the better of him and he didn't entertain the idea out loud. He could really do with some sex though; it's been a while since anything notable. He texts back.

I think we'll . . .

And just at that moment, a cyclist crashes into him. The guy falls off but quickly picks himself up and gets back on his bike and speeds off. Was he embarrassed? Escaping someone? Jason doesn't give a shit, all he cares about is the fact that his phone flew out of his hand and disappeared down a drain.

Tara, and her number, gone.

FUCK.

Tara

As the train passes through Seven Sisters, I look around me. My carriage is empty. I've got that heaviness inside me. That dull thud of my libido like a heart thumping in my underwear.

I could wait until I get home to give it what it wants, but then here I am. Alone on a train. Gently drunk and reeling off the back of an electrifying encounter. It's been so long since I've felt this fluttering of excitement. Why wait?

I see a copy of the *Metro* on the seat and lay it over my lap, then slip my hand inside my trousers and then into my underwear. My head falls back against the wall of the train and I think about Jason's body pressing against mine. I imagine us in that doorway, naked now. My legs wrapped around his waist as he pushes me against the door, not caring if anyone sees. Totally locked into my fantasy, I rub hard, it feels so good. My knees fall apart and I feel cool air filter through my pubic hair as the newspaper falls to the floor. The train starts to slow. I'm running out of time, but I can't and won't stop. I press harder, think harder, breathe harder until I come harder than I have in a long, long time. The train slows down. I know I have to move. Just one more second in this moment.

I hear a sniff.

My eyes bounce open and I see a kid – white, blond, in a tracksuit. He's holding a phone. Taking a picture? Or God, is he actually *filming* me?

'What the fuck?' I scream as I launch myself at him. But as the train stops I'm jolted forward and end up face down in the aisle with my trousers around my ankles. The youth's feet disappear as he runs off the train.

'PERVERT,' I scream to a closing door.

What the hell did I just do?

2

Cam

Over a breakfast of black coffee and scrambled eggs on toast with an enormous dollop of ketchup, Cam is sitting at her kitchen table wearing a t-shirt and knickers, making a few finishing touches to the column she's been writing since Mark left to go to the gym at nine a.m. As she's reading through it, searching for missing commas and spelling mistakes, her doorbell starts ringing so aggressively she thinks there must be a fire. Launching herself into her bedroom to pull on some leggings, she runs to the intercom saying, 'What? What?' only to hear her sister say, 'Cam, it's Mel. We were on our way to the Heath and thought we'd come to say hi.'

She buzzes them up, instantly hearing the stampede of Mel's three children racing up the stairs. She opens her door and in pelts Max, eleven, Tamzin, nine, and Jake, four. They all run straight to the window and start naming all the London landmarks that they can see in the view.

'Morning,' she says as they pass her. 'MORNING, AUNTY CAM,' they shout in reply.

Behind them comes Mel, trudging up the stairs, weighed down with beach bags and a cool box. 'Here, let me help you,' says Cam, rushing to help her.

'This is the most un-kid-friendly flat I've ever been to; how many stairs are there? Oh, Cam, you haven't got a bra on!' says Mel, disapprovingly.

'There are forty-six steep steps, it's an old building and I don't have kids so it's fine for me. And I am not wearing a bra because I'm at home. Alone. Or at least I was.'

'I know, but still. You could have put one on before you opened the door.'

'Mel, you're my sister?'

'Yes, but, the kids . . . anyway.'

Cam shuts the door and sarcastically mouths, 'Welcome' under her breath.

Mel drops all of the bags onto the floor, puts her palms on her lower back and arches backwards. She lets out a loud sigh but it doesn't hide the sound of her cracking bones. She looks exhausted.

'The place is nice,' she says, looking around. 'It's big, won't you get lonely?'

'Absolutely not,' Cam says. 'Tea?'

'Better not. I'll need a wee in the park if I do.'

'Right,' says Cam, putting on the kettle anyway. She fancies more coffee, and is grateful her bladder allows it. 'All well?'

'Not really, Mum is worried sick. She thinks that your website is inappropriate and she's too embarrassed to go to her ladies' club because she thinks all the other ladies think you're a bra-burning lesbian!'

'Well I guess that would explain why I'm not wearing one.' Cam gives Mel a 'touché' look, and thinks back to the post she wrote last night about having a younger lover. Her mother will hate it, but at least it will help with the lesbian part.

'Is there anything you can do to make her feel better, it's literally all she talks about?'

'Mel, there is nothing I can do to make Mum feel better, I am who I am. I've told her multiple times not to read my blog but she keeps doing it. If it tortures her so much she should just stop.'

Mel waddles over to the window. 'OK kids, five minutes. I want to get to the park before it gets busy and someone steals our tree.' She turns to Cam. 'I need to sit in the shade or my blood gets too warm and my veins bulge.'

Cam looks at her sister and isn't sure what to say. She looks terrible. Mel never really coped with having kids, not physically or emotionally. She used to be sporty and have a great body, but progressively after each kid she got fatter and fatter and now she's a hefty size eighteen. Unfortunately, she carries most of her weight on her bum and thighs, so she suffers from chafed skin during the summer months and is largely uncomfortable on hot days. She's very pretty, possibly even beautiful, but the stress of life and a lack of sleep, as well as coping with three kids, makes it hard to spot the smile that used to attract so many boys at school. She got post-natal depression after every baby, and her marriage is holding on by a shoestring. Cam is sure Mel's husband, Dave, is having an affair, and she doesn't really blame him. Mel's turned into a complicated person with a lot of anger issues in regards to how her life turned out. She's the best advert for not having kids that Cam has ever seen.

The truth is, Mel is more like Cam than she would ever like to admit. She was never maternal, she never needed to be in relationships to be happy. But she was weaker when it came to standing up to tradition. Their mother saw no future for her four daughters other than marriage and babies. The two eldest, Tanya and Angela, were happy to conform. They both married guys they met at university and have seven kids between them. Tanya teaches yoga and Angela runs a daycare; it's all pretty sickening and ideal in Cam's view. Like they read *House & Garden* and try and live within one of the pictures. But Mel, like Cam, wasn't designed that way. She was clever, academic and top of the class. She wanted to study law and work in the city. She had plans well beyond being a stay-at-home mum. But then she met Dave and got pregnant with Max. She stupidly told their mother, despite Cam warning her not to, and the guilt laid upon her for even considering an abortion was too much for her to fight against. So she had a kid at twenty-six, even though she didn't want it. And ever since then, she has lived a life that she wasn't supposed to live.

'So, kids, you excited to go to the park?' Cam asks, walking over to see them. They all turn around, like monkeys in an enclosure who know they're being watched.

'Why don't you have a boyfriend?' asks Tamzin, a mini version of Cam, even down to the massive hands.

'Maybe I do have a boyfriend,' Cam says, not willing to take any shit from a monkey.

'No, you don't. Mum said you might like girls,' Max states, casually.

'Max, that was a private conversation between me and Granny,' Mel says sharply, trying to silence him with her eyes.

'Then why did you say it when we were all at the dinner table?' Max says, closing that conversation. It's no surprise to Cam that her mother and sister talk about her when she isn't around. She is all they talk about when she is *in* the room, why on earth would they stop when she isn't?

'Guys, one day you will be grown-ups and you will see there is much more to life than having boyfriends and girlfriends. Like having lovely homes and jobs that you enjoy,' Cam says, spreading her arms as if to draw attention to her gorgeous new apartment. They all turn back to the window. 'Do you like it?' They don't answer. Kids are so unobservant, Cam observes.

'I want to get married and have three children,' says Tamzin, proudly, looking back over her shoulder.

'Or maybe you won't, maybe you will change your mind, or maybe you won't meet anyone that you love and you'll happily while away the years on your own in a nice flat surrounded by expensive art without the fear of a little monster drawing on it with a marker pen?'

Mel rolls her eyes at her little sister. 'She's not one of your "women don't need men" crew Cam, every little girl wants the same dream.' Her wind up is triumphed by her son.

'I hate art,' says Max, moving towards Cam's laptop. He

broke her last one by jumping on it because Cam's connection wasn't strong enough to illegally download *Kung Fu Panda*.

'No way,' she says, snatching it out of his way. 'You can't go anywhere near that.'

'Why? Has it got porn on it?' Max says, very rudely.

'Max! How do you know about porn?' interjects Mel, looking genuinely aghast.

'From Aunty Cam's blog. She wrote about how porn was good for you.'

Cam looks at Mel with a guilty face. Mel looks back at her with an angry one. 'What? Oh come on, it's not like there were pictures! And I didn't show him my blog.'

'No, but he looks at it whenever he goes online. It's out there, Cam, anyone can see it. Can't you write about other things? Stuff that won't psychologically damage my children if they read it?'

'Oh calm down, he's not damaged. And perhaps you need to sort out your parental settings.' They both turn to look at Max, who is now pulling a moonie out of Cam's window, while Tamzin is banging on it to get the people on the street's attention. Jake is watching and learning.

'You better put that away, Max,' Cam says. 'I've heard little boys go to prison for exposing themselves around here.'

Max pulls up his trousers. He's a cocky little so-and-so but in that childlike way, he looks like he is debating if what Cam just said is true. He obviously doesn't want to risk it.

'OK, well, I suppose we better go,' says Mel, looping the bags back over her wrists and making a 'huggghhh' noise as she bends her knees and lifts them. 'SO great you live so close to the park, lucky you. I hate the tube, it's so hot, my veins can't take it. Come on, kids. Park, now.'

'Look, I have to work for a bit, but why don't I come join you in the park today?' Cam says, wanting to be with them all, but not in her lovely new home.

'Sure,' says Mel, and herds the kids together. They run down the stairs, leaving Mel struggling with the bags. 'Please put a bra on!' she shouts and trudges behind.

Back at the kitchen table, Cam, as usual after seeing one of her family members, feels alive with motivation. For some, being misunderstood by the people closest to them would lock them in a box, make them insecure, shy away. But for Cam, it's been the inspiration for almost everything she has ever done. She's been gently tapping on her mum and sisters' shoulders most of her life saying, *accept me, I'm different from you, but I'm happy*. Yet for whatever reason, they've never been able to do it. She knows her mother has a hard time reading her blogs, and as much as she tells her she shouldn't, Cam also loves that she does. *HowItIs.com* is her place to say everything she needs to say, to speak her mind and not be belittled by what society, or her mother, deems as normal. She's proud of who she is. Not fitting in has been the catalyst to her success. It's time to write a blog for anyone who is happy to feel alone in a crowd.

Does anyone want to hear a love story? It's not one that has ever been told before. It's called, Cam Stacey and her great love, The Internet. Let me start at the beginning . . .

Once upon a time, there was a girl called Cammie. She was generally quite good at things at school, working hard and keen on doing well. She had a rebellious streak, in that she smoked fags and kissed boys and drank too much cider, but as a whole, she was a pretty good kid.

She wasn't one for trying to be cool, but by not trying to be cool, she probably came across a bit like she was trying to be cool. She wore tight trousers and band t-shirts when the other girls were wearing short skirts and low-cut tops. She didn't have many close friendships. Instead, she sat around talking about music with boys, rather than gossip sessions with the girls. All in all, she got through her teenage years without too much trouble; girls found her a bit intimidating, boys probably did too. All she wanted was a bit of peace and quiet. With three older sisters at home, leaving the house was like a holiday, and she didn't want to fill that time with too many people, so she generally kept herself to herself.

Yes, you've guessed it, Cammie is me. Here is how the story goes on . . .

I left school, went to uni, and studied English. I was one of those people who read everything on the course modules. I was never without a book, and I had a freakish tendency to read multiple newspapers a day from cover to cover. Why? Because I knew that I had to be a writer. I knew I had to absorb words to be good at it. It was the only way that I was ever going to get the billions of thoughts and opinions that were in my head, out. In a way that anyone would understand. Because socially, I really sucked.

I did what all aspiring writers did back then, and I wrote pages and pages of articles, printed them off and sent them to editors in yellow envelopes. I never got any replies. Then, this amazing thing happened . . . they called it ***email****. Suddenly I could send my work as attachments to emails, so I did that, but still, I never got any replies. And then I read an article about this little-known hobby that they were calling 'blogging'. This woman was blogging about her family. Her husband was a photographer, she was beautiful, their kids were cute and their dog was fluffy. So every day, she got her husband to take an adorable picture and she posted it with a note about what they did that day. It was kind of sickening if I am honest, not my thing at all. But then I read that 30,000 people checked in every single day to read what she had to say. And I knew this was the answer for me.*

So, Reader, I married him! By ***him****, I mean, the Internet. And by* ***married****, I mean I built a website. And then, we started making babies. (You get the picture by now. By* ***babies****, I mean writing blogs.)*

I found my voice online and that helped me find my voice inside. I wrote and wrote, and every day, without fail, I posted something. Whether it was something I was feeling, or a reaction to something in the news. And then, I made everyone I knew read it. I had flyers printed that I put on cars and through letterboxes. I emailed the link to every editor of every paper and magazine, and I posted the link on thousands of people's MySpace pages. It became my life; it became an addiction. If I wasn't writing, I was promoting. I didn't need editors of newspapers to notice me, I was getting an audience all of my own. And look at me now. I have one of the longest running lifestyle blogs in the UK. HowItIs.com started sixteen years ago next week and it's still going strong. Over half a million people read my blogs each day; that's a bigger readership than most print publications.

I'm telling this story for anyone who has a voice but doesn't know how to get it heard. You don't have to be a social butterfly, you don't have to be charming, overly confident, beautiful or thin. All you need to have is something to say.

The Internet is the love of my life, because it allows me to be who I want to be. Words that would get stuck in my mouth tumble out of my fingertips with total ease. I'm not sure what I would have become if I didn't have this as an outlet. And you know the best bit? I can connect with hundreds of thousands of people every single day, without even having to say a word. So go for it, post your feelings online. Even if no one reads it now, there is a little piece of you out there that will last forever, it's kinda magical!

Cam x

Tara

'Mum, the cotton wool keeps falling off,' says Annie, as we walk up to Trudy's door. There are two birthday helium balloons tied to the handle and a little Post-it note saying, 'LET YOURSELVES IN, PRINCESSES'.

My head is thumping from too much booze and almost no sleep. I can't get the image of that guy's face out of my head, his camera aiming at me like a gun that was loaded with shame. And Jason still hasn't texted anything since before I got on the train; how did I get that so wrong?

'Mum?' pushes Annie. 'I feel silly.'

I turned up to my mum's house at eleven thirty this morning armed with an empty cardboard box, a Pritt Stick, a sheet of orange card, a piece of elastic, a white hat, some white tights and six packets of cotton wool balls. It's amazing what you can muster from a Tesco Metro when you have to create a fancy dress costume for a six-year-old. I cut a hole in the box for Annie's head and covered the whole thing with cotton wool balls. I made a carrot nose out of the orange card and elastic and with the tights and the hat, she looks great. OK, not great, but the best I could do.

'Snowmen are round, not square, Mummy.'

'Annie, it's OK. You look snowy.'

'But why am I a snowman, it's the summer?'

'There was a snowman in *Frozen*, wasn't there?' I say, which doesn't seem to help.

We go in. It's clear the party is happening in the garden; the shrieking of excited children is tearing through the house. I should have taken more Nurofen.

The house is nice. A very large Victorian terrace with tidy bookshelves, a massive TV and a posh navy sofa with a big doll's house in front of a bay window. I'm surprised Amanda has such good taste, and her husband obviously earns loads because, apart from two large chests of practical-looking drawers, all with neatly written labels describing what toys they contain, the place looks impressively un-IKEA.

'Annie, Annie,' yells Trudy as she runs excitedly into the living room, followed by three other little princesses in their perfect, shop-bought fancy dress frocks. I feel instantly sorry for Annie. She looks ridiculous in comparison.

The other girls take her hand and drag her outside into the garden, where a small bouncy castle is being challenged by around fifteen extremely excited six-year-old girls. To the left of it is a long table with a blue tablecloth and plate after plate of blue and white foods. I want to eat all of it.

At the far end of the table are about twenty adults, men and women. Mums and dads. Why do I get so nervous in these situations? My hangover anxiety tells me that I have been the topic of conversation until now.

'Hello,' I say, approaching the table.

'Tara,' says Amanda, coming over all friendly, as if the uncomfortable moment at the school gate never happened. It's a little unnerving. 'Wine?' she says, offering me a glass of white. I swear everyone has stopped talking and is smiling at me in that awkward way that people at parties do while they are waiting for you to make eye contact with them so they can say hello. I quickly look around them all, and mutter hello so they can get on with their conversations. 'Well?' pushes Amanda, waving the glass of wine under my nose. I think for a second, but my face must speak volumes because she retracts the glass and says, 'Too early to drink?'

'Oh, no, never too early. I just had a big night last night. Feeling a bit shaky.'

'Oh come on, hair of the dog, it works wonders,' says a man in a blue shirt approaching us.

'This is Pete, my husband,' she says. Something in her face shows me she is angry with him.

'Hi,' I say, reaching my hand out to meet Pete's. He is tall, with a mouth that takes up a lot of his face, and really flirty eyes.

'I could whip you up a Bloody Mary,' he says. 'I was a bit shaky myself this morning. I've got some already made up in the fridge?'

'You know what, that would be perfect. Thank you!' I say, as he goes inside.

'Annie's costume, it's . . . it's brave.'

'Thanks, Amanda,' I say, taking that as a compliment and making it clear I have her name right now. 'I like to encourage her to be her own person, rather than just do whatever everyone else does.' We look over at Annie. She is stepping out of the box and into a princess dress. 'It doesn't always work.'

'Sure.'

We stand together, pretending to be engrossed in what our children are doing, trying to think of something to say, but something negative is in action between us. It's cosmic, out of our control. I don't have the energy to fight it.

'Here you go,' says Pete, handing me a Bloody Mary and breaking the silence.

'Wow, celery and everything. Cheers.' We chink glasses, and I take a big sip. It's delicious.

'OK, well, have fun,' Amanda says, walking away, as if she has hit her limit on what she can handle from me. 'Pete!' she says, ordering him away. I can't help but notice him glance at my tits as he goes.

'Hello, hi, hey, hi, hello,' I say, walking over to the table of food and the small crowd of people around it. 'Mmmmm, bright blue cupcakes, yummy,' I say, taking a paper plate and loading it full of food. Everyone is looking at me with 'isn't she fascinating' faces. There are as many dads as mums. I feel very conspicuous. Very solo. How is it I can be so confident at work, but put me in a group of parents and I want to bury my head in the birthday cake?

'A Bloody Mary and carbohydrates, that can only mean one thing,' says Tracey, Gabby Fletcher's mum, coming over to me. We've chatted a few times before; she's generally quite friendly but also has that air of primness about her that so many women seem to get when they get married and have kids. Even the wildest ones, like Sophie, even though she doesn't have children. They used to be hard drinking, slutty drug munchers, but now they're boring, safe, and married to men who would implode if they knew the things they used to get up to. I get the impression from Tracey that she has a past she doesn't want to admit to. She always takes a second to answer questions, as if she is reminding herself of the right thing to say. Maybe I'm imagining it, maybe not.

'Yup, killer hangover. This table has everything I need on it.'

Pause.

'I haven't had a proper hangover in years, I just couldn't do it with my two,' she says, and the rest of the parents mumble in agreement.

'Oh, I know. My mum has Annie on Friday nights, so I can go out and have a sleep in. I'm not sure I could handle it otherwise.'

Tracey glances back at the group. I wonder if she's been sent over to get information.

'And I suppose you can do weekend swaps with Annie's dad too? I mean, God forbid anything ever happen with me and James, but a bit of child sharing must be nice?'

It's not unusual for people to presume that Annie's dad and I split up. It is unusual for me to be asked about it in front of an audience of mums and dads at a Disney-themed birthday party. This topic gives me extreme anxiety at the best of time. Mix that with hangover fear, and I suddenly realise that my face is very sweaty.

'Oh, actually Annie doesn't have a dad,' I say, stuffing half a blue cupcake into my mouth and hoping she moves on.

'Oh. Yes, some of the girls and I were just saying, we don't really know much about you, we just wanted to get to know you a little better.'

Girls, I think. Why do women refer to themselves as *girls*? It's so weird.

'Oh, right,' I say, eating more cupcake.

'So, was it a bad breakup?' she asks, after watching me chew and swallow the whole thing.

'No, nope. No, we were never actually together.'

The other mums have now moved closer. I wonder how many cupcakes I can get in my mouth at one time, so I don't have to speak.

'Oh, sorry I shouldn't pry!' Pause. 'So, what, just a fling?'

I could just say yes, but as the Bloody Mary kicks in and joins last night's alcohol that is still buzzing around my system, I have an unfamiliar wave of bravado.

'Nope. Not a fling, a one-night stand. Well, there was a bit of flinging, I suppose. In that he flung some sperm up my vagina and into my uterus.' I laugh, thinking that was pretty funny. Then I look at all of their faces, and realise it wasn't.

'That's quite the image,' Tracey says, picking up a cupcake she obviously has no intention of eating. 'So he didn't want to be involved?' she asks, like a human lie detector that I know I won't beat.

'Nope. Actually he never knew. I never told him.'

Silence. For what feels like a very long time. I eventually realise this isn't one of her weird pauses, she just has no idea what to say. My nerves keep speaking.

'Anyway, now I'm dating and looking for love, not sperm. Real, actual love. So don't worry, your husbands are safe, ladies!' I let out a raucous and crazy laugh. *What am I doing? Who am I being? Why the hell did I say that about their husbands being safe?*

'Pete,' shouts Amanda across the garden. 'Pete, let's get the cake.' I hadn't realised that he was standing behind me again.

The crowd of parents disperses and spreads themselves into small groups around the garden. Every wife is making some sort of physical contact with their husband. I am left standing at the table alone, me and approximately 40,000 calories' worth of blue puddings. I feel like the smashed-up sausage roll that nobody wants to eat.

After a minute or two, my anxiety wins.

'Annie, Annie, come on, we have to go,' I say, rushing over to the bouncy castle and elbowing parents out of my way to get my daughter.

'But Mummy, we haven't had the cake yet,' she says, looking embarrassed and worried that I am serious.

'We'll have cake at home. Come on, grab your cardboard box.'

'But . . . '

'ANNIE, now!'

She does as she's told, mortified that I just shouted at her in front of her friends. I don't care, I'm too embarrassed to deal with judgement from these people. I also think I might be sick.

I grab Annie's hand and hurry through the house, feeling like I'm escaping an avalanche. As I open the front door, Vicky Thomson is standing there, her fist up to start knocking. I jump about three feet into the air.

'Tara,' she says, 'are you leaving? God, I'm so late. Is the party over, why have you got a blue mouth?'

So many questions. I push past her, dragging Annie by the hand.

'OK, well, bye. And we should do coffee, I've written up a few more ideas, I really think one could . . . '

But I've strapped Annie in and driven away before she has the chance to finish. When I get around the corner, I feel a little calmer. Then I look in the rear view mirror and see Annie's face.

My little princess is crying her eyes out.

Cam

'Hello, yeah I've been waiting for my pizza for over an hour . . . Yes, it's Stacey . . . What? I spoke to you myself? . . . Oh, forget it, I'll call Domino's.'

She hangs up.

'That is so rubbish,' Cam says to Mark, who is also very hungry but not the type to get annoyed. 'It's going to take ages to get here now.'

She storms over to the kitchen and aggressively opens and slams shut all of the cupboards and the fridge. They are all empty.

'Babe, you get so hangry,' says Mark, infuriating Cam a little with his youthful slang.

'I've been craving pizza all day,' she says, huffing.

'Well then, let's go out and get some?' Mark suggests, flippantly.

'What, and bring it back here?'

'No, let's go eat somewhere. It's Saturday night. Date Night!'

Cam goes a little cold. *Let's go eat somewhere?* As in, they sit opposite each other? In a restaurant? With clothes on? Making conversation? Is that possible?

Before Cam has the chance to question it, Mark is standing by the door, ready to leave. 'Come on then, I'm starving,' he says.

She picks up her keys, slips into some flip flops and follows him out. This is actually happening.

As Mark reads the menu, Cam stares at him. It's been a few months since they met in the line at Whole Foods, they've had sex in every position imaginable, but she has no idea if he even has a middle name. Sitting opposite him now, she can't think of a single thing to say.

'I'm going for the meat feast, I don't even know why I bother to read the menu. What about you?' Mark asks, putting the menu down and nodding at a waiter.

'Me? What about me?' Cam asks, worried he's asking her to express some feelings.

'Er, what pizza you going for?'

'Oh, a Hawaiian, always.'

'Nah, can't do fruit on pizza,' Mark says.

'Oh right,' replies Cam, making a face that she thinks shows she is enjoying getting to know the small details of who he is, despite finding this terribly awkward.

It's not that she doesn't like Mark, or doesn't like spending time with him. But she's actively avoided traditional dating for most of her adult life; it isn't what she's good at. She'd rarely choose to sit opposite someone she didn't know really well for an entire meal. A drink, probably. A coffee, fine. But a meal? A proper date? She's not good at this. She's good at being at home, in her pants, making general conversation between sex sessions. In that environment she has props, distractions from intense emotional interaction. But now here she is, sitting opposite her fuck buddy of a few months, realising for the first time that the age gap is actually a thing. She feels conspicuous. Like an older man with a young hot blonde. Out of bed, this feels a bit silly.

They order.

'So what did you do today?' he asks, as they wait.

'Oh, um, I went to the park with my sister and niece and two nephews. We swam in the pond, it was nice,' Cam says, shoving two olives into her mouth.

'Ah, nice. I've got two nephews. Jacob and Jonah. Both want to be called JJ, so I just call them JJJJ, like Ja-Juh, Ja-Juh, and they find that really funny.'

'That's hilarious,' says Cam, hiding her feelings by spitting olive pips into her hand.

'They love me. I can pick them both up at once. They call me Uncle Hulk,' Mark says, holding his arm up, bending his elbow, and flexing his biceps.

Cam smiles. He's so nice, she doesn't want to be rude, or mean, but . . .

'So how old are yours?' he asks, being completely acceptable and acting as any normal human being would in this situation. But it's too much for Cam. She's not sure why she's finding this so excruciating, but she is. She can't do it. She just can't.

'Mark, I'm sorry. I'm not feeling great, maybe sunstroke or something. Can we get the pizza boxed up and take it home?'

Mark doesn't seem bothered. He still gets pizza, he still gets Cam – as far as he's concerned, it's all good.

'Sure,' he says, calling over a waiter to ask for the pizza to go. Cam instantly relaxes, and fills the time by getting her wallet out of her bag and counting out some money. 'I'll get this,' she says. Mark happily accepts.

As they leave, Cam thinks again.

'You know, maybe I'll just go home alone. I'm sorry, I think the heat really got to me today. Then not eating, and chasing kids around all afternoon. Is that OK?'

'Of course, babe,' Mark says, understandingly. He opens a pizza box to make sure she takes the right one. 'Want me to walk you home?'

'No, I'll be OK. Thanks though,' she says, appreciating how nice and easy he is, and wondering why she can't bring herself to sit through a meal with him.

'Will you go out tonight?' she asks.

'Probably, I fancy a dance,' he says, further clarifying the vast contrast in their lifestyles. Cam wonders if he'll pull later. Someone closer to his age, who also works in a gym, who is happy to chat about stuff. She knows she isn't allowed to care.

'Have fun,' she says as he walks away.

'Thanks babe,' he calls back. She walks home, slowly.

Back at her kitchen table, laptop in front of her, half a pizza to her right, and a cup of tea to her left, she thinks about what to write about. She knows her relationship with the world through the Internet is better than it is with it in person, but does that matter? Why should she have to be great offline, when she can be everything she wants to be online? It's not like she has no contact with other humans at all; there is her family, Mark, and of course she *has* friends. Sure, she conducts most of her relationships on email, but it's not like she's literally alone, like an old person in a home that no one comes to visit. She could go out if she wanted to, she just doesn't want to.

She sits for a minute, and thinks about that.

Does she want to? Or has she become so consumed with her online profile that she's forgotten how to communicate face to face? She shakes her head. No . . . no, that isn't how it is. The Internet allowed her to be everything she wanted to be. She's happy living through her fingertips. In her virtual world she is bold, brave and powerful. In the real world, she kind of sucks. Her relationship with the Internet is nothing to be ashamed of.

There, she has something to blog about. Cam gets to work.

Being alone doesn't mean I am lonely.

I don't remember the last time I felt lonely, but I am alone all the time. I think it stems from being brought up in a busy household, and living most of my life in my head. The truth is, I probably have the same fear of being surrounded that most people have of loneliness. Being alone doesn't scare me. In fact, it makes me really happy.

Being lonely is actually quite hard, if you fill your life with things you love. For me, the things I love don't take me far from my front door. I enjoy walking, and watching movies, and seeing family and those kinds of things. But the rest of the time, when I am alone in my home, my thoughts and work occupy me plenty.

When I am alone, I just get on with things. I do all sorts, ranging from acts of vanity to writing words. As I sit here in my kitchen on a Saturday night doing the latter of those activities, I thought I might share some of the other things I do when there is no one else around.

Sometimes, I might sit at the kitchen table and pluck my bikini line with tweezers. Or I put a little vanity mirror on a table by the window, and use the brightness of the daylight to inspect my pores. I squeeze little blackheads and pluck out dark hairs from places on my face that they shouldn't be. This leaves me looking all blotchy and unsightly, so I probably wouldn't do it if there was someone else around. I'll finish that process with a face-mask, that I leave on for ten minutes while I email friends.

I'm brilliant at emailing people. I'd write letters if actual handwriting didn't give me wrist cramps, because I love the idea of old-school pen pals. I write school friends huge catch up emails, and I send them all the time. And they write back with just a few sentences, and I always feel really proud of myself for being so good at staying in touch, even though I would never make the effort to actually see them face to face. I also spend ages reading all of the emails I get from you guys, and a good portion of my time replying.

I cook myself meals, and sometimes really go to town on what they might be. A few nights ago I made myself a chicken Thai green curry from scratch, including the paste. Then I sat in my window seat and I ate it while looking out over London and listening to Tapestry by Carole King. I followed that by reading almost half of a novel about a North Korean refugee, before going to bed and writing a blog with a cup of peppermint tea. In the morning, I woke up at ten a.m. and finished the curry. Cold. There was no one there to judge me, so I just did it, and it was perfect. I spent the rest of the day doing DIY with my dad.

This is my life now, and how it has been for a really long time. I am alone, but never lonely. I don't know if I could ever be lonely, because I love being alone. I think when you've truly mastered the skill of enjoying your own company, happiness just comes.

Cam x

She uploads the piece and tears off a huge piece of pizza. Usually she feels a sense of calmness when she's written a good article, but Cam can't quite shake the jitters she's feeling from earlier. The weakness she feels when she's in the wider world. How can the virtual her and the real life her be so different? Taking the pizza with her into her bedroom, she slips between the sheets and eats it. Looking around her room, she thinks how nice it would be to have a small armchair in the corner, one with a fun print on it, just for show. Maybe she'll go looking for one tomorrow, that would be the perfect way to spend a Sunday. Still chewing, she lets out a massive pizza-perfumed fart, turns off the light, and falls fast asleep.

Sunday

Tara

Annie and I are snuggled up on the sofa watching a movie, like we always do on rainy Sunday afternoons. My phone beeps and I jump up like a wasp just landed on my leg, giving Annie a huge fright. Suddenly we are both off the sofa, and standing in the middle of the living room.

'What, Mummy? Who is it?' she asks, a little frightened.

'It's just Sophie,' I say, glumly. And sit back down.

Did he text yet?

No.

Need cheering up ? You can come over? Bring Annie. Carl is here, but that's OK.

Maybe later. I'm too busy dying of shame right now x

OK, well come if you can. I like Carl seeing me with kids x x

I consider telling her about the guy who filmed me on the train, but I don't even know how I would explain that to Sophie. It's giving me the creeps so badly, I'm really trying to block it out of my mind. But I keep visualising him in his living room wanking away to it, or even worse, posting it on his Facebook page so all his spotty little mates can wank over it. It's so weird to think that someone out there has that footage and I have no idea who he is. Oh God, me having an orgasm, *on camera*. It's just the worst thing I can imagine.

Maybe he was just taking a photo? The newspaper didn't fall off my lap until pretty near the end. It might not be as bad as I think. I just have to forget about it, pretend it didn't happen, or it's going to taunt me for the rest of my life. There is nothing I can do about it now, so I need to focus on the other things in my life, like the fact that I totally imagined how much Jason liked me. Urgh. Today is not good. Annie wants to do stuff, and I feel so low I can't get off the sofa. There is a standoff.

She was so upset about leaving the party early that she refused to come out of her room yesterday afternoon. I felt so gross that after some pitiful attempts to coax her out, I just lay on the sofa eating Pringles, like a teenager going through a breakup. Eventually I took her up some dinner and let her eat it in her room. Why is it that kids find eating away from a table so exciting? She came downstairs after that, and we played Snap until bedtime. When she was asleep, I got back to my carbohydrates and a bottle of wine. That's probably why I feel even more horrendous today.

'You said we'd go to the park today,' Annie says, not even looking at me, arms crossed as she stares at the TV. We have *Chitty Chitty Bang Bang* on, we've seen it a hundred times.

'I know. Sorry, Annie. Mummy's not well. Come on, what do you want to watch, anything you want, I don't mind?'

'I don't want to watch TV. I want to go out.'

I look at my phone again even though it didn't make a noise. *Why hasn't Jason texted me?* Maybe he thought his message had sent? But then he'd be waiting for an answer from me and he'd look and see it hasn't. No, he decided to stop writing. But why? I want to text him again, say something cool, easy, funny? But I can't bring myself to. The least I can do for myself is retain some level of dignity by not saying anything else mortifying. Annie huffs loudly.

'I'm bored inside, it isn't even raining,' she says, staring at my phone like it's another child that is taking me away from her.

'OK, I'm sorry, I don't feel well,' I say.

We sit in silence for a few more minutes. I know she isn't watching the film, I'm not either, but we both stare at the screen anyway.

'I'm hungry,' she says, eventually. 'I want to go to the park and get an ice cream.'

'Can't we just have one day where we sit around doing nothing?' I realise I'm sounding like the child and tell myself to grow up. I am a mother, not a lovesick teenager. I must parent and stop moping. I skulk into the kitchen. There is a plate of chicken in the fridge, I think it was from Thursday night's dinner; it should be fine. I flop a big dollop of mayonnaise into it and stir it up, then squash it between two slices of bread. I sprinkle a few Pringles onto the plate next to it, and pour her a glass of water.

'There,' I say, offering it to her. 'I made you a sandwich. Chicken mayo, yummy. Eat up and then we'll go out.'

She takes a few bites and swallows hard. 'It tastes weird, Mummy.'

'Oh Annie, please will you stop being so grumpy and just eat the sandwich!' I snap, instantly regretting it. But I feel so tired, and embarrassed, and I need to wallow in all of those emotions until they go away. I look at Annie, she looks so upset. 'Oh baby I'm sorry, I . . . '

'You're SO mean!' she shrieks as she throws the plate on the floor, the sandwich popping open and mayonnaise splattering everywhere. She storms out of the living room and flies up the stairs. Her bedroom door slams and makes the house shake. That's the first time she's ever done that, I couldn't feel more terrible. I throw a tea towel over the mayonnaise and pretend it isn't there. Covering my face with my hands, I tell myself I have to be strong, this is not Annie's fault, our weekends are precious, and I can't waste one just because I am a total loser. We'll go to see Sophie, everything will be fine. I'll make up for yesterday. I have to be strong.

I look at my phone again as I plod up the stairs. Still nothing. Why hasn't he texted me?

Stella

Last night was shit. Halfway through my stir fry, Phil came back and sat in the living room with the TV on so loud I could barely think. I stood in the kitchen for ages, calming myself down. I wanted to go in there and rip the TV out of the wall and smash him over the head with it. Why is it him that's so annoyed? Is it his whole family who died? His body that is under threat? I stared at the back of his head from the kitchen door and mouthed everything I wanted to scream at his face. He is supposed to be the strong one. He is supposed to take care of me, to make me feel better. That is the person he was when we met. That is who I thought was moving into my home. He was the one who persuaded me to get the test, with his 'I'm here for you, baby' and 'It's better to know.' And now we have the result, he is the one who isn't man enough to deal with it.

But I held myself back. And I thought about what I want. And I don't want to be alone, and I want to have a baby. So as I so often do, I swallowed my pain, I took off Alice's lovely skirt, I went and sat next to him, put my hand on his leg, and I told him I was sorry. For what I should be so sorry for, I'm not entirely sure. But he turned the volume down, and he accepted a plate of food, and we sat and we watched a movie side by side.

Now, a day later, we are at the kitchen table, eating the roast beef that I just prepared in a further attempt to stop him leaving me. I am running out of conversation; no friends to catch up on, no work gossip, no family news, and I'm trying to avoid the b and the c words.

'Did you know that if you Google "What if I die with no legacy" the first four results are about what happens to your Facebook account after you've died?' I say, with a small piece of meat stuffed into my left cheek.

'I didn't. No,' replies Phil, taking a sip of red wine.

'Apparently, now you can nominate someone to be your "legacy contact", and then they can take control of it after you've gone. So basically I'd give you my login and then you could change my pictures and accept friend requests and stuff.'

'Why wouldn't you just shut the page down?'

'Who?'

'You?'

'Well, I'd be dead,' I reiterate.

'OK, then why wouldn't the legacy contact just shut the page down? A Facebook account is no good to you when you're dead, is it?' Phil says, bluntly.

I take a moment.

'What if it's all you leave behind?'

'Well that would be pretty depressing, wouldn't it?' says Phil, obviously hoping this conversation stops soon.

'Maybe that's all I'll leave behind,' I say, pushing him to respond.

'OK, Stella. Do you have to talk like this?' Phil blurts, standing up from the table and taking his plate over to the sink. He drops his head. 'I can't have more of these casual conversations about death, it's wrecking my head.'

'Sorry,' I say, even though I'm not. I creep behind him and put my arms around his waist. We stand like this for a minute or two, Phil's body stiff and uninviting. I undo his belt.

'I want you,' I say gently as I take his flaccid penis into my hand and try to work it into something functional. I don't remember ever having to do this at the beginning of our relationship. It's standard now.

After a long silence, it's finally hard. 'Come to bed,' I say, taking him by the hand and leading him into the bedroom.

As I take off my jeans and knickers, Phil lies down. He pulls his trousers down a little but leaves his underwear on. I crawl on top of him. 'I might need a little help,' I say, seductively putting my fingers into his mouth. He sucks them and turns his head to the side. I run my wet fingers around the opening of my vagina, a move he taught me, that he used to like to watch. I position myself above him and lower until he's inside me. He keeps his head to the side. I move slowly up and down, not taking my eyes off his face. I try harder, making the noises that used to turn him on. I lean forward and kiss his neck, then his cheek. I kiss the side of his mouth as I groan and move faster, but he refuses to look at my face. He's managing to retain an erection but he's not moving, he's not offering anything. I keep going, ramping up my speed a little but getting nothing back from him.

'Phil, come on,' I bark, frustrated. 'Just fuck me, will you!'

Phil pushes me off and onto the bed. I roll and face the

other way, covering my face with my hands. It's too embarrassing to bear.

'I'm sorry, Stell,' he says, sincerely. 'I'm just really full.' A lie.

He gets off the bed, does up his jeans as he goes into the living room. I hear the TV go on.

Tara

Sophie and I used to work for an agency that supplied waiting staff for posh people's parties. We'd serve miniature Yorkshire puddings with horseradish cream, or other such pretentious tiny things, to London's society crowd. We dealt with a lot of pretentious arseholes, but we also got to snoop around their houses. Huge Notting Hill townhouses and massive Sloane Square apartments. They were another world from what we were used to in Walthamstow. Our families did well by our local standards, we were the upper end of the scale for where we were from, but nothing in comparison to the people who had these parties. They seemed like something out of the movies, and they lived in a London that we didn't recognise as ours. We used to laugh about how we would be if we lived that way. We fantasised about wearing wild dressing gowns, marabou slippers, wafting around our mansions with glass after glass of champagne. It was a ridiculous dream, but every time I arrive at Sophie and Carl's house, I realise she is living it.

I pick Annie up so she can ring the doorbell. It's Victorian, so quite stiff. Her little fingers struggle to push it, so I put mine on top of hers and say, 'One two, three.' We hear the perfectly tuned, beautiful bells of Big Ben that their £400 doorbell bellows out whenever anyone pops round. Sophie's voice booms out of a speaker, 'Hang on, just upstairs,' but as she says it, we hear heavy footsteps walking towards the door. Annie holds onto me a little tighter, which makes me feel so good. She's been angry with me all day. But in that way that kids do, when a shred of fear from the outside world creeps in, she knows her mummy is the one to make her safe. I squeeze her back, happy to be a team again, as the door slowly opens.

And there is Carl. All six foot two of him. His dark hair neatly cut and parted at the side. His fifty-one-year-old, well-looked-after body hidden underneath a cream V-neck jumper, with a checked shirt poking out from underneath. I'm not sure what you'd call the trousers he has on, a casual chino? This is him when he's relaxing at home, but he still looks smarter than most of the men I know when they're at work.

'Hey Carl, so nice to see you,' I say, stepping inside and kissing him on each cheek. I feel under surveillance, like I could say something incriminating to piss him off. I remind myself I am a parent, that he is not my husband, and it actually doesn't matter if he likes me or not. But still, I feel judged.

'Hello Tara, Annie; welcome. Sophie is somewhere, come in,' he says, warmly, reminding me that most of my opinion of Carl comes from Sophie's paranoia.

'Hiiiiii,' says Sophie, coming down the large staircase. She looks fully the part and as beautiful as ever. All casual in black, but impeccably styled.

'Aunty Sophie!' says Annie, letting go of my hand and running over to her. They've always got on great. Sophie is childlike by nature, so connects well with kids. I am pretty certain this would not be the case if the kids were her own. It's another reason why marrying Carl suited her. He has three boys by his first marriage, and no interest in having any more.

'Hello sweetheart,' she says, picking Annie up and giving her a huge kiss. I see her shoot a look to Carl, to make sure he is watching. She thinks him seeing her with children makes her seem responsible in some way, I think. 'Shall we go into the kitchen?' she says.

In the kitchen, a huge white three-sided cube that opens up to a sprawling and perfectly preened garden, Carl goes over to a wine fridge that is four times the size of my actual fridge and says to Sophie, 'Maybe a 2008?'

'Lovely,' she replies.

As he opens it, Sophie opens the back doors so that Annie can burst into the open air and run around the flower beds. She gets to do no such thing at home, because my garden is basically a shed with no roof on it. I do love seeing her play happily, a gentle reminder that maybe I am doing OK at being a mum.

'So, did he text?' Sophie asks me, as Carl puts three enormous bulbous wine glasses in front of us. He puts three fingers' worth of wine in mine, three fingers' worth in his, but as he's pouring Sophie's, she puts her hand up as if to stop him putting so much in hers. That is the first time in the history of my existence I have ever seen her do that. Carl looks impressed. Sophie looks at me and winks.

'No, not yet,' I say, tasting the wine. It's unbelievably delicious, like the smoothest, creamiest, most perfectly chilled drink I have ever consumed. I bet it cost £50 a bottle. I drink it slowly, despite wanting to neck it. 'I obviously gauged that completely wrong. He hasn't contacted me all weekend, I'm gutted,' I continue.

'I presume you're talking about a young man?' says Carl, like an old dad.

'Yip! Tara went on an Internet date on Friday,' Sophie says, as if she is telling Carl of a new phenomenon that the kids are doing.

'Actually, that's not quite what happened. I went to meet the guy from the Internet but I ended up with a guy I met at the bar,' I say, correcting her, then wishing I hadn't because that didn't sound great. Carl looks confused, and I feel dirty.

'I don't think I could ever date someone I met on the Internet, I'd be so worried that they would expect something from me on the first date,' says Sophie, like butter wouldn't melt. My jaw falls open and I stare hard at her, as if to say, 'I'm sorry, what character are you playing here?'

'I was never much of a dater,' she continues. To which I have to stop myself yelping, 'No, you were just a shagger!' What is this rewriting of history she has to do to keep her husband happy? I know what it is; it's a fear of him leaving her and her being left with nothing. But would he, really? He's a bit of a pompous snob, but I don't think he's that bad.

'So, hang on,' interjects Carl. 'You were going to meet

someone on the Internet but ended up with someone at the bar?' He looks more intrigued than judgmental, but Sophie still looks nervous.

'Yes. I went up to the wrong guy. By the time I realised it was the wrong guy we were already getting along really well, so I just stayed there with him.'

'And what about the other guy?' Carl asked.

'He left with someone that looked like a prostitute, so he looked pretty happy,' I say, looking at Sophie, as if to say, '*You* might lie about real life, but I don't.' I can see this terrifies her; she's wondering how to separate herself from my debauchery.

'God, we are so different,' is what she goes with, causing me to spit out about £2.50's worth of wine all over the solid white glossy kitchen table that seats twelve people.

'Tara, careful,' she says, getting up to fetch a cloth, with which she mops up my mess. I feel like I'm fifteen and sitting at a table with my friend's parents who think I'm a bad influence.

'Sophie, we are not that different. Are we?' I say, not willing to take any further unnecessary humiliation this weekend; I think I've hit my peak after Jason and Wankgate. She stops wiping and looks at me. Carl is behind her, and she looks deeply into my eyes as if to say, 'Please, just go with this.' But why should I? Why should I sit here and be made to sound like some old slapper when she was basically 'Miss Trollop of Walthamstow' from 1998 through to 2010? Just as I am about to say something brilliantly clever and collected to set the record straight, Annie runs into the kitchen.

'Mummy, I think I'm going to be sick,' she says, looking as green as the garden behind her. And then, like an earthquake shattering a dam, she projectile vomits all over Sophie and Carl's perfectly pristine floor.

3

Cam

Cam's article about not being lonely got shared 42,000 times, retweeted 18,000 times and discussed on *This Morning*. She is thrilled. This all helps raise the bucks she can haggle from her advertisers, and proves to her that even though she is relatively old now, well, old compared to Mark and his beautiful body, *HowItIs.com* is still as relevant as it ever was.

But coming up with content every day is hard. She needs to find a balance of outrage, opinion and personal detail. Blogs with a good dose of all three are smash hits, and she thinks she has just the one to follow on with this buzz. She's been wanting to write it for ages, but needed to get it word perfect. Having spent the weekend obsessing about the most horrendous attempt at dinner out with Mark and if her lack of social skills is a problem or not, she knows the time is right. This isn't about him, it's about her; about taking control of her life in the bravest, most honest way possible. She *is* happy, her choices *are* right, and it's important to her that everyone understands that. Cam knows what she is about to say will get a strong reaction. From her readers, of course – but mostly from her mother.

HowItIs.com

Why I Don't Want Children

I don't want kids. And no, I'm not sad or selfish, or self-obsessed or mean. I'm a kind, funny, thirty-six-year-old who was loved by both of my parents and who gets plenty of sex. I'm attractive, fit, healthy, a great lover and good friend. I've never been sexually abused, I've had happy relationships, and I like myself very much.

I just don't want kids. That doesn't mean that I am not very nice.

I also don't hate children, and to be honest I am spooked by people who say they do. When other people who don't want kids say that to me I think, **you were a child, I was a child, we need children.** *They are only little adults. They are not something you can hate. I believe that people who hate children actually hate themselves more. I do not hate myself; I just don't want children.*

I am an aunty, and I love my nieces and nephews very much. I am not, however, desperate to be relevant to them in any way more than aunties who have their own children are. They are not my surrogate offspring. They are just my nieces and nephews. I'm a fun aunty who visits, plays games, teaches them inappropriate words and leaves by bedtime. They like me, I like them, but I don't want to make them feel that if they ran away from home they could come and live with me in my absolutely incredible new Victorian flat which is, in many ways, my very own baby.

There are lots of reasons why not having children works for me. I am a writer and spend most of my time alone, as I've previously mentioned. I love that part of my life so much, and I know I'd have to fight for it if I had a child. Writing is my therapy, my way of connecting with the world. It fulfils me in so many ways that I have never felt like anything is missing as long as I have a thought in my head and a pen or keyboard to get it down. I believe that if I had a child and struggled to find the time to write, then I would feel like something **was** *missing. So why would I want to do that?*

Of course I know that if I did have a child, I would experience the kind of love that would probably fill in all the gaps and solve all the worries that I have, but they wouldn't give me the time I have to do the other things that I love in life. So really, I can gain nothing from having a child, because I would lose so many of the things that are important to me. Solitude, travel, late nights, lazy weekends, sex on the couch in the middle of the day, to name but a few.

I read about women whose lives are caving in around them because they can't find a man to reproduce with. And others who have re-mortgaged their houses as they try round after round of IVF. I also know mothers who are blissfully happy, but also those whose careers have suffered, along with their self-worth, and the unspoken truth is that they probably won't get either of them back. My life is free of any of that. I am in no hurry to settle down, I do not feel empty, nothing is missing. You probably think I'm selfish. I think I'm a revelation.

Family ask me if I worry I will feel unfulfilled in the future because I never had kids. To which I think, ***are there not billions of women out there who feel unfulfilled because they*** *did* ***have kids?*** *Isn't choice basically what feminism is all about? How can we look back over the past five hundred years, at how women were knocked into second place because they were the ones that had to bear the children, and not agree that it is a reasonable reaction to want to remain child free?*

As a society, we have to stop valuing women on whether they have babies or not. My decision not to have a family of my own will mean that some people will always think I've failed, that I am tragic in some way. But there is nothing tragic about my life, because I love everything about it, and I'm especially excited for my future.

I look forward to your emails.

Cam x

Stella

Monday morning

'Stella, thank fuck. You have to unblock my computer; I need to get on the Internet,' says Jason as he comes, frantically, into the studio. It's nine a.m., he's never this early unless we have a shoot.

I knew this would happen, and I'm not doing it. He sent me an email after he left on Friday making me promise that no matter how much he begged, I must not unblock his computer until his book is finished. He sent me all of his passwords for his email and all his social accounts. 'You are in control,' he said, 'You are the boss.'

'No way. "Under no circumstances", that's what you said,' I remind him, my head throbbing from crying myself to sleep until three a.m. Phil slept on the couch.

'Well, things have changed. I need to find someone.'

'Jason, you said you would do exactly this. So no, sorry. There's no point in us making arrangements like that if you break them. You're locked out of the Internet until you've written the book. What is so urgent?' I ask, nosily.

'I met a girl on Friday night. She was awesome. I took her number, and just after we said goodbye this guy on a bike smashed into me and I dropped my phone down a drain.'

'Oh, that's annoying. Did she take your number?'

'Yes, we were texting.'

'Great, then there is no problem. I'll order you a new phone and she'll no doubt text you. Also, if you saved her number it will probably be on iCloud and you'll have it anyway. So, get back to work and be patient. No Internet, like we said,' I say, bossily. It's not always easy being Jason's PA, he takes some controlling. Luckily it's the part of my job that I enjoy the most; it's not like I have any control over my own life.

He is visibly calmer upon hearing that this woman's number isn't lost forever.

'And maybe playing it a bit cool could be good?' I continue, slightly out of turn. But I've seen Jason have multiple disastrous dating experiences because he tends to move way too quickly and freak people out. His old-school romantic tricks have a tendency to plummet with the kinds of women he likes. He likes to send flowers, and although the idea of that is nice, he often sends them to women at work. For some of his dates, who work in quite male office environments, this hasn't gone well.

One, who he apparently had a great time with, worked quite high up at Morgan Stanley. He sent her roses to work the day after their first date and she called him, livid, saying she never wanted to see him again because he'd embarrassed her so much. Jason couldn't get what the problem was. I told him that women who work in male environments don't like to make an issue of the fact they are female. Sending flowers was like passing her a big flashing sign that said, 'I AM A WOMAN WITH FEELINGS, TREAT ME DIFFERENTLY'.

He said he understood, but then sent flowers to the next woman he dated anyway. She had a similar reaction. He is who he is. There is something so endearing about how much he adores women.

He goes into his office and throws his rucksack on the floor. I hear him growl with frustration. He's quite cute when he's stressed, especially when it's over a girl. I feel so shitty today, so angry with Phil, but I can't help but find Jason amusing. It's so sweet how he pines for love. I long to be noticed the way he observes the women he falls for. I sometimes think I could do a naked cartwheel in front of Phil, and he'd just say something about the weather. He's lost so much spark from when I first met him. He was so charming, so confident, so happy. The worst thing about this is that I know *I'm* the one who has drained it out of him, and I do nothing to make it better. I'm cordial, I'm polite, I try to keep it sexy, but I don't connect. Not really.

I watch Jason as he sits in his chair and runs his fingers through his hair. His wrinkles are deeper, because his face is all tense. I get up and go to the door.

'Hey,' I say gently. 'Thanks so much for the champagne on Friday, that was really nice of you.'

His face falls back into place, as if momentarily forgetting about this mystery woman.

'Oh, you're so welcome. Did you have fun?'

'Yeah, it was nice. Good food. My friend is pregnant, so it kind of became about that.'

'Really? She gave you that news on your birthday? Selfish bitch, it should have been all about you.' He winks at me with his right eye. There are more wrinkles around it than the left, from being scrunched up looking down a lens. I've always thought that was really cute.

'Coffee?' I ask him.

'Go on then.'

As I wait for the kettle to boil, I text Phil.

Last night was weird. Hope you can still make it later?

He texts back right away, saying he'll be there.

Jason makes me jump, appearing behind me.

'Stella, please unblock my computer. I want to find Tara.' He really isn't giving up on this one.

'No. Sorry, Jason, it's not happening. Take a couple of days with no devices to just get on with it. How far are you past your original deadline now? Weeks, right? If she's that good, she'll wait. I'll order you a new phone, her number will be there and you can text her then, OK?'

'How long will that take?' he asks, impatiently.

'I'll get straight on it. Tomorrow, maybe the next day. OK?'

'OK.' He walks away, looking notably morose. I call after him.

'So who is she then, this Tara?' I ask, intrigued to know who has got him so besotted this time.

'I met her on Friday night. We had this amazing time. Like,

I always have a good time on dates, but there is always the feeling that it's all down to me, my effort, you know? But it wasn't like that with Tara. It felt so, so mutual. I took her number and then that fucking maniac smashed into me and I watched my phone disappear down the drain. I was halfway through texting her back, it's so frustrating.' He walks back towards me to take his coffee from my hand. 'I never even got her surname. We actually managed to spend a whole evening together and not talk about work or the weather, we really got on. Try and find her, will you?' he asks, pathetically.

'Find her? Where?'

'The Internet?'

'You want me to find some girl called Tara on the Internet?' I ask, thinking he must be joking.

'No, not just *some* girl called Tara. *The* girl called Tara.'

'Well, do you know where she works?'

'TV.'

'Do you know anything about her? Any defining details that might make her stand out on the Internet – because there are quite a lot of people on there and I could really do with some direction?' I say, a little worried he actually thinks I can do this.

'Well, I know that she is forty-two. She's about five foot eight with long thick brown curly hair, gorgeous freckles, size ten-ish. She works in TV, has a six-year-old daughter, and lives in Walthamstow. That's it. If you'd just let me use the Internet, I'd find her!'

'No, not happening, sorry. You pay me to control you, so I am controlling you.'

Jason puts his head back into his hands and lets out a huge exhalation.

'Look, I'll order your phone and you can call her then. OK? For now, crack on.' I watch him walk away like a kicked dog. I almost cave, but stick to my guns. I want this book to be done, it's boring around here with no shoots to organise. I'm spending way too much time on Facebook getting pissed off about how annoying everyone is.

I log in. So many status updates, so much sharing. People with new jobs, people losing weight, people having babies. Some are angry at the government; others are cracking jokes. I wouldn't know what to write, even if I did break my Facebook silence. What would I say? 'Desperate for a kid but my boyfriend won't sleep with me'? Or 'My twin sister died and now I have no idea how to live my life'? or 'When I die, there is a good chance that no one will remember I ever existed because I have never done anything that's made any lasting impact on the world'?

I decide it's probably best I don't say anything, and click on to *HowItIs.com* to see what Camilla Stacey has to say for herself today.

Being alone doesn't mean I am lonely.

Sure, I think. *It's alright for some.*

A calendar reminder pops up on my screen for five p.m. 'MAMMOGRAM' it says.

As if I would have forgotten.

Tara

'Sorry I'm late,' I say to Andrew as I walk into the office on Monday morning. 'Annie was up all night with a sick bug so I had to take her to my mum's.'

I feel horrible. The weekend was shit. Annie was so ill. The chicken I fed her was completely rotten, I realised this morning when I smelt it properly. On the way home from Sophie's she was crying and begging for it to stop. She puked all over the inside of the car, up the stairs and all over her bed. I watched her like a hawk until she eventually fell asleep in my bed at five a.m. Mum came and got her this morning and I came to work even though I should have just taken the day off. I felt so guilty, but I honestly couldn't face another day feeling like the crappiest mum alive. Now I'm a walking zombie but I just need to get on with work and forget about what was possibly the shittiest weekend of all time. Apart from meeting Jason, which was so amazing, and I still can't believe I misinterpreted it. But I clearly did. Thinking about it makes *me* want to projectile vomit. And then the guy on the train, urgh! I don't really want to be at work either, but saying that, Andrew seems to have decided not to make me feel guilty about being late, which is unusual.

'It happens,' he says. 'Nice weekend?'

He sits back in his chair and crosses his arms, a weird and zany smile on his face. If he is flirting with me, he can seriously do one.

'It was OK, thanks. You?' I reply, finding the casual chit chat with someone I usually spar with quite awkward.

'Oh you know, it was quiet. I didn't have any adventurous journeys or anything like that.'

'OK, well, sometimes chilled weekends are nice,' I say, deliberately not asking a question, hoping that our talk is over.

I put my laptop on my desk, then take off my cardigan and put it on the back of my chair. Andrew leans forward and stares at me.

'What?' I say, bluntly. He's really annoying me now, I'm not in the mood for his games.

'No, no, nothing,' he says, pretending to read something on his laptop. I instinctively check my seat for a whoopee cushion. There is nothing there.

'Oh, you're here,' says Adam, walking in. He also has a weird look on his face that makes me think I should check underneath my desk for cameras.

'Yes, sorry, Annie got—'

He interrupts me. 'I thought you might want to stay on the train all day, seeing as how much you love trains.'

What? Weirdo. I ignore them both, then Samuel appears behind Adam. They all watch me as I log in to my computer.

'What? Why are you all watching me?' I ask, starting to get ratty. I hate the way they try to intimidate me, it's really annoying.

'She doesn't know, does she?' says Samuel. 'She hasn't seen it. Oh my God, this is going to be beautiful.'

'Seen what? What's going to be beautiful?' I ask, with a little excitement that I try to hide, as it's obviously a big deal.

Andrew comes over to my desk, and leans over me to get to my laptop. I pull my jumper up over my shoulder to cover my skin. He types 'MailOnline' into Google. I'm racking my brains as to what I'm about to see. I would never admit this out loud, but I'm wondering if one of my shows has been nominated for an award.

The *MailOnline* website opens. In huge letters on the home page I see the words, 'ALL ABOARD THE LOVE TRAIN! *Tube shame as woman is caught MASTURBATING on the Victoria Line*.' And just underneath it, a video link and the static image of me with my trousers around my ankles and my hand in my crotch. They've pixelated my hand, but my face is as clear as anything.

'Oh my God,' I say, as my heart starts pounding so strongly in my chest that I have to swallow hard for fear of it coming up my throat. 'Oh my God.'

I just stare at it. Andrew presses play on the video but I slam my hand down on the mouse to stop it.

'That's you, having a good old wank on a train,' clarifies Adam. 'Even I wouldn't do that.'

'Oh my God. Annie,' I say, pathetically. 'My mum, my DAD.' I drop my head into my hands.

'Yup, that's one you probably don't want your dad to see,' Andrew says, patting me on the shoulder like I'm a dog.

I feel so hot, like my blood is actually boiling. The weight of people looking at me feels like a hot towel that's been thrown over my head, and I can't get it off. My breathing gets short; I can't draw in the air that I need. What is happening? Bev's hand appears in front of me, it sets a glass of water down on my desk. I try to pick it up but my fist won't clench, it rattles out of my hand and the water spills everywhere. I feel coldness seep through my skirt, and see Bev on the floor next to me mopping it up with a tissue. I can't hear anything. Am I underwater?

'Tara Thomas, Train Wank Woman,' says Andrew. 'It's got a ring to it.'

'No, wait,' says Adam, laughing. 'Thomas the Wank Engine!'

Their laughter is like a swarm of bees surrounding my head. How do I escape it? I have no words, no way to defend this. So I just run. I get up, grab my bag and I run for the door, down the stairs and onto the street. As the fresh air hits my face, I suck it in like it's my first breath in years. I am bent double on the pavement, I close my eyes and there it is, the image of me on the train, my hand in my pants, masturbating. How can I make it go away? I can't. It will never go away. I know this world enough to know that. I know how these things spin; it's my job to spin them. I look up and the brightness hurts my eyes, my brain is begging for darkness, desperate to shut down. My skin starts to burn, like an atomic bomb has exploded and I shouldn't be above ground. It's not safe for me out here, everyone is an enemy, infected with something that can kill me. I have to get home. I throw my arm into the air and hail a cab. When one pulls up, I clamber in and lie across the back seat. Has the driver seen it? Has everyone seen it?

My phone beeps. I can't bring myself to look who it is.

The driver keeps looking at me in the rear view mirror.

'What?' I snap.

'Sorry love, you just look like you're going to be sick. Do you need me to pull over?'

I sit up.

'I'm OK,' I say, looking out the window. We pull up at a traffic light, and someone who is about to cross the road makes eye contact with me. I duck again. *What if they know?*

'Are you hiding from the police, love?' the taxi driver says, jokingly, but also with concern in his tone.

'No, but please just get me home as quick as you can. I need to be in my house.' Ten minutes later, I am home. I double lock the door. The house feels cold; I'm not supposed to be here, I'm supposed to be at work. It wasn't expecting me. It feels small, claustrophobic, and there is the distant smell of sick. I sit on the stairs.

No. No, this isn't real. I don't deserve it to be real, why would this happen to me?

Maybe because I wanked on a fucking train. WHAT was I thinking?

I walk into the kitchen, turning on the heating on the way, I'm so cold. I put the kettle on. *This isn't real.* I take long, slow breaths as I try to ignore the calling of my laptop in my bag. I need to hold off looking. These last few minutes are important; I must treasure them, before I see the severity of this thing that isn't real yet. I wait for the kettle, I make some tea. I take it over to the kitchen table, get my computer out of my bag and open it. As it loads up, I stay calm. There is air in my lungs. Whatever happens, I will survive.

I type in my password.

My daughter's face appears as my screensaver, little folders all over it with key words reflecting various elements of my life. 'Photos', 'Annie Medical', 'Research', 'TV Contributors',

'Financial'. These secret little files that keep me in order, but I know that my life has just gone beyond my desktop. The Internet icon stares back at me like a red boil I need to burst.

I click on it.

I log onto *MailOnline*, and there I am. Clear as anything on the home page, having a 'good old wank', as Adam so beautifully put it. I click through to watch it on YouTube. I press play.

I see myself lost in the throes of ecstasy. My head is back, my tongue is licking my lips. My hand and crotch are pixelated but there is an undeniable dark mass representing my pubic hair. The *Metro* newspaper is next to me on the floor. If only I'd have held it with my other hand!

The video is only thirteen seconds long, but shows me making eye contact with the camera and throwing myself forward as I realise I'm being filmed. It is the clearest, most undeniable image of my face. I look into my own eyes; the desperation is shattering, my attempt to grab his phone futile. I land face down in the aisle of the train, like a deranged animal that's been shot with a tranquilliser gun. The guy filming me ran off the train backwards, so the final shot is me on the floor with my trousers round my ankles. It then it cuts out and the words, 'Play Again?' appear over the picture of my face.

I look to the bottom right. It's had 946,873 views.

It's only 11.30 a.m.

I log on to Twitter. #WalthamstowWankWoman is trending, as CCTV footage of me stumbling off the train at Walthamstow Central has been released. I shut it down instantly, I can't bear to look any more.

My life is fucked. Fucked. There is nothing I can do.

I sit with my head in my hands in my kitchen. The silence sounds like cymbals crashing in my ears. What am I supposed to do next? Call someone? Who? I have no idea. I feel like outside my front door is too terrifying to contemplate.

WALTHAMSTOW WANK WOMAN?

Of all the accolades!

Nearly one million people have seen me masturbate. God knows how many more by the end of today. So rarely in life would someone ever give in to an urge like that, and then to get filmed, it's just so unfair. This doesn't make sense.

I think of Jason. That speech bubble drove me nuts all weekend. He obviously already thought I was into crazy shit from asking if he had 'any special requests', now he's probably seen this. He must think I'm some slutty, crazy animal who turns down sex but has weird creepy wanks in public places; I mean, my God. If I was a man this would be illegal. Fuck, maybe it *is* illegal? I quickly type, 'is it illegal to masturbate in public if I'm a woman?' A *Guardian* article comes up; the first thing I see is that the penalty for masturbating in public in Indonesia is decapitation. I throw up a bit in my mouth. Then keep reading.

It is an offence for anyone to 'wilfully and indecently' expose his 'person' in a street or public place to the obstruction, annoyance or danger of residents or passengers (N.B. references to a 'person' mean 'penis').

Well, I don't have a 'person' and I wasn't being dangerous or an obstruction. And I thought I was alone! I can find nothing on what happens if you're a woman caught publicly masturbating when you're not an actual porn star. As I sift through Google, the only evidence I find of a woman ever masturbating in public are articles about me. And there are *hundreds* of them. Nearly every news outlet has covered it; everyone from *Sky News* to Buzzfeed, all either laughing, or questioning my sanity. One even says 'Is it any different because she is a woman?' I click on the article and see multiple comments from online users saying things like 'It's no different, anyone who is willing to expose themselves that way is a danger to society.'

I think about Annie. Her school. Her teachers have done a great job at pretending not to judge me, but this will tip them over the edge. What if they report me to social services? What if social services see this? I look at my front door, an inch thick of wood protecting me from a stampede of judgement. I'll never go out there again. I can't.

My phone beeps. It's Sophie.

Wait, is this real? Is this actually really happening or is this some weird TV stunt?

It's real, help me.

Meet me tonight, our bar. 6?

I don't reply. I'm never leaving the house again.

Oh, God. I feel like someone died. Like I died. Like I have to arrange my own funeral. Grief and logic are battling in my brain. The girl in me wants to sit and cry. The other parts –

the mother, the producer – know I have shit to sort out. People to tell, accounts to close.

I stand up. *Come on, Tara, you can get on top of this.*

OK, Annie. How do I deal with her? I text my mother.

Mum, I've come home. Really sick, please can Annie stay until tomorrow?

She texts back instantly.

Of course love, you must have caught Annie's bug, get better.

She doesn't really go on the Internet. She reads the *Daily Mail* but only the physical paper, hopefully I won't make it into that.

OK, next. I go back to my computer, and log on to Facebook. I have 145 Notifications and forty-three messages. The video has been posted on my page multiple times with comments varying from, 'Is this one of your documentaries?' to the more piss taking, 'You're such a wanker.'

I delete them all, check my privacy settings and make my timeline private so nobody can post on it.

Next, work. I look at my email account. As expected, there is an email from Adam already.

'Are you planning on coming back? We have a lot to do. I suggest you get a taxi.'

I can't think of anything to say. All I know is, I am never going back to that office. I don't reply. The grief is starting to overtake my logic now. A few minutes of clarity was enough, but reality is now kicking in. And yes, it's grief. Grief for the life I had, that I know I don't have any more. How can I? This isn't just a drunken night where I acted like a dick in front of friends and need to say sorry; this is strangers, colleagues, the media.

I should have been at home with my kid, not out exposing myself. And to think it was the one night I actually tried to do the right thing. I was going to go home, after that blissful bubble of a date, and I was going to look forward to seeing Jason again. I was going to play it right, be mysterious, take it slow. And now him and half the world have seen me partake in what is being presented as the grossest sexual act imaginable. I still can't believe this was me. *What was I thinking?*

Actually, I know what I was thinking. I was thinking about Jason, and how great he made me feel. And that maybe I had actually met a guy I could fall in love with, someone who accepted me for who I am. But most importantly, I was thinking I was alone.

And now I am alone and mortified. I'm worried that if I start to cry I just won't stop. I have no idea what the world is about to unleash on me or, to my utter shame, my six-year-old daughter. I have to hold it together. I text Sophie back.

Sophie, can you come here instead? I can't leave the house.

Sorry babe, I'll be in town already and then I have a dinner. Come, you'll be fine. Everyone can't have seen it yet?

Why can't she go out of her way for me, even just this once? But sod it, I need to talk. And she's right, I suppose. Not *everyone* will have seen it *yet*.

See you there at 6

FUCK!

Cam

Cam, wearing just black cotton knickers and a non-wired bra, looks up to see Mark standing naked at the bathroom door with a towel hanging over his erection. She stares through him while sucking a pen.

'How do you feel about women masturbating?' she says, not really looking for an answer.

'I love it when you masturbate, babe. Like you love it when I do.' He tosses the towel to the side and starts to touch himself. Cam reverts her eyes back to her computer and starts typing 'women masturbating' into Google. She is instantly met with an abundance of hardcore porn sites.

'Not me,' she continues, thinking aloud. 'Just women masturbating generally. Is it OK?'

Of course Cam knows it's OK by her standards, but she's throwing the question out there to society. Only society isn't actually in the room, so her young and unworldly lover is a little confused by the question.

'Do you want me to watch you?'

'No, Mark. No, I'm just asking if it's OK for women to masturbate, publicly. Is it different from men?'

'Well, I—'

'No, Mark. You don't have to answer. It's rhetorical.'

Mark doesn't know what rhetorical means, so walks over to the bed, hoping to end the conversation by resting his penis on her bottom lip.

'I have to work. I'll text you tomorrow, OK?'

Mark gets dressed and leaves without a peep. When the door shuts, Cam watches the Wank Woman video again.

She tries to put herself in this woman's shoes. Would she ever do it in public? In front of sexual partners, masturbating is hot, but when caught doing it unaware it's . . . creepy? Would she feel differently if it had been a man on the train? Why do women never talk about it? This whole thing is making her really uncomfortable, she can't help but feel sorry for this . . . Wank Woman. As everyone on the Internet seems to be judging or laughing, Cam is having a different response.

Cam thinks carefully, her fingers resting lightly on her keypad. Then, she writes.

I just sexually abused someone. And the chances are, you probably did too.

You've seen the Wank Woman video, right? That thirteen-second clip of a woman on a train, touching herself before she realises that she is being filmed? The clip that has, at time of writing, been viewed by 1,345,876 people. The clip that has no doubt changed a woman's life forever.

I, like everyone else, clicked on the video with intrigue. You try and keep me away from a catchy headline like 'WALTHAMSTOW WANK WOMAN'. And I watched and I started to laugh, but then I watched it again, and didn't find it funny at all. And then I watched it a third time, and felt angry at myself for ever seeing it at all.

There isn't a single news outlet in the country that isn't either laughing at this woman, calling her insane, or making her out to be some pervert. But that isn't what I see at all. I see someone who clearly thought she was alone, doing a very private thing, being filmed against her knowledge and then being publicly humiliated. And you know what? I don't like it. I don't like it at all. She may have been on a train, but she wasn't trying to be seen. The look on her face when she realised she was being filmed isn't funny, it's heartbreaking. The person who filmed her is not only a pervert, but he is an arsehole. He indecently filmed her against her will, and we are all guilty of abuse for watching it.

Human beings get up to all sorts of debauched and sexually intolerable things all the time, but they get away with it because most people aren't unfortunate enough to get caught. This poor woman wasn't even doing anything that wrong. She wasn't waving her vagina in people's faces, rubbing herself against them in the street, flashing her boobs at passers-by; she was simply trying to get away with a quick moment of private thrill in the wrong place. And now she's a national joke.

I feel sorry for her. You should too.

Before you watch that video again, before you forward it to your mates, I ask you to imagine this woman now. No doubt hiding in her house, too scared to go outside. Crying, alone and afraid. So embarrassed that she can't face even her nearest and dearest. Of course there is the chance she isn't, that she finds this all funny and got caught on purpose, but we all know that isn't true. You only have to look at her face at the end to know the consequences of this footage will be high.

I urge you to rethink your attitude towards this. It's not just a case of a woman being caught; it's a case of a woman being exploited.

Think about it.

Cam x

Tara

I race towards Sophie and throw my arms around her. 'Oh my God, Sophie, help me. What have I done?' I need my friend, a friend, *any* friend, to help me make sense of all this.

'Oh, Tara, I can't believe it. I mean, that video, it's so graphic,' she says, not helping.

'I thought maybe he was just taking a bloody picture. At

worst I thought he might show it to his mates, put it on Facebook but then take it down because his mum told him to. He was a kid, like, eighteen, or something. How did he manage to do this? Jesus, it's usually pictures of cats that go viral, not forty-two-year-old mums,' I say, drinking some of the champagne she had already ordered me.

'Well, to be fair, your pussy kind of stole the show,' she says, laughing to herself.

'Sophie, no! Please.'

'Sorry. But wow, the moment you realised you were being filmed. That was priceless.'

'Sophie, seriously. Just try to say things that will make me feel better. Just try, OK?'

'Sorry.'

'Work was horrible. I can never go back there. The bastards didn't even try to help me.'

'Help you, how could they help you?'

'I don't know, support? Suggestions. Anything. Instead they just laughed, called me names, it was like being at school. FUCK. Sophie, I have a little girl, I have a career. I need this to go away.'

Sophie takes a sip of her drink. She looks like she has something to tell me.

'What?' I ask her. 'Oh God, what?'

'Nothing, it's just— I'm not sure I can see you until this has all died down.'

'Why?'

'Because Carl saw the video at lunchtime. It made him really mad, he said he always got the impression that you were a bit like that and now his imagination is running wild as to what we used to get up to. He was all like, "If she's masturbating on a train when she's forty-two, what the hell were you two doing when you were in your twenties?"'

I can't believe she is saying this, and OK, maybe Carl is that bad. But she should be sticking up for me.

Rage starts to consume me. I don't know why I put up with Sophie and her crap idea of what friendship should be.

'Well why don't you tell him the truth then? That you fucked pretty much everything with two eyes and two legs for most of your premarital life, and that I was usually left on my own waiting for you?'

'OK, Tara, don't be like that.'

'Or about how I raced you to hospital three times to get your stomach pumped?'

'OK, you don't have to . . . '

'Or how I counselled you through two abortions, or how you deliberately used to seek out married men so that you didn't have to commit to anything more than just their wallet?'

'OK, now you're just being mean.'

We sit quietly. She looks at her watch, as if she needs to be somewhere.

'I'm sorry, hon, it just makes things really complicated for me. I've got a different life now and I don't want your mistakes to ruin that. I'm so sorry.'

'You're a terrible friend,' I say, meaning it. She always has been. I don't know why I stuck with it. I feel too shocked to feel betrayed. But if this is Sophie's reaction – *Sophie*, who's done worse things than this, on all forms of public transport – this must be bad.

'OK, you're upset. Hopefully by the time we get back, you'll have calmed down.'

'By the time you get back?'

'Yeah, I've booked us two weeks in Bora Bora. We need a holiday and this seemed like perfect timing, seeing as your face and fanny are all over the news. I need to get Carl as far away from it as possible. Classic distraction. It should have died down in two weeks . . . I hope.'

Two weeks, that feels like an eternity. What the hell is going to happen to me in the next two weeks?

'I'll let you know when I'm back, see how you're doing,' she says, downing her bubbles and walking away. I don't have the energy left to shout abuse after her.

I sit with my elbows on the bar, and drop my head into my hands.

'Aghhhhhhhhhhhhhhhh,' I murmur quietly. 'Aggghhhh, aghhgghghghg, aghghghghghh.'

'Excuse me,' says a woman's voice behind me. I turn to her; she is looking at me as if she's trying to pinpoint where we met. 'I don't mean to be rude, and please excuse me if I am wrong. But my friend and I were just wondering, is this you?'

She holds up her phone. It's a freeze frame of me with my head tossed back and my hand in my pants. What is the correct response in these situations? I don't know, but the only one I can offer is to run out of the bar, with my hand over my mouth, and throw up into a drain outside.

*

Back home, I look in the fridge. It's almost empty apart from some milk, a block of cheese and the leftover roast chicken that I now know to throw away. In the freezer there are two pizzas, a bag of peas and a gel eye mask. In the cupboard there are two tins of soup, a few tins of beans, some pasta, some rice, some crackers and a tube of Pringles. I calculate that I have around three days until I'll have to leave the house to get food. Maybe things will have died down by then. Maybe not.

Annie. My baby. *Oh God.*

Maybe Mum can bring her here after school tomorrow, they can bring food? I'll pretend to be sick. No, that's ridiculous.

Fucking hell. What the fucking fuck am I going to do?

Stella

I stand naked in front of the mirror in the examination room, my huge boobs hanging in front of me like horse's heads. My large brown nipples are like snouts, pointing subtly up at the end. My small waist is hidden by them; my wide hips are complemented by them. Alice and I used to stand side by side, comparing every tiny detail and difference like they were small secrets only we knew. We were like the hardest game of Spot the Difference, identical to anyone but us. We loved our bodies, and I still do. Which is why the prospect of losing pieces of it is so terrifying, of it being different to Alice's. I need it for my memories.

I cup the ends of my breasts in my hands and push them up a little, to where they used to sit. They haven't sagged much since I was a teenager, but enough to mean I could never get away with not wearing a bra now. With my cleavage pumped up, I turn slowly from side to side and smile as I remember the low-cut tops I used to wear in my party days. A memory of me and Alice dancing on a podium in Ibiza comes into my head. We'd been up for twenty-four hours and had pulled a couple of brothers who were loaded and kept pumping us full of Ecstasy and tequila shots. We were trying to dance sexily on the podium but Alice lost her footing and we both ended up in a heap on the floor. Alice got a black eye, and I got a broken arm. We spent the next eight hours in a Spanish hospital surrounded by other wasted people with similar injuries. Because we were still so high, we laughed the entire time. That's the kind of fun we used to have, all the time.

I look at the scar across my forearm. An everlasting memory of that brilliant holiday. And then, finding the sensation of joy uncomfortable, I clench my hand around my boobs and yank them both backwards, slamming my elbows down to hold as much of the flesh under my arms as I can. I look at my body now. Breast-less. Nipple-less. Sex-less. This is how it will be. My vagina will be a dead end.

'OK, are you ready?' says the nurse, coming back in and walking to the mammogram machine.

I lift my elbows and my breasts flop back into position, swinging and bouncing off each other as they find their place back on my chest. An anger burns inside of me like indigestion. Why my mum? Why Alice? Why me?

'OK, lift your breast and lay it on the plate,' says the nurse. I do as she says, thinking how ridiculous the command 'lay your breast on the plate' is. Also I know exactly what to do, this is my second mammogram. Ever since I heard the word 'positive', it's been constant appointments, smear tests, blood tests, squashed boobs. The BRCA gene means that cancer could appear quickly, so until I have the surgery, they are monitoring me carefully. Nothing is private any more. It's my body but someone else, or some*thing* has the control.

'OK, now I'm going to bring the other plate down, it might squeeze a bit.'

'It's OK,' I say, with an air of impatience, 'I know how this works.'

'Just wanting you to feel as comfortable as possible.'

'As comfortable as possible? While you squash my tit to be as flat as a pancake so we can find out if I have cancer or not? It's hardly a spa treatment, is it?'

'OK, let's just get this over with, shall we?' says the nurse.

I am terrible for making things harder on other people when I feel out of control. I know it isn't nice. I do it anyway.

The machine takes a few pictures.

'You have lovely big boobs,' the nurse says.

'Thanks. I like them.'

'That's nice. Doing this job, you see how many women don't like their breasts. It's sad.'

'Not as sad as when the ones that *do* like them have to have them sliced off, I imagine?'

There is an awkward silence. Something else I am good at creating. The nurse realises that what she said was potentially a little insensitive, considering the scenario, so just cracks on with taking the pictures in a bid to get me out as quickly as she can. I suppose it's not her job to deal with the complex psychology of these situations.

'OK, you're all done. If you get dressed and wait in reception, Dr Cordon will be right with you for your consultation.'

Out in reception, Phil is sitting there, reading a leaflet.

'You came?' I say, surprised to see him. But to be fair to him, he's never missed one of my appointments.

'Of course I did. Sorry I was late, you'd already gone in by the time I got here,' he says, sweetly, but without really looking at me.

'It's OK. You wouldn't have come in there anyway; you don't need to see me getting touched up by a robot.' I laugh, he doesn't. 'Dr Cordon is going to see us soon.'

'Great.'

'Great. What are you reading?'

He passes me the leaflet.

Preventative surgery saved my life

Inside is a picture of a woman with her husband and a child.

'When I found out I had the BRCA gene, I feared for my family. I felt like a ticking bomb. There was no question what I should do. I booked in for the surgery immediately. My husband was very supportive; I knew he'd love me, regardless of my body. Now I can live my life and I don't live in

fear of leaving my little boy without a mum. I feel so lucky that the surgery was an option for me and my family.'

'I wonder what my testimonial would say in a leaflet like this,' I say, trying to have a joke with Phil. 'Something like, "*I had the surgery because my mother died of breast cancer and my twin sister died of ovarian cancer. There wasn't really any choice for me unless I wanted to die too. Oh, and I never had any kids, so in the grand scheme of things my death wouldn't really matter anyway. So I should probably not have bothered and just kept my boobs so at least I would have died with my body intact rather than with half of me missing and being alone . . .*"'

Whoops. I had intended that to be funny.

'God, Stella. When you talk like that it makes me feel so uncomfortable,' he says, taking the leaflet back from me.

'Sorry, that just kind of came out. I should have added that I have you, and that you make me really happy. And that you have supported me?' We both know I'm lying. I put my face close to his and he moves his cheek towards my lips so I can kiss it.

'Stella?' says Dr Cordon's voice. We are both relieved for the interruption.

Phil and I walk into her examination room and sit next to each other on the two chairs next to her desk.

'So, how are you two?' she asks.

'Good, yeah,' says Phil.

'We're OK,' I clarify.

'Great. We won't get the results from the mammogram

back for a week or so, and I really want that to be your last. At your age too many can actually be detrimental, and your breast tissue is too dense to get very clear results. If you decide to go against the surgery idea, then we will do a yearly MRI instead, OK? It is much more accurate.'

Dr Cordon had booked me in for a mammogram because last time we tried to do an MRI I had a severe panic attack. The noise, the memory of watching Alice go into one of those machines, it all got too much for me. I never want to have one.

'I want the surgery,' I say, causing Phil to shift in his seat. 'Even though I am terrified.'

When Mum was having her last bout of chemo, she was so sick. Alice and I were sitting on the bed listening to her vomit constantly for fifteen minutes. When she came out, she made us both promise that if we could ever do anything to avoid that happening to us, then we must. Unfortunately, Alice didn't get the chance to make any decisions. Her cancer appeared and then she disappeared. It was all over in under a year.

'I'm sure,' says Dr Cordon, sympathetically. 'And what is it that troubles you most?'

'Oh, you know. Just that I'll be disfigured and infertile. It's all pretty daunting.'

Phil sniffs. Dr Cordon and I both look at him, to make sure he's not crying.

'Yes, right, of course,' Dr Cordon says. 'But because of the aggression of Alice's ovarian cancer, and also your mum's breast cancer, and that they both developed at such a young age and that Alice was your identical twin . . . ' The word 'was' hangs in the air like a dark cloud that won't blow away. ' . . . I am particularly anxious about your situation. Have you two thought any more about having a baby? I know we discussed it last time you were here?'

Both Phil and I scramble for some words, but come up with nothing. I'm not going to be the one to tell her that he has refused to have sex for a month.

She senses tension, and moves it along.

'Like I said in our last appointment, I'm comfortable with holding off the surgery for a year or so, to give you the chance to have a baby naturally. I'd monitor you very carefully throughout. If this result comes back clear, then there is nothing to say you don't have time.'

'Do I, though?' I ask. 'Alice was dead by the time she was twenty-six. How do you know I have time?'

'OK, I don't. You know that the positive gene result means you have an eighty-five per cent chance of developing breast or ovarian cancer in your lifetime. Your mum and sister's ages at passing show that the risk in your younger years is also very high. But if you really want a baby, then my view is that you go for it. You might never get cancer; fifteen per cent says you won't. We don't have to do the surgery at all . . . '

'No, I want the surgery,' I say, boldly, again.

But I want a baby too. So, so much.

'OK, so my advice is go home, work on getting pregnant, and stay focused on the fact that right now you are a healthy young woman. We can do the surgery when the baby is born. What do you think?'

'Yes,' I say, looking at Phil, who says nothing but nods unenthusiastically.

'And if it doesn't work, we can look into freezing your eggs, and then you can have the surgery and have a baby further down the line. But if you're quick, maybe you can do it all naturally, just the way you want. OK?'

'OK,' I say, feeling pumped after a little pep talk. 'We'll try.'

'So, shall I make that tuna bake tonight then?' I ask Phil, as we arrive home. He has barely said a word in the Uber.

'Sure.'

'And there is champagne in the fridge. The one your parents sent me for my birthday, we could drink that, relax a little?'

'Sure.'

'Great, I'll make a start on dinner. Why don't you chill for a bit?'

God, he is being so grumpy. Who was it that just got reminded they have an eighty-five per cent chance of getting cancer?

I wash my hands, and then get to making the food. I can feel him hovering and it's making me uncomfortable.

'I can't do it any more, Stella,' he says softly, standing behind me as I get three tins of tuna out of a cupboard.

'Do what?' I reply, as if he's going to tell me he doesn't know how to open bottles of champagne.

'It's just so much pressure. The gene, the operation, the baby,' he continues, his voice getting stronger.

I turn to him. He's crying. This is really happening. I wonder what to say, but then I remember what my mother used to tell me. She said if someone is about to hurt you, let them say everything they need to say – so when they are done, you can tell them to shut up if they interrupt you.

'I wanted to support you, so much, but this has taken it to another level. You don't connect with me; you don't see how this is hard for me. You sat with Dr Cordon last time and told her that you wanted a baby, that we were going to try for one. But you never even asked me if it was what *I* wanted. And now I feel like if I don't give you the baby then you'll be miserable forever and I don't think you've taken any time to consider how that might feel for me. I'm not ready for kids, and this isn't how I want to do it even when I am. I'm sorry, but I don't see how it is good for either of us for me to stick around while you go through this.'

'OK, Phil. Let's not have a baby then,' I say, slamming the tuna down on the work surface. 'I just won't have a baby, fine.'

'But that's not the problem, is it, Stella?' he says, gaining more confidence. 'The problem is you can't love me because you're so full of grief and anger that there's no room for anything else.'

I gently lay both my hands on the work surface and stare at the spice rack on the wall. That was a really horrible assessment of my character.

'I think we should break up,' he says, clearly determined to say the things he needs to say and not allow emotion to get in the way. 'And I know that makes me look terrible and like I'm abandoning you, that I'm cruel and selfish, but you know that if it wasn't for you testing positive to the gene we would not be trying for a baby. We'd probably not even be together. So I'm ending it – because no matter what you decide to do, us pretending to be in love with each other just because it would be easier if we were is not the right thing, for either of us. I think what you're facing is horrible, but I can't carry on this way. I'm sorry.'

I want to scream in his face. This relationship was supposed to make things better, not damage me more. He came into my life all compassionate, full of, 'I'll help you, I'll support you, I'll take care of you.' What else is someone like me supposed to do in that situation? I'd lost the people I loved the most and there was this guy saying, 'Hey, you don't have to be alone.' I threw myself at him, saying all the right things, doing all the nice things, all the stuff you're supposed to do in relationships to make the other person happy. I cooked, I worshipped him in bed, I made him laugh. What more could I have done?

I could have actually loved him.

'I'll come back and get my things while you're at work,' he says, getting up. He walks over to the door but turns just before he leaves. 'You should just have the surgery, Stell. Learn to be alone. I know this has been awful for you, but you need to work out who Stella is without Alice. You're not a twin any more.'

'GET OUT,' I screech. 'Why the fuck would you say that to me?' I pick up a vase from the table and launch it across the room. It smashes as it hits the door behind his head. 'GET OUT,' I scream again, watching him leave quickly as he fears for what I might do next. I'm not even sure myself.

The bomb inside me has exploded.

4

Cam

'In my day, the jokes were funnier,' says Cam's dad, as they turn on to Carlisle Street and arrive at The Toucan pub. 'Now it's about who can be cruder, who can say the most racist, aggressive or politically inappropriate thing. The laugh comes because the audience doesn't know what else to do with themselves, not because of a well-constructed and cleverly written joke. Comedy is losing its soul. Anyway, the usual?'

'Yes please,' says Cam, sitting on a barstool that is shaped like a giant pint of Guinness. Her dad orders a stout and a pint of lager. The lager is for Cam. They've just been to a Tuesday night comedy gig, a tradition they have held for around ten years. Her mum hates comedy clubs, always has, which is one of the main reasons her dad had to stop working in them. Cam couldn't bear the idea that he didn't get to be in the clubs any more, so every Tuesday she takes him to one and they have a pint or two afterwards. She loves it; she's more herself with her dad than anyone else. This evening they went to see a newish guy at the Soho Theatre who the critics are calling, 'The Next Russell Brand'. He spoke about little more than his sexual conquests, itchy balls and his fantasies about interracial orgies. Her dad is right – it was gross, tacky and shit.

'The millennials love it though, Dad. They're growing up in an unedited world. They can see anything at any time of the day and people in entertainment think they have to match that, so they get more and more extreme. I see it all the time in journalism too. Lots of people writing stuff to get noticed, rather than stuff they actually feel. Most of what is being said is just the fearful result of some writer who is scared of not getting any more work. I do it myself sometimes.'

'You do?'

'Kind of. I mean, I don't make anything up or pretend to be someone I'm not like a lot of people do, but I know I have to play a game. I have to entice and provoke. No one wants normal, or sweet and fluffy. People want grit, dirt, drama. But they want it to feel spontaneous, like it's my real life.'

'Yes, well you certainly create drama,' Cam's dad says, taking a glug of beer and raising his eyebrows. She knows exactly what he means.

'Has she read it then?'

'Yup, she's read it alright.'

Cam knew the column about not wanting kids would go

down like a smack in the face with her mother. Her mum has never wanted to hear it, no matter how many times she has tried to explain how she feels.

'She thinks there is something wrong with you.'

'You mean she thinks I am a lesbian?'

'In her mind that *is* something wrong, unfortunately.'

Cam looks at her dad; this funny, energetic, liberal, gentle, kind man, and wonders how he ended up with someone so completely different to him in so many ways. She loves her mum so much. She admires her greatly for her strength, determination and dedication to her family but the truth is not something she can avoid – her mum is an arsehole.

'How have you done it, Dad? For forty-three years?'

'Ahh she's not so bad when you get her on her own,' he says, smiling. 'It's just a shell, she's all slushy on the inside. You know that really.'

Cam nods. Of course she's seen her mum's softer side over the years. It's there, somewhere.

'Your mum is a good woman, Camilla. She loves you very very much, that's all. She had a dream for all her girls and you don't want to live it. She's still getting used to it.'

'I want her to be really proud of me for everything else.'

'She'll get there. She will,' her dad says, reassuringly. He looks like he has something he needs to say.

'Oh go on, what is it?' Cam asks, with a good idea of what it is.

'Look, don't get mad. Just tell me really, why do you not want to do it? Have a family?'

'Dad! For God's sake, not you as well!'

'Oh come on, you know I don't care if you do or don't. But I'm curious to know, is it anything we did?'

Cam doesn't want to answer. But if he really thinks it could be his fault, she can't have that.

'It's nothing you did, Dad. Look, I'm sure if all the layers were stripped away it would have *something* to do with us as a family. The life I think you could have lived on the road, or me being bossed about my entire childhood by three really overpowering sisters and only feeling truly in control of myself when I was alone. Or maybe because I worry I'd not be loving enough, like Mum. Or because I hid in a cupboard one too many times as a kid, or blah blah blah. But also maybe it's none of those things. Maybe it is just really, genuinely who I am. Does everything have to be because of something? Aren't some things just because?'

They both sit quietly for a minute, sipping their pints, thinking about that. Then a big smile creeps across his face.

'She looked so beautiful when she got pregnant with Tanya; I didn't want to miss a minute of it. Sounds pathetic really, doesn't it? But it's true, I loved having a wife and a family. My old man didn't want anything to do with me most of my life, and then your mum came along and she never let me out of her sight. Christ, she got jealous. But I think I'd been wanting that to happen my whole life. And then Angela and Mel, then you came along, and for once my life was all about family. It was hard work but I was so bloody proud of you all I didn't mind working at the school. Everything was better than that basta—' He stops himself from getting upset.

Cam puts her arm around her dad. She hates to hear about her grandfather, he was such a brute. But he's right, her mum is soft under that brittle surface. It makes Cam so happy to hear her dad speak so affectionately about her. As an adult she doesn't have to deal with her mum every day, but he does. She likes to be reminded that their marriage is a happy one; it means she'll always love her mum, no matter what.

'I'm sorry your dad was mean to you,' she says, putting her forehead against his.

'Ah, what can you do? I think he made me a good dad. I know how much your parents can screw you up, I never wanted to do that to you girls.'

'What the hell are you talking about?' Cam says, finishing her pint with one huge gulp. 'My therapist said you're totally the reason I'm so fucked up.' She digs him in the ribs. He laughs.

'Me and my sisters did a good job of trying to screw each other up though. Those fights!'

'The fights! I had to pull you off each other so many times,' her dad says, shaking his head at the memory. 'Boys are rough but girls, girls are vicious.'

'I know! Angela actually drew blood on my arm once. She grabbed me so hard, I still have a bit of a scar. But I'm grateful for it. I think having to defend myself to three older sisters made me tough in the world I'm in now. My sisters were nothing compared to some of the female journalists I've had to deal with over the course of my career.'

'You're right. Do you remember when that awful woman

from the *Mail* wrote that piece about you, saying that you were a disgrace to feminism because you—' he clears his throat, 'because you write about boys the way you do. I don't know what is wrong with women, the way they pit themselves against each other. You girls fought but you were a gang. Remember the time Tanya punched that girl who called you a lesbian at school?'

'I do, but let's be honest, part of that punch was frustration at me because she wondered if it was true. I love you, Dad,' she says, putting her arm around him. 'You're my feminist icon.'

'No matter the fights, you girls are a team. You will always have each other. That's what family should be, the people who are there for you, no matter what you do.'

'True that! One more for the road?'

'Sure.'

As the barman pulls their pints, Cam's dad puts his hand on hers. 'You haven't really got a therapist, have you?'

'No, Dad. No, I'm OK in my head. It's everyone else that is crazy, not me.'

'That may well be true, love. I can't argue with that!'

Stella

It feels like the night Alice died. That night, I was completely alone too, and knew no one else was going to come home. I sat here, in the flat, and stared at the front door. I wanted to run at it as fast as I could and knock myself out. It wasn't that I wanted to die, but I needed a pain I could understand. Something physical that could be treated, rather than the emotional agony that I had no idea how to fix. I ended up slicing a knife into my arm instead, right along the line of the scar I got that night in Spain. Like cutting through my memories, trying to make them into something else. It didn't do what I thought it would do, but it did mean I ended up in A&E getting stitches again. I've never cut myself since. But that doesn't mean I have found a way of coping.

I wasn't born to be alone. I came into this world three minutes after Alice and we weren't more than a few feet apart until we could crawl. I spent my entire life, until I was twenty-six, with my sister. Even when we had our own rooms we chose to sleep together, it was only having boyfriends that meant we were apart. And then she died and there I was, in our home, looking into the abyss of my life, not knowing if I would ever have someone to be close to again.

Then, a year later at Jessica's wedding, my first big social outing since Alice's funeral, I met Phil. Because a lot of the same people that were at the funeral were there, they all wanted to talk about Alice when they were drunk. So when I realised that Phil fancied me I locked myself onto him, and didn't leave his side all night. He seemed to like me, despite my darkness. We met up the next day, and he made me all these promises and I stuck to them like glue. He wasn't the guy I imagined myself with – he wasn't Alice – but he was a ticket out of solitude, and so I went for it with all I had.

And look at me now. Sitting alone at the kitchen table, half a bottle of red wine in front of me, the other half in my belly, and nothing but Facebook to remind me that I should have more people in my life than I do.

I pour more wine and drink it quickly. I don't have an addictive personality, but I can rarely deny myself the emotional freedom that drinking alcohol offers me. I log in to Alice's Facebook account.

When I'm feeling sad, and I really need to cry, this is the first place I come (after the wine). Her messages still feel so alive to me, her silly banter with friends. Arranging nights out, then laughing about them the next day. But there is one message that is really hard to read. The one she sent to all her friends to tell them she was dying. I never saw it until after she'd gone, because she didn't include me in the list of people she sent it to.

Hello to all of my wonderful friends. I have some news.

As you know, I've not been well. Some of you know why, but some of you don't. It's time for you all to know that I have cancer, and it's not going away.

I know you're going to find this sad and it is, it is so so sad. I haven't had time to come to terms with it because it's all happened so fast. I'm in shock, I feel cheated, I feel angry and sad and all of those things. But I also feel grateful. Grateful that I didn't die in an accident and not get the chance to tell people how I feel about them, or say my good-byes.

I'm sorry for the group message, but typing this more than once isn't something I want to spend my very short time left doing. But I wanted you all to know a few things.

1) *I am dying really happy. It's been short, but I've had a good life. The one I wanted.*
2) *Even through the sadness of losing my mum, my friendships and my sister have given me so much joy. If you received this message, you gave me joy, so thank you.*
3) *I got to work at an animal shelter for five years and simple as that might sound, it was all I ever wanted to do. Please look after your pets and donate to animal charities in my honour.*
4) *I'm not scared. This is happening quickly, and I am in pain, but I am not scared. Apart from one thing; my sister. I want to ask you all to do something for me, because I need to know she won't be alone. Stella isn't dealing with this very well and I understand why, because if it was her dying, I wouldn't deal with it well either. But I'm going to die and we can't avoid it. She's going to go into a hole when I've gone, and she's going to cut you all out and do her best to suffer alone. Please don't let her. Please go and see her, talk to her, make her get out. She will get through this if she has people to help her, so I am asking you, my friends, to help her. For me. Thank you.*

That's it. That is my parting message – on Facebook, how modern! I'm sure I'll see you all before I go; let's deal with that however we feel in the moment. But my hope is that we laugh about our past rather than cry about my future.

Also, don't be shocked. I look like I'm fucking dying.

Alice x x

I wipe tears from my cheeks and pour more wine. I was so loved. So protected by her. Right up until the last minute, Alice's life was wrapped around me, making mine OK. But as soon as she died, that was gone. It took no more than a year for all of those people to stop bothering with me. Sure, I turned down every invite, I rarely answered my phone, but weren't they supposed to push through that? Understand that my healing would take time, guide me out of my 'hole'? They think writing public messages on my Facebook page on my birthday is what she asked them to do? It's pathetic. They call themselves her friends, but they never committed to her dying wish. I hate them. Fake, soulless shits who use her death to get attention on this stupid website.

I pour the rest of the bottle into my glass and drink it. I click on Melissa Tucker's profile and scroll down her page. She's received so much sympathy for the post she wrote on my birthday about missing Alice.

'I'm so sorry for your loss,' says one person.

'You are so strong for building your life around this,' says another.

I look at her photos, there are countless ones of her and Alice that she's posted recently with messages like, 'Still miss this lady', and 'I had the best nights of my life with Alice'.

God, she's so annoying. I come out of photos and just as I'm about to leave her page I accidentally click on the ADD FRIEND button.

I'm logged in as Alice. *Oh shit.* I quickly open a new Internet window and type, 'How to cancel a Facebook friend request'. My connection is being slow. Hurry up! OK, there it is . . . *Go to their page, hold cursor over FRIEND REQUESTED and click* CANCEL *on the drop down menu.*

Right, I go back to Facebook. I see the FRIEND REQUESTED button, but just as I am about to click it, PING, a notification pops up saying, 'Melissa Tucker has accepted your friend request'.

Oh, God.

A message comes up instantly.

'What is this, some sick joke? Who is this?'

I panic. If she looks at the page, she'll see that I left a message on it just a few days ago wishing Alice a happy birthday. That will make me look mental, or she'll know it's me. What can I do?

I deactivate the account.

It's gone.

No more green dot.

Wednesday

Tara

I'd been awake for four minutes before my left eye opened this morning. Eventually I had to prise my eyelids apart with my fingers. Four-day-old mascara had welded it so tight that at minute three I almost accepted that I would never be able to use it again. I wasn't even bothered.

Since yesterday, I have slept in my bed once and the rest of the time I have sat on the sofa watching TV and Googling myself. I've eaten both frozen pizzas, most of the cheese and the Pringles. My tongue has turned a weird shade of yellow and I feel like I've drunk an entire glass of salt. I keep going into the kitchen to get water but forgetting what I went in for, so then I just sit back on the couch again, wishing I wasn't so thirsty. The air is hot and thick, it's like I'm wading around in a bowl of sad soup.

I have told repeated lies to my mother about being sick so that I don't have to face the reality of life. And I live in hope no one at the school gate would utter a word to her, if they have seen the video. Hopefully I will be protected by their own embarrassment to say what I did out loud. But I miss my daughter, so, so badly. And I need some vegetables. I'm going to have to leave this house soon.

I feel like the entire Internet is obsessed with me. I've been trending on Twitter for days, and I've been discussed and written about by almost every female-focused TV show and website. People think I'm mentally ill, that I did this because I'm crazy. Women who know nothing about me are discussing how I was probably abused and how they 'shouldn't judge' (even though they are), 'as you never know what a woman has been through to get to the point that she does something like that'. They think I'm broken. That I did this as a cry for help, or because I'm deviant, or a pervert. I've read reasons for my actions that I could never have thought up in my wildest dreams, they're writing everything but the truth: that I thought I was alone, I felt horny, so I masturbated. I mean, why can't anyone just take it for what it is?

In the whole Internet I have only found one article that's on my side, written by Camilla Stacey. I nearly died when I saw it. I'm such a massive fan of hers, it's so bizarre reading about me on a blog I've been reading for years. But even she is getting shit on Twitter for supporting me. People really hate me.

The video has had over three million views. I'm a meme that's been shared over 500,000 times. It's a picture of me with my head rolled back and my hand in my crotch with the words, 'WHEN YOUR PHONE RUNS OUT OF JUICE' across it. I read an actual article explaining why this meme was so 'powerful', how the human race has become so wildly addicted to smart phones that they 'panic wank' if they run out of battery. When you are the subject of a juicy topic of social scandal, you realise how fucking crazy everyone has gone. Any moron can get an article published giving their hot take on something like this. It's only a matter of time until they know my name, what I do. Or what I *did,* should I say. I'm never going back to that office.

The weird thing about the past twenty-four hours is that I've had no contact with a single human but I've felt completely surrounded. I don't think there is a corner of the earth that isn't talking about me. I'm trying to be logical. I remember when Pram Push Woman was the biggest thing. A video went viral of a woman pushing a pram into the middle of a motorway and then running off and leaving it there. It caused a pile up of three cars because the drivers obviously thought there was a baby in it. It turned out, there wasn't. She'd just done it to trick people. Even she couldn't explain why she had done it. The only thing she managed to squeak out when asked by a journalist outside her house was, 'I just wanted to see what would happen.'

Luckily no one died, so I think she got away without any criminal charges, but God knows what she's doing now. Who would employ her? Who would date her? Who would leave her alone with a child? She was the biggest story on social media for a whole week, but then it was gone. You never really hear about Pram Push Woman any more, but that isn't to say she's alright.

I keep telling myself this will pass, that people will move on, because nothing stays interesting for that long. I didn't try to kill anyone, or pretend to try to kill someone. But the problem is, sex trumps everything. I think what I have learnt is that men get treated like individuals, no matter what they do. But when women do something like this they get spoken about like they've let the side down, like they have personally set feminism back a peg or two. It's all about the *why*. *Why did she do this, what led her to it? What does this say about women?* Rather than just accepting it was a moment of sheer joy and ecstasy that has been turned into a moment of deviant madness. My video is the greatest study of female sexuality of the past year.

Maybe there *is* something wrong with me. I wonder what I'd think if I saw the clip of someone else doing what I did. What presumptions would I make? I'd certainly laugh about it, send it to a few friends, be aghast and make judgements. Then what would I do? I'd probably get on with my day and not really care, but be thrilled if someone brought it up so I could laugh about it and judge her some more.

But would I care? I don't think so. So why should anyone else care about me?

But they do. I know they do. Everyone who doesn't know me thinks I'm a lunatic. God knows what the people outside my front door think. But I have to go out there. I have to see my daughter. I can't just lock myself away and not deal with that.

I text my mum.

Mum, I'm feeling better. Maybe I should pick Annie up later?

I try to sound as un socially shamed as possible, not wanting her to suspect anything is wrong. I've been analysing her replies to see if I detect any hints that she knows about what's happened, but I'm pretty sure she hasn't. I'm sure it's just a matter of time, though.

She would love that darling. She missed you very much x

I honestly believe that if I didn't have the responsibility of a daughter I might never step outside the front door ever again. I'd have to earn money, but I'm sure as hell never going back to work again. I'd probably just capitalise on my new brand and wank on a web cam for truck drivers in America. At least I'd be utilising all of my skills.

Adam has been emailing constantly and I have about forty missed calls from him. I can't even look or listen to them.

Another text pops up from my mother.

Oh, while I have you. I'm just finalising the details for your dad's birthday party on Friday. Let me know if you have any last minute suggestions?

Oh fucking hell, I had totally forgotten about that! *My dad. Oh God, my dad.*

I'm at such a loss of what to do. How do I make this go away, when the world is so against me? How can I turn this around? I look back onto *HowItIs.com* and read Cam Stacey's article again.

'There isn't a single news outlet in the country that isn't either laughing at this woman, calling her insane, or making her out to be some pervert. But that isn't what I see at all.' Is she my only hope? I see her email address on the Contact page, and the words, 'Write to me, I love to hear from you.'

And so, because I have absolutely nothing else to do other than Google my own name and cry into an empty pizza box, I do.

Cam

Cam's column about not wanting children appears to have caused quite the stir. *Sky News*, *BBC Breakfast* and *This*

Morning all asked her to go on, but she only agreed to *Female First* on BBC Radio London, because she can't be bothered with the Twitter backlash of going on TV. So many people read her blog, but apart from a few very carefully selected pictures she posts, her image isn't hugely out there. That's intentional. Every time she goes on TV, no matter what she is discussing, all anyone on Twitter goes on about is what she looks like. It's so boring. They tear apart her hair, her face, her big hands. Even when people are complimenting her, she still wants to tweet back, 'STOP GOING ON ABOUT WHAT I LOOK LIKE AND JUST LISTEN TO WHAT I HAVE TO SAY.' She wants to be known for her opinions, so writing and radio suit her just fine. Also, she can hide her nerves if no one can see them.

Arriving at the BBC, a woman with a clipboard comes to meet her in reception. She's got a navy knee-length skirt on, a white shirt and a blue cardigan. Her hair is mousey and shoulder length, she isn't wearing any make-up and she has reading glasses on top of her head. She's probably around thirty-five, and looks like she loves libraries. Comparatively, Cam feels like a giant and looks like she loves mosh pits. She's wearing skinny jeans, a taupe t-shirt and a black leather biker jacket with chunky boots. The weather is hot, she wants to take her jacket off but her sweat patches feel pretty bad, so she leaves it on, grateful for the aircon. She didn't wash her hair this morning because she couldn't be bothered to dry it. That's another bonus of radio.

'Hi Camilla, I'm Philippa. Thanks for coming on the

show, we're all really excited to have you. Did you get your pass?'

'Yup,' Cam says, proudly, holding it up.

'Great. I'll take you up.'

In the lift, Philippa pretends to read whatever is on her clipboard to fill the silence. Cam is surprised by the lack of conversation. She'd start it herself, but her stomach is in knots at the thought of live broadcasting. She also has a paranoia about disappointing people when they meet her in real life. She's so feisty, cool and funny on her blog, constantly getting emails from fans saying she is their hero, they wish they could be more like her. And although that is who she really is inside, she needs the help of a keyboard to get it out.

When they step out of the lift, there is a door to get through, it needs a fob. Philippa pretends to struggle with it, but it's obvious she is just buying time. She eventually seems to give in to the voices in her head.

'OK, I shouldn't really say this,' she says, turning from a meek librarian to a someone with a bit of fire behind her eyes. Cam is a little startled by it.

'Your column about not wanting kids was so amazing. I've never wanted children and it's been hard to say that out loud sometimes, because of judgement. So, thank you.'

'Oh good, thanks.' Cam wonders what is coming next. That wasn't worthy of the prefix, 'I shouldn't really say this.'

'Look, you should know this. Janis doesn't understand women like us. She's doing this feature because she knows it will get a big reaction from the listeners, but she won't have your back if they call in and get nasty. I just wanted to warn you, you'll have to stick up for women like us. It's what you do, I know, but seeing you face to face I want you to know how much I appreciate it, that you say what so many of us are too scared to say. I can't be honest about who I really am here, I'd lose my job if she knew that I'd rather be single forever than have a husband, but you don't have to lie about anything, you don't have a boss like Janis to answer to.' Cam's mother flashes into her mind, and she wonders if that is true. Philippa looks quickly from side to side. 'I get so paranoid this building is bugged.'

'Right, well, thanks for the heads up,' Cam says. She was not expecting that from Philippa. She's got something of the Clark Kent about her. Also, talk about pressure, her palms are suddenly very sweaty.

'OK, if you just wait in here, I'll come get you when it's time to go in,' Philippa says, showing Cam into the green room, which is actually a white room with no windows, three chairs and a bowl of nuts.

Cam takes a seat and checks her Twitter feed on her phone. Her piece supporting 'Walthamstow Wank Woman' has bombed.

@CamStacey Oh do give over . . . you're telling us not to watch a video of a woman having a right old frappuccino on a train? She loved it mate. She wants us all to watch it.

@CamStacey I usually love you, but you've lost me with this, sorry. Am I supposed to sympathise with a pervert? #disappointed

@CamStacey Then I should probably go to prison because I can't stop watching it! It's HOT. Love the PUSSY.

She looks at the stats for her site. It's had half the hits that one of her pieces usually gets, almost no retweets. This is so unusual. Cam feels deflated by it. She hates it when her posts don't rate, but really? People are that jaded that they can't see what has happened to this poor woman?

She checks her email to see if there is anything notable. There is an email from a 'Tara Thomas'. The subject reads, 'Thanks, from Wank Woman'. Cam opens it immediately.

Dear Camilla, I'm a bit short on words right now, but just wanted to say thanks for the piece you wrote. I can't tell you how good it felt to read one thing that wasn't about me being crazy or a pervert. I don't know if you'll read this, I hope you do. Thanks again, Tara (aka Walthamstow Wank Woman) x

Tara saw her piece, and it made her feel better. That's the greatest affirmation of her job she can imagine. Reminded that what she says counts, Cam tells herself she really has no need to be nervous.

'We're ready for you,' says Philippa, coming back in. 'Can you turn your phone off and come with me?'

Cam does as she says, and the knots return to her stomach. As they walk down a long corridor towards a thick door with a red light above it, Cam thinks about what Philippa said about feeling judged for her decision not to have kids.

'What do you think about Wank Woman?' she asks, testing her.

'Oh God, I can't stop watching it,' Philippa says, 'the look on her face is priceless.' Philippa opens the door and enters the studio. Cam shakes her head slowly as she follows. Such hypocrisy. Why can nobody else see it?

The studio is small and dark. Thick fabric walls make it feel like an air raid bunker. *You'd be safe in here if something went down*, Cam thinks.

Janis is sitting at a round table. She looks to be in her mid-fifties, frumpy with shoulder-length wispy hair. There is a microphone with a pop shield in front of her, and two on the other side of the table. Janis points at the chair opposite and, smiling, urges Cam to sit down. Cam does as she is told. The microphone feels like a thousand eyes, and the knots in her stomach tighten even more. She takes off her leather jacket, and keeps her arms down.

'I'll be with you in just a minute,' Janis says quietly, covering her mic and leaning way to the left whilst making a circular motion with her wrist, as if trying to wind up the current caller, who is giving a long-winded answer to whatever Janis asked her about the controversial sex scene on *Emmerdale* the night before. After another ten or so seconds, Janis has had enough and cuts the caller off.

'OK, well, we must move on otherwise it will be time for tonight's *Emmerdale* and I won't have had time to chat to my next guest. Thank you, Sandra.' Janis rolls her eyes in a jovial way and smiles again at Cam.

She seems nice, fun even, what was Philippa talking about?

Janis continues. 'Now, sitting opposite me is a young woman who doesn't want children. She says she isn't sad, or selfish. That she has no issue with intimacy and men. This, very attractive I might add, woman says it's a decision that she has made, that it is her right not to have children and that society shouldn't have such a problem with that. Please welcome blogger and founder of *HowItIs.com*, Camilla Stacey.'

Cam clears her throat and takes a deep breath. Her mouth is dry, so she takes a sip of the glass of water that's in front of her, presuming it's there for her.

'Hello, Camilla dear, how are you today?' says Janis, kindly, if not slightly patronisingly, but absolutely not meanly.

'Good, thanks,' says Cam, still with some water in her mouth. A little bit trickles down her chin and drops onto the felt table, creating a few dark spots. She doesn't risk taking another mouthful. She swallows properly and looks to see Philippa through the window in the next room, her eyes like a mum watching her kid in a soccer match. Proud, but also saying, 'Don't lose. Don't you lose!'

'So tell me about what happened to make you not want to have children. Can you pinpoint a moment in your childhood that may have triggered this in you?' says Janis.

'No, not really,' Cam says, knowing she should elaborate but needing the guidance of continuous questioning to get her through her nerves.

'Surely a pretty girl like you could have any man she wanted?' Janis probes.

'Oh, well, I'm not sure the way I look has anything to do

with it. I was raised in an environment where it was normal for women to have children, all three of my sisters do,' Cam says, happy with her methodical response, feeling a little more confident.

'Yes, but what was the moment you decided not to be a mother?' Janis pushes.

'Well there wasn't one, really. I just always knew. A bit like being gay I suppose; you don't decide who you fancy, you just do.'

'*Are* you gay, dear?'

Oh wow, she's one of those, Camilla thinks. Just like her mum. But this isn't her mum. This is someone she doesn't care about upsetting. Her nerves take a back seat, and the Cam that her readers love comes to the surface. She sits up straight, nods subtly at Philippa.

'No, *dear*, I am not gay,' she says, boldly.

'OK, well as expected our phone lines are hot with callers who want to know more about this, so I think we'll go straight to them,' Janis says, 'Mary in Balham, are you there?'

'Yes, hello Janis. Camilla, don't you worry that one day you'll retire and regret choosing your career over children?' Janis rests her elbows on the desk in front of her, and aims a vacant smile at Cam as she waits for an answer.

'Me not wanting children isn't just to do with how much I work. Some of the most successful women I know are mothers. Some of the most successful women in the world have kids. Women can have it all . . . I just don't want it all.'

Janis leans her head slightly to the side and raises her eyebrows.

'OK, thank you, Mary. Let's go to Laura in Hertfordshire. Hello, Laura?'

'Hello Janis, love the show. Camilla, I know that you're single, other than the lover you have written about, but are you really just saying you don't want children as self-defence against those who might say you're only not having them because you never found "The One"?'

Cam lets out an inaudible sigh and says, 'No, I am not saying I don't want kids to defend myself. If I wanted kids and couldn't find a man I'd look into IVF, or adoption. I'd ask a gay friend to give me some sperm. There are loads of ways to skin a cat, I just don't want children.' She is proud of herself, speaking like she writes. Her readers will be happy.

'Well, I think comparing having a child to skinning a cat says a lot about your feelings towards motherhood. Maybe as that clock inside you slows down, you'll have a change of heart. I'm not sure there's much more to say after that,' Janis says, looking at the clock and then to Philippa, who looks to Cam and begs with her eyes.

Nope, Camilla thinks, *that can't be it.* She's not getting up early and sitting in rush hour in the back of an Uber for forty-five minutes to be on air for three minutes and told she doesn't know her own mind. *Screw that.*

'You know,' she says to Janis. 'I don't get it. A woman comes on and tells you that she doesn't feel like she "needs" a child, and you and your listeners can't take it in. Why is that? Why is it that since admitting to this apparently unbearable thing, I have been asked to go on nearly every news sofa to discuss it? Is this really such breaking news?'

'Well,' Janis says, looking nervous; her guests don't usually answer back. 'I suppose it's just unusual, that's all. For a woman to choose to not want children, rather than have that opinion forced upon them. You can't argue that it isn't normal, dear?'

Cam squirms at the word 'normal', and continues.

'Yes, it's unfortunate that we have been conditioned to see an alternative to motherhood as not normal. But you do all realise that some of the most brilliant women in the world don't have kids, right? Oprah, Gloria Steinem, Helen Mirren, Dolly Parton? Do you think their lives carry an air of tragedy because they never had children? I don't. I'm sure they all had different reasons for not doing it, some maybe couldn't, some didn't want to, but these women's lives are not empty because of that. I think it's important we take the lead from our heroes and for everyone to stop valuing women on whether they do, or do not, become mothers. The irony of yours and your listeners' opinions is that it is *you* boxing women in to these roles, not men. It's highly un-feminist of you.'

She looks up at Philippa, who is trying to hide a grin.

A few seconds of dead air are a long time in radio.

'OK, thank you to Camilla Stacey, editor of *HowItIs.com* and strident . . . non-mother,' says Janis, wrapping up, not even looking up at Cam as she is led out of the studio by a trembling Philippa.

'You were amazing,' says Philippa, exploding with joy as the studio door shuts behind them. 'Shit, let's get downstairs, these walls have ears.'

They walk the rest of the way with Philippa making a

squeaking noise as she tries to keep her joy in. Cam wants to roar with frustration. As they get to reception and the front door of the building, Cam turns back to Philippa and says, 'You know, you could tell Janis she's an arsehole yourself.'

'Sorry? No I can't, I'd lose my job.'

'So? You know what you want in life, you know who you are. Stop hiding behind all this,' Cam says, reaching forward and tugging on her cardigan, 'this weird disguise, and be honest with yourself. Don't conform because of people like her. What's the point?'

'This look works here. I love my job.'

'Do you, though? You love having a job where you feel you have to lie about who you are every day? Where your boss makes you feel irrelevant because you're brave enough not to do what society expects of you, but you let her silence you anyway? Speak up! What's the point in having strong opinions if you don't live by them?'

'I, but . . . '

'There is no "but". Women can't keep complaining about how society treats them if they just take being told they're wrong all the time and don't react. You telling me Janis was an arsehole is fine, but *I'm* not the one who sees her every day and lets her get away with it. Do something, say how you feel. Nothing changes if you don't.'

Philippa looks at the ground like a schoolgirl that's been told off, but then raises her head. 'It's different for you, everyone listens to your opinions. I've got so much to say but I haven't earned my right to say it.'

'I say this stuff to encourage women like you, not to speak

for you.' As Cam goes to leave, she says, 'And stop watching the video of Wank Woman. You have no right to call yourself a feminist if you do.' Philippa nods.

In an Uber, Cam gets out her phone, there is an email she's been desperate to send.

Tara, I am so glad you emailed me, and so happy you saw the piece I wrote about you. How you holding up?
Cam x

Before she even reaches home, she gets a reply.

Hey Cam

How am I holding up? OK, let's see. I can't get to sleep no matter how many antihistamine or Nytol I take. When I eventually do drop off, I wake up with night terrors because I dream that someone is filming me in my bed, and I can barely remember what fresh air smells like. So all in all, I'm holding up pretty shit.
How is your day?
T x

Tara

The doorbell goes and I wake up with a start. I was sleeping bolt upright on the sofa with the TV on, the remote control is in my hand and there's a piece of cheese on my thigh. There is a bad smell. It could be me; it could be the cheese. My left eye is struggling to open again. I am completely disgusting. I really need to wash but the idea of a shower seems too stressful. The doorbell rings a second time.

I look at my phone. No texts from my mother, and she would have let me know if she was coming over, she's good like that. Who else would just show up? Before I put down my phone I look at the text conversation with Jason again, the speech bubble still hovering there like some cruel joke. Why do I care, it was just one night? I know I need to get over it. I don't feel like I'll ever move on from any of this. The doorbell rings again, this time followed by a loud thump. I consider not answering, because whoever it is, I really don't want to see them. But a fourth ding-dong and more aggressive banging lets me know I can't ignore it.

I slump into the hallway and look at my front door. Jets of daylight are creeping in from the tiny gaps around the sides. I reach for my sunglasses from the drawer of the little French table in the hall. I can already tell that my left eye won't be able to handle raw daylight. As I get closer to the door, I hear a man's voice.

'Tara Thomas,' he says. 'We can hear you in there. Can you open the door, please?'

Next I hear the unmistakable crackle of a walkie-talkie. When I open the door, two police officers are standing on my doorstep. A large plump man, and a short skinny woman.

'Tara Thomas?' says the man.

I nod. Despite my sunglasses, I'm squinting quite aggressively.

I can also now confirm that the smell is coming from me, not the cheese.

'We're here to take you down to the police station,' he continues. 'We just need to ask you a few questions about your little incident on the train last Friday night.'

'Am I being arrested?' I ask, realising I look ridiculous in sunglasses but also so pleased I am wearing them.

'We just need to ask you some questions, Ms Thomas,' says the skinny woman cop.

'Can I just get my things?' I ask, not knowing what the protocol with getting arrested is. Are they going to handcuff me? Put their hand on the top of my head as they push me into the car like they do in the movies?

They wait for me on the doorstep while I get my keys, my phone and a coat. I don't even put them in a bag. I've forgotten how to leave the house.

In the back of the police car (they didn't put their hand on my head to guide me in), I look at the back of their heads. They probably don't think I can see, but they keep looking at each other and laughing. I'm pretty sure the woman keeps hitting the fat man's leg, and I'm pretty sure it's because he keeps making fun of me.

I feel a bit like I'm in a taxi; the back seat is blocked off by a black plastic wall with a Perspex window separating our heads. As the crackle of the police radio fills the car I sit back and look out of the window. People on the street are looking in at me; one of my neighbours is peering out her window, trying to get a glimpse of the filthy criminal in the back of the cop car. What will they think when they see it's me, have they seen the video? I realise how serious this is, and the situation I am in. Will I go to prison for masturbating in public? From underneath my sunglasses, bulbous tears roll down my cheeks. I feel sick with fear and regret. They came to my house. How did they know it was me? I won't be able to hide now. Even when the press dies down, my name will have been dragged through the mud. Will I have a criminal record? Will I go to prison? Even that creep Shane Bower will laugh at me, and to think I believed I had the power over him. I look at my hands and they are shaking. I haven't felt this level of fear in my entire life. Telling my dad I was pregnant was terrifying, but not like this. I wanted to keep Annie and that gave me strength to make it clear to him I was doing the right thing. But there is nothing I want about this. No good can come of it. I am just shamed, publicly, globally, and I am so, so frightened.

I sit alone in the interrogation room waiting for whatever it is that is about to happen.

The door opens. The fat man and the female officer come in. She takes a seat, he stands behind her. She starts to speak.

'OK, Ms Thomas, I'm Officer Flower, and this is Officer Potts. You have the right to remain silent. Anything you say can and will be used against you in a court of law. You have the right to a lawyer. If you cannot afford a lawyer, one will be provided for you. Do you understand the rights I have just read to you?'

'Yes,' I say, like a little girl in the headmistress' office.

'With these rights in mind, do you wish to speak to me?'

I feel like I'm in a movie. *How is this happening to me?* I want to get out of here, I want this to go quickly. If they are going to arrest me, no lawyer can help. Exactly what I did is on video, it is what it is.

'Yes,' I say, trying to be a grown-up.

'OK, good. Now, want to tell us about Friday?' she says, her elbows on the table, fists together and her fingers interlaced.

'I got filmed on a train when I thought I was alone,' I say. That's the truth.

'And for the tapes, what were you doing on that train?' Officer Flower says, probingly. The male officer makes a strange grunting noise and puts his hand to his mouth. He either stopped a sneeze or a laugh, I can't be sure.

'I was masturbating,' I say, releasing myself into the pinnacle of humiliation as my shame floods the room and sweeps up my self-respect like a gigantic tidal wave.

The fat man cop makes the noise again, this time letting out a little more than he intended to, clarifying that it is, indeed, a snigger.

'That's right,' says Officer Flower. 'And why did you do that?'

Why did I do that? The very question I've been asking myself since this whole ordeal began.

'I don't really know. I just felt . . . '

I look at Officer Potts. I contemplate holding back but considering where I am, I realise there is no point. 'I just felt . . . horny.'

This sends him over the edge. He lets out a full-scale guffaw and Officer Flower scrapes her chair back and turns to look at him scathingly. 'Officer Potts!' she says, like she's his mum and he's a little boy who just laughed at his sister's boobs. 'Martin, do you need to leave the room?'

He pulls himself together with a medley of sniffs, posture readjustments and fake coughs. 'No, no, absolutely not. All good.'

Officer Flower turns back to me. 'Ms Thomas, you were on a train. You do realise that this could come under the category of indecent exposure, don't you?'

'I do now, yes. But I thought I was alone. When I saw that kid filming me I felt completely violated. I wasn't trying to be seen. I can't believe that out of me and him, *I* am the one being questioned.'

'That's right, blame the guy,' Officer Potts says, like a ventriloquist, as he rolls his eyes and lets his gaze settle on the wall to his right. Both Officer Flower and I shoot a look at him, in a strong but unspoken moment of female solidarity.

'Look, I'm just saying that if she was a man this would be a clean case. Indecent exposure, public indecency, lewdness, there's no getting away from it,' the fat twat says.

He's right, I suppose. There probably shouldn't be different rules for men and women. But I really hope that there is.

'Ms Thomas,' Officer Flower continues. 'Did you do what you did with the intentions of being seen?'

'No, I really didn't.'

'Did you know the young man who filmed you was on the carriage?'

'No, I didn't. I still don't know where he came from. I swear he wasn't there when I got on the train.'

'Have you ever done anything like this before?'

'No, never.' That's a lie. I had sex with a guy on a train once. I also gave the same guy a blow job on the back of a bus. But that is very, very different, it was years ago, and mentioning that would not help. I say no again, just to reiterate.

'Right, well then, I am happy to put this down to a moment of personal misconduct. We all have them. The fact is, there were not more than two other people present. You clearly were not trying to receive attention and your regret seems palpable. Ms Thomas, can you assure me that we will not receive any more footage of you doing anything like this on public transport again?'

'Yes. I won't. I really, really won't. I have a daughter,' I say gently. 'I just want to protect her.'

'I'm sure you do. OK, then I think we can leave this here.' Officer Flower gets up.

'Wait, that's it?' Officer Potts splutters.

'Yup, that's it. You can leave us now, Martin. Come this way, Ms Thomas.'

As we walk down the corridor, she speaks quietly to me. 'He's new, tact isn't his strong point.'

'I suppose me being here means the press can identify me?' I say, having a little experience in the relationship between the police and the press because of my job.

'I'm afraid it probably does, yes.'

'Why is this happening to me?' I say, pathetically, feeling

oddly safe in this cold, bright corridor. Officer Flower stands in front of me and puts her hands on my elbows.

'Listen to me,' she says, looking into my eyes. 'This will pass. You did something very questionable; people are going to roll with this until the snowball is pretty big. But it will pass, everything always does. I see people come in here who have done much worse things and they serve their time and then they live their lives.'

'"Serve their time"? Am I going to prison?' I feel a ball of vomit shoot up my throat, but swallow it back down.

'No, but it might feel a bit like that for a while. Your time will be played out publicly but I'm going to give you some advice. Do what is right for you, respond in a way that makes you feel comfortable. You can take control of this and you can come out the other side. Do what is right for you, and your daughter. And Ms Thomas, can I say something, woman to woman?' I nod. I like Officer Flower. I want her advice. Any small crumb of comfort would be welcome right now. 'Take a shower, OK? You smell of cheese.'

'Oh, yes. Sorry.'

'It's OK, I've smelt worse. Now, I can get someone to drive you to wherever you need to go. Is there anywhere you can go where you won't be on your own?'

I tell her my mum's address.

In the back of the police car, I ask if it's OK for me to look at my phone, and the cop driving me says yes. He looks young and new, still at the stage of being polite because he's nervous. A ridiculous character trait for a police officer.

I'm so happy when I see I have another email from Cam Stacey. I've been thinking about her a lot.

Tara, you can't control what other people do, but you can control how you deal with it. This will get better, I promise. Cam x

'Mummy!' shouts Annie running to greet me as soon as I walk in the door. She flops into my arms and it feels so, so good. The smell of her head, her warm body, that cuddle that means nothing but love. I hold onto her like we are about to say goodbye, not like we are saying hello. We've never spent so long apart. I know instantly that it can't happen again.

'Mummy, are you better?' she asks me, her big brown eyes looking so worried. 'You don't smell right.'

'I'm so much better,' I tell her. How would I even begin to tell a child the truth? One day I'll have to. I hold her hand as I stand up. 'Come on, let's go and find Nan.'

'You're here,' says Mum, walking towards me from the kitchen. Her arms reach out for me, but the expression on her face changes as she looks at me and realises the mess I am in. I look into her eyes and those boulder tears start falling again. 'Mum,' I mouth, trying to hold it together so Annie doesn't notice.

'Let me take Annie upstairs,' she says, jumping into action like mums so naturally do. I go and sit in the kitchen while she takes my daughter to her bedroom. After a few minutes, she startles me by speaking from the doorway.

'So what is it? Breast, bowel?'

'What?' I ask, wondering why she's listing body parts.

'What cancer do you have? It's cancer, isn't it? That's what's wrong?'

'God, no, Mum! I don't have cancer.' I realise she's crying. I must have terrified her. Why do I suddenly feel like I'm about to tell her something worse than me having cancer when of course it's bloody not?

'Oh thank God,' she says. 'No one survives cancer, no matter how much they try to tell you they do. So what is it, darling? What have you—' She stops speaking as she has a lightbulb moment. Her face turns from concerned to annoyed. 'You've done it again, haven't you?'

'What?'

'You're bloody pregnant again, aren't you?'

'No, Mum. I'm not pregnant. Please stop guessing. Mum, I've been caught doing something really bad.'

'Oh God, you've shoplifted? What did you take? Was it clothes? Cosmetics? A television?'

'Mum, no, I haven't stolen anything please, will you stop guessing.'

She sits down next to me. She's managing to stay quiet, but I can tell her mind is running through possibilities like a random results generator.

'Mum, I've been filmed doing something and it means I'm going to be in the papers.' I've said the first bit, I'm nearly there. *I can do this.*

'Filmed doing what? Did you hurt someone?'

'No, Mum, I didn't hurt anyone. I got filmed doing something sexual, and it's gone viral.'

'Gone viral? Well what is it? AIDS?'

'For God's sake Mum I don't have AIDS. It's gone viral, as in it has spread across the Internet. As in, millions of people have seen it.'

'Oh,' she says, having no grasp of the Internet and what any of that means.

'Mum, on Friday night I met a guy. A really great, brilliant guy and we got on so so well. At the end of the night we were going to go home together but I said no. I wanted to wait, play it right. But . . . '

'Well, that's good. I told you you shouldn't sleep with them all.'

'Yes, Mum, I know you did. But I liked him. A lot. Physically. You know? I really fancied him. And when I got on the train I . . . Mum, I'd had a few drinks and I didn't think anyone else was there so I . . . '

'It's OK love, you can tell me anything, you know that,' she says, leaning in then leaning out when she gets a whiff of me.

'I masturbated on the train and a stranger filmed me doing it.'

If there was a dictionary with pictures my mother's face would be the image used to describe HORROR. Her skin goes from plump and pink to pale and sullen, the blood draining at lightning speed to her hands, which are suddenly engorged and veiny as she throws them to her cheeks and opens her mouth. I give her a moment to adjust. But she doesn't, she remains deadly still, looking like the 'Face Screaming with Fear' emoji.

'Mum, you have to say something.'

A long, high-pitched squeak comes out of her. I can't be sure from where.

'Your father . . . ' she finally says.

'I know, he won't like it. But Mum, I have so much more to worry about than Dad. The police—'

'The police?'

'Yes, the police. They came and took me to the station this morning. It's OK, they are not pressing charges. But the media might not be so lenient. I've been trending on Twitter since Monday . . . '

'Trending, what's trendy about masturbating?'

'No, Mum, trending on Twitter means . . . you know what, it doesn't matter. But everyone is talking about it, and now it will probably go into the actual paper, and they have my name, so it might also be on the news. And your friends might see it. And Dad's friends. And everyone we know, and somehow we are going to have to cope with that.'

Her hands come down from her face. 'Where is the video now?'

'It's online.'

'Can I see it?'

'Mum, I don't think that's a good—'

'If the entire world is going to see the video, Tara, I think I need to see it myself, don't you?'

'Mum, you heard what I said, didn't you? I'm masturbating on a train. It's not fake, I am really doing it. Are you sure you want to watch that?'

She insists. As much as the idea of this is torturous, a part of me wants to get as much over and done with as possible.

If she doesn't watch it now, I'll just be dreading the moment that she does. Fuck it. I get her laptop and search for the video. WALTHAMSTOW WANK WOMAN. It comes up right away.

'Are you sure?' I ask her, one final time as my finger hovers over the touch pad.

'Oh Tara, just press play on the sodding video, will you?'

So I do.

5

Cam

'Come on, Cammie, it will be fun,' says Tanya on the phone. 'We haven't done anything just the four of us in ages.'

'I hate spas,' Cam says, rejecting the idea of a bonding exercise with her sisters, and hating the cliché of ladies getting their nails done together. 'Can't we just have a day at Mum and Dad's? I'll get a takeaway for everyone or something?'

'No, Cammie, the whole point is that we want to get away from the kids. Come on, if Mel doesn't get a full body massage her veins will explode and wipe out the human race. She's a fucking mess, do it for her. Do it for Mel's veins.'

'OK, OK, stop, they make me gag. I'll do it. I'll spend an afternoon in a posh spa with my mean sisters, I can't wait.'

'We love you really . . . little Cammie, all grumpy and alone, loves her sisters when they phone . . . '

'That's a rubbish poem,' Cam says, smiling. 'I will join you for an afternoon in the spa because if I don't, you'll talk about me all day and make things up about me.'

'Yup, we probably will. OK, I'll book it. And hey, you OK to pay for it? I know you're raking it in?'

'Of course. I'll pay for everyone if you promise to be nice?' Cam loves being asked to pay. Her finances are an undisputable triumph.

'Oh but Cammie, you're such fodder for us tired old mums. OK, I'll text you later when I've booked somewhere, love you.'

'Love you too, bye.'

Cam hangs up, and goes straight to her Twitter feed. There are countless messages of support after her performance on BBC Radio London.

@CamStacey HERO.

@CamStacey Finally someone exposed that frumpy old bat, Janis, for being such a grumpy old twat. #TwatBat

@CamStacey MY VAGINA IS A ONE WAY STREET. The only way is UP #withyousister #babiessuck

@CamStacey Saw you on TV once. Great tits. You'll hang on to those if you don't have a kid. My wife's are a mess. Dave x

Camilla should be happy, but she's not, she's irritated. Philippa was this great girl with a head full of strong opinions, but too spineless to act on them. That shit drives Cam crazy. If women are reading her work and still not being confident enough to take command of their own lives, then she isn't being direct enough. She needs to write a blog that will get women, like

Philippa, itching to go to work to tell their boss, and society, to go fuck itself. She gets to work.

HowItIs.com – A Call to Action

I think women need to stop talking about how hard being a woman is and live by the example they want to set. Every time I look on Instagram or Twitter there is another post about how hard it is being a working mum, how hard it is being a woman who works in the city, how hard it is being a woman and having to be beautiful. It just goes on and on and on. What's more, most of these posts are written by successful or famous women right at the top of their game. Their beauty made them rich but they don't want to be objectified for it, they earn more than most men but still go on about how hard their industry is, they have all the childcare they want, but they can't juggle family and work.

You might be scared, and I understand that. The consequences of speaking out are high. You can't afford to lose your job, you have a family to support, rent or a mortgage to pay. But what if? What if you speak up and get what you want, or a compromise is found, what if something does change? Taking risks is what moves us forward. When you're in a rut you have two choices, you stay in it, or you fight your way out. I'm not saying put your security on the line, but I am encouraging you to at least investigate a possibility, if there is one, for things to be better. Say when things are wrong, speak up when you are put down, take control of your own destiny.

I think we've got feminism to this place where there is too much talking and not enough action. If I was a guy, I'd just say, 'OK, if you want me to stop treating you differently because you're a woman, stop going on about being a bloody woman.'

We all know what the problems are, where the challenges lie, what needs to change, so let's live by the words we preach rather than just say them on social media, let's be active in making a change. By actually changing the things around ourselves, we change the world. If you don't fight your own corner, you can't fight anyone else's. Be who ***you*** *want to be, get what* ***you*** *want, and the position of women in the world will change. By helping ourselves we help others. It's true. If you all went to work tomorrow and told your boss what you want, the pay gap would start to close. And so on and so on. As an individual, you can change the world; why wait for someone else to try to change it for you?*

I'm worried that there are too many women out there who know the difference between right and wrong but don't have the guts to say it to the people in their own lives who are causing the problem. What is stopping you? Who are you afraid of? Men, why? Other women? Well, that's just dumb. The reason men progressed above us in society is because they dominated us with actions and attitude. It's that simple. To re-address the balance, we have to do the same thing. If someone is overpowering you and stopping you getting to where you want to be, then STOP letting them do it. If someone is objectifying you for your sexuality, STOP allowing yourself to be objectified. If someone is stopping you get what you want, tell them. If they still get in your way, move on. Stop using victim language like, 'because I am a woman' and 'being a woman is hard because' at the start of every sentence about your success, or lack of. Take being a woman out of the equation and just go forth and conquer. You have the power to shape your own destiny, you have the power to dictate how people treat you. You have the power not to be made to feel small, put down, or intimidated. As Ghandi said, 'Be the change that you wish to see in the world'. Everything that happens to you is in your control, because you control how you respond.

Don't apologise for who you are, and don't take shit. Don't be a victim. Feminism needs you to step up. Get what you want. Just go out there, and take it.

Cam x

It usually only takes a few minutes for responses to start pouring in from Cam's blogs, but today she feels too impatient to sit and wait. Needing a distraction, she reads a new email from Tara. This friendly correspondence is exciting her a bit. The tone of the emails is so casual, it's intimate and honest. She can't be sure why it feels different from correspondence with other fans, but it is. Why is that? It could just be the thrill of something that she wrote having the desired effect, or maybe it's the idea that she is secretly conversing with the most talked-about person on Twitter. Or maybe it's simply because Cam gets a good vibe from her new email buddy. And no matter how content she tells herself that she is in her solitude, there is space in her life for a friend like Tara Thomas.

Hey Cam

So I'm sitting in the back of a police car as they hauled me in to discuss my 'indecent exposure on the Victoria Line, eastbound train'. They decided not to press charges and now a policeman who is about ten years younger than me is driving me to my mum's house.

So that's all giving me the confidence boost I need.

This is all so surreal. This time last week I produced documentaries about people, now I feel like the whole world is making one about me. 'The Thomas Show'. It's got a ring to it. Kill me now!

Tara x

'*A documentary maker?*' Cam says to herself quietly. She doesn't know why, but she knew Tara would have a cool job.

She realises that the world only knows her as 'Wank Woman' but now Cam is one of the few people who knows her real name. She types 'Tara Thomas, documentary maker' into Google. A headshot of Tara on IMDB comes up right away. She looks a little less dishevelled than in the video, but it's unquestionably her. Long brown curly hair, freckles, a button nose and deep brown eyes. She's quite unique looking, not easy to hide. The page reads:

Tara Thomas: Producer, Field Producer, Development Producer

Credits:
My Boss Touched Me Up – in Production – Producer/Director
I Married a Fraud – Producer/Director
Women's Lives Matter – Producer/Director

Cam is impressed, her credits are awesome. She spends an hour or two speeding through clips of Tara's work; it's clever, thought-provoking and full of confidence. She can see now that Tara's job will be almost impossible with the new credit of 'Wank Woman' added to her CV. Cam had always loved the idea of being a TV producer but her social skills meant she couldn't work with contributors. She feels even more sympathy for Tara now.

Hey Tara,
I just looked you up. You're a big deal, your shows sound so good. Look, this will pass. I'm sure it feels like it won't, but of course it will. There

are scandals all the time, but they get boring eventually. Someone else does something and the public move on to that. Maybe I could get filmed rubbing myself sexually against one of the lions in Trafalgar Square, to distract attention from you? Would that help? But really, this world moves at a terrific pace. One minute something is there, and then it is gone. Hang in there, Cam x

Hey Cam
You're right, it will pass. But something tells me this is just beginning. The police coming means people know who I am, it's just a matter of time until the press reveal my name and the true weight of global humiliation is upon my shoulders. How are you supposed to react to this?

Oh, also my mum just watched the video. You can imagine.
T x
p.s. Leave those lions alone, you weirdo.

Tara!
Oh GOD! Welcome to my world. Every blog I write seems to mortify my mother more and more. She's read about me masturbating so many times I think she thinks it's all I do. Which is 50% true, I suppose. I spend a lot of time alone ;)

Maybe we should start a club 'The Embarrassing Daughters' Society'?

Sorry about the whole police thing. Glad you didn't go to prison, C x

Yeah, me too. This will all be hard enough to explain to my daughter when she grows up. Not sure how I manage that without her thinking that a woman touching herself is a criminal offence. X

You have a daughter, how old? I presume you're single? Hope that doesn't offend you . . . just . . . you know . . .

Not offended. Yup, a six-year-old called Annie. And nope, no partner. A single mum with a lot of explaining to do x

A daughter? A single mum? Wow, Cam thinks. The press will go to town on that! She wonders how different her blog would have to be if she did have kids. Would she have to stop writing about sex, because it would be seen as inappropriate? She reads over the article she just posted and questions herself. Can she really comment on how it feels to be a working mother? How hard it is, how it feels to have someone else pretty much raise your kid? Not really, she has no idea. Her mother never worked, her sisters don't do nine-to-five jobs. It's all very well for her to think women should stop moaning and get on with it, but what does she know? If Tara had got caught wanking on a train and she didn't have a kid, this would eventually blow over. But because she's a mum, this will stick. That's how the world works, mothers have to behave themselves. Another point that makes Cam feel even more determined not to reproduce.

Tara, you don't need to explain yourself to anyone and you'll find a way to help your daughter understand. I'm here if things get tough, email me anytime. I've got your back, Cam x

Tara

I had to leave Mum alone in the house for a minute. She went into actual shock and I feel shit enough without watching her face go from white to purple and back again as she tries to think of something to say. There is nothing to say. *Her daughter wanked on a train*, end of conversation.

As I walk out of the house, I instinctively hunch my shoulders over like someone who is up to no good. I grew up on this street. It's quiet, so my friends and I used to play in the road, something I can't even imagine suggesting Annie would do now. She's not allowed beyond the front door on her own; it's depressing how much the world has changed. The Internet has petrified us all. Never more for me than now.

As I get to the end of the path, I see Mrs. Bradley and her son, David, heading towards me. They live two doors down, which tortured me for most of my teenage life because Mrs Bradley was my headmistress. Living on the same street as your headmistress is terrible; you simply cannot be a rebel, no matter who your friends are. Mrs Bradley and my mum always got on really well, she'd pop round on Saturday mornings for tea, which I hated more than anything else. Mum always made me come down to say hello, but then I'd hide upstairs until she'd gone. She always brought David with her, which made things even worse.

David was in my class, we called him 'special needs' back then. Or 'spastic', which now makes me feel terrible. We didn't realise anything was wrong until we were ten and he kept taking his trousers off at school. We all called him a pervert, and he got picked on and laughed at and called 'weird' and a 'freak'. Mrs Bradley came under pressure because all of the other teachers wanted him to be expelled, but she was the headmistress and couldn't bring herself to do it. Eventually she had to, and he went to a special school, and over the next few years people started to understand him a little better. We all felt like total shit for taking the piss out of him when we realised he actually had a condition, but hey, we were kids, what did we know?

Sophie, of course, found the idea of terrorising him with her sexuality thrilling, and one Saturday morning after she'd stayed over and Mrs Bradley was downstairs, she made me go down to ask if David would like to come and listen to music with us. I'll never forget the look on Mrs Bradley's face, she was so touched. 'Oh, Tara, that is so kind. I'm sure David would love to, what do you think, David?'

David didn't say anything, just stared at the floor. But when I went to leave, he followed me. I turned back to look at Mrs Bradley and her eyes welled up. When David and I got to the top of the stairs, Sophie was standing there with her top off, jiggling up and down so her boobs were going everywhere. I thought he was going to be sick, he started making this weird noise, like a sea lion. His arms went really straight like they were stuck to the side of his body, while his top half kept planking backwards and forwards so hard, I thought he was going to fall down the stairs. I yelled at Sophie to put her top back on and Mrs Bradley came running up to see what had happened. Sophie nose-dived into my bedroom, so I was left to try and explain why her son was going mad.

'He has these fits,' she said, putting her arm around him and helping him downstairs. 'He has these fits.' She led him straight out the front door and took him home.

Mrs Bradley stopped bringing him with her on Saturdays after that. I have no idea if he ever told her what happened, or if he kept it to himself. But he has avoided me ever since, and I think that is totally fair enough.

'Hello Mrs Bradley, hello David,' I say, as they walk towards me. If I'd have had more time, I'd have run across the street and hidden under the seat of my car until they'd gone. Apparently David has never been able to get a job and so still lives at home and spends the majority of his time watching YouTube videos. Has he seen it? Maybe.

'Tara, love, how are you?'

The simplest question suddenly has the most complicated answer. So I lie.

'I'm fine thanks. You?'

David is staring at the ground. I'm trying to gauge him. Has he seen it? What would he say if he did?

'Ah yes, we're ticking along. Very much looking forward to your father's birthday party on Friday.'

'Oh, you're coming? I ask, even though I knew she would be. Mum has invited people to the house, she's going to do her cottage pie and a salad buffet. It will be a few family members, some of Dad's mates from his club and some neighbours. Nothing big or fancy, but I want to be sick every time I think about it.

'Great. See you there then. I have to run,' I say. David is freaking me out; he usually at least looks at me but he's now moved behind Mrs Bradley. Even she seems uncomfortable with this particular level of social awkwardness from him.

I hurry away, and into my car. I call Mum and promise to pick up Annie later. I want to get home as quickly as I can. Now the press knows my name, and where I live, it's just a matter of time before it's published and I want to see it when it is. But shouldn't I be hiding under my car, pretending the Internet isn't real? What is it about this torturous experience that makes me want to read everything? See everything? If the world is going to talk about me, I need to know what it's saying. A relentless feeling of 'I need to know . . . I need to know.' I wonder if this is what it feels like to be Kim Kardashian? To be fair, she's a great example of someone who turned it around after a sex tape went viral.

I get home and search my name in Google. Just my TV credits, my Twitter account and my LinkedIn profile come up. Tara Thomas is still just a woman who makes TV shows, but not for long. For three hours straight I click REFRESH, REFRESH,

REFRESH on the *MailOnline* website. And then, as if it happened suddenly, it's there. My name in big, bold letters. My face looking completely fucking awful. My bright pink front door gleaming in the background. Jesus, I didn't even know anyone had taken the picture. My life, exposed.

WALTHAMSTOW W**K WOMAN REVEALED
By Alex Mixter for MailOnline

*Walthamstow W**k Woman REVEALED. Tara Thomas is a 42-year-old single mother of a 6-year-old girl who hid the existence of their child from the father.*

After days of speculation, the identity of the mysterious woman who was filmed touching herself on a train before alighting at Walthamstow station last Friday night is finally revealed. The woman, who entered the underground network at Tottenham Court Road and alighted at Walthamstow, has been named as Tara Thomas, a 42-year-old single mother who never even told the child's father that she was pregnant. A source close to Ms Thomas told the MailOnline; 'Tara never questioned her decision to keep the baby, it was what she wanted, so she didn't think twice. As far as she was concerned, the father didn't need to know.'

Thomas has a history of making TV documentaries

that expose the lives of individuals who do not seek public attention, but in this bizarre twist of fate she appears to have turned the tables and put herself into the spotlight. Many have speculated that this was a cry for help from a lonely woman struggling with the pressures of single motherhood. Our expert psychologist, Raj Singh, believes that this video exhibits the behaviour of a woman who is desperate to be noticed and could indicate Ms Thomas is on the edge of a nervous breakdown, a statement that appears to be corroborated by erratic behaviour at the school gate and at work. MailOnline contacted her place of work, Great Big Productions, who were keen to disassociate themselves with her actions. 'We are a respected production company making quality programmes about modern society. We have a zero tolerance to explicit sexual activity. We are baffled as to what led one of our employees to behave this way in public. With our history of holding people accountable for their crimes in our programming, we saw it as our duty to announce her identity to the police. We now no longer work with Tara Thomas and have removed all credits from our current productions,' says Adam Pattison, MD of Great Big Productions.

Thomas is the only child of Peter and

Stephanie Thomas. She was born and raised in Walthamstow where she currently lives with her 6-year-old daughter. With no previous convictions for indecent exposure, the police will not be pressing charges at this time. Officer Flower of the Met Police says, 'We are confident that releasing Ms Thomas without charge is the right decision. She acted out of character and in a way that she deeply regrets. This is no longer a police matter.'

Do you have any information on Tara Thomas? Contact the MailOnline news desk at . . . '

Who told them all of that stuff about how I had Annie? Those bitches from the school gate? Saturday is a real blur. I know I told them about the one-night stand but did I tell them I never told Nick? I can't remember. I obviously did. Those cows. I bet it was Amanda. And what the hell does Adam mean, 'We now no longer work with Tara Thomas and have removed all credits from our current productions'? Is he actually kidding? He better not have taken my name off the sexual harassment doc; that's been over a year's work for me. And what an arsehole for dobbing me into the police, just to make them sound good as a company. I can just imagine the HR meeting where they discussed how this was gross misconduct and all laughed. Well, fuck them! I hated that job and they will be utterly shite without me. And if I'm honest, I just have no fight left. How has everyone turned against me in such a short space of time? I've always felt like the world can't touch me because of Mum and Dad and Annie, my team. But suddenly I feel a million miles from them too. I'm out here on my own – my existence has been reduced to a thirteen-second video that's on a constant loop.

But now it's not even about what I did on the train, it's about Annie. This isn't fair, Annie is only six, and our history is just that, history. What's important is that she's happy. And she is; she's really, really happy. What if the other kids know about this? They'll tease her and it will be all my fault. I can't bear it. How could things have got even worse?

I promised Annie I'd pick her up and bring her home tonight, she called me to say she misses me. I feel so guilty but maybe she should stay at Mum's another few nights. Maybe the press are outside my house, they'll no doubt want a picture of me looking cranky and evil again. I can't expose her to that.

The house phone rings and nearly gives me a heart attack.

'Hello?'

'Tara, it's Mum.'

'Why are you calling the house phone?'

'I was worried maybe our mobiles were being tapped.'

Oh, bloody hell.

'Mum, don't worry about that. No one is tapping our phones.'

'It's just that our names are in the paper – and they're all hacking nowadays dear, did you not see Hugh Grant on *BBC Breakfast*? He was terribly angry. It feels like we are under surveillance.'

Even more guilt consumes me as I realise it isn't just my

life that's being smashed apart by all of this.

'Mum, please don't worry, it's not going to get to that. The story was the peak of the hype, it will only get calmer from here,' I say, lying. I think this is just beginning. I hear a huge crash in the background, then a man shouting, more crashing and a smash. 'Mum? Mum what is that, are you OK?'

'I'm OK. That's your father. He's smashing things in the kitchen. He's read the article, Tara. And he's seen the video.'

'He's seen the video, how?'

'I showed it to him.'

'You did *what*?'

Oh *God*. My dad has seen me wanking? Seriously, every time I think this can't get more excruciating it gets taken to a whole new level.

'I just thought he should. I'm sorry if you disagree but I thought if he just saw it for himself, then we could all work out a way to move on.'

'Dad should never have seen that video.'

'Yes, I realise that now.'

There is another massive crash from the kitchen.

'Tara, I have to go. He's into my special crockery. I've had it for forty years . . . Peter, not those, please . . .'

The phone goes dead.

This is the worst day of my life. Hands down. I don't know what to do. What are you supposed to do when this happens? In five days, my life has been turned upside down. This time last week I had a great job, my daughter and I were just ticking along, doing our thing, I was secure, happy. Now nearly three million people, including my mother and my father, have seen me masturbate, I've lost my job, I've been branded like a criminal for keeping a child in the way that I did. Even my work is being criticised as tabloid sensationalism, and the general attitude seems to be that I deserve all of this because of every choice I have ever made. All this from one tiny moment where I gave in to temptation. How is this possible?

I've never felt like a terrible mother until now. Even compared to the other mums, I've never felt that Annie would have been better off with anyone else as her parent. But now I'm hiding in my house and she is living streets away with my parents, probably wondering what the hell I am doing – and I have no idea how to explain it to her. She'll be at school now telling her friends I'm not well, and the teachers will be talking in the staff room about me and what a disgrace I am. And without her even knowing, they will be watching her, waiting for her to do something reactive so they can blame me for messing up my daughter's head.

I can't let this happen. No matter what people are saying and how much I want to crawl into the cupboard under the sink and drink all of the household cleaning products, I have to keep my shit together, for Annie.

I'll go food shopping. I'll fill the fridge and cupboard up with all of our favourite things and I'll pick her up from school with my head held high and we will continue to live our lives. Cam was right, I don't have to explain myself to anyone. I can take control. I can write the life I want to live. I'll find another job, maybe something online. I could do surveys, or be an examiner. One of those jobs where you just get sent a load of stuff that needs checking. I'll sell things on eBay, antique jewellery. Maybe I'll even design some, I've always wanted to do that. I don't know, I'll work it out. What's the alternative? There isn't one. I have to pull my shit together. For my daughter.

I race to the front door and leave the house before I have the chance to second guess myself. I'm met with cameras. 'Tara Thomas?' says a loud voice as a bright flash goes off in my face. As my retinas re-focus, I see a camera pointing right at me, a man behind it, his face scrunched up as he peers down the lens.

'Why did you do it, Tara?' he says, as I see another man run up behind him, also with a camera. More flashes, more clicks. My ears pop like I'm on a plane and my vision goes blurry from the lights.

'I, I . . . ' I stop speaking. Pram Push Woman comes into my head, her dumb quote, 'I just wanted to see what happened' flashing in front of me like a ticker of BREAKING NEWS on the TV. I know I mustn't say anything.

I power through, like I'm walking through rolling waves that are coming over my head. I lead with my left shoulder, keep my head down to protect my eyes and I charge and keep charging. The local Tesco is only a few minutes away. They can't follow me in there, eventually the flashing lights will stop and I'll walk up and down the aisles and I'll get all of the things that Annie likes best. KitKats, Monster Munch, Edam cheese. I'll be ready for when she finishes school, and we will get on with our lives and eventually all of this will be over.

But these men are so close to me. It feels like they're going to push me to the floor. I keep going. Tesco is close. I can get there. They'll disappear, these men, because I'll make them disappear.

When I reach Tesco, the silence that surrounds me as the doors close again makes me feel like I'm in a dream. I walk forward like I'm on a conveyor belt and sense multiple other shoppers glancing at me, but I'm scared to look up in case they look me in the eye. Being looked at directly isn't something I can deal with quite yet.

Does everybody know?

I pick up a basket and loop it over my arm.

Grapes.

I draw my elbows in towards my body.

Butter. Milk. Cheese.

I turn a corner, someone walks past me and knocks my basket. They say sorry and carry on walking, I don't turn to see if they look back but I presume that they do. I'm hunched over, I must look very weird.

Cheerios. Nutella. Marmite. Honey. Jam. Dry roasted peanuts.

The basket is getting heavy.

Someone else bangs into me, or did I bang into them? This time, they get annoyed. 'Watch it,' they say, but I don't turn to look at them, I just keep going forward. Am I walking, or is the floor moving? I turn another corner. The beep beep beep of the tills gets louder. More people, now standing still in a row. Something about the stillness worries me, they are so close to me, they do not move. The cold air turns fiery hot and I feel sweat start to pour down my face. I'm sure I hear laughter. 'It's her, look it's her.' More laughter. Is everyone in

Tesco laughing at me? I'm so hot and my chest is closing, the lights become so bright I close my eyes just enough to see the basket over my arm. My heartbeat is suddenly so loud that I can hear it over the beep beep beep and there is a pain across my body that makes my head throw itself back and then a bang so hard that the lights shut down and the people disappear and the noises fade away and then everything is gone.

Beep. Beep. Beep.

There is noise before there is light.

Beeeeep. Beeeeep.

My eyes blink quickly as they adjust to the very bright lights above my head. Just as they are coming into focus, the silhouette of my mother's face appears above me. 'Mum, why are you in Tesco?' I ask, acknowledging the coincidence, despite my drowsy state.

'You're not in Tesco, dear,' Mum says, stroking my hair. 'You're in the hospital.'

I sit up much faster than my body can handle, my head thumps and I lie straight back down. 'What happened?'

'The doctor thinks maybe you had a panic attack, then you hit your head on the way down. You've been asleep for a few hours now. He thinks maybe you are exhausted?'

I remind myself that I have barely slept since Monday, and nod gently. I go to touch my face and see there is a tube in my arm. I don't know if it's real but my face feels so small.

'It's a drip,' my mother tells me. 'He says you're severely dehydrated. Your blood sugar was so low, like you hadn't eaten for days.'

That also seems true.

'Where's Annie?' I ask, looking to see if she's there.

'She's at home with your father. She's OK.'

I'm relieved, then horror kicks in.

'Oh, God. Dad. How's he doing?'

My mother pushes another pillow behind my back so that I can sit up more. She takes a while to respond.

'Not great, but it all comes from love. He's worried about you, of course.'

I let out a loud and exasperated groan.

'He'll come around,' she says. 'He always does.'

'After seeing videos of his daughter masturbating? When was the last time he came around to that?'

'It's certainly a new challenge, I won't deny that.'

She pours some water into two plastic cups and takes a sip from one as she stares at a painting, clearly building the confidence to say something rather than experiencing the art.

'The school called me today,' she says, turning to me. I sense the call wasn't to pass on their regards.

'They've seen the video, of course.'

'What did they say?' I ask, dreading the answer.

'They asked if you were alright.'

I'm surprised, I wasn't expecting them to care.

'In the head,' my mother clarifies.

'Oh. And what did you tell them?'

'I told them that you were fine. But that you were under a lot of pressure.'

'Why did you tell them that, Mum? I'm not under any pressure. At least, I *wasn't*.'

'They needed a reason, Tara. I had to say there was something going on that led you to do that, otherwise they'd think it was just who you are. So I said you'd been under a lot of pressure at work, had a few too many drinks one night, which you very rarely do because you usually have Annie, and that you did something that you hugely regret.'

Despite me wanting it all just to go away, for people to accept it and move on, I still find myself feeling so angry about having to claim madness or apologise for simply responding to a sexual urge when I thought I was alone. I turn away and close my eyes. My head still really hurts.

'They are worried about Annie,' she continues, 'So I said that she would be living with me and your father for the foreseeable future, and they agreed that was a sensible idea. She's a good girl, they don't want to cause any trouble for you or her.'

Before I even get to open my eyes, there are tears streaming down my face.

'I'm a good mum,' I say, my face soaking wet, lips quivering as I try to stop the tears, in a vain attempt to hide my pain.

'Why don't you come and stay too?' Mum says, carefully. She knows that offering me too much help and suggesting I need it can often cause tension. But not this time. I need to be a mum, and I need my mum to be one too.

'Yes please,' I say, weakly.

I don't want to be alone.

6

Stella

I'm in bed. Alone. Huddled under the covers, eating tuna pasta bake. The temperature has dropped again; the air is chilly. Putting the heating on seems silly when it's May and just me. So it's dinner in bed for one. How tragic.

I've been in bed for three hours, just staring at the walls. Occasionally getting up for more pasta bake. Occasionally going for a pee. Occasionally sitting up and screaming at the door.

This used to be my mum's room, then it was Alice's room. Then it was mine and Phil's room, and now it's just my room. Mum bought this flat while Alice and I were at uni. We kicked up such a fuss when she said she wanted to sell our house and downsize. But then we came and stayed in it one weekend and loved it. Mum was in remission after her first bout of breast cancer. We had no idea in that joyful moment that it was about to come back in her other boob and kill her within a year.

It's the garden flat of a Victorian townhouse in Stoke Newington, with its own entrance. It's got big windows, a fireplace in every room, and it's lovely and bright. I've never achieved anything in my life that would mean I deserve a home like this, but I guess that's inheritance for you. My wages easily cover the small mortgage Mum left us with, and sharing it with Phil meant that my main expenses were just bills and food. I guess I'll have to pay for everything now, which is intimidating. But it's not like I have a kicking social life to fund, or anyone to go on wild holidays with, or absolutely anything fun or interesting that would require a big budget. And I suppose now my chances of having a baby have been dashed, I won't be needing to save for that either.

I'm not going to have a baby. I keep saying it to myself, but it's not getting easier to handle. I mean, I know there are other ways, I could freeze my eggs or adopt, but neither of those options are how I want it to happen. I want to do it naturally. I don't want having a kid to feel like something I had to buy. But the threat of cancer, the fact it already took my mum and sister so quickly and the reality of what I'm like to live with are three big reasons why that dream will probably never happen for me. So maybe that is that, I'll die alone, and leave nothing behind, not even a child. And what will the people who knew me say on their Facebook pages when I've gone? Nothing like what they said about Alice, I know that.

I can see it now from Phil:

R.I.P. Stella, you were emotionally unavailable, moody, impossible to reason with and controlling. You were so obsessed with your dead twin sister that your life was stuck in time. You lost all your friends, and then lost me because you turned into such a bitch to be around. If you'd have stopped wearing your sister's clothes like I told you to, you'd probably have been OK.

Or what about the girls from school?

Stella Davies died in her sister's shadow. We always preferred Alice because she was way more sociable and friendly, but as they came as a duo we just had to accept that Stella would tag along. When Alice died, we all stopped bothering with Stella because without Alice, she was really shit. RIP Alice. Oh, and Stella.

The only person I get on really well with is Jessica and she isn't even on Facebook, so I can't count on a gleaming personality review from her either. I suppose maybe Jason would say something nice, but then he knows so little about me even that would be pretty basic.

R.I.P. Stella, you were a great PA. Really bossy and organised. Thanks for all the coffee and do you have any other skirts, because you wear that bird one WAY too often? J x

All in all, I think it's fair to say that the Internet won't break the day that I die. Sitting at the kitchen table at my laptop, I look at Facebook but quickly close my page. I hate not seeing Alice's green dot welcome me and I still feel a little raw after nearly getting sprung by Melissa. She messaged me the next day to let me know what happened.

Hey Stella, just thought you should know that I think someone has set up a Facebook account in Alice's name. They added me as a friend but now the page has vanished. What sicko would do that? Don't they know how hurtful that is for me? Anyway, I thought you should know in case they do the same to you. Hope you're well, Melly x

Melly? Gross.

I haven't replied. If I ever see her again, I'll just say I never go on Facebook any more. Instead, I log onto *HowItIs.com* to see what Camilla Stacey has to say tonight. I've religiously read her words for as long as I can remember, but recently her smugness has started to grate on me. I read her latest post, 'A Call to Action'.

'Get what you want. Just get out there, and take it.'

Oh yeah, because life really is that easy? Cam Stacey doesn't live in the real world. She writes this idealistic, self-adoring nonsense about how you should love yourself, be who you want, get what you want. What does she know? Life seems so easy for her, her money, her success, her joy in being alone. Who wants to read about someone else who is nailing life? I'm not sure I do any more.

I have come to discover that very often the best therapy is seeing other people in pain. It's why society is so obsessed with celebrity gossip, and why soap operas are so depressing. Hearing about other people's shit makes you feel better, less alone – and that is the problem with Cam Stacey, it's all so bloody perky. She loves her body, her life, her childlessness, her job. She tries to disguise her smugness as positivity but it's not, it's smugness. How did I not see this before?

I log off her site, and onto *MailOnline*. I need to read about celebrities with shit lives, that always makes me feel better.

Wait . . . what?

WALTHAMSTOW W**K WOMAN REVEALED

The woman, who entered the underground network at Tottenham Court Road and alighted at Walthamstow, has been named as Tara Thomas, a 42-year-old single mother who never even told the child's father that she was pregnant. A source close to Ms Thomas told the MailOnline; 'Tara never questioned her decision to keep the baby, it was what she wanted, so she didn't think twice. As far as she was concerned, the father didn't need to know.'

Hang on. Tara? Last Friday? Works in TV? Six-year-old daughter? Oh my God, Jason went on a date with 'Wank Woman'? I saw this story at the start of the week, it was all over Facebook. I watched the video when Jason was in his office right behind me, I thought it was really uncomfortable to watch. Some woman clearly being filmed without her knowledge. I agreed with Camilla Stacey that it was creepy and exploitative and stopped following the story. Which was hard, as it's been everywhere. But that was *the* Tara? The one that Jason was so desperate to track down? It would seem so, I'm sure he said she had long curly brown hair, freckles, and she definitely lived in Walthamstow. That description matches Wank Woman perfectly. How could Jason not have seen this?

I guess at least now I know he's been sticking to his deadline and not looking at the Internet, because no one who has been online in the last few days could have avoided the global sensation of 'Walthamstow Wank Woman'. Holy shit, I feel like I just got handed a grenade.

Cam

Lying naked on her new shag pile rug, Cam is feeling pretty smug, her call to action piece is trending. Lazily scouring Google for new feminism blogs, it's like more pop up every day. What is flattering but annoying is that most of them cite her as their inspiration. There is one called 'One Night Stance' where a twenty-three-year-old blogger called Julia Rylan does online interviews with various women about their relationships with casual sex. A woman called Becky Martin has a site called 'The IVF Crowd', all about women above the age of thirty who are having children by themselves. And another, by Jemma Osbourne, called 'All Work No Play', about her life as a working mum. They have all got over fifty thousand followers on Twitter and there are hundreds of comments under each post, proving to Cam that their readerships are huge. When she started out there was no competition; now there are so many writing in the same field as her. She needs to focus her writing if it's going to keep its position as the 'Number 1 Voice for Forward Thinking Women'. What would the book be? What makes *HowItIs.com* different?

Her phone rings.

'Mother!' Camilla says confidently, answering it. She visualises her in the hallway on her landline phone, dressed in M&S trousers with a long M&S cream cardigan. Her 'house shoes' on her feet. Also from M&S.

'I heard you on the radio.' There is a pregnant pause. Cam knows her mother well enough to know that when she allows a space for Cam to speak before she has made her point, she doesn't really mean it's OK for her to speak. 'Everyone in Brockley is talking about it.'

'Mum, everyone in Brockley is always talking about everything.'

'But everyone is not always talking about *you*. And why did you have to write that one about the twenty-eight-year-old? If you're going to have a sexual relationship like that, it doesn't have to be broadcast news, does it?'

'I wrote it so people don't think I'm sad and lonely.'

'But you *are* sad and lonely, Camilla. You always have been.'

'Mum, one day you'll realise that I am happy. I just find my own company riveting,' she says, holding the phone between her ear and shoulder so she can paint her toenails with a peachy nude.

'I know. That's why you hid in the cupboard under the stairs for two whole days. I thought you'd been kidnapped.'

'I was seven. I can't keep apologising for it, I'm thirty-six.'

'Some people wrote terrible things under the article. One man even called you a whore.' Another pause, short, but definitely pregnant. '*Are* you a whore, dear?'

'No, Mum, I just don't want children. You have forty thousand grandchildren, please stop acting like I am letting you down.'

Cam softens her voice a little, genuinely tired of saying the same old thing. 'I want you to be proud of me for other things, Mum. I do other really great things.'

'I am proud of you, but can't you get a column in *Red* magazine and talk about fashion? You love all that.'

This is a prime example of how Cam's mother boxes her into all female stereotypes in her head. Cam really couldn't give two shits about fashion.

'I want to write about things that matter, Mum. It's important that women who make unconventional choices speak out, or the world will never change.'

'You're like that Gloria Steinem in the Sixties.' Cam smiles. For her mother to compare her to Gloria Steinem means she sees her in a political capacity, and that *is* progress. 'She went on about feminism and ended up alone as well.'

Or maybe not.

As Cam tries to think of a way to end the call, Mark appears from the bathroom. She holds both a toe, the bottle and the brush in one hand, and pushes her other hand to her lips as if to tell him to shush. He doesn't say a word. Instead, he puts both of his hands on his hips and shakes his hips from side to side so his penis makes a slapping noise on his upper thighs. She wonders if he practises all of these little penis tricks when he is home alone, they are so well executed.

'Mum, I have to go. There's a bird stuck in my bedroom.'

'OK, Camilla. But please, no more of the twenty-eight-year-old, OK?' But Cam has already hung up.

'I trimmed my pubes so you can see my dick better,' Mark says. He's more proud of his body and his penis than Cam is of anything she has ever said, owned or done. He is a young, handsome, cut-to-perfection man who has no idea what a lack of self-confidence feels like because he's never encountered one. They have the most phenomenal sex.

'Shall I shave your pussy tonight?' he asks, lying down beside her and stroking her pubic hair. He is so young and sexual that he wants to try everything, and he continuously watches porn. Soft, easy stuff. The kind of softcore that's on TV late at night, not horrible, sexually abusive porn that so many people watch on the Internet. He's got a constant erection, but a well-meaning one. 'A penis with a conscience', as Cam likes to think. He's not pushy, and she imagines he'd always wait to actually hear the word 'yes' before he had sex with anyone. He's a good guy, just so young and too handsome for Cam to take him seriously for anything other than sex.

Also, she has no desire to behave like a porn star just to please him.

'No, I don't want you to shave my pubes. You can go down on me for twenty minutes before I have to get on with some work, though?'

'I can do that, or if you want to work I could whip us up some food? Or run out and get a pizza? You can work for a bit, I'll watch TV, then we can just eat and hang out?'

'But I have to work,' Cam says, flirtatiously, trying to entice him down.

'I know, babe. I know you have to work. That's why I'm saying you can work now, and when you're done, we can hang out.'

Cam stiffens, she doesn't want this, she doesn't want him encroaching into her alone time, that is not what a fuck buddy is supposed to do.

'Mark, sorry, I don't like having a time limit on how long I can work for, OK? Maybe you should just go now, you think? We can hang out, or fuck, or whatever, tomorrow. Cool?'

Mark knows there isn't much point in trying to change her mind. She's made it clear from the start that work comes first. He gets dressed.

'Will you go out?' she asks him, as he goes to leave.

'Nah, not in the mood. I'll just have an early night,' he says, defeated.

'I'm sorry, OK? I just have to work.'

'Yeah, yeah I know, you mentioned that. Maybe leave me out of this one though, OK? My mum reads your blog, that last one about me was embarrassing.'

Cam sits up straight and moves her laptop to the side. 'You read that?'

'Of course I read it.'

'God, I'm sorry, I never even thought for a minute that you would,' she says, feeling genuinely horrified.

'It's OK, just don't write my name, OK? I'm not really a public person. And maybe leave out stuff about my dick. My mum's got a dodgy heart. I'll see you tomorrow then?'

'Yeah. And Mark, I'm really sorry I wrote about you without telling you. That wasn't cool. Mark?' she calls after him, but he's gone.

FUCK! Cam says to herself. *He's told his mum about me?*

Stella

I deactivated my Facebook account and I miss it. It might have driven me crazy in some ways, but I've spent hours and hours over the past few years clicking on profile after profile, stalking various people's lives. It's been pretty much all I've done since Jason has been on his deadline and now, I have nothing else to do. How pathetic is that?

I think maybe I enjoyed the jealous hate that swirled inside of me when anyone posted baby pics or wrote posts about the joys of family life. That fireball of rage kept pushing me through the day, it gave me something to think about. To worry about. To be passionate about. Because I want to be passionate. I don't mean sexually, I mean about something, *anything*. I have nothing that motivates my day now, other than the actual logistics of my job. But it's so quiet here right now, that after I've made myself a cup of tea and Jason a black coffee, I'm kind of done. I've organised everything in the office to the point of craziness, created well over thirty completely pointless spreadsheets and even started putting together a list of who Jason needs to send Christmas cards to. Now all that is done, I can't think of another single thing to keep me busy apart from wallowing in my past, and now my present too. I can't quiet the ticking biological bomb that lives in my mind as much as it does in my genes.

I get a cereal bar out of my top drawer. Food doesn't taste of anything right now; I'm just eating to pass some time.

I miss Alice. I was never bored when she was alive. I'd call her to talk about what I was having for lunch, she'd call me to tell me she was going for a wee. We spoke or texted all day about the tiniest details of our lives. Long, pointless conversations whilst on our way to work, just so we weren't alone. Ever. My arm would ache from holding the phone to my ear so much. We'd talk on the way home, only to hang up when whoever was already in opened the front door and we could see each other's faces. Then we'd get into bed that night, and if we were in separate rooms, we'd text until we fell asleep. I look at my phone. I've sent three text messages in the last three days. One to Phil, telling him he forgot some socks and that I was throwing them away. One to Jason, asking if he wanted me to pick him up a croissant on the way in, and one to my next door neighbour telling him to stop filling the rubbish bins with his Amazon Prime boxes. What a tragic trail of communication that is. But that's my life. Tragic.

I find the article about Tara again. I need to read about someone else whose life is shit.

'Stella, did my phone arrive?' says Jason, appearing out of his office. I quickly shut my laptop.

'No, not yet. I'll chase them now. How's the writing going?' I ask him.

'Getting there.'

I know I should tell him about Tara, but I don't know where to start. *'Yeah, so, Jason, the girl you like is a global wanking sensation?'*

Nope, I just can't. Not just because I'd have to find the words, but also because I'd have to show him the video, and I think watching what is essentially soft porn, with my boss, might be crossing unnecessary boundaries. Not to mention what it will do to his concentration. Jason has to finish this book; he doesn't know it yet but him losing his phone is a blessing in disguise. Keeping him in check also gives me a purpose, which I need right now. So I am not backing down. I look at him. He looks so, so sad.

'I'm getting I'm-going-to-die-alone vibes,' he says, looking at the floor. I stand up and walk over to him, putting one hand on his shoulder like a father would to a son in an old-fashioned movie. I'm not sure I have ever intentionally touched Jason before, other than shaking his hand when we first met. With just the two of us in here, it feels quite intimate.

'Ahhh, I'm sure you won't, Jason. Guys like you don't die alone.'

'You're so lucky, Stella. Having a relationship. I know you'll probably think I'm a sad case, but I get so lonely. Like I've got this big gap inside me that I can't fill. I should be married with a kid right now but I'm still meeting strangers in bars and holding out for text messages like some stupid teenage boy.'

He's so emotional, it's really disarming. I'm not sure I've ever met a guy who displays feelings in the way that Jason does. Phil was tender and thoughtful but not like this. Jason makes me feel like I could talk to him, tell him how I'm doing. Like a friend. But no. I am his PA; I do not, and shall not, explain to him that I am also, with very little doubt, going to die alone.

'I know I only met her once, but there was something about Tara. The connection was real; I know it was. She's exciting,' he says, looking at me with sorry but sweet eyes.

I suppose *exciting* is one way to describe her.

'Come on, you've been in solitude for a few weeks. You're bored, maybe lonely? That's why you're feeling down. Come on, hang in there, it will be over soon. When this book is in you can get back out there again,' I say, walking back behind my desk and taking a seat. It always amazes me how logical I am about organising Jason's life; I'm sure I come across as really together. No wonder he has no idea about who I really am – I hide it very well when I'm around him.

'You're right, of course. OK.' He starts to walk back into his office. 'Maybe I should just get on Tinder and broaden my horizons,' he says, looking back and smiling sarcastically, although I suspect he is genuinely wondering if he should.

When he's gone back into his office, I open my computer and read the article about Tara. 'As far as she was concerned, the father didn't need to know.' Why is this line playing on my mind so much? So, she just had a one-night stand, got pregnant and kept the baby, it was that simple? I wonder if she planned it. Because you *could* plan that kind of thing, I suppose. If you *really* wanted a baby . . .

I search the App Store for Tinder and download it. I set up an account and start swiping.

Just for the heck of it, of course.

Cam

'"The Face of Childless Women", are you kidding me?' barks Mel as she storms into the reception of Dream Spa where

Cam, and her sisters Tanya and Angela, are waiting.

'Excuse me?' asks Cam politely, wondering why Mel has just, quite aggressively, thrown a copy of *The Times* at her.

'Look, top left; it's you and your crusade. Look!'

'What is this? Give it to me,' says Tanya, the eldest of the four sisters, snatching it from Cam's lap. She reads aloud.

Camilla Stacey, The Face of Childless Women

By Susan Miller

After a career of punchy articles and provocative tweets, journalist, blogger, women's rights pundit and founder of *HowItIs.com*, Camilla Stacey, seems to have found her new position as the Queen Bee of the childfree.

'"Childfree"? They make it sound like we're in parent prison,' interjects Angela, the spikiest of the four.

'We kind of are,' says Mel, 'but wait, she hasn't even got to the best bit yet.'

Tanya continues:

After a series of emotionally explicit postings on her feminist website about her decision not to have children, Stacey followed on her pledge to educate society of the value of childlessness by battling it out with the rather conservative listeners (and host) of *Female First* on BBC Radio London.

When referring to some of her childless heroes, Dolly Parton, Oprah Winfrey, Gloria Steinem and Helen Mirren, Stacey said, 'I think it's important we take the lead from our heroes and for

> everyone to stop valuing women on whether they do, or do not, become mothers.'
>
> The interview welcomed a wave of cyber cheers as Twitter praised her for her support of the 'non-mothers', one follower even awarding her with the accolade, 'The Face of Childless Women'.
>
> It's about time we had an icon to represent the fastest growing social demographic in our society today; the female NON parent.
>
> Of course, there are the naysayers. Traditionalists who believe that a woman's place is at home, and that it is her obligation to reproduce to continue the evolution and growth of the human race. But as Stacey has so rightly put it, 'There are lots of humans, and plenty of babies being born. If you decide not to do this, we're gonna be OK!'
>
> All hail our new queen, Camilla Stacey, The Face of Childless Women. Take your crown, girl!

'Holy shit!' gasps Cam, taking the paper back from Tanya. 'This is major.'

'Major embarrassing, you sound like a dried-up old hag,' snaps Angela. 'What's next? The Face of Mad Cat Women? The Face of "Fucking Hell I'm Suddenly Eighty and I Haven't Left the House for Forty Years"?'

Tanya, Mel and Angela all laugh, then stand over Cam like witches round a cauldron. No matter how big she feels in her online life, Cam always feels like a little girl when she's with her sisters. Tanya sits to her left, Angela to her right. Tanya puts her hand on Cam's knee. 'Are you sure this is what you want, Cammie? I know we complain about being tired and it being hard work, but we wouldn't give up our kids for the world. You'd love it, if you opened your mind to it. It's not *that* bad.'

Angela leans in to her. 'We just wonder if you're using the no kids thing to hide something else, you know, something . . . '

'Oh just say it,' snaps Mel from a seat opposite. She's gently rolling a compression stocking down her left leg. 'She thinks you're a lesbian. Are you?'

'I have been telling you I'm not a lesbian since I was a kid, guys, what more can I do? I write about sex with men, I *have* sex with men, what more proof do you need?'

'Is that true then? You are actually seeing a twenty-eight-year-old? You didn't just make him up for your blog?'

'Of course I didn't. Yes, he's real. Very real. Getting realer, in fact,' Cam says, thinking back to Mark leaving and his feelings being hurt.

'What does that mean? He's your boyfriend?' asks Angela.

'No, no he's not my boyfriend. Not at all. God, no, he's a kid. I just mean, you know, the more time you spend with someone the more you get to know them, I suppose.'

'Ooooooh, Cammie's got a boyfriend, Cammie's got a boyfriend!' The three sisters start chanting, giggling and taunting her like it's twenty-five years ago and she's just been asked to a school disco. This scene is all too familiar. Cam doesn't need Sigmund Freud to work out where her social issues have come from.

'OK ladies, are you all here?' says a pretty blonde in a white cotton uniform. 'Come this way.' They all pick up their bags, and follow her into a changing room.

'OK, I have you all booked for private massages followed by pedicures at the same time, is that right?'

'Yup, that's right,' confirms Tanya.

'Actually, can I swap my pedicure for a foot massage, please?' asks Cam. 'A private one?'

'Oh, Cam, come on,' says Mel. 'The whole point is that we spend time together. Sit with us and have a pedicure.'

'No, I hate that. Looking at all of your feet, it makes me feel sick. It reminds me of when you used to wake me up by putting your toes in my mouth. I'll pay for everyone if you let me have my treatments on my own. We can go for a drink afterwards and you can carry on ridiculing me then?'

'Will you pay for that too?' asks Angela, boldly.

'Yes, I'll pay for that too. Just spare me your feet, please.'

'OK, but tell your therapist not to add extra time just because your feet are so massive,' says Tanya, jokingly.

'Oh you're so funny!' says Cam, pulling off a sock and throwing it at her.

They all undress. Cam, without much thought, takes off her leather jacket and pulls her black t-shirt over her head.

'Jesus, Camilla. You could have warned us we were about to get our eyes poked out,' says Mel, taking her underwear off under a towel. 'Do you ever wear a bra?'

'I didn't want to have to put one on after a massage. I like to be free.'

'Bra free, childfree, boyfriend free, have you ever committed to anything other than your laptop?'

'Yes, actually. I committed to the home that I own, and the business that I run, and the writing that I do. Not like you three, tied down by husbands and babies. I am free as a bird to do my things, and I am happy, so please can we just spend one afternoon together where you stop acting like some days you don't envy my life?'

There are a few moments of awkward silence while they continue to take their clothes off.

'I can't be as free as you, you're right,' says Mel, stepping out of her knickers. 'Mainly because of this.'

She drops her towel, revealing a body battered by pregnancy and childbirth. Veins like biros popping out of her legs, breasts like empty tote bags, stretch marks like a dartboard across her belly. Her sisters aren't sure if they should be laughing or not.

'I also pee when I sneeze,' Mel adds, causing them all to crack up laughing as she grabs the towel and wedges it between her legs. 'Shit,' she says. 'And when I laugh.'

'Come to my yoga class, for Christ's sake,' says Tanya. 'Your pelvic floor is a mess!'

'OK, which one of you is Camilla?' says a different girl with brown hair and the same white cotton uniform. She is not sure what she just walked in on, but she's doing her best not to look at the woman who she thinks might be peeing into a towel.

'I am,' says Cam, tying the robe and dropping her phone into the pocket.

'Cam, no, come on, you can't take your phone for a massage. Can't you stay off the Internet for an hour?' says Angela, who isn't even on Facebook.

'Yes, I can. And when that hour is up and it's time for my

foot massage, I will blog about the massage. Because that is how I roll, OK?' Cam sticks her tongue out at them and follows the therapist.

'My name is Sandra, I own this place. If you mention you were here we'll give you fifty per cent off,' the therapist says. 'I love your blog.'

'Sure, thanks!' says Cam. Yet another perk of the job.

After a blissful hour-long full body massage, Cam's brain is ready to get back to work. 'Can I sit up for the foot massage, so I can be on my phone?' she asks.

'Sure. I won't disturb you. I know how you don't like to chat.'

Cam buckles at the intimacy. Here she is in a tiny room with a stranger, who knows the intricacies of her life because she's read the words that Cam herself put out there to the world. It's the second time this week that has made her feel weird.

'OK, look up and smile. Tweet time,' Cam says, taking a photo and posting it.

Best foot massage ever at @dreamspa. Ask for Sandra, she has magic hands #dreamspa #magichands #askforSandra

'Thanks,' Sandra says. 'It's a tough business. Competitive, you know? I set this place up after I had my little girl. Her dad didn't stick around and I was left with nothing. It started as just manicures and now it's a spa. Turned it around in the end. Anyway, sorry, you get on. Let me know if it's too much pressure.'

'I will, thanks. That feels nice.'

Cam settles back and checks her email. There is one from Tara.

Hey Cam

So yeah, my name is out there. I guess there is no hiding now. Also, I passed out in Tesco and ended up in hospital. And yup, officially back living with my parents at the age of forty-two. So feeling really great about myself right now.

How are you? I loved your piece about women stepping up. I guess it's not always that easy though. I keep having moments where I think I can pull things together and get my life back on track, and then I realise that the universe is out to get me, and I don't have the power to do shit. They even seem to have erased me from work, which is the only place I ever felt totally on it. Is this just my life now? Help.

Tx

Cam leans forward and looks at Sandra. 'It must have been hard,' she says, 'to find the energy to make this place work, when you had a kid and were on your own?'

Sandra looks up as she rolls her knuckles around the inside of Cam's left ankle.

'Yeah, it was. But when you have a kid you have to get it together. I'm not saying it makes life harder than if you don't, but it's not just about you. At the end of the day anyone can turn their life around if they put their mind to it. I believe that.'

Cam closes her eyes for a second, as thoughts swirl around her head. Her eyes ping open as inspiration strikes. She opens *HowItIs.com* on her phone, and gets to work as Sandra applies the perfect amount of pressure to her feet.

You can always get your life back, no matter what!

Everyone is in their own rut at some point, and when you're in it, it can feel like life as you knew it, or hoped it would be, just isn't going to happen. But that doesn't mean it has to stay that way, or that you have to accept a raw deal. Everyone has the power to turn their life around, it's really just a matter of good decisions.

When sadness is dominating your life, when you are so consumed with negativity that you can't see the wood from the trees; in those times it is the job of someone close to you to remind you that everything will be OK one day. But if you don't have that person, then I'll be the one to tell you that everything is going to be alright, if you decide you want it to be.

Take prison, for example. The whole point of prison is rehabilitation. Criminals are reprimanded for what they have done, locked up as punishment and taught a lesson for their crimes. All with the intention that they learn from their mistakes and go back into the world at the end of their sentences to live relatively normal lives. If the worst people among us are able to rebuild themselves after being incarcerated, then the rest of us absolutely can too.

Sometimes life presents itself with the kinds of challenges you never think you'll overcome. Heartbreak, humiliation, losing a job, someone you love or your health, these are all things that happen to so many people. They are darkly 'normal', yet they can rip us apart and subsequently life can feel impossible. But the truth is, you can turn anything around with the right mentality. Your attitude to everything, from life to death is what defines how the experience is for you, and those around you. Keep your attitude good, and you can get through anything.

GO on, turn your life around, you can do it!

Cam x

She posts it, then replies to Tara's last email.

Tara, see my last blog. It's all about good decisions – so what are you going to do next?

7

Tara

'I can't believe this,' Dad says, as Mum feeds his arms through the sleeves of his jacket. 'How can I enjoy myself when everyone has seen it?'

'We had this organised well before any of this happened, Peter. It would look bad to cancel,' Mum says with a tight mouth but at full volume, as if that will make her inaudible to me.

'"Look bad to cancel"? How can we look worse? And why do we have to go to the pub, I thought we were having a dinner here at home?' Dad says, looking in the hallway mirror and straightening his collar. He's a proud man; I know this is killing him.

'We were, dear. But you smashed three of the dinner plates, two side plates, one serving dish and my china cake tray. How can I have a dinner party with half of my best china missing?'

Truth is, I wish he *would* cancel it. A 'small gathering of our nearest and dearest in our local pub', as Mum put it, is as tempting to me as a gunshot in the face right now. But I'm doing it, because my mum has been so awesome, and I want to make her happy.

'Is Katya here?' I ask, coming down the stairs.

'Yes, she's watching *Coronation Street*,' Mum says.

I go into the living room and Katya is sitting, drinking tea and watching TV. She's been mine and Mum's cleaner for six years, and babysits for Annie sometimes when I go out. I told her not to come to mine this week, because the house is so disgusting and I need to clean it before she gets there. She's around forty, Russian, tall, blonde and a bit trashy in the way she dresses. She's also hard as nails, never had kids and never talks about love. I trust her entirely.

'Hey, Katya, how are you?'

She gives me an angry side eye, then focuses back on the TV. She's wearing a leopard-print top with skinny jeans and ankle boots with pointy toes. She always wears bright pink lipstick, which I think is hilarious when she is essentially spending a night in alone watching television.

'Annie is asleep; she was wiped out. She didn't eat much dinner, so if she wakes up for any reason you can make her some toast, but I doubt she will. Katya?'

'I can't look at you,' she says, sternly. Her accent is very strong.

'Why?' I ask, even though I know why.

'For years I have cleaned your dildo!' she says, standing up and getting agitated.

I step much closer to her. 'My dildo?'

'I worry about you, that you get none of the sex. So every week I come, I clean your dildo, I make sure it is clean for you and I leave it in your drawer and all so you have sex and respect with yourself. And then you go on a train and you do those things for everyone to see? Why you do that?'

'Wait, you clean my dildo?' I ask, slowly.

'Every week, I clean it with the polish.'

'With furniture polish?'

'Yes.'

'Jesus.'

Sophie got me the dildo for my birthday present three years ago. I have never used it. No matter how little sex I get, I've never been able to get turned on by a piece of rubber. And thank God; I'd probably have died of toxic poisoning by now with half a gallon of Mr Sheen being wedged up my vagina.

'Katya, you don't need to clean my dildo, OK? And you don't need to worry about me and the sex I get.'

'The sex you don't get, more like.'

'OK, the sex I don't get. You don't need to worry about it.'

'I won't clean it for you any more,' she says, huffily, as she sits back down.

'That's OK. Will you look at me?'

She turns her head slowly to the left and looks up. We make eye contact.

'There,' I say. 'Great. OK, we won't be late. In all honesty, I hope I'm home in under an hour. See you later.'

'Goodbye,' she says, gazing back at the TV. 'I will not clean your dildo one more time.'

'That's fine with me,' I mumble as I leave.

'OK, shall we go?' says Mum as I walk into the hall, my grown-up mind telling me to face the world head on, the child in me wanting to lock myself in the cupboard under the stairs and never come out. Social paranoia is a new emotion for me. I'd literally rather bathe in cockroaches than sit in a pub with my parents and their friends.

'Yup,' I say, putting on a brave face and a denim jacket. 'Let's get this over and done with.'

I knew this was a terrible idea. Sitting around a large round table in the back room of our local pub are me, Mum, Dad, Mum's best friend Gloria (Mum's 'sexy friend'), her husband Simon, and two of Dad's mates that he drinks with at the bar, Ron and Malcolm. Also there is Mrs Bradley and David. There is a buffet table covered in food against a wall. No one has touched it.

'Well, happy birthday, mate!' says Ron. 'What is it, the big nine-oh?'

'Oh ha ha,' says Dad, sipping from his pint of stout. He doesn't want to be here, it's screamingly obvious.

'Well, I have news,' says Gloria. 'Tina is pregnant.'

'Oh that's wonderful,' says my mother. Everyone raises a glass to Tina, Gloria's daughter. Then we all go quiet again. Ron keeps looking over at me. Whenever I look back, he winks. Ron is seventy-six. I want to throw up.

'Yes, they'd been trying for ages. So we are all thrilled.'

'Not that I like to think of them "trying",' says Simon, referring to sex, which makes everyone look at me, then look away and blush.

'Sorry, I . . . ' he says. Like I'm German and someone mentioned the war. Everyone goes quiet again.

'OK, come on, we might as well deal with this head on,' says my mother, suddenly, putting her drink down firmly on the table. 'As you all know, Tara was videotaped doing something very personal on the train last week.'

'Mum, no, what are you doing?'

'Quiet please, Tara. It's your father's birthday and we can't all sit here in silence pretending this isn't happening.'

Oh, Jesus.

'We've had a very hard week. The newspapers have written about us and we are all very embarrassed. But as a family we thought it was important to not cancel tonight, as we want to move on from all of this. So may I suggest we all raise a glass to my wonderful husband, Peter, on his seventy-second birthday?'

Everyone does as she says, and I wonder if anyone would notice if I ran out of the room to be sick.

'Thank you,' says my mother, as she sits back down. My dad looks like he's sitting on a thousand drawing pins. Everyone goes quiet again.

'I touched myself in public once.'

'Gloria!' spits my mother. 'What are you saying?'

'Oh, no one saw me, but I thought it was wonderful. Very exciting. Of course I didn't get filmed; we didn't have camera phones in those days.'

Oh my God, no, this isn't happening.

'She's a wild one, alright,' says Simon smiling at Gloria, who looks very proud of herself. My dad removes himself from the table and starts cramming small ham sandwiches into his mouth over at the buffet table.

'I've had the occasional squeeze outdoors myself,' says Ron, making Gloria laugh and my mother's jaw smack her thighs. 'There's nothing wrong with that, good on ya, girl,' continues Ron, looking at me and winking, like I just did well in a maths exam.

'OK,' I say. 'We don't need to talk about this.'

'We've even done it in public, haven't we, Simon?'

Oh for fuck's sake.

'Sorry everyone, I'm not sure this conversation is appropriate,' says Mrs Bradley in her haughty headmistress voice, gesturing towards David, who is clearly about to have a breakdown at the mention of sex. This is the second time I've been involved in David being exposed to sexual content. He's going to have a full-scale episode every time he sees me from now on.

'What's the matter, David?' says Ron. 'Still not popped your cherry?' Him and Malcolm burst out laughing. Dad turns sharply and silences them with his eyes from the corner of the room. He is comfortable with being around men and has spent hours of his life in this pub talking about sport and work, but he's never been able to cope with crass, laddish behaviour.

'Yes, please, let's try to keep the conversation away from S-E-X,' says Mrs Bradley, looking nervously at David, waiting to see if he gets worse or calms down. I notice that even though David is looking down, his eyes are edging towards me.

'Right, well, now that's out the way, shall we eat?' I say, really needing this to move on. I get up and head over to my dad at the buffet. Everyone else stays seated and continues with the awkward silence. I might have to give up trying; this evening is obviously doomed. But then my mother starts to speak again.

'OK, well if you must know, Peter and I did it on a beach in Portugal once, so I guess everyone has had their fair share of public fun, haven't they?' she says, as if she didn't want to be left out.

'Oh for the love of God,' says my dad, dropping a plate full of stale buffet foods and crouching down to pick it all up.

'Peter, please, will you be careful with the bloody crockery!' shouts Mum, and I can't help but laugh. This is all completely ridiculous.

I kneel down and help him pick up bits of buttery ham off the disgusting pub carpet. 'Happy birthday, Dad,' I whisper. He manages to look at me for a second, but it doesn't last long.

'We were on a private beach and under a towel,' he says, abruptly.

'Dad, seriously, we don't need to share any more, OK?'

'Yeah, sorry, love,' he says, standing and reloading his plate. I hope that is the end of the Over Seventies Confession Club meeting I seem to be stranded at.

After a short while longer we've all managed to eat a little, have a couple of drinks, and keep the conversation off sex, but the tensions are still high. Ron has been trying to edge closer to me for twenty minutes; the more he drinks, the more his eyes glint like a coyote eyeing up a cat. God knows what nuggets of sexually inappropriate wisdom he is planning to spray me with. So as he begins to make his move over to the empty chair next to me, I make a sharp exit to the toilets, where I spend a long time sitting with my head in my hands, not caring what anyone thinks I am doing. When I come out, David is standing right in front of me, blocking my way. His black curly hair is hanging gently over his face, his skinny, tall frame suddenly surprisingly intimidating. I take a sharp intake of breath and slap my hand to my chest.

'David, my God, you made me jump. This is the ladies, the gents are over there,' I say, pointing down the corridor.

'I saw your boobs,' he says, like something from *The Walking Dead*.

'What? No, David, that was Sophie. You saw Sophie's boobs.'

'Your boobs. In the shower. January seventeenth, 1998, at eight sixteen a.m.'

OK, this is creepy. He's obviously had a dream he thinks is real?

'No, David. You saw Sophie's boobs, you came upstairs with me and she flashed at you, OK?'

I try to get past him, but he blocks my way.

'Your boobs. The door was open, you were there. In the shower. Soap.'

'David, did you sneak in on me in the shower?'

He says nothing and stares at the floor, then looks up at me with strong intentions in his eyes, puts his arms around me, offering the stiffest hug I have ever had, and says, 'I love you.' He then turns around and walks, with purpose, back into the function room. I remain motionless by the toilet door. After a few seconds I exhale the huge breath I've been holding in, and smile. Normally I'd be freaked out, but honestly, I really needed that.

Saturday Night

Stella

Tinder is so addictive; it's certainly taken my mind off Facebook for an evening. I've been lying on my bed swiping left for the last three hours. Man after man, potential after potential, but I need to stop being so picky, and remember I only need to meet them once.

With this in mind, I swipe right on James. He's thirty-four, his bio says he runs an artist's studio. He likes art and artists and he is looking for someone to 'get cultural with' in London. He doesn't sound too bad. Good genes. Actually, he sounds a bit like Jason. We are a match, apparently. He sends me a message.

Hey Stella, love your pic, but where is your bio? I can't date a girl without a bio, you could be anyone ;)

He's right, I need a bio. I start to write one.

My name is Stella. I am an identical twin but my sister died and I . . .

No, I can't lead with that, it's too depressing. I try again.

My name is Stella, I'm a PA and that's it really. I own a flat though, so that's one bonus. And I've got great boobs but not for much longer because I have the BRCA gene and that means if I don't have my entire reproductive system removed soon I'll probably die of cancer.

Oh come on, Stella. *Positive!*

Hey, I'm Stella, I own a really nice flat and have a really nice job. I mean, it's not the kind of job that means anything, more support for a great boss who is achieving loads. I just organise his diary, and boss him around and make him coffee. It's a nice job in a nice place but it's hardly going to change the world. I mean my boss might, he's brilliant, but it's nothing to do with me. I'm also desperate for a baby before I become infertile, and my twin sister is dead.

Bloody hell, on paper my life is so shit. Apart from my flat, which I love but don't feel proud of because I didn't earn it, I can't think of a single positive thing to say about myself. All the good things are under threat. Everything happy is dipped in sadness. I'd need to write a bio full of lies to make myself sound dateable.

*

Or . . .

I log out and set up another account. This time I use Alice's name, and a nondescript photo where you can't really see her face. It's a close-up of her eyes looking to the side and directly into camera. I love it so much. I stare at it for hours sometimes, it's really useful when I need to cry. OK, let's see if this feels better.

Hey, I'm Alice. I currently work in an animal shelter but I am training to be a dog trainer. I did a degree in psychology but realised I find dogs way more interesting than humans so I switched the species that I study. I love my job, and want my own dog-training school one day. I love music festivals, lazy Sundays, my friends and my sister. We are identical twins . . . I'm the fun one!

I quickly delete the last line; there is no need for me to be down on myself when I am not even being myself. I'll keep it simple. I post the bio. It was so much easier to write than my own. She'd probably have her training studio by now, she wanted it so much.

I start swiping right on all the guys who I think Alice would go for, and I wait for a match. Within minutes, alerts start coming in. Alice's eyes are as alluring as they ever were. Everyone always said that, but they never said it to me. I used to think that was odd, considering our eyes were exactly the same. But I guess it's what is behind them that people are drawn to.

Hey Alice, I work with animals too. Which shelter are you at?

Oh God, my heart leaps up my throat. What do I say to that? What if he knew her? I ignore his message; I can't even go there. London suddenly feels so small. Maybe I should stop this. But I can't. Another message comes in.

Hi Alice, I agree, animals are better than people. Fancy a drink?

I'd forgotten that the point of this is actually to meet someone. My heart is racing, I'm so hot all of a sudden. Blood is rushing through me like I've just run a race. I stand up and take off my cardigan, stretch out my arms and shake them, then sit back down and take a deep breath. OK, come on, Stella, be brilliant. *Be Alice*. I hit reply.

Hey, I said more interesting, not better ;) A drink might be nice . . .

I quickly read his profile, he doesn't work with animals. It feels safer. His name is Scott, he's thirty-four. He's got dark hair, a straight nose, a nice smile. He's cute looking, and works in the city. Looks *and* brains, my baby would come from a good place. Maybe this could work.

It looks like we are within a mile of each other, shall we be spontaneous? I'm free now if you are?

Oh wow, here come the heart thumps again. Can I do this? Really? A date?

Sure, 9 p.m.? Jaguar Shoes, Kingsland Road?

Oh Christ, what am I doing? I take some long, slow breaths and tell myself it doesn't matter. I don't have to do anything. I can just come home. If I like him, and he seems like a good guy, then maybe I can try this. I reply before I change my mind.

Done!

I open the article about Tara again. 'A one-night stand'. 'She never even told the father she was pregnant'.

Maybe it *can* be that simple. Is it cruel if he never even knows about the kid?

I go into the bathroom, wash my face and put on some foundation, a little blusher and draw two long black lines along my eyelids, doing little flicks at the ends, just like Alice has in the photo. I go back into the bedroom and get her bird skirt out of the wardrobe. I wear it with a silky black t-shirt and a little pair of low red heels that Alice used to wear all the time. I'd told Phil I'd given these away, but really they've been hidden in a box for the past year. I look nice. I look just like Alice. I wish it was as easy to put on her personality.

As I leave the flat, I think back to what Camilla Stacey said in her article. *Women need to take charge of their own lives, go find what they want, and take it.* OK, Camilla Stacey, I'm going to do just that. I'm going to take what I want!

I see him as soon as I walk into the pub, he looks exactly like he does in his photo. Scott is tall, cute, casually dressed but looks like he might feel more comfortable in a suit. If I was to be critical I'd say he looks pretty boring, but I'm not going to be critical, because his personality isn't what I am after.

'Hello,' I say. 'I'm Ste—' Shit, I stop myself just in time. 'I'm sssstarting to think this is a good idea,' I say, covering my mistake, and cringing at how cheesy that sounded. But he doesn't seem to care.

'Alice, hi. It's absolutely a good idea. What would you like to drink?'

'Vodka please,' I say off the top of my head, trying not to show that being called Alice made me want to fall down and bang my head on the ground.

'OK, anything with it?'

'Just ice.'

I feel so stupid for just ordering a neat vodka that I pretend it was no mistake. When I get it, I have to work hard not to scrunch my face up with every sip.

'So, where did you grow up?' Scott asks me, after twenty or so minutes of discussing the weather, local highlights and how great Tinder is. I told him I'd been on loads of dates but with no success; I have no idea what the right answer to the question, 'Have you had many Tinder dates?' is. I imagine most people would rather not be asked.

'London, born and bred. My sister and I went to school and uni here.'

'Oh wow, so you could be on *EastEnders*?' he says, laughing at his joke. At least I think it was a joke. I don't have an East London accent; Jason even calls me posh. Scott sees I don't find it funny and asks, 'Is your sister older or younger?' moving on the conversation.

'She's my twin,' I say, finishing my first vodka and ordering another one, this time with a splash of soda. 'My identical twin.'

I wasn't going to mention that, but I don't seem to be able to avoid it. It's the only thing that makes me sound interesting.

'Oh wow! I've always found identical twins fascinating. Did you do terrible things when you were younger, and date each other's boyfriends? I dated a girl once whose mood swings were so dramatic I used to joke she was an identical twin and that the nice version of her was my girlfriend and the moody one was her evil twin sister who hijacked her life because she hated her own.' He laughs so hard at how ridiculous that would be, and I honestly don't know where to look.

'That would be crazy,' I say, smiling reassuringly. 'No, we never did anything like that.'

'So what is her name?'

'Stella.'

'And does she work with animals too?'

'No, she's a PA. She doesn't really know what she wants to do.'

'Funny isn't it, how you can be identical but so different?'

'Yeah, it's really funny.'

'So, are you completely identical?'

Why do people always ask that? Is there some confusion about what the word 'identical' actually means? I need to move this along.

'I have to be up early,' I say, squinting my eyes a little. I think it's suggestive, but he seems to think I'm dissing him.

'Oh, OK. Cool. Sure. Sorry. Fair enough, I suppose. I guess it's hit and miss with the Internet isn't it.'

'No, I mean. We should probably go back to yours quite soon?' I say, surprised by my own forwardness. But he ticks all the boxes for a prospective father of my child, so I think we should just get on with it.

'Oh. Oh wow, I thought you were trying to get away from me. You want to come back to my place?'

'Yes,' I say, 'shall we go?' I step off my stool, and start to walk to the door. 'Come on, then,' I say, calling him to follow me. Like a well-trained puppy, he does.

Back at his place, he pours us two glasses of wine and we sit on the sofa. 'You live alone?' I ask, wanting to know before I attempt to have sex with him in the living room.

'Yup, I haven't lived with anyone since college.'

I look around his flat. It's modern and organised. The decor isn't particularly interesting, although he's obviously got money. It always amazes me how some people mistake expense for style. But I try not to judge; it doesn't matter, I won't be back here after tonight. I put my glass down on the coffee table, and move towards him. Putting my hand on his upper thigh, I start to kiss him.

'You're so forward,' he says, my tongue in his mouth.

'I just really fancy you,' I say, keeping him focused.

I feel that he's hard, so I crawl on top of him and grind. My head tells me to go quickly, but my body has its own thoughts. My hips slow down as the pleasure controls them. I loop my hands behind his neck and push myself down and around on his cock. He pulls my t-shirt out from the skirt and pulls it over my head. I undo my bra and let my boobs fall towards his face. I feel him buckle as he looks at them. 'Fucking gorgeous tits,' he says, before filling his mouth with my right nipple. He sucks hard and I want it harder. Phil couldn't treat my body this way since I got the results. This is how it was before my sexuality was threatened with death.

I lean back, putting my hands on his knees to give him the best view of my breasts that I can. I want him to see them, to feel them, to smother them with his mouth, his hands.

'Suck them,' I tell him, and he pushes them together and glides his mouth over each, back and forth and back and forth, until my nipples are rock hard. I feel a tear roll down my face when I imagine them gone. I wipe it away.

'I have to fuck you,' he says, pulling my face back to his.

'Yes,' I say, as I step onto the floor, undoing my skirt and pulling down my knickers, letting them both drop to the floor. He pulls his trousers to his ankles, and reaches to the back pocket for his wallet, then gets out a condom.

Shit.

'It's OK,' I say, getting back on top of him and guiding him in. 'I'm on the pill.'

But he pulls his hips back, and rips open the condom.

'I never have sex without one,' he says. Trust me to get a good boy.

He rolls it on. I pull away. What is the point now?

'What's the matter, Alice?' he asks. And everything goes into slow motion. I look at his face, just a guy, a normal guy. And who am I? A fake, a liar, a broken idiot. I could split on this plan. Make my excuses and leave. But what Cam Stacey said is going over and over in my head. *Go out there, and take it. Take it. Take it.* So I think of a Plan B, and I lower myself onto the condom, and I roll on him, and I whisper in his ear, and I push my breasts into his face, and I work hard until he fills it with my future. And when I know that it's done, I step onto the floor. I roll it off gently with my fingers. I say, 'I'll take care of this,' and I pick up my clothes and go to the bathroom, where I flush an empty toilet, just for effect, and tie a knot in the condom before slipping it into the pocket of the skirt. And when I come out, I remind him I have to be up early. I give him a fake number. And I leave.

While in an Uber heading home, I delete Tinder. At home I lock myself in the bathroom, despite being the only one home. I take the condom out of my pocket like it's a little shrew that I found in the garden, and I prod it with my finger so the creamy fluid slops around in its little bag. Then, cutting just below the knot with a pair of nail scissors, I hold it steady as I take my knickers off with my left hand. I lower myself to the ground and roll back onto my shoulders. I let my knees fall towards my face, my vagina is facing up, my lips are spread and I pour the sperm into the gap. When the condom is empty, I wait.

How long does it take?

I should have read more. I have no idea. Is there a right way and a wrong way to do this? After a few minutes, I gently roll myself back down, squeezing my pelvic floor as if to hold it all in. But as I stand, the sperm flops onto the bathroom floor. I put my foot in it and slip, crashing to the ground, banging my head on the corner of the bath. I quickly scramble back up to my shoulders, now there is sperm in my hair, on the side of my face. Is there anything inside me at all? I stand up. If I put my knickers on, will they catch it?

And then I jump. I swear I see Alice standing behind me. But no, it was my own reflection. I stare at it, the sorry state that it is. A stranger's sperm running down my leg, onto my sister's skirt that is crumpled on the floor. What would she say if she knew?

I get into the shower, take the head off the hook and push it inside of me and hold it there for as long as I can stand it, until the water runs clear. Until I am sure every last sperm has gone. Then I put the shower head back, and watch the water run down my chest and over my breasts. I can't imagine them not being there, being replaced by aggressive scars that would terrify men rather than turn them on. No matter what happens to me over the next year, the reality is that I will lose my breasts and my ovaries before I'm forty. It isn't a case of if, but *when*. I turn the shower off and rest my forehead on the wall, then clench my fist and draw it into my stomach. I grind my knuckles against myself until it hurts, then I pull my hand away and thump myself again. Grabbing my skin with my fingers, I twist and pinch and hope the physical pain will take the mental pain away, even just for a second. It doesn't.

I get out, stepping over the sperm on the bathroom floor, and throw my wet body onto the bed. What does it matter; I'll just sleep on the other side, now that I am alone.

I cry myself to sleep.

8

Camilla Stacey – HowItIs.com - Why Childlessness Could Save Feminism

The only thing that really ever separated men and women was that women got lumbered with the wombs, right? The fact that the babies grew in the women's tummies, then got pushed out of their vaginas and fed from their breasts gave men a right to delegate women to be the primary carers of children. I am sure it made perfect sense to everyone at one time for the females of the species to abandon all other ambition and commit to a life of motherhood. But what if the woman didn't have a child? Then, other than what we have been indoctrinated to believe – as in, that a woman's function is to have children and if she doesn't she is somehow incomplete – what really separates a man and a woman in terms of what they can achieve? What they should be paid? Whose boss they could be?

Nothing.

The truth is, a woman without a child is as available and capable as any man. Even more so, possibly, as many of those men will have families to get home to. But childfree women, we are free as birds to crack on with whatever job is in hand. No tie to a home, no pressure to be anywhere else. We could literally take over the world with all the time we have. Which is probably why a lot of men like to put childless women down, call us heartless, selfish, presume we are lesbians. They have to rationalise that there is something wrong with us, because the reality of the threat we pose is possibly a little too terrifying to bear?

I am not trying to encourage more women to choose childlessness, but I am encouraging those who do to wear that badge with pride. We, the childfree, can bridge the gap between men and women and achieve true equality, because there is nothing that makes us unequal. We can boldly say that men are no better, stronger or more worthy of status, money or power. Women with children are rock stars, women without children are superheroes. Together, we can take over the world.

'I basically just solved feminism,' Cam says to herself as she reads the blog post back. She's on a roll, her new accolade is gaining momentum, she's a hero among her childfree fans.

But with all her success, there is always someone trying to kill the fun.

An email pops up from Samantha Byron, Head of Advertising at L'Oréal, Camilla's main sponsor. Cam dreads Samantha's messages; they're always urging her to be boring, or safe, or write something she doesn't want to write. Samantha has no imagination and she's really tedious. But even though Cam has final say on all content and creative output of *HowItIs.com*, as L'Oréal is her main sponsor, she has to at least pretend to take their notes on board.

Samantha took over from Susan Jeffries around six months ago and it's been a challenge ever since. Susan was cool, mid-thirties, she had a kid when she was in her twenties, didn't want more. She was single, feisty, untraditional and really funny. She took such pride in L'Oréal sponsoring Cam's website, but quit when she got a job in the New York office, and Camilla was gutted. They used to go for wild boozy lunches and all Susan's notes ever said were, 'More of you, more of you . . . whatever you are today.' It was unusual for Cam to feel so at ease with someone, especially someone who was essentially her boss, but she liked Susan. They were friends. She misses that relationship.

Samantha, on the other hand, is a dull, play-it-safe jobsworth mum who probably only had sex three times in her life to make her three babies. She has no sense of humour, she hates other women, and she can't even bear to call herself a feminist because she thinks feminism is 'scary'. The working relationship is stiff, and happens predominantly on email. She also always says 'we' when she means 'I' and ends all of her sentences with question marks.

Dear Camilla

We've all seen and enjoyed your writing this week, and of course the piece in The Times is wonderful exposure for the site? We do feel it necessary to mention though, that we are concerned about alienating the many women who are not onside with your new accolade?

As a working mother of three I'm not sure I would want to check in with a website that promotes a lifestyle I can't myself participate in? Does that make sense? It might be an idea to keep HowItIs.com balanced to appeal to a broad spectrum of women as it always has. And we think you are at your best when you keep things light and fun, nothing too heavy or political. We women have enough to worry about, don't you think?

I'm sure you understand?

Thanks,
Samantha.

'Oh blah blah blah,' says Camilla out loud, to no one. This is going to be massive for the site, that piece in *The Times* was a game changer, and it wasn't the only one. *Grazia Daily*, the *Independent*, *Emerald Street* and *Glamour* have all done stories about Camilla, leading with the line 'The Face of Childless Women'. It's going to be huge, and just the USP she needed to keep her ahead of the game. Competition mounts daily; if she doesn't reinvent herself she'll be knocked off her pedestal by some millennial who writes about Tinder and partying on Molly. Cam could be the voice of a growing demographic, but stroppy old Samantha would rather she wrote about fluff? It's so frustrating. But she has to keep her advertisers happy, and annoyingly, maybe Samantha is right, while she becomes a hero to some, she might lose the attention of others. She needs to write something that keeps the mums on board. Maybe even something that gets her own mother on board. Anything is worth a try.

Cam writes.

Camilla Stacey – HowItIs.com – Mothers and Non-Mothers, Let's Quit with the 'Them and Us'

Can we get one thing straight? Yes, I am a woman who does not have or want children, but that doesn't mean I hate mums or motherhood. There is a lot of vitriol online at the moment, and it's aimed at mums who dare to post happy family pictures and pictures of their kids on Facebook. This has never bothered me; I've always thought it's quite a nice thing. But I've seen people complain about it, saying it's an unfair representation of what parenting is really like. Making other mums feel guilty for struggling, or non-mothers irrelevant for not being able to conceive, or contributing to society's notion that women are in competition with each other. Really, is that what you actually think?

If you do, I think **you're** *the one with the problem, not the happy mums posting pictures of their cute kids.*

Everyone knows parenthood isn't really represented by the photos people put on social media. Mums aren't going to post pictures of the moment a midwife scooped their poo out of the birthing pool with a colander, are they? Or write a status update about healing vaginal stitches, or having to perform a manual evacuation (Google it) on a constipated one-year-old. Why would they tell us about how their anus practically turned inside out during birth, and how ever since their poo just falls out, unannounced? Or how they can't walk up, or down, a hill without wetting themselves, or that their varicose veins ache in hot weather? They are hardly going to bleat on about the sleepless nights, the fact that they are never able to pee without an audience, or that their child still wears nappies at the age of seven.

Who wants to read about that on Facebook? We all know motherhood isn't glamorous, so let's allow people to celebrate the joy online, and deal with the copious amounts of shit behind closed doors. As a non-mother, I feel the least I can do is click 'like' on a happy family photo.

But some people are so riled by happy photos and I find that really odd. I even saw one woman on Twitter say that the women who had time to post pictures of their kids on Facebook were 'jobless idiots'. That's right. An actual woman, a journalist in fact (shocker), wrote that about other women who take twenty seconds to post perfect pictures online. Yes, many mothers are jobless and yes, they may have made that decision themselves. As much as I can't personally relate to that, or imagine it for myself, I am not behind feminism turning against mothers. How terrifying and ugly is that? I have three older sisters who have multiple children, I see their blood, sweat and tears as they do their best by these little people who demand everything, need everything, scream at ***everything****. Anyone who calls a mother a 'jobless idiot' is a heartless cunt. End of conversation.*

My mother was a housewife. I don't think she's pathetic, I actually think she's amazing. She raised four kids on a caretaker's wage and it was impossible at times, but the pictures on the mantelpiece in her house don't represent that, they represent the happy moments. No one needs to know that hours after the picture of us all frolicking by a pond in the summer of 1983, my older sister disappeared into the pond and had to be dragged out and resuscitated by my father. We all thought she was dead, and my mother's guilt for allowing it to happen still haunts her today. Of course she survived, although we all think she is a little slow (sorry, sis), but that was the reality of having four kids. There were terrible times where my mother and father lost control of us. The picture is on the mantelpiece because it reminds my mum how lucky she is that my sister didn't die that day, it's actually quite sombre, despite how blissfully happy we all look. If there was Facebook back then, that would have been the picture she posted – not the one that my other sister took of the moment my half-dead sister vomited up a load of green algae.

Mostly, it's hurt women, who want kids but can't have them, who get upset about mothers' photos. I guess I kind of understand this, it must be like rubbing salt in a wound, but what is the answer? Do we ban the joy of motherhood from the Internet so as not to hurt anyone? And then what? Do we just ban joy? Will people who are dying of cancer say that images of people in good health are offensive? Will they become angry and abusive to people who are not dying? No, we can't get to that.

I'm sorry for all the people who want kids and for whatever reason can't have them. That must be agony and I do understand why you get sad. But you can't blame the women who do. It's not fair. They are, after all, simply continuing on with the human race.

Many women don't choose childlessness, and it's for them that I want to be a beacon of positivity on the matter. For them there will be grief, of course, such sadness for the thing they always wanted that they might not ever have. But I want those people to know that if they don't have kids, their lives don't have to be empty. There are a million ways to be happy, so don't give mothers a hard time for spreading joy. Just find a way to be as happy yourself.

Have a great weekend,

Cam x

Stella

'Morning!' says Jessica, all spritely and annoying. I'm on the bus on the way to work, it's full but I got a seat. I'm a bit wet because it's raining outside, and there is a very large woman sitting next to me rubbing her big wet raincoat against my jeans. Answering Jessica's call gives me an excuse to squash up against the window, to create more space for her enormous arse.

'Hey,' I say back, quietly.

'You OK, babe?'

'Yeah, sorry. Just on the bus.' I feel a little conspicuous as people look at me, so put on some sunglasses to hide my swollen eyes. I couldn't stop the tears coming this weekend, I just cried and cried and cried.

'Oh God, I couldn't be on a bus right now, my morning sickness is so bad. It's horrible, Stella. When you get pregnant you won't believe it, it's like constant food poisoning and I'm sooooo tired, I could fall asleep standing up, like a cow.' She laughs at herself, and I hear Mike laugh in the background. 'Anyway, I'm just calling because I have a favour to ask.'

'Oh, what is it?' I ask, feeling a little boost at the idea of someone needing me for something.

'I have to go to John Lewis to get all our baby stuff, a cot, onesies, bottles; oh God, the list is endless. I don't want to go at the weekend because it will be hell in there, but Mike has to work during the week, so I was wondering if you'd come with me, can do any day soon? You said you were quiet at work. We could go for cake after?'

'Oh,' I say unenthusiastically, imagining myself having a full-scale emotional breakdown in the baby section of John Lewis, but also knowing I should get out of my own head, and do something that doesn't involve sobbing alone. So I say yes, and tell her to let me know when.

'OK, amazing, thank you! I'll text. Love you, bye,' she says, sounding delighted.

'OK, bye,' I say in a fake happy voice. I try to say 'love you' back, but it just feels weird.

The bus comes to a stop, and a load of people get off, including the fat woman next to me. I feel my own bum spread across the seat as I now have full use of it. A woman with a pram gets on, parks it just in front of me and sits down. She's skinny and looks tired. Her baby is screaming.

'She's been like this all day,' she says to me, looking despondent. I nod and smile then turn to look out the window. She reaches into her bag and pulls out a rice cake. 'There,' she says, sternly, giving it to the little girl who shuts up immediately like she's just been drugged, looking at the rice cake after every bite as if baffled by its diminishing size.

'You got any?' she asks me.

'Any what?' I say back, thinking how rude it is to ask me for food.

'Any kids?'

Oh.

I look out the window for a moment, remembering how Alice and I used to discuss city living, and how you have small interactions with hundreds of people a week, none of whom you'll ever see again. Whether on public transport, in a lift, waiting in a queue or walking down the street. Strangers' lives connect for brief encounters that may or may not affect your day. We used to joke about making up characters for ourselves, being someone different for everyone that we met. How fun that would be; that no one would ever know the truth of who we really were. In a big city, you can be anyone you want to be.

So I turn to the lady, and I look her in the eye, and I say, 'Yes, I have two. A one-year-old and a five-year-old. Is it just the one for you then?'

'Wow, yes, just the one. You started young. So you know all about this shit then. This brat just lay in the middle of the road in a solid plank, screaming like she'd just been run over and refusing to get up because I tried to put a shoe back on her. A *shoe*. You'd have thought I was trying to pull her foot off.'

'Oh dear, poor you,' I say, as if I fully understand. I imagine myself grappling with a screaming child. Maybe mine won't do that. She's probably not strict enough or something, the kid knows it can get what it wants. I'll be firm but fair, it can't be that hard to reason with them.

'Oh yes, been there,' I say, smiling. 'My eldest didn't wear shoes until he was three, he just refused. Little sod.'

She seems comforted by what I say. I feel a little disappointed in myself for bitching about one of my imaginary babies. 'But he's excellent at maths,' I add, feeling better about it.

'At five? Wow, maybe he's a genius or something. So what are their names?' she asks me, causing me to cough in an attempt to buy me some time.

'Oh, um, Jason and Alice.'

'Ahh, lovely names,' she says, and I realise I should ask her the same.

'Yours?'

'Oh, Shania. As in Twain. I'm a massive fan.'

Shania? Christ, no matter this kid is so pissed off.

'So is your fella any good? Mine's bloody useless,' she says, reaching forward and handing Shania back the rice cake that she just dropped on the floor of the bus.

'Oh, he's not been involved for a while. We actually broke up when Jason was around one. We got back together for a bit when he was three but it wasn't going to work, he doesn't want to be a dad. I got pregnant with Alice that time but he never even knew about her, still doesn't. I prefer it that way.'

'Wow,' she says, looking impressed. 'Good for you. The hardest thing about my life is my husband. Having the kid is tough and everything but him, wow, he's another level. I envy you doing it alone; I sometimes think it would be easier.' She smiles at Shania, who is getting to the end of her rice cake. 'Truth is, she could scream the fucking house down and I'd still love her. Know what I mean?'

I nod, and she gets up. 'OK, this is our stop. Say bye to the nice lady, Shania.'

Shania waves at me as she is told. I wave back.

'You're a strong woman,' says my new friend who I'll never see again. 'I admire you, I really do.'

I sit there on the bus, watching her lower the wheels of the pram onto the pavement, and I think about what she said. *I envy you doing it alone; I sometimes think it would be easier.*

That was just what I needed to hear.

Tara

I feel like I'm fifteen years old again. I'm sat in my old bedroom at my mum and dad's house, hiding under my duvet, waiting for a boy to call. Only back then there were no stupid mobile phones, so none of this would have happened. I'd never have sent Jason a slutty text, I'd have given him my number and he'd have phoned me the next day. I'd never have been filmed wanking, I'd never have been haunted by a speech bubble or sent rape threats on Twitter. But mobile phones have made life disgusting.

I keep looking at my Twitter page. This time last week I had seventy-nine follows, now I have 614,000. All of those people just waiting for me to say something, probably hoping I've drunk myself into a crazy stupor and that I'll give them more material to laugh at me about. The most annoying thing is that my last tweet before I knew any of this was going to happen was . . .

Spent my day with a pervert and it was magic #moresoon #tease #sogoodatmyjob

Of all the things to say before getting filmed masturbating on a train. All of my followers were just mates from school or people I've worked with, so I didn't think twice about it. I only really used Twitter to keep up with the news and stalk contributors; now I am the news.

The tweets have been horrendous. It's pretty intense when you're lying on your bed reading your daughter a story and *@BigGunnerz 'Bitchez like you are gagging for it luv. I'd rape you double sides on that train but you'd still want more'* flashes up on your home screen. Annie started reading it out loud before I realised what she was saying. I grabbed the phone out of her hand. But just as she was going to sleep she asked, 'What's a rape double?' It made me shudder with fear. Some guy has taken such a huge amount of notice of me that he is willing to write, publicly on Twitter, that he wants to rape me in both of my holes? At least, I presume that's what it means. How angry is this guy? Angry enough to come and wait outside my house? I told her it was a type of ice cream, put her to bed, and logged in to my settings to turn notifications OFF.

I can't bring myself to shut down my account though. I

feel I need to know what people are saying about me. I know I could cut out a lot of this pain by not looking online, but how realistic is that? Tragically, I think it's best that I am aware. And that means reading violently aggressive comments about how I look – 'frumpy' 'pale' 'sick in the head' – how I have behaved – 'Slutty' 'Mentally ill' 'Pervert' – and how I chose to have my daughter – 'Slutty' 'Criminal' 'EVIL'. But the worst are the ones from other women, the passive aggressive vitriol that they try to disguise as sisterly; those are the ones that cut the deepest.

@TaraThomas123 From one mother to another, do what is right for your daughter and tell her who her father is. She has a right to know. You have no right to keep them apart.

@TaraThomas123 I'm sure you love your daughter, so why rob her of her truth?

@TaraThomas123 You should be ashamed of yourself. Call yourself a mother?

The truth is, I can just about take what people throw at me for the actions that I took. I can handle being called a slut, and I can cope, kind of, with aimless threats online. But every time anyone mentions my daughter, a guilt creeps through me that makes me feel physically sick.

Maybe they're right; maybe I should tell her? I always presumed one day I would, she'd need some kind of explanation. But I was going to tell her I wouldn't know how to contact him, more for him than her, if I'm honest. And maybe that is really terrible of me as a mother, because I remember exactly where he lives. I think I just always presumed that at some point I would meet someone and Annie would have a father figure in her life. I suppose I can give up all hope of that now, who is going to want to be in a relationship with Wank Woman? Other than @BigGunnerz.

I type Jason's name into Google, like I have so many times over the past week. I found him immediately when I first Googled him at the weekend, just searched for that *Times* article and there he was, Jason Scott. His work is incredible. The detail he captures; the stories his pictures tell. The way he reads a person with his lens is so powerful, like a book that needs no words to tell the story – his photos take you on a journey.

I have been staring at our text chat like it's a door that he's sitting just behind. It's like being on a diet and being locked in a room with a box of doughnuts. The temptation to text him is killing me.

I just don't know if I believe that he didn't feel the same way that I did, and also, he seemed so liberal. Not that any amount of liberal means someone would be OK with dating a person who has been seen wanking on a train by the entire world, but from the small amount I got to know him, I'd say he was more the kind of person to say something cheeky than not say something. Maybe I just scared him off a bit? That would be fair, I suppose. 'Any special requests' could be read all kinds of ways. He might think I'm into electric probes, dungeons or anal beads? Maybe if I just explained myself, said

I didn't mean anything too kinky? Make it clear I'm up for kinky stuff if he is, but I'm not a fetishist or anything. But how do you get that across in a text? And then there is the video, that he has probably seen. He'd have spent the weekend thinking I was a crazy sex perv then seen that, which basically confirmed it.

I should let this go, walk away, but I can't. I can't stop thinking about him. I have to text him. But then, what if he still doesn't reply? I'm not sure my self-esteem could take it. But then, how could I feel worse? Things literally couldn't be worse. So I reach for my phone. I go to our conversation. And I text him. Fuck it.

'Love?' Mum shouts up the stairs, making me jump and snapping me back into my real world.

'Yeah,' I shout back.

'I'm going to go into town. Would you like anything from Marks and Spencer's?'

'No thanks,' I reply, then hear her come up the stairs anyway.

'You sure love? I could get you the hummus, or those little cocktail sausages?'

I shake my head. I haven't been hungry for days and Mum keeps trying to feed me.

'You need to eat, love.'

'Mum, I know I need to eat. I have been a human for forty-two years and so have a lot of experience with the "food is fuel" procedure, I'm just not hungry, OK?'

'OK, love, no need to be snappy, it's probably just because you're hungry. I'll get the hummus.'

'For fuck's sake, Mum. I am not angry because I am hungry, I am angry because I am Walthamstow W—'

'No, Tara, no! I can't hear it any more, OK? I'm having a little shot of whisky every night because of this. I can't hear it any more. Now, would you like some bloody cocktail sausages or not?'

We both stare aimlessly at each other. Unlike my teenage self, who would sit in this very room and be stroppy all the time, I care about not hurting her. I calm myself with a deep breath.

'Yes, please, Mum. Thank you,' I say, very politely.

'Right then,' she says as she goes back downstairs. I hear the front door open, then close with a little more force than normal.

I look at my phone. Nothing. Urgh, why did I text him, I feel even more stupid. An email comes in from Cam Stacey.

Hey, just checking in, you still alive?

Hey Cam, my mother is showing signs of alcoholism and force feeding me sausages. You get the idea.

Loved your piece on being able to turn life around by making good decisions. I'm trying to be proactive, in little ways, but not an awful lot of opportunity is presenting itself right now.

I'll eat the sausages and start with that.

Thanks for checking in, it means a lot to me,

T x

I sit for a moment with my phone in my lap, thinking if I don't look at it for two whole minutes, maybe there'll be a text. After eighty-five seconds I pick it up. Nothing.

Bloody hell, Jason – just text me will you?

Stella

I reactivated my Facebook account. I couldn't help it. I just needed one more look, one more session of torturing myself with other people's joy.

I sit at my desk, scrolling through my feed, getting more and more hateful with every status that I read. Groups of friends, happy families, big achievements. It's like rubbing my face with a handful of wasp stings. Why do I do it to myself?

Imagine their faces if I was to write the truth about what I did this weekend. How would that sit among the marital bliss and the joy of motherhood?

Can people handle the truth? I type it to see how it looks.

Met a guy on Tinder this weekend. Collected his sperm in a condom then tried to get myself pregnant with it. Changed my mind halfway through, so douched, but if any of the little swimmers made it I'll be sure to post relentless pictures on here. Have a nice week!

My cursor hovers over the POST button. Imagine the uproar, the drama it would cause. What is that little voice inside of me telling me to *do it, do it for the thrill*? But I don't, of course. It isn't attention I want, it's relief. I deactivate my account again. They really need a more severe solution for people who have legit Facebook addictions. I can reactivate and deactivate whenever I want; it is literally impossible for me to get rid of it permanently, so I probably never will.

But I'm going to try to stay off it. I will. I will, I will, I will.

My puffy face feels raw, my swollen eyes sting. Phil used to say it would be good for me to cry; I feel like calling him to tell him how wrong he was. Letting things consume me in that way didn't get anything out, it just reminded me how ultimately shit everything is. I don't feel relieved; I feel infested with grief. There is no positive end in sight for me, and crying doesn't change that. Maybe I should just book the surgery? Accept it? The thought of it makes me cry even more.

'Stella, did my phone arrive?' says Jason, appearing out of his office too quickly for me to sort myself out. 'Jesus, what happened?' he says, and I quickly put my hands to my eyes, as if to push the tears back in.

'I'm fine,' I say, 'just tired.'

'You are not fine. What happened?' he presses. I can see he's not quite sure what to do, he's never seen me show much emotion before. It's always him who is flapping around making a drama out of everything, with me supporting him however I can.

Realising that I can't pass tears off as normal, and knowing how much I hate it when people do public displays of emotion and then act all 'nothing' about it, I tell Jason the only part of it all that I'm willing to share.

'I split up with my boyfriend,' I say, feeling an unfamiliar sense of relief for being emotionally honest, but also annoyed that he'll think I am so upset about the most trivial part of all this.

'Oh Stella, I'm so sorry.' He steps closer. Is he thinking about hugging me? I'm not sure what the boundaries are in a situation like this, him being my boss, us being alone. He hovers backwards and forwards, then eventually puts a hand on my shoulder. We're both relieved he found a solution.

'I'm sorry,' he says, because that's what you're supposed to say and he's a good person. 'I always presumed everything was happy on the home front.'

'Yes you keep saying that, and it's not,' I say, snapping. The more he tells me how perfect he thinks my home life is, the more it feels like I've failed. He senses my tone.

'I don't mean to be rude when I say it, I just . . . I should stop speaking. You're just always so consistent, it's hard to believe things weren't OK at home. That's all. Sorry if that's out of turn.'

'I don't feel very consistent.'

'You always seem so in control.'

'You pay me to be in control. If I didn't control you, you'd never get anything done.' I smile at him. He nods in agreement.

'Hey, well if you need any advice on how to be a single loser, just ask. I'm a pro at this, I get dumped all the time.'

'OK. Thanks,' I say, the tears drying up a little. This is probably the most intimate conversation I've had with anyone other than a doctor in about six months. It feels good. Good to be open with him. We spend eight hours a day, five days a week together and although we get on well, it's work, not a friendship. We talk, but mostly about him, and the basics about me. The last few weeks have been particularly cosy. Because of his book deadline, the studio, which is usually alive with models, editors, stylists, journalists and make-up artists, has been dead. I have so little to do that I'm spending most of my days reading the Internet, trawling through Facebook and getting myself in a state, realising that everyone seems to be happy except me.

Jason asked me not to take this time as holiday so that I could keep him motivated. All that has involved is an Internet ban, multiple cups of coffee and a few words of encouragement. But it's given me too much time to think, during a period of my life where I should probably be trying to distract myself from me.

'OK, well, just let me know if I can help. We're good people, and good people don't die alone. We'll find love, and have families, and be incredibly happy and fulfilled. At least, that's what I keep telling myself,' he says, his gentle eyes giving me a shot of reassurance, along with a bolt of something else that I can't quite identify.

'Thanks,' I say, scrunching my eyes as an idea creeps into my head.

He puts his hand on my shoulder again. At first it feels wrong, inappropriate or awkward. But then my hand reaches up, and my fingers lie gently over his. My body relaxes as I accept the comfort that this small gesture is offering me.

'The guy's an idiot, Stella. If I had a girlfriend like you, I'd never let you go.'

He goes back into his office, and I sit very still at my desk.

Woah.

I shake my face, as if to stop my brain from carrying on with a train of thought that I know is wrong. But it's too late, my imagination is in motion.

Could I have a baby with Jason?

The sound of the doorbell cuts through the air and snaps me into reality. I buzz up a delivery guy who passes me a small box with Vodafone written on it. I sign for it, and walk slowly back to my desk.

'Is that my phone?' Jason calls from his office. He's desperate for Tara's number. Without much thought, I find myself replying, 'No, not yet. Just the post.' I hear him huff with disappointment.

'I'm shutting your door, OK? So you can concentrate,' I say, pulling it shut.

'Yes, boss!'

I take a seat at my desk and quickly unwrap the phone. I put it on silent, and turn it on and go through the set up. I go to settings and restrict the Internet. He'll need a password to get it back again, and I'm not going to tell him what it is. As the phone wakes up, various messages come through. Good luck messages from his mum, a couple of mates asking him to go for drinks. He hasn't missed anything too important. I go to his Facebook, a few of his friends have posted Tara's video on his page, asking if he's seen it. I delete all of his social apps. And then a text from 'TARA' pops up.

Hey, look, I'm sorry if I came across like a dominatrix crazy pervert. I had a really great night with you and I'm not sure I'm willing to accept that a connection like that can be ignored just because I'm an Internet sensation for publicly exposing myself. I'm quite normal, I promise. And I'd love to see you again. Tara x

I have to stand up and walk away from my desk. I think of Jason in his office, his deadline, his eyes, his hand on my shoulder. *If I had a girlfriend like you, I'd never let you go*. Those words. From a man I know, who is desperate for a baby, just like me. I pick up the phone. I open Tara's message, I write a reply, I press send. My stomach whirls. There is that thrill I've been looking for. Acting for myself, taking my life into my own hands. It feels fucking fantastic. I block her number, then delete it, before knocking on Jason's door.

'It's here,' I say, joyfully.

He looks so happy. I give it to him and walk away slowly as if absolutely nothing is happening that should require my attention.

'It's not here,' he yells, storming out of his office a minute later and looking wildly distressed.

I play along.

'What's not there?'

'Tara's number. It's not saved. I thought you said it would be in The Cloud?'

'Oh Jason, come on now, it must be there. Let me have a look. Tara, right?' I say, acting all innocent.

'Yes.'

'Hmmmm, are you sure you spelt it right?' I ask, scrolling through his address book.

'How else would I have spelt it, it's T-A-R-A.'

'It's not here,' I confirm. 'Maybe you didn't save it? Did you save it?'

Jason grabs his phone back. 'I don't know now, do I? I was drunk. I texted her, does that mean I saved it?'

'Not necessarily.'

'I don't know how I couldn't have saved it . . . but maybe I didn't. Oh for fuck's sake.' He throws his phone down on the couch in his office and storms over to the window, with folded arms. He looks genuinely devastated. 'Give me the Internet, I'm going to find her.'

'No, absolutely not. You won't get your book finished if you're heartbroken.'

'I won't be heartbroken, I'll be in love? Give me your computer.'

'Jason, look, sorry to say the obvious but maybe she didn't feel the same way about you. She could have found you online, right? I've been checking your email constantly and there is nothing from her, your email address is on the website. And she hasn't texted, it would have come through by now.'

Jason's smile lines shoot towards the floor as he realises I am right.

'But we were texting! Then the guy on the bike came and . . . we were so into each other.'

'Then why didn't you go home together?' I ask, pushing it.

'She . . . didn't want to.'

I raise my eyebrows as if to say 'there you go' and sit back in my chair. Jason slumps back into his office like an exhausted bear that just lost a fight. I did him a favour; if he found Tara and saw what she'd been up to he'd never get his book written. My idea is less distracting. He won't even know it's happening.

Tara

I'd given up hope of getting a reply to my text but then there it is, on my home screen. *Jason.*

I'm too scared to read it in case he doesn't want to see me again. If he does, then why is he only replying now? What if he is telling me to leave him alone? I feel like I'm about to open my exam results.

I run into the bathroom and look at my face. I brush my hair. I put on some mascara, and some lip balm. Looking better will make me feel better if I'm about to get dumped by text by someone I only knew for four hours. I tell myself that whatever he says just doesn't matter, he's not a part of my life, this guy doesn't have to hurt me. I am beautiful, I am strong, I can deal with this.

But who am I kidding? I have thought about him constantly since Friday. I know we only met once but it was good. It was really, really good. I tear back into my bedroom, pick up my phone and open the message. I might as well just rip this plaster off.

Tara, sorry to say but I think you misread the signs. It was nice to meet you but I'm not sure I see this going anywhere. Sorry to mess you about and good luck with everything, J.

Misread the signs? What? No, I didn't. You can't misread signs that press up against your leg and tell you they want to fuck you. How could he be like this? I knew there must have been something wrong with him. Guys that good aren't just single for no reason.

You know what? Screw him. I don't need a man like that. I need a man who is tough enough to handle how I had Annie, and tough enough to handle the fact I am an Internet sensation and global joke.

Oh, God.

I'm going to be single forever.

Men are way too egotistical to cope with either of those things. I might as well just sew up my fanny and marry God. I don't see any way out of this. It's been ten days and it's not dying down. Every time I dare to look at Twitter I've got thousands more followers and #WankWoman is still trending. A parody account – @ShitWankWomanSays – has over 400,000 followers and whoever it is posts tweets almost every two hours along the lines of:

Had five minutes to kill before a meeting today so I just cracked my vag out and had a good old frig about it **#WANKWOMAN #SHITWANKWOMANSAYS**

I even saw that HarperCollins had tweeted them asking to get in touch about a possible book deal. This has no sign of going away. It's only a matter of time before there is merchandise. I'll be the next Grumpy Cat, all over gift shops. Who will get the profit? Some dweeb with a Twitter account who wanks while he plays computer games, probably. Why is everyone acting like I'm the only woman in history to touch her own clitoris?

I have another email from Cam. Which, apart from my daughter, is the only thing getting me within reach of a smile right now. She is so nice. Not that I thought she wouldn't be, but you know what they say, 'You shouldn't meet your heroes.' Not that I've actually met her, but it kind of feels like I have. I feel like I could tell her anything.

Hey Tara
I've been thinking about you. A lot, actually. I'm having a day where I feel like relationships will always be complicated, no matter how simple you try to keep them. Know what I mean?

Anyway, just checking in, how you holding up? Cam x

I reply right away.

Hey, I feel exactly the same way. I thought I'd kept things simple, at home anyway. Now my closest relationships are the most complicated and I still don't understand it. Loved your piece on mothers Vs non-mothers, we are all the same really. How am I holding up? Not great. I have the fear, I can't sleep, I am too scared to go outside, the boy I like thinks I'm crazy, I think I'll be alone forever, my best friend is shit, my mother is showing mild

signs of alcoholism, my father has seen me masturbate. Oh, and I am pretty sure I am unemployed. You?
T x

I read that back. What a depressing state of events when you write an email trying to be funny, then realise all of the shit things you put in it are actually true. Whose life am I actually living right now? It doesn't feel like mine. I have an email from Adam. I open it, despite wanting to ignore any correspondence with him or anyone related to my old life.

Subject: Sky News interview
Tara, a mate from Sky News got in touch asking how to contact you. They want to do an exclusive. Probably good money. I gave them your email and number. Oh, and I found someone else to do your job, she promised she wouldn't wank on a train and make the company look bad, so she's in. Also she's taking over overseeing the edit on the pervert show so I'm giving her the exec prod credit. Obvious reasons why it can't be you, don't get your knickers in a twist about it.
Adam.

THE TWAT.

I hate him. There was a tiny part of me that thought maybe he'd value my work enough to protect me on some level? I got that company BAFTA nominations and worked my arse off on my shows. At least I'd have hoped he would give me the credit I deserve, or protect me enough not to give my email address to *Sky News*. Can't he see the entire world has turned against me? I took his misogynistic crap on the chin for years because I actually sympathised with him for not having the balls to admit to his sexuality. I took so much; I just took it and took it and took it because at the end of the day, it didn't matter. His derogatory comments didn't stop me doing anything. I was good at my job, I had the freedom to make the shows I wanted to make, so I just let it slide. I let him dump his denial all over me on a daily basis and now? Now he can go fuck himself.

Adam.

That was a really shitty thing to do. This is my personal email so please stop handing it out to journalists. Also, that show will do really well and it's down to me, you know it. So put me back on the credits or I'll tell everyone that you are GAY.

Tara.

There. Fuck him.

I sit and wait for a reply. Nothing.

Five minutes later. Nothing.

An hour later. Nothing.

Now I feel guilty. I get a reply from Cam.

Hey. Me? Oh, I think I'm realising that you can't control other people's emotions, no matter what you want for yourself. Listen, one thing I've learned in the billion years I've been putting work out into the public domain is that today's news is tomorrow's chip paper. I realise that no one reads newspapers any more and stuff on the Internet lives forever and can't be wrapped around a soggy piece of battered fish and some salty chips. BUT people move on, things move on, and you will move on. We are so young (I read you were forty-two? I'm thirty-six, same age really). I look at my mum and dad and feel like my life hasn't even started yet; there is so much I will do by the time I get to their age. You should feel the same. Whatever has happened in the last few weeks is the beginning of something new, no matter how catastrophic it feels. You'll find a way to turn this around to make it work for you.

After everyone is laughed out, they'll move on. My dad once told me to look for opportunities in everything and I've lived my entire life with that in mind. Don't hide, keep your head up and keep your eye out for a way to spin this in a way that works for you. You can do it! Cam x

Another email pops up. It's from Damien Weymouth.

The front door slams so loud it makes me jump. Next I hear the thud thud thud of Annie racing up the stairs. Is it end of school already? Christ, I'm still in my pyjamas.

'Mummy, Mummy,' she says, jumping up onto the bed. I feel like a patient. I pretend to look happy.

'How was school?' I ask her, taking off her coat as she cuddles me.

'I did painting,' she says. 'Look.'

She hands me a sheet of A4. There are four people on it, one is little, so I presume that is her. She confirms it for me. 'So who is this?' I ask.

'This one is Grandpa,' she says, pointing at the stick figure with nothing on. 'This one is Grandma,' she says, pointing to the stick figure with a coloured-in triangle for a skirt. 'And this is you,' she says, pointing to a stick figure with nothing on but a long black triangle hanging from its shoulders.

'That's me? And what is that?' I ask, pointing at said triangle thing.

'That's your cape.'

'My cape? Why do I have a cape?'

'Because you're Wank Woman,' Annie says, confidently.

I didn't think it was possible to have an awkward silence with a six-year-old, but there it is.

My daughter just called me Wank Woman. Can this get any worse?

When Annie is in the kitchen eating dinner, I run up to my room to email Cam back, like she's a guy I fancy and I am fifteen years old. For a few minutes, I forget about Jason. The truth is I have as much of a gap in my life for a good friend as I do for a lover, and the prospect of it excites me just as much. Sophie hasn't texted once since she got to Bora Bora, and what's weird is, I don't miss her. She'd be stressing me out at a time like this, saying all the wrong things, going on about herself. It's actually been quite nice getting a break from it. I need a friend, but one that can focus on me for five minutes straight without butting in to talk about what hair colour to do next.

Despite how horrible that video is making me feel, and how confused and miserable I am about Jason, there is this little thing that's glowing. Aside from Annie, I mean. Something else that is keeping my humour alive, that is giving me something to focus on that isn't the state of my life. It's my emails with Cam. She just seems to get me. I can laugh about all this in a way I wouldn't dare with anyone else, and what she replies is real. Actual engaged, kind and useful advice. Like a real friend would. I'm not quite sure how Cam Stacey from *HowItIs.com* became my new friend, but I am so so glad she did. I go to her email to reply, but am distracted by the one from Damien Weymouth. I want to delete it out of protest, but the subject line is pretty alluring.

Subject: ***Exclusive Interview Opportunity with Sky News £30k fee.***

Dear Tara

I've been watching your story with great interest. I'd like to offer you an opportunity to set the record straight, as I am sure you are being hugely misinterpreted by the Great British (great global?) public.

I'm proposing an exclusive on-screen interview with Sky News where you can tell your side of the story. Very often in these cases of public shaming, an apology is all the public needs to move on. Showing emotion and regret can gather the sympathy that is needed for people to accept that you acted out of character, and that you are remorseful about the way that you behaved. I have conducted interviews with many shamed high-profile celebrities who needed to set the record straight. In light of the magnitude of public interest in you, Sky News have offered a prime time TV interview to go out as a special within their news programmes.

I'm sure you are feeling like life may never be the same again, but hopefully you'll see this as an opportunity to get things back on track. I should mention, there is a notable fee for this, £30,000, for a morning of your time. Think about it.

I look forward to hearing from you.

Damien.

I read it again, then look back at Cam's email.

Don't hide, keep your head up and keep your eye out for a way to spin this in a way that works for you.

But me, in front of the camera? I'm not sure I can do that. Not on purpose, anyway. But maybe Cam is right. I do need to turn this around, and saying it in my words might be the best way? I shudder at the thought. TV is vicious, I know that, but what other options do I have?

I go back downstairs to see Annie. I'll think about it. £30,000 is hard to ignore when you just lost your job.

Stella

I don't know why I am going through the 'Archive' section of Cam Stacey's website when she's been pissing me off so much lately, but I remember an article she wrote ages ago about women taking charge sexually, and I really want to read it again. After an hour of torturing myself by reading more about her perfect FUCKING life, I find it.

June 2009: Women Need to Take Charge of Their Sex Lives More

I have a confession . . . sorry, Mum!

Last week, I was in an airport. My flight was delayed for an hour and I was hungover from the night before, and on top of this, I was monumentally horny. Like, the kind of horny where I felt like a wild animal. I was charged by my loins, only able to think of one thing. I walked around that airport trying to sniff out prey, ready to pounce on the first penis I saw. And then I saw one. This really gorgeous guy, standing alone by a window, watching the planes outside. I went up behind him, acutely aware of the sound of my own breath. I think I was going to straight up ask him to do me in the toilet. I started to make my approach, and as I got within a foot of him, licking my lips, panting at the thought of getting off, an equally-as-gorgeous woman joined him with two Starbucks cups and I had to back away. My mission was unsuccessful, but I loved the feeling of being so overwhelmed by my sexuality, and the entire scenario has been a fantasy of mine ever since. Partly because recalling that level of horn is thrilling, and partly because of the joy it gives me to think of women going out into the world and getting the kicks they want. It's what we should do – act on our impulses, give in to temptation, be reckless and act a little bit sexually selfish sometimes. You know, like men do.

OK, so maybe this isn't quite relating to my current situation, I'm not going to hit on Jason because I'm horny, but it all amounts to the same thing really; me getting what I want. But if I'm going to pull this off, I need to know a bit more about him.

I take him in a coffee, and ask him if he needs anything else. He says no, and that he's about to start a new chapter. I get the impression he won't leave his desk for a while, so I head back to mine, log into his email and get stuck into his personal life.

From what he has described there is a bit of a theme, he likes them tall with long brown hair, successful and emotionally honest. I'm not too far off that. I'm not short, at five foot seven, I have long brown curly hair, and I could pretend to be emotionally honest if I needed to be. Jason is pretty consistent in how he is with women in his messages. He's sweet, and he definitely likes to talk about things. One email conversation reads,

Hey, loved last night. Could have talked to you all night
Jason

Hey, yeah me too. Sorry if I told you too much about me. It felt good to talk.
Sal x

Please, I'm a guy that likes to talk about feelings. My work is about capturing emotion; I didn't want you to stop. J x

I make a note – Be Open.

The next email conversation I find is with another girl, and this time it's sexy. For a moment I think I can't bear to read it, but then I realise I'm going to have to get over that if I am to have sex with him myself. My plan is to make this happen on the day I ovulate. I can't afford to mess this up, and knowing what he likes in bed will ensure my success, so I go ahead and read it.

From Michelle:

I'm wearing a black pencil skirt, four-inch heels, a tight blouse and no underwear. I'm surrounded by my colleagues but all I can think about is what you did to my pussy this morning. I had fun, Michelle x

From Jason:

You're so sexy. I'm sitting at my desk. I can see my assistant in the next room so have to hide that I'm pulling my dick. Imagining you on your knees, with me in your mouth.

I slap my hand against my mouth, JASON! Eeewwww, while I was there! But OK, OK, he's way more sexual than I imagined. This might be easier than I thought. If I open up a bit, and ramp up my sex appeal it should work out OK. He's sensitive, but he's seriously red blooded.

An email alert pops up in the top right of my screen. It's letting me know that Camilla Stacey has posted another blog. I don't know how she does it, she must do nothing but write!

Camilla Stacey, HowItIs.com: I Did Not Waste My Womb Just Because I Didn't Use It . . .

Oh here we go, what crap about not wanting kids is she spouting now?

I love your emails, and I read them all. I see it as part of my job, and want to know how what I write affects people. And I can safely say that I have never been so inundated with messages since I opened the can of wombs (ithankyou) and admitted to not wanting kids. Happily, a lot of you seem encouraged by what I have to say, but of course, there are many of you who aren't. For those of you who are giving birth at the thought of my vacant vagina, I am sorry that my choices offend you. But at the same time, stop pushing your traditional opinions onto me, step forth into the modern world, and bore off.

Now . . . one suggestion that has popped up after my articles and in my inbox multiple times is that I am 'wasting my womb'. That's right. Because I have a womb, that I didn't ask for, I am 'disrespecting the power of being female'. Because to have this empty sack and not use it is apparently unthinkable.

But wait, I did not order this piece of equipment from Amazon. I was embedded with it at birth, and unlike an oven (the household object that seems to be compared to the female reproductive system the most), I cannot simply use it, take out the contents, eat them, and get on with my day. I think we are all aware that parenting lasts a lot longer than a jacket potato.

So no, I won't use it for what it is capable of, but that isn't to say I haven't used it my entire life. My womb is what makes me a woman. How can that be a waste?

'Oh fuck you, Cam Stacey,' I say standing up and kicking my desk. My hand automatically lands on my belly. This time next year my womb will be gone. My breasts too. Everything that makes me a woman will be thrown into a furnace and destroyed, while Camilla Stacey sits in her posh new apartment with hers fully intact. How is that fair?

'Everything alright?' yells Jason from the other room.

'Yup, sorry, just broke a nail.'

But seriously, what is she doing? Someone with a life as perfect as hers can't write about this stuff. She thinks she's being empowering, but most women who don't have kids *don't* choose it. She isn't paving the way for a growing demographic, she's rubbing our faces in what we can't have and it's really pissing me off.

I look behind me to check Jason isn't coming, but he's busily tapping away, clearly on a roll. I click on the 'contact' button on Cam's website and it automatically opens a new email.

To: Camilla Stacey
From: Stella Davies

Maybe your womb isn't a waste, but do you know what is? The air you breathe. Why don't you shut up with your 'Woman Almighty' preaching and get a real job? You've got no right to sit in your ivory tower and write like you have a clue. You don't. Why don't you just stop?

Send.

I sit still for a minute, as I visualise the 'ping' of her computer, alerting her to a new mail. Maybe she is sitting there now, will she see it right away? I feel anxiety pouring out of my fingertips as I imagine her reading my words and feeling as shit about herself as I do.

It feels really, really good.

9

Cam

Cam is feeling shitty – bad cramps, and nausea. Her remedy is two Nurofen and a ginger tea. She doesn't need to be anywhere; that's the joy of working from home, for yourself and living a life online. London lights are flooding her living room with their gorgeous orange glow, so with a blanket over her shoulders, she reads through emails from her readers, knowing that despite the belly ache, this is the only place she wants to be.

Dear Camilla

I just wanted to say thank you for your piece on acting on your opinions. My boss has been belittling me for so long. I'd go home every night and moan to my housemate about it. We'd drink wine and slag him off and I'd be honest about how he made me feel. But then I'd go in the next day and let him do it to me all over again. It all stemmed from a fear of losing my job, but you made me realise that I hate my job.

So, on Friday morning I registered with a recruitment agency, and on Friday afternoon I went into my boss' office and told him I was leaving. When he asked me why, I said it was because he was rude. And rather than use victim language, like you said, I just told him that I feel more qualified than him, and that wasn't very inspiring. He was totally stumped, it was magic. The agency already have three interviews for me next week, so I'm out. And I'm already feeling better. Thank you!

Martha x

And another . . .

Hey Cam

Every morning I have to walk past builders at the end of my road and every morning they embarrass me by shouting things like 'Nice tits' and 'Smile love!' I always skulk past and go red and wish I'd gone the long way. Anyway, yesterday morning it was really sunny, and after reading your article I just thought 'fuck it', and I stopped, lifted up my top and shouted 'THANKS, LADS'. Their faces were priceless. They were so embarrassed they nearly fell off the scaffolding. This morning, they didn't say a word. THANKS x

Cam chuckles to herself. She's always wanted to flash her tits at builders but to be fair, she's never had the guts to do that. As she sifts further through her emails, one name keeps appearing. It's usual for fans to email her regularly, but this 'Stella Davies' has sent a few. She clicks on the latest.

I see right through you. Your self-serving posts about feminism mean shit. You have no idea about struggle. Your perfect life, your money, your regular sex. You don't represent me. You cause pain, you don't take it away like you think you do. Shut the fuck up, or who knows what will happen.

Woah! 'Who knows what will happen?' Is that a threat? She looks at the other messages. This 'Stella' calls her a 'bitch', a 'liar', a 'disgrace to women'. Who is this woman, and why is she taking this time to be so angry? Threats and aggression are commonplace online, but at what point should Cam report someone? Surely not until they are waiting outside with a bucket of acid? Stella clearly hates her more than most people who get upset by what she writes.

Hormones are giving her the fear. It's probably fine, just some lonely, sad nutter who will move on when she doesn't get a response. Cam shuts down her public email, and looks at her work inbox. There is a message from Samantha Byron. Just what she bloody needs.

Dear Camilla

We are very happy with the latest site figures but we were thinking that maybe it is time to recruit some guest writers for the site? We would like to suggest a mummy blogger, to set a balance between your childlessness and normal women?

Looking forward to your thoughts on who that might be? As a start, I'd like to recommend Maria at ***Bubbsywubbsy.com****? She's one of my personal favourites. She's hilarious and does great recipes for the little ones. She also gives great advice on which TV shows are best for development and toys that encourage academic nourishment. Anyway, take a look. We think she'd be ideal?*

Samantha x

If her entire life wasn't centred around it, and if she didn't feel so sick, she would throw her computer out of the window in a fit of rage. How fucking dare she 'normal' her? Cam logs onto **BubbsyWubbsy.com** and it's as grotesque as she imagines. The home page is pale pink with pale blue writing. On the left is a picture of an ugly baby, to the right a little box saying 'Funny Mummy Moment of the Day'. Underneath that, 'I got halfway to the park this morning and realised I still have my slippers on. Uh oh, mummy brain! Luckily the dog didn't notice.'

Cam hates this fluff. She can't think of anything worse in

the entire world than having someone like BubbsyWubbsy Face blogging on *HowItIs.com*. She takes a few deep breaths, she needs them anyway, it helps with the nausea. She's about to reply to Samantha, when the urge to be sick becomes unbearable. She runs into the bathroom and vomits.

Stella

I pour boiling water into my Pot Noodle and sit on the sofa. This is always where Phil sat, my spot was the chair. The cushion has dipped in the middle from the hours and hours he sat here watching football after I'd gone to bed. I haven't even turned the TV on since he left. The thoughts in my head take up most of my time, the Internet fills the rest.

I can't finish the Pot Noodle. I saw it in the corner shop and thought I could remember the taste, Alice and I used to eat them all the time without Mum knowing. We loved them, but the taste isn't how I remember it. I chuck it in the bin and sit at my laptop at the kitchen table. I log onto *HowItIs.com* and look through Camilla's old blogs. One called, 'Why I Love Having Small Tits' pops out. I remember reading it at the time and thinking it was cool she was being positive about having small boobs, now it makes me want to kick a dent in my fridge. It's from 2006.

The truth is, men think they love big boobs, but actually, they love big confidence more. I have it under strictest confidence that the sexiest women are the ones from the French movies whose boobs sit proudly on their chests like little shuttlecocks. They have no bounce, they do not require a bra, and they are natural. This isn't to say if you have big boobs men don't love those, of course they do. But if you have fried eggs, like mine, then you're still hot. All guys care about is that you have boob for them to feel. It's you that makes the issue out of what they look like.

'All guys care about is that you have boob for them to feel'? How does Camilla Stacey know how to hurt me?

I email her again.

You're such a smug bitch. 'My perfect life'. 'My hot lover'. 'Everything going the way I want it'. That isn't real. You know what is real? Death.

I log onto Facebook for the first time today. Scrolling through other people's joy, I feel less impelled to read every status. I don't need to emotionally self-harm in that way, not tonight. For years, I've written post after post of aggressive abuse that I'd never have the guts to send. But now I've found my release, Camilla Stacey can take my anger, she probably doesn't read it anyway.

I also have a plan.

I log off Facebook and write, 'How to get pregnant' into Google.

To get pregnant you must have sex on the day of, or days surrounding ovulation.

As I read on, I learn that out of the entire month, you can only really get pregnant for about five days, and even then you have the most chance on three days. Why didn't anyone ever tell us that in school? That would have saved me a ton of pregnancy scares. I search 'How do you know when you are ovulating?'

Most women ovulate on day fourteen of their cycle. This is calculated from the first day of your last period. However, everyone's cycles are different, so be sure to calculate your own cycle. Over the counter ovulation kits are very accurate.

Over the counter ovulation kits? I need equipment for this? I had no idea getting pregnant was such a science. I try to get the image of me pouring sperm into my vagina out of my head. It was pointless. That doesn't help with the shame.

I'll go and buy an ovulation kit before work tomorrow. *I can do this. I can make this happen*. I snap my computer shut, turning off the only light source in the room other than a few red and green spots from the kitchen appliances. I hadn't realised I was sitting in the dark.

Tara

Dinner times have been terrible. After I've put Annie to bed, my mother has insisted that we all sit around the dining table in front of a ridiculously extravagant meal, all designed with the intention to distract from our reality. Our reality being that I haven't left the house in seven days. That my personal hygiene is at an all-time low. That my father has tried, but finds it almost impossible to look me in the eye. And that now 5.6 million people have watched me masturbate.

Tonight, when we've exhausted the amount of times three people can compliment a lasagna, more silence fills the air until I dare to break it by broaching the subject of my life.

'I had an email from *Sky News* today. They've offered me thirty thousand pounds for an exclusive interview that they would broadcast during the news.'

My dad thumps the table and a spoon flies up and lands on his lap. He rests his elbow on the table and drops his forehead into his hand to support him, while he sighs and huffs. I turn to my mother and continue.

'I'm worried about money.'

My dad sits a little straighter. No matter how angry he is, he knows he can't support all of us forever. Money is a legitimate reason not to leave the room in another strop, like he has almost every time I have opened my mouth for anything other than food for the past two weeks.

I'm over it. I know he's upset about it all but it's my life that is ruined, not his.

'They say if I apologise, then it will get better.'

'*Are* you sorry?' says my mother.

'No,' I say, causing my dad's anger to return in the form of an actual growl. 'And I don't want to apologise, but maybe

I should.' Another slam of the fist. This time a couple of peas bounce off his plate and onto the table. 'I have to think about Annie. And I'm going to have to work again one day. If I say nothing, it will brush over in terms of people talking about it, but what is the reality of my life after that? Who will employ me? Who would let their kid come over to play with Annie? Who would date me? I don't want that video to be my legacy, so somehow I have to reclaim my life. Maybe if people see it from my point of view, they'll understand that I'm not some sex-crazed lunatic.'

That was the straw that broke the camel's back; my dad is up and out the door in seconds. I can't deal with his anger at the moment, I just need support.

'I think I should do it,' I say to Mum, who would never walk away from me, no matter how embarrassing she thinks I am. 'I know the TV world; I'll speak in un-editable sentences. I'll say things that show I'm not crazy. I know it won't make all of this go away any quicker, but at least I'll have said my bit. What else am I supposed to do – sit back, do nothing and let the whole world create a version of me that doesn't exist?'

'It could backfire,' she says. And she's right. It could. But I don't see how things could get worse. 'I've Googled famous apologies and they *do* work,' I reply. 'Hugh Grant said sorry after getting a blow job from a prostitute, Tiger Woods said sorry after having sex with pretty much everyone, Bill Clinton said sorry after he lied about his affair with Monica Lewinsky. All of those men have gone on to thrive since their scandals; people can move on. Life *can* continue after being shamed.'

'I suppose so,' my mother says. 'But those men had popular

public profiles beforehand, long careers they could fall back on. And of course, there is the obvious.'

'What's the obvious?' I ask.

'They're *men*. People don't like women being overtly sexual. There is one rule for men, and another for women. It's the way of the world, darling. I don't think it will change.'

My mother's defeatist attitude to the progress of feminism is the rocket up my arse that I need. I excuse myself and go back upstairs. I reply to Damien Weymouth's email.

Dear Damien,

Let's do it.

Tara.

What have I got to lose?

Cam

Cam carefully pours boiling water into her hot water bottle, and screws on the lid. Wearing light blue denim leggings and a big white shirt, she lies back on the chaise longue and pushes it against her belly. These cramps are strong. It's like her womb is speaking to her. 'Don't act like I don't exist,' it would say. *If wombs could talk.* She laughs to herself, despite the gripping. She needs to blog but for once doesn't feel like writing. She looks in her 'Emergency File'. It was for moments like this that she has sat writing on cold wintery days, writing blog after blog to cover her back.

She wrote this one some time last year, when a well-known tampon company got in touch and offered a pretty feeble amount of money to advertise on *HowItIs.com*. They said in the email, 'We think your website is a perfect match for us, because you could really become a spokesperson for periods.'

A spokesperson for periods? What even is that? Would she be *The Face of Periods*? Cam thought it was a ridiculous idea and never even replied. On top of this, Cam hates periods. She had the contraceptive implant put in her arm a few years ago with the hope that they would stop, but they never did. Some months they come and go, some months they wipe her out like flu. As she is sitting here tonight feeling like her uterus is about to burst through her belly button, anticipating menstruation to come flooding at any moment, this blog feels like the perfect piece to post.

Camilla Stacey, HowItIs.com: I Don't Want to See or Hear About Your Period. Period.

Before I begin, there are some things I want to say:

1) *I do not think women should be embarrassed about periods.*
2) *I think shame around periods is terrible.*
3) *I hope that all young girls who get their periods feel they can talk about it and are educated and they don't feel embarrassed.*
4) *I don't think women should have to pay for sanitary protection.*

5) *I think period pain is a legitimate reason to take the day off work.*
6) *I think men humiliating or dismissing women over their periods is shit.*

I think all of these things, but that doesn't mean I want to:

1) *see YOUR period*
2) *make an announcement every time I change my tampon*
3) *see adverts with actual periody women on them, making me dread mine even more.*

Let me explain myself.

Seeing Your Period

Artist Rupi Kaur put a picture up on Instagram of her lying in bed with bloodstains on her clothes, quite obviously from a period. No big deal, it happens to everyone. I've bled through so many clothes and in so many places and fully appreciate it's normal, but I don't know if I want that image popping up in between photos of avocado on toast on my Instagram feed. You know I'm no prude, no subject on this blog is not tackled head on. I pride myself on being un-shockable and open minded, but I think I draw the line on visuals of stuff that comes out of other people's bodies. Feminist issue or not, it's just eeewwww.

I think we should talk about periods more. I don't think that means we should SEE periods more.

Announcing Your Period to the Room

I read some weird statistic that one in three women feel they have to hide their tampon up their sleeve at work, and that this was considered a problem. Help me understand, what are we supposed to do, yell, 'HEY GUYS, I'M OFF TO STUFF THIS UP MY BIG BLEEDING FANNY' every time we go to the bathroom? I do so very hope not. But now I've read this, I am worried that people really do think hiding tampons is problematic. If I choose not to announce my period to the room, will I now be seen as someone who is ashamed of my period? Because I'm not. Or someone who has given into society's misogynistic view of menstruation? Because I haven't done that either. I just like to keep what I do on a toilet to myself. Sorry if that is not helping your version of feminism.

Periody Women on Adverts

The way so many women hate sanitary protection adverts baffles me! If you search for articles on it, you find hundreds of feminist writers in uproar because the women in the tampon adverts are being sporty and happy while they demonstrate how effective the product they are advertising is. HOW is that so offensive? What should the alternative be?

I think it's great to see that my tampon won't leak if I climb a mountain, but it seems that some feminists want a more honest portrayal of periods in the adverts. Like what? A spotty, bloated girl eating a tub of ice cream with Nurofen sprinkled on it, crying at Dirty Dancing after routinely dumping her boyfriend after too many Pinot Grigios? Oh God, who wants to see that?

I'd argue ***that*** *is actually more insulting than women achieving quite impressive sporting goals. My periods are a pain but I'd rather not be represented by the media as mental or ill every time I have one. I like the 'get up and go, no need to mention it, this doesn't hold me back' vibes of period ads. I think that is the best way to stop men thinking we are incapable because we menstruate. What says, 'this makes me no different from you' more than jumping out a sodding plane to a great tune with a massive smile on your face?*

If I was a man, that would make me ***want*** *a period.*

I look forward to your emails (kind of). I won't open anything with an attachment ;)

Until tomorrow,
Cam x

Stella

Mum would have loved grandchildren. She always said having twins was tough but that she loved babies so much she never wanted us to grow up, even when we both cried our heads off and she hadn't slept for days. Mind you, she also always said that Alice was a really easy baby, and that if we had both been like me she probably would have lost her mind. It's weird hearing things about how you were as a kid. Really it means nothing and is no reflection on who we are as an adult, but it was still *us*, and I never liked hearing about me being a difficult baby. I guess I never understood how Mum couldn't resent me for it; apparently I screamed and screamed. She never expressed any anger towards me about it, but deep down I always knew she preferred Alice.

Mum encountered so many bad things in her life. Her own parents were awful, she never had any luck in love. But when she was dying, she said she felt whole because of us. I've never forgotten her words, 'I never needed anything but you girls.' They stuck with me. They gave me hope that one day I might feel fulfilled, because the truth is, even before she died, and before I even knew about Alice's cancer, I was already struggling with who I was.

Maybe it was just that I lived in the shadow of my brilliant sister. Identical to me in every way on the outside, but almost my polar opposite on the inside. I was dragged into the spotlight because of her infectious character. If she had been more like me, the Davies Twins wouldn't have been the girls everyone wanted to hang around with, they'd have been the girls everyone wanted to ignore. I lived most of my life pretending to be like Alice, copying her, mimicking her excellence. When she'd gone, I couldn't remember how she did it.

Now I just cling on to those words my mother said – 'never needed anything but you girls' – and I know that having a child is my only real chance of happiness. Even the thought of it changes my mood.

I think I'd like a boy. *Girls are so complicated, what if I had one like me?* I think, chuckling to myself at my desk. I wonder if you can do that? Choose which sex you'll have. I Google it.

For a Boy Baby, try the following . . .

Male sperm are thought to be stronger and tougher than their female counterparts. So there are a few ways you can help them along.
** Cough syrup, apparently the ingredient that thins your nasal mucus also thins your vaginal mucus, meaning the boy sperm have more chance of breaking through.*
**Acidic conditions are said to kill boy sperm, so the prospective mother needs to go on a high alkaline diet.*
**Weight loss apparently encourages conceiving a girl. So don't lose weight. Bulk up, if anything.*
**Doggy style is the best position for conceiving male children. Deep penetration, so those strong boy sperms have easier access.*

```
*Drinking a shot of coffee beforehand is said to make the Y chromosome more active.
*Having an orgasm during intercourse is said to give the male sperm a head start.
```

Wow, OK, so there is. So aside from getting him to have sex with me, all I have to do to have a baby boy by Jason is drink loads of cough syrup, eat tons of vegetables, put on some weight then get him to have sex with me from behind, just after he's drunk a coffee, while I am having an orgasm.

I mean, how hard can it be?

'Fuck this,' Jason shouts, storming in and making me leap three feet into the air. I quickly slam shut my computer. 'I'm trying to focus on writing but I can't stop thinking about her.'

'Who?'

'Tara!'

Oh, shit.

'I know it seems crazy, but she was just amazing. Confident, in control, successful, sexy as hell. I know I'm a walking cliché but there was just a connection. I want her! I'm going to trawl the Internet until I find her, it can't be that hard. Tara, TV, Walthamstow. She'll be there somewhere.'

'No, Jason. No Internet. You promised,' I say, trying to lay down some guilt about the book. It's been relatively easy to keep Tara's video out of his sight until now, but if he searches for her, he'll find her right away and that would totally ruin my plan. I have to keep him offline until it all dies down.

'Stella, please move. I am using your computer,' he says, firmly.

There is a gentle tussle, but I am determined not to let him online. He clings onto my laptop while I try to pull it away, but eventually he wins and I'm forced to stand to the side. He's typing those fatal words into Google. TARA. TV. WALTHAMSTOW.

This cannot happen. He cannot find Tara. He has to get me pregnant.

I grab a glass vase from on top of the filing cabinet behind my desk and throw it on the floor, it smashes everywhere. Jason tuts but is unperturbed. I can see the pages loading. All is about to be lost. Should I push him off the chair? Throw a glass at the computer screen? Take my top off? No, fuck, shit, aaaaaaar, ahahahah . . .

'Jason!' I shout, falling to the ground, unsure if what I am thinking will actually make it past my lips. But then I am saying it, I'm just bloody saying it.

'Cancer! Jason, I have cancer!'

Total stillness.

Jason turns to look at me just as a picture of Tara appears on the computer screen behind him. He doesn't turn back to see it, he's too much of a good person to do that. He stands up and comes over. Kneeling down to join me on the floor, despite the glass slivers, he hugs me, with no thought for what the boundaries should be. The comfort of his cuddle eases me into whatever mess I just made. The power of affection overrides the tap-tapping of guilt. I deserve a few moments of this.

'Stella, no,' he says gently. 'Cancer?'

'Yes, cancer,' I reply. Breathy, pained, committed. He wipes a tear from my cheek, presuming I am crying because of the fatal illness I just told him I have. Actually, it's because glass is cutting my knee.

He lifts me up, and leads me over to the couch. As we pass my desk, I push the laptop closed before he sees Tara's haggard face.

That was close.

'Here,' says Jason, coming back in from the kitchen and handing me a cup of tea. I quickly reassume my 'I've got cancer' face. 'Don't you need to work?' I say, as if shunning his attention.

'Writing can wait,' he says, generously. 'Is tea enough, do you need something stronger, wine? Whisky? Shit, what am I thinking, you can't drink wine.'

'NO, wine is fine,' I say, a little too desperately. I correct myself, 'I mean, it can't get much worse, can it? A little wine can't hurt.' I really need a drink.

He goes over to a little bar in the corner of the studio where we keep booze for clients, and opens a bottle of red. 'If I found out I had cancer I'd probably go on a massive drug binge and smoke a whole packet of cigarettes. I'd think, *fuck it*.'

'Oh, you couldn't be more right. Trust me,' I say, taking a huge glug of wine.

'So I want you to start at the beginning, OK? How long has this been going on, I mean, when did you find out?' Jason says, settling next to me on the sofa. I know I have to tell him things, it's one of the things he finds attractive in women. Emotional honesty . . . I need to give him some.

'My mum got breast cancer when she was in her early

forties, she died when she was fifty-two,' I say, as Jason pours more wine into my half empty glass. 'My twin sister and I—'

'Oh, I didn't know you had a twin sister,' Jason says, interrupting, possibly realising I've worked for him for nearly a year and he's not made any effort at all to get to know me.

'Yes, Alice and I took care of Mum, she had so much treatment. Double mastectomy, chemo, radiation. It was brutal. She was battered by it for years, and then we were told that nothing was going to work, and that the cancer had won.'

'Shit, Stella, I'm so sorry.'

'Yeah, it was the most bizarre feeling, the last five years had been so terrible that we all talked about how we wished we hadn't bothered with treatment. Alice and I organised a funeral for her, she wanted the memory of her pre-cancer life to be the theme so we both wore her old dresses from the Seventies and asked all of the guests to wear the brightest colours in their wardrobes.'

'That's adorable,' Jason says, taking a sip, happy for a glimmer of joy in what is otherwise a pretty bleak story. 'The traditional black is so depressing.'

'Yeah.'

'So where is your sister?'

I pause. *Does he need to know it all?*

'She's dead,' I say, drinking some wine, deciding I might as well lay it all bare.

Jason puts down his glass and leans forward to put his head into his hands. 'Stella, I don't know what to say.' I see a tear on his cheek. That's understandable, I suppose, what I am telling him is horrendous.

'Yeah. A year or so after Mum died, Alice started to feel really ill. She had this constant pain in her belly and was so tired all the time. So we went to the doctor and they did loads of tests but couldn't work out what it was. And then they found out that she had stage four ovarian cancer. It had spread to her liver and was incurable. She was dead within six months,' I say, finishing my wine and putting the glass on the floor.

'And what about your dad, is he around?'

It's funny, I think so little about my father that I am surprised when Jason asks after him. But of course he would, it's normal for people to ask where someone's dad is. One day I might be telling our baby about Jason, and what will I say? What are my intentions if this does actually work? Will I even tell Jason I am pregnant? I don't know. I don't want to hurt him, but I also don't want things to be complicated. I could just quit work, say working with him after we had sex was too difficult for me. I never have to see him again; he never has to know. I could remortgage the flat, live off that for a few years and then get another PA job somewhere else. I'll work it out.

'I never knew him,' I say. 'He left soon after Alice and I were born. Twins are a lot of work, he couldn't take it apparently. Mum was always pretty open about not fighting for him to stay. She said it's best to be alone than surrounded by people who don't love you. So that was that, she raised us on her own. I wouldn't have a clue where he is now.'

'Do you care?'

'Not really. If I'm completely honest, I never think about

it,' I say, realising for the first time in my life that so much of who I am has been shaped by the fact that my dad never stuck around. This is the danger of talking about feelings; you realise that your life is more fucked up than you thought.

'I never even asked you about your life,' he says, visibly disappointed in himself.

'It's OK,' I say, comforting him. 'I'm your assistant, you employed me to look after you, not to be my counsellor. And really I didn't want to talk about it. The job has been really important. When I met Phil he got me out of a dark place, convinced me to work. I didn't know what I wanted to do, I just wanted to be distracted, so he suggested that I worked as a PA where I focused on someone else, other than me. It's when I go home that things get complicated.'

'So when did you meet your boyfriend? Sorry, ex-boyfriend.'

'I met Phil two years ago. He was the first person I'd really spoken to about Alice and he was so supportive.'

'And he just left you? What a prick.'

'Yeah, well I guess there was a lot of pressure.'

'Did he know you have . . . does he know you have cancer?'

I pause. I could backtrack, say that I worded it wrong. That I was sorry but I forgot to add the bit about the gene. But you can't take back the words 'I have cancer' once they are said.

'Yes,' I say.

'Wanker.'

'It's OK, it's going to be a tough ride and I guess it's best I just do it alone, rather than have someone around me who doesn't really care.'

'Well, I care, OK? I'll help you.'

'You have a book to write, mister,' I say, trying to sound like I'm not desperate for him to impregnate me.

'I do. But I'm here for you, I really am,' he pauses, clearly unsure if what he is about to say is OK or not.

'What?' I press.

'You could stay at mine tonight if you don't want to be alone? I have a spare room, it's clean, I promise. Believe it or not, I have a cleaner.'

I have to be careful if this is going to work. I don't want to push things too fast.

'I better go home, but thank you. I have my first treatment tomorrow morning, so if it's OK I'll be late? Apparently it's just mild, I should be OK to come in,' I say, impressed by my improv skills.

'Jesus, Stella – take the day off!' insists Jason, but I know that if I leave him unattended, then he'll find a way to get online.

'No, really. The doctor says I'll be OK and I'd rather come in than be at home alone. Really, I need life to continue as normally as possible for as long as possible, I should only be an hour late, if that. My appointment is at eight a.m.,' I say, looking forward to a lie in, I slept so badly all weekend.

'Would you like me to come with you?' he asks, because he's a great guy and that is what great guys do.

'No, really. I'm OK to go alone. And look, I'll let you know when I need you, OK? We don't need to talk about this again, the focus should be your book, that has to get done, OK?'

'You're so selfless,' he says, putting his arms around me, obviously feeling like the perimeters of our relationship have opened up and that friendly physical contact is absolutely acceptable. 'Thank you for sharing all of this with me and really, if you need me for anything, just call. I'll leave my phone on all night in case you need anything.'

'Thanks, Jason. But it's business as usual, OK? I don't want you to treat me any differently.'

That was maybe the biggest lie of them all. I want him to treat me so differently that he bends me over his desk and gets me pregnant.

But of course, I keep that to myself.

10

Tara

I kiss Annie goodbye, and Mum and Dad take her to school. I'm nervous, and they can see it. I go back up to my room and lie on my bed, I close my eyes and try to clear my head, but it's impossible. I'm terrified, my hands are trembling and I feel like the blood is all in the middle of my body, like it's been sucked away from my skin. I email Camilla.

Hey
I think I've fucked up. I said yes to an interview on Sky News, they are about to arrive. I sold out for cash. What have I done?

She writes back straight away.

Tara, don't panic. It's OK. It's OK to say your bit, just don't apologise. You don't need to apologise. Women do not need to apologise for being sexual.

Good luck, you'll get through it. TV is your world, just be you and you'll be fine x x

Don't apologise? That's the entire fucking reason I agreed to do this. If I don't apologise, what the hell else do I say? The doorbell goes. *Shit*. They're here.

I'm dressed in a black polo neck and jeans, as neutral but respectable as I could manage. When I open the door there are nine people with cases and bags and lights and even though I have worked in TV for over ten years and should have known what to expect, I am shocked and intimidated as they walk into our house and turn the small living room into a mini TV studio.

I make everyone tea and try to be hospitable. I paid for Mum and Dad to go to a museum, lunch and a matinee in the West End; I couldn't cope with Dad's hyperventilating and Mum cleaning out the Marks and Spencer picnic section to feed the crew. The crew are all very good at acting like nothing is a big deal; the trick with good TV is that no one mentions anything about the issue until the cameras are rolling. This means the contributor, who may not be used to being on camera, doesn't say things like, 'as I said earlier' or even just miss chunks out, for fear of the people in the room thinking they are repeating themselves. Another trick is that the host has no contact with the contributor until the cameras roll, so I'm not surprised that Damien himself isn't here yet.

It is so bizarre to be the subject of the show. I know all the tricks. I know that as soon as I am out the room they are talking about me. I know that they are all going to leave and tell everyone they know what I am 'really like'. So I am careful not to act nervous or insecure. But I am finding the close proximity to strangers excruciating.

I sit on a chair in the kitchen, as a young girl whose breath smells of Tic-Tacs paints my face with a variety of products.

'I love MAC foundation,' I say, breaking the ice, because she's obviously been told not to talk to me about anything personal and that's clearly killing her.

'Me too,' she says, happy to speak about make-up. 'It's so good. And their new neon eyeshadows, have you seen those?'

'No, I'm not really a neon eyeshadow kind of person,' I say. 'I actually don't wear much make-up, I keep it pretty natural.'

'Yes, I Googled you and saw that so I—' She stops, realising that by admitting to Googling me she has just confessed to seeing the video. And now her hand is trembling and I have no idea how she's going to put mascara on me without stabbing me in the eye. We say nothing else until the make-up is done.

At eleven a.m., Damien walks into the house.

'Tara,' he says, warmly. He's about five foot nine, stocky, and looks like he gets his hair cut far too often. 'Thanks for doing this. I think it looks like we are ready to go, how are you feeling?'

'You know, a bit like I wanked on a train and now I have to go on national TV to talk about it,' I say, managing to make myself laugh for the first time in a while. Damien doesn't really laugh. I clock it. I never engage with any contributors' humour if I have the intention of stitching them up. I'd never want them to say afterwards that I was two faced, because I was so nice before the cameras started rolling and then I fired uncomfortable questions at them from behind the camera. I suddenly feel suspicious. Damien tries to move things along and goes into the living room to take a seat in my dad's armchair that has been pulled up close to my mother's chair as if they are going head to head.

'Can I get you miked up?' says a sound man, holding a radio mike in front of me. I drop the cable down my top and catch it out the bottom, he connects it to the pack and attaches it to the back of my jeans. And suddenly I am filled with such fear, and such regret that I want to scream GET OUT to them all and get back up to my bedroom where I can hide and Google myself and not have to endure actual human interaction.

Think of the money, I tell myself, and I must. This is for Annie.

'OK, I think we're just about there,' says Damien, suggesting I come over and take a seat.

He's in my dad's chair, I'm in my mum's chair. It feels symbolic somehow, although of course the crew didn't know whose chair was whose when they set up the shot. As the cameraman makes a few tiny adjustments, and the make-up girl dashes in to brush my nose with powder, Damien shuffles his notes. There are about ten pages on his knee. I feel like my future depends on what they say.

The room is silent. The cameraman says, 'Action.'

Damien talks to camera.

'Hello, and welcome to the special interview with me, Damien Weymouth. Now, unless you have been living under a stone, you will have heard of my guest today. Twelve days ago, Tara Thomas was living a normal life, working in television and taking care of her daughter, Annie.'

I flinch when he says 'Annie'. Something about her being named on TV feels so grim.

'But now, this single mother of one's life is anything but normal. Branded a "scarlet woman" by the *Mirror*, a "traitor to feminism" by the *Guardian* and a "shameful example of a mother" by the *Daily Mail*, Tara Thomas is not only a national hate figure, but a national joke. Trending on Twitter for a record ten days, in just one week she has lost her job, moved back in with her parents and ended up hospitalised after a severe and public panic attack in a local supermarket. Today, feeling humiliated, vilified and like life may never be the same again, she is here with me, Damien Weymouth, to give her side of the story. Tara, how are you feeling?'

His gaze is like a laser beam. That introduction was horrendous. I sound pathetic, and even though I feel pathetic, I don't feel *that* pathetic. I open my mouth, but all that comes out is a weird croak that Damien cuts off quickly.

'I'm sure it's hard to find the words. So let me ask you some questions, and I have to say,' he puts his hand up to the camera, 'off the record, if at any point this gets uncomfortable for you, you just tell me and we will stop. If I ask you something you don't like, just let me know and we will move on, OK?'

I say OK. But I know he's lying. I've said that a thousand times at work. That is the host or producer's way of manipulating contributors to feel like they are on their side. They are not. If I say I didn't like a question, he will see that I am becoming emotional and know to push that particular subject as far as he can, in the hopes of getting some tears. It's a classic tactic. I am not stupid and I won't fall for it. He drops his hand and carries on.

'Tara, take me back to that night. The night on the train. Where had you been previously to that?'

'I'd been on a date and I was heading home,' I say, thinking that part at least sounded quite normal.

'Had the date been bad in some way? I mean, I don't want to make any assumptions but you were going home alone. Were you upset?'

'No, actually. I'd had a lovely time.'

'OK, so you're on the train, having had a lovely time. And then what happened?'

'We all know what happened. That's why I'm here, isn't it?'

'In your own words, please. For anyone watching who didn't see the video.'

'OK, I— I masturbated on a tube train.'

The whole crew take a sharp inhalation. It's hard to tell if they are shocked, or holding in laughter.

'That's right,' continues Damien. 'And why did you do that?'

'I just did, I can't be sure why.'

'And would you say that is how you live your life; by succumbing to your urges, doing things your way, when you want to do them? Is that a trait of yours?'

'No, I wouldn't say so. I think I generally consider other

people before acting for myself. That's just part of being a parent, isn't it?' I say, thinking that sounded fair.

'Hmm. We have a clip from a short interview last night that I did with your old employer, Adam Pattison from Great Big Productions. I wouldn't say he completely agrees with that.'

'Wait, what?'

Damien tells a short guy in a baseball cap to play the film and I am urged to look at a tiny TV screen to my right. Adam's face appears.

'Tara was good at her job, there is no doubt about that. But part of the skill set for the kinds of programming she makes is being able to detach from other people's pain. She did that very well. She would also lash out sometimes, and say incredibly cruel and unfair things, accusing people of being things they are not. Just out of nowhere, usually on email, which I thought was cowardly. She's like a snake, she'll slither along quietly and then SNAP, that tongue shoots out and stings. She could be very hurtful.'

My mouth falls open. 'That fu—' I stop, thinking twice about giving a visual on the crap he just spouted about me. Damien carries on.

'So, would it be fair to say that you live a life based on what is right for you, and not anyone else? Like having a child by someone and never telling them, for example?'

'We're not here to talk about that, though? I'm here to talk about what happened on the train, and how my life has been turned upside down since,' I say, leaning my head away from the camera, as if that would stop them filming this bit. I know it won't.

'We are, and of course we will get to that. But firstly I think it's important that we establish your nature, what led you to that moment of public indecency. And I'd like to start with the way you had a child, because the viewers will want to know how you told yourself that was acceptable.'

'I'd really like to just talk about the masturbating part, please. That's what we agreed.'

'And we will, but first, did you deliberately have sex with that man with the hope of getting pregnant?'

'No, I didn't. Now, please can we talk about me on the train?'

'And when you found out you were pregnant; did you consider his feelings at all?'

'Please,' I continue, 'I'm not here to talk about my daughter, or how I had her. That isn't anyone's business but mine.'

'Well I'm not sure that's entirely true, is it? Her father is somewhere out there and the poor man has no idea.'

'The "poor man"? He's not a poor man. He had a nice house and he got laid. Now, please, can we get back to what we agreed.'

He puts his hand up again, as if speaking off the record. 'I'm just asking you the questions that the public want to know, Tara. If there are stones left unturned, this won't be over.' Annoyingly, I know he's right.

'But OK, we'll move on for a minute while you get yourself together.' He sits up straight, and gets back into arsehole mode.

'How does it feel to have the public judge you in this way?' he asks me.

'It's awful, it really is. I've cried more than I've ever cried in my life and I made myself sick because I could barely eat a thing. Everyone seems to have this perception of me and it just isn't true. I'm a good person, and a good mum, and to be a hate figure like this is really upsetting, and very confusing.'

I'm happy with that. Not too desperate. Articulate, precise and true.

'You must deeply regret what you did?' Damien asks and I find myself freezing. Cam's words come flashing into my mind. *Don't apologise. Women do not need to apologise for being sexual.* I realise she's right. There are many things I should probably say, but sorry isn't one of them. I can turn this around.

'I wish I had waited until I got home,' I say with a small smile on my face. He does not smile back.

'And you must be very, very sorry?'

'Not really, actually. I want people to know I'm not mental, but I'm not sorry for touching myself when I thought I was alone.'

Damien looks twitchy, he shuffles in his chair, trying to think of manipulative ways to seduce me into a grovelling apology. But I won't, I won't say it. No matter how persecuted I feel, my future depends on the decisions I make from now on. I can't change that my dad saw the video, I can't turn the Internet off, but I can control how I cope with this publicly, and as far as that is concerned, I have two choices. I allow the public to win by begging for forgiveness and basically offering myself as comedy fodder for the rest of my life, or I own my own life and don't diminish it by apologising. I mean, apologising? Who would I actually be apologising to? Sitting in front of Damien, some chubby TV twat who thinks he has one up on me because he believes acceptance from strangers is more important to me than acceptance of myself. But it isn't, so I just don't do it.

'Tara,' he pushes, 'is there anything you would like to say?'

I sit still and look at my knees, as if building up to the breakdown he is hoping I have, and then I lift my head and say, 'Yes. It's such a shame I got into so much trouble over it, because I had a really fantastic orgasm. Are we done?'

11

Cam

Cam wakes up slowly; she feels terrible. The air is thick and musty in her room as she gets out of bed and opens the curtains and a window. Cool summer morning air flows in, and sunlight creeps over the London skyline, flooding the room with its luminous rays, but the usual high it offers her isn't there today. This early summer brightness makes her feel worse. She gets back into bed, and curls into the foetal position.

'Errrr,' she says, in a groggy voice.

'Still feeling ill, babe?' says Mark, waking up next to her. He'd come over late last night with crisps and Diet Coke, as she thought they might have helped with the nausea. They didn't. He reaches over to gently stroke her boobs, and her reaction is to smack his hand away.

'Woah, what was that about?' he says, understandably taken aback by the violence.

'Sorry,' she mumbles, putting her hands to her boobs herself to investigate the swelling and the pain that she's suddenly aware of. 'PMT,' she confirms.

She rolls onto her back, exhaling through pursed lips, and feels sick again. She gets up and goes to the bathroom, where she vomits instantly.

'You OK, babe?' calls Mark from the bedroom.

'All good now,' she calls, casually, as she goes to clean her teeth. But a thought is lurking in the back of her head. The implant was supposed to last for three years; how long ago was it she had it put in? Two? Three? . . . *Four?*

She drops her toothbrush on the floor, and bangs her head as she reaches down to get it.

'FUCK EVERYTHING,' Cam shouts, using it as an excuse to be emotional.

'What's the matter, babe?' Mark says, suddenly appearing at the bathroom door. She turns to look at him, not knowing what the right thing to do is. When she opens her mouth, she doesn't know what is going to come out.

'I think I'm pregnant,' she says.

'What?' replies Mark.

Cam stares at him, as if he's going to tell her it can't be possible.

'What do we do now?' he asks instead.

'I don't know; I've not done this before. Get a test?' suggests Cam.

'OK, shall we go now?'

'OK.'

They get dressed without saying a word, both with glazed,

zombie-like looks on their faces, feeling like total strangers, despite months of physical intimacy.

When she's dressed, Cam sits on the end of the bed and puts her head in her hands.

'Don't worry, babe, if it's happening, we'll do the right thing,' Mark says, being a great guy. Cam gets up and steps away from the support. She has a feeling that her idea of what constitutes 'the right thing' and his idea of 'the right thing' are probably very different.

'You know, you don't have to come. I'll be OK. I'll get a test, and if it's positive I'll text you later, OK?' she says, feeling like she needs to be alone and regretting telling him.

'No way, I'm coming. We're in this together.'

'No, Mark, please. I'd really like to be alone, OK? I'll text you later.'

'Babe, it takes two to ta—'

'Mark, please don't say tango. Were you going to say tango?'

'Yes.'

Cam pushes a long, slow breath through her tight mouth. She might be sick again, or maybe she just needs some air.

'Mark, I'd really like to be alone, OK? I'm feeling really sick, I'm sure it's a false alarm, and that I'll do the test, take some Pepto-Bismol, get my period and all will be fine. OK? Please, go to the gym, I'll let you know later.'

Mark thinks about arguing, but he knows Cam well enough to know that when she says she needs to be alone, there is no negotiation.

'OK, but call me, OK? Not text.' He puts on his denim jacket, and goes to the door. 'This doesn't scare me, you know.'

'I know,' Cam says as he leaves.

That's what I'm afraid of.

In Boots, Cam takes one of every type of pregnancy test they have and drops them into a basket. There are five in total. She also grabs a big pack of Always Ultra to throw anyone who might be spying on her off the scent. At the check-out, she looks down and bobs gently up and down on the balls of her feet, doing all that she can to show the cashier she's in a hurry. The cashier looks around to make sure her superior isn't listening.

'You must be very excited to want to know five times?' she says, smiling sweetly.

'Yeah, really really excited. I'm also in a hurry, sorry, can you . . . '

'I understand. I was the same, just desperate to know. And to think there is this movement where women are deciding not to have children. It's so sad.'

'What movement?'

'Oh, I read this awful article by this woman who says she never wants children. Trying to make other women follow in her footsteps. It's not right. I have two and wouldn't change it for the world.'

'Yes, well, everyone is different.'

'Well, fingers crossed for this test then.' As she scans the pregnancy tests, her perfectly swept-up ponytail swings from side to side, making Cam feel sea sick.

'I actually don't want to be pregnant,' she blurts out. 'If I am, I won't keep it.'

'But . . . '

'I'm sorry if you find that upsetting, but I have the right to make that decision and not feel I can't admit it.'

'I just . . . '

'Stop judging me!'

'I'm not, I . . . '

Cam snatches her card out of the card reader, grabs the bag of pregnancy tests and sanitary towels and storms out of Boots. Standing in the street with a carrier bag in her hand, she can't stop the tears from rolling down her face. She has no idea why she is crying.

'Fucking hormones,' she says to herself, as she wipes tears from her eyes.

Back at home, in her empty flat, Cam gets a coffee cup from the kitchen and pees into it. Sitting on the toilet, with the cup on the floor between her feet, she unwraps each test and drops all of them in at once. After a very long three minutes staring at the ceiling, she pulls the first test out. Then the next, then all the rest at once.

'FUCK IIIITTTT,' she screams, squeezing her head with her hands.

The Face of Childless Women is pregnant.

12

Stella

As the plain circle indicating NO HORMONES appears on the ovulation test, I learn that I am not ovulating again today. It's OK, I can wait. This will happen, and it will be perfect. I wrap the test up in loo roll and put it in my bag. Coming back into the studio, I sit at my desk and take a huge glug of cough syrup right from the bottle. I imagine it thinning my vaginal mucus as it slops down into my guts. I've also brought in a high-alkaline, roasted vegetable bake for lunch. I'm doing all the things I can to ensure I conceive a boy. I realise this is a little obsessive, but I might as well do everything I can.

Jason is busy writing. I think of him in his office, tapping away, his penis resting casually between his thighs, unaware of my plans to ravish it. Am I being cruel? I don't think so. Men waste sperm all the time, tossed into the atmosphere like the dregs of a cup of coffee down a sink. They have no emotion toward that sperm, why should they have any emotion toward the ones that get used for their intended purpose?

I am approaching this whole thing with a completely guilt-free attitude. Yes, Jason wants a baby, but he doesn't want one with me, and I don't need him beyond the obvious input he needs to have. My mother didn't paint a glamorous picture of being a single parent, but she certainly painted the alternative as worse. I can do this alone; I *want* to do this alone. Forcing Jason to have a baby with someone he doesn't love isn't right. But deciding to keep a baby after a one-night stand with him is fair game.

If there is anything I can take from my relationship with Phil, it's that two adults who don't love each other probably shouldn't have a baby together. Or at least, they shouldn't stay together if they have a baby.

I'll miss him though. Jason, I mean; I like seeing him every day. His handsome face, his charm, it's all really nice to be around. Maybe there will be a way for me to have it all? I could say it's someone else's baby? But then he'd think I was slutty, sleeping with him and someone else so close together, and how would I prove it wasn't his? What if he wanted a paternity test? No, I'll need to quit work. He can't know about the baby. Maybe we can stay in touch over email. I can write to him in a year and say I had one, but lie about when? Or maybe I just have to accept I can never see or speak to Jason again. The joy of motherhood will override the sadness of losing my job and not seeing him; it's a small price to pay for my life falling into place.

I'm enjoying this. This feeling of being preoccupied. I

sprang out of bed this morning, rather than my usual heavy slump. I have a mission, a purpose. I feel interesting. The only problem is I can't tell anyone what I'm doing. For once I'd love to write a Facebook post; I have so much to say. But no, people wouldn't get it. They'd think I was mad, deluded, they wouldn't even try to understand. But I am itching to tell my story to someone.

I guess there is one way I can share . . . I open my email.

Hello Camilla

So you probably think I'm some angry, crazy woman because I send you the messages that I do. But I'm not, really. I mean, I've got my shit, but I'm actually quite together. And what is crazy anyway? Is crazy letting life pass by without taking what you want from it? Or is crazy doing whatever it takes to get what you want? Is crazy only crazy when you hurt someone else? Like, when a tree falls, does it only make noise if there is someone there to hear it? A person can only be crazy if another person thinks it, right? Because to me, what I am about to tell you, is completely sane.

Camilla, I am going to sleep with my boss. Not because I love him, or want him, but because I want a baby. I'm going to do what you said in your column, and take what I want. I don't want to hurt him, he's a good guy, so he never needs to know. Women get accidentally pregnant all of the time –

don't you think, deep down, that it's usually not an accident? Women pretend it is, but they know exactly what they are doing. So don't judge me like you judge everyone else. You wouldn't understand how I feel, because you say you don't want children. You can't even imagine what it's like for someone like me, someone who wants a child so desperately but may never have the chance, because I can't find a person who loves me enough to share the experience.

I'm doing this alone. Getting what I want. Living the life I want to live, for ***me****. Isn't that what you've always told your readers to do? For once, you might be actually right.*

I press send.

For years I've sat here at my desk, with only grief and Jason's schedule to occupy my mind. Now I have my own thoughts, my own future. Things have become so clear to me and my purpose is taking shape. My legacy is in motion. I get a text.

Hey babe, how about John Lewis tomorrow lunchtime? Do you think Jason would let you take an hour and a half to help me? You said things were quiet? Jess x

No problem, see you there at 1 x

Ooh, I can't wait to look at all the baby things!

Alice and Mum flash into my head. They look disappointed, they're telling me not to get carried away. *But I'm doing it for you as well,* I want to scream. *I'm doing it for our legacy.*

Tara

When the crew left and the house was quiet, I felt proud of myself for not apologising for what I did on the train. The atmosphere in here was horrible when the cameras stopped rolling. No one could look at me, like I had done the most unforgivable thing. What happens to people in these situations? How is it that something they would laugh about in the pub becomes so horribly serious when faced with the person who did it? Has no one on that crew ever masturbated? Why the superiority? I might have laughed along with them if they'd tried it.

I've interviewed so many perverts and even when I know they really are as bad as people say they are, I still manage to be human about it. I still look them in the eye. I still manage to be myself around them. I have never treated anyone the way that I've been treated over this.

But it's clear that what I did on that train isn't even the story any more. It's *me*; the mother, the sperm thief. That's all anyone cares about now. Wanking is just a way in to talk about the way I had Annie. That's why people hate me. And I can't change that.

I'm so scared for my daughter. What if kids at school taunt her about not having a dad? The other kids come from such normal homes; to my knowledge, none of the parents from Annie's class are even divorced. She'll be treated as different; her friends will turn against her. All little children want to do is fit in, and I've made her stand out for all the wrong reasons. I want to make this as easy on her as I can, but maybe everyone *is* right. Maybe the answer to that is her knowing her dad.

This morning, as I was getting Annie ready for school, she told me that one of her classmates told her that her mummy didn't love her as much as other mummies love their kids, because she never picks her up. Apparently, this kid's mummy had said that '*some mummies* are too busy loving themselves to love their children'. Apparently *some mummies* are bigger arseholes than I thought. To think those women made me feel the way they did at that stupid princess party, before they even knew what I had done on the train. I can only imagine what they think of me now.

But Annie shouldn't suffer, so I promised that I would pick her up from school myself today. And now I am in my car opposite the school gate, and all of the other mums are standing there waiting for their children, and I feel sick with fear. This is my first public outing in days. I feel like I've escaped prison and that big scary people are out there trying to hunt me down. I know I have to get out and join them, because my daughter's happiness depends on it. I am wearing jeans and a hoody, the hardest thing in my wardrobe to criticise. They talk about the school playground being a tough place for kids, but the other side of the gate isn't any easier.

As I approach, I feel like I'm swimming towards a school of sharks. The mums see me, and go into slow motion as they part, leaving a huge gap in the middle for me to stand in. There are around nine women, but it feels like there are hundreds.

In around ten minutes, the doors should open. *I can do this.* I have taken worse. There is nothing that these women can say to me that hasn't already been printed, tweeted or said on TV. I've heard it all. *Come on, Tara, this is for Annie.* I must not get back in that car.

I stand very still and stare at the door, but I can see them twitching in my peripheral vision. They are shooting looks to each other. The judgement feels like a massive raincloud. It's about to burst, I can feel it.

And then it begins to rain.

'Uh oh, here she comes, Walthamstow's answer to Rihanna,' says Amanda. I'd recognise her snooty voice anywhere. 'Unbelievable!' she exclaims. There is a low hum of agreement. Their energy builds and I feel like I'm surrounded by an alien life force that is connected by an aura that I can't see. They are getting stronger as a group. I can't fight them.

'My daughter saw the video,' says someone else in a concerned voice, maybe Tracey? I can't be sure. A flurry of sighs and gasps fill the air. 'Her friend's older brother was watching it with his mates and they showed it to her.' I can feel this woman looking at me, and my head is pulled around to face her by whatever force it is that these women have. 'So my daughter has seen a mother that she recognises, masturbating on a train. How do you suggest I explain that to her?' she continues. The question is obviously aimed at me.

There is a long pause as they all burn holes in my head

with their eyes. Am I actually supposed to answer her? I feel like I'm back at school for real, and suddenly realise how insignificant online bullying is in comparison to when it is happening to your actual face. I'd take a Twitter rape threat any day; this shit is real. I long for that door to open, for Annie to run out. For her to feel joy because I am there, and for me to hurry her to the car so we can get the hell out of here.

'That poor little girl, she'll have to live with this shame for the rest of her life,' says Amanda, and a switch inside me flicks. It's like all the lights go on.

Poor little girl? Excuse me?

'And what is it that makes you Mum of the Year?' I say, going up to Amanda's face. My eyes are squinting a little, it feels like my soul is coming back to life.

'Oh don't you try to intimidate me. Women like you . . . '

'"Women like me"? What does that mean? You mean women who have children because they want them so much that they are willing to do it alone? You mean women like me who work their arses off so that their child can go to the best school, and live in a lovely house, and have everything they ever need? Is that what you mean, by "women like me"?'

'"Everything they need"? A child needs a father, that is what they need,' snaps a very stressed-out mum who looks like she's going through a divorce. NOT that I am judging.

'Maybe. Maybe the one thing Annie doesn't have is a father figure, but what she does have is a mother who is teaching her that she can live her life her own way. That she has the power. I may have had my child under what you consider to be questionable circumstances but I'm raising an individual, not a clone of every other girl in her class. So you—'

I'm cut off by Amanda. If she compares me to Rihanna again, I'll knock her out.

'She has the power? The power to what? Masturbate in public, is that really what you think power is? And stop talking to us like a bunch of housewives. You came to my house, and looked around, saw how nice it all was and just presumed my husband provided it all for me. How dare you.'

'What? No I didn't,' I say, quieting down, knowing she is right, I absolutely thought that.

'Yes, you did. It never occurred to you that *I'm* the one that earns the money, did it? I pick Trudy up every day, because when I got pregnant I launched my own business so I could manage my own hours. My husband doesn't earn a penny. Which is why I kicked him out last week after the party, because I've had enough. So stop acting like you're some hero for having a job, we all have our shit, OK?'

The others might as well start cheering. Amanda just kicked my butt and I can't think of anything to say back. I just stand still, staring at the ground like I am a little girl and she is my angry teacher. After a few seconds, I start to walk back towards my car. I wanted to be there for Annie, but I can't take this, I just can't. Just as I reach my car, the fire inside me reignites and I charge back to them. I make them all jump with my return.

'Hey, you lot,' I shout at their backs. They turn around in unison and I hold my stare. 'I did not go out that night to masturbate on a train, and I certainly didn't ask to be filmed, and for my life to be turned upside down. But that is what happened, and because of that I've just had the worst two weeks of my life. I've had rape threats, police at my door and I've developed quite a severe case of agoraphobia. I'm a global joke, my family are desperately trying to keep it together. And I now face the very real threat that I will die unloved by anyone other than my daughter. I am so scared for my future that I cry myself to sleep every night and the only thing that gets me up in the morning is how much I love Annie, and how much she loves me. So when you judge me as a mother, you scar the only thing that I have left. My life is now entirely centred around her being OK, so please don't tell me that she will suffer, when I am so focused on making sure she doesn't. I am an excellent mother. I thought I was alone. I was really unlucky that someone was there to film it. OK? I didn't deserve to have my life destroyed and neither does Annie for *my* unfortunate mistake.'

They all look at me with pity, which I marginally prefer to staring at me in judgement. None of them feel the need to speak.

'Amanda, I am sorry I made presumptions about you, OK?'

She holds her stare. Some of the others nod. The silence seems to go on forever.

'You could make a bloody TV show about this,' says Vicky Thomson, who I didn't realise was standing behind me. I'm so grateful to hear her voice. I turn, and she smiles at me like I just did really good.

The school doors burst open and the children swarm out, dragging the tension with it. Annie runs right up to me and hugs my legs, as if she knew to show them all how much she loves me.

'Mummy, you came,' she says, so happy that I'm here.

She smiles the whole way home.

Later that night, I lie on my bed in a pair of blue Marks and Spencer pyjamas that my mum bought me. Mum and Dad are both downstairs with the TV on so loud I am surprised Annie can sleep. I replay the scene at the school gates in my head. Amanda was right, I *had* judged them all from a thousand paces. I assumed I was better than them, more worldly because I worked in the media, maybe. And that my struggles made me different, better in some way for coping and making it work. How am I just realising how awful that was of me? I've always loved the idea of female solidarity, but I haven't experienced much of it because of the friends I have chosen and the places I have worked. One poxy text is all I've had from Sophie since she scarpered on holidays.

Hey babe, amazing here, I'm so brown. Hope things are OK . . . did your dad watch the video yet?

I didn't answer. I know she'll know about all the press that's been happening, because she calls *MailOnline* her 'Bible' and knows intricate details of celebrities' lives before they do. There is no way she won't have been checking in. What kind of friend is that? Some surrogate sister she turned out to be. I thought she'd be there for me in the middle of the worst shit storm of my life – instead she's topping up her tan in bloody Bora Bora.

But then there is Camilla. The one who stuck up for me publicly, the one who has written me countless messages of support. The one who feels like the truest friend I've ever had, but who I've never actually met. We're like old school pen pals, sharing intimate details of our lives and feelings through letters, or emails as the modern world would have it. I can't help wondering if that friendship could be the same offline?

Cam's often written about her fear of social encounters. How she would avoid face to face meetings at all costs. But really, her anxiety can't be that bad, not when she lives out her life so publicly. And to be fair, I come out in hives at the very thought of seeing people right now, so she'll probably come across like Davina McCall compared to me. I want to meet her.

Hey. Look, I know you don't like awkward social situations. I can appreciate that more than ever right now. But I'd love to meet you. If you were up for it. I'm not sure where all of this has come from, but I feel like I need someone, and I think the person I need is you.

Too weird? We could wear gas masks and communicate via the medium of dance, if that made it easier? Let me know, T x

Camilla replies immediately.

Tara, not weird at all and yes. Please. I think I need you too. Wednesday night? I'll bring the gas masks. C x

As I'm replying with a few suggested times and venues, my bedroom door creeps open.

'Mummy, why do old people have the TV up so loud?' says Annie, rubbing a little soft elephant against her cheek.

'Come on, come in here with me,' I say, pulling the covers open and getting into bed. She climbs in next to me and cuddles up.

'Do you want to sleep in here with me tonight?' I ask her. But she doesn't answer, she's already nestled in and is closing her eyes. I lie awake for well over an hour, *News at Ten* booming up the stairs reminding me that my *Sky News* interview is going out soon. The dread of how they will edit it threatens to keep me up all night. But I inhale the smell of my daughter's hair, and I snuggle up as close as I can. I can be sad about not being in love, and I can be angry at Sophie for not giving me what I need, but the truth is as long as I have Annie I will never be alone, and for that I have to feel grateful. I squeeze her a little too hard and she wriggles away from me. I lie on my back and look at my phone, I go to the conversation with Jason and before reading it again I just delete it. I got it wrong, it's time I accepted it. *He's just not that into me*, as the saying goes. I look again at Cam's email. 'I think I need you too.'

Maybe female solidarity is coming my way after all.

Stella

'Excuse me, where are the sheepskin baby comforters?' says Jessica to a John Lewis 'partner'. She is holding the longest list of baby essentials I have ever seen. Actually, it's the only list of baby essentials I have ever seen. Does she really need all of those things? Bath tub, Moses basket, bottle nipples . . . nipple cream? Is the cream for the bottles, or her boobs? I have no idea; this is a whole new world. The 'partner' points to a wall and we head over there. They are out of the one she wants, and she looks genuinely panicked.

'Maybe you can get one online?' I say, reassuringly.

'Maybe. Jesus, there is so much to think about. When you get pregnant you can just have all of my stuff. It will save you the hassle.' She zooms off to the changing bags and starts investigating the internal pockets of a really ugly grey canvas one. It feels weird, having the plans that I have, and acting like there is nothing going on. I am busting to say something. For once, I have news.

'This one looks good,' she says, picking up a disgusting rucksack with little bows all over it. 'It's got a wipe-clean changing mat and a special pocket for dirty nappies.'

'Yeah, but it's hideous,' I say, wondering if she is really willing to abandon all sense of style so quickly into the process of parenting.

'It's not that bad, those bows are quite cute, no?'

I choose not to respond. She's got that crazy look in her eye that pregnant women and brides get. It's best just to let them crack on. She puts the ugly rucksack on her back and zooms off to the baby bottles. I follow slowly.

'So how's it going anyway?' she asks me, checking her list and then reading the packets of bottle nipples.

'How's what going?'

'You and Phil? I couldn't help but notice the tension between you guys the other night. Everything OK?'

I guess this says a lot about how little I've been thinking about Phil; I'd totally forgotten to tell Jess about us breaking up.

'Oh, no, things weren't great. We actually split up.'

'Oh Stella, my lovely. I'm so sorry,' she says, pushing the nipples back onto the hook and cuddling me. I try to cuddle her back but the rucksack won't let me. I'm pleased, I'm not a hugger.

'Oh, I'm fine. It was a long time coming. Things haven't been right in ages. I'm fine. Happier, actually.'

'I just can't believe it, I was sure you two were going to be together forever,' she says, her eyes welling up. Which is completely ridiculous and not at all what I am comfortable with. 'Sorry, I'm quite emotional at the moment,' she says, wiping her eyes.

'Jess, seriously, I'm fine. It's for the better. Things are better.'

'But how are things better? You're alone. What about having a baby, I thought you were going to have a baby?' She rests her hands protectively on the top of her bump, maybe to show me what I'm missing.

She looks at me like I am a tragic case of something so sad that she can't think of the words to describe it. I know what she is thinking. She is thinking that I am going to die alone, that now, I've lost everything and everyone. That she has a husband who loves her, and a baby on the way, and a perfect life and she won't know how to talk to me about it because she thinks my life is so awful. But I don't want sympathy.

And I don't want anyone thinking I am a lonely mess, and so I say the one thing that I know will wipe that look off Jessica's face and stop her acting like my life just ended.

'I'm pregnant too,' I say, smiling and putting my hand on my tummy. 'Don't be sad, I'm having a baby as well.'

Ooops.

'Oh my God,' she says, giving me another cuddle that I can't reciprocate because of the rucksack and also because I don't want to. She is clearly stunned and going through the motions of what you are supposed to do when someone gives you this news, but it doesn't take her long to look worried and confused.

'Wait, so you got pregnant and then broke up with Phil? Does he not want kids? I always thought he wanted kids?'

'He does want kids, but not with me. And I don't want them with him. It's not Phil's baby,' I say, looking proud.

'What? You were having an affair? Then whose baby is it?'

I look her in the eye and raise my eyebrows. I am urging her to guess. She can do it, I know she can.

'Wait, no, surely not?' she says, working it out. I nod slowly, with a very naughty look on my face. 'Jason?' she asks.

'Yup!' I say, proudly. 'I'm having Jason's baby. We've been seeing each other for a while and it just happened.'

'I don't get it. I should be so angry at you for cheating on Phil but I could tell you guys weren't happy, so this is obviously the right thing. You're having a baby. Oh my God, here, look, this is the list of stuff you need. Shall we both just get it all today?'

There is that look again, that crazed, glazed stare that brides and mums-to-be get when they can't think about anything else but weddings or babies. It's kind of terrifying. I'll never be like that.

'Oh no, today's about you. I'm only a few weeks gone. I shouldn't have told you really.' I say this to cover my back. If I don't get pregnant this month, I can always just tell her I lost it.

'Oh, sure. Of course. What did Jason say when you told him?'

I wonder what to say to this. Jess wouldn't understand the whole 'doing it alone' thing. She needs romance to engage with anything. I know she's taking this well because she finds Jason so utterly dreamy; I don't want to shatter that illusion for her. I'll work out the bit about him not being involved later.

'Oh he was thrilled, of course. Shocked, we both were, but absolutely thrilled.'

'God, I love him. What a guy. I can't deny I'm a bit jealous, he's just the most delicious thing. Stella, wow, I mean you landed on your feet there.'

'Thanks, I think so too.'

'Poor Phil though, he . . . '

'No, Jess. No "poor Phil", OK? We hadn't been good in ages, he wanted out, so did I, everyone wins, OK?'

'OK,' she says, with one hard nod, signifying that she gets it, and will not mention Phil again. 'OK, well we have to get a little something today? Look, what about this?' She holds up a bib with little monkeys all over it.

'Sure, OK,' I say, smiling. 'Go for it.'

'Great, I am officially the first person to buy your baby a

present. Done!' She throws it into her basket and refers back to her list. 'OK, nipple pads . . . ' Linking her arm with mine, she laughs, 'Where are those sexy sods then?'

And just like that, for the first time since Alice died, I feel a sense of belonging.

Cam

When Cam is with her mother, she feels completely powerless. Everything that she stands for in the rest of the world means nothing, because her mother doesn't care about any of it. Or at least, that is what she wants Cam to believe.

'It's a very impractical rug,' she says, pointing at Camilla's shag pile. 'It will be ruined in no time, with people walking all over it.'

'No one walks on it though, it's only me here. I lie on it.'

'A rug that only gets laid on. It's a show rug? That's a bit silly. But I guess it's nice to lie down on after hiking up all of those stairs.'

'Yes, Mum, it's a show rug. And I love it,' Cam says, putting the kettle on. She knew her mother coming over to her flat for the first time wouldn't be easy. She needs to let her get all the criticism out of her system before she can pay any compliments. It usually takes around two visits, but because of the splendour of this amazing flat, Cam suspects it might take three this time.

'How are you feeling, love?' says Cam's dad, as they follow her into the kitchen.

'Rough, actually. Sick, crampy.'

'Well, what is wrong with you?' asks her mum, taking over the tea making.

Cam watches her pour boiling water into cups, and drop the tea bags in afterwards. It's how her mum has always made tea, and Cam thinks it tastes rubbish because of it. But she's never told her mum that she's wrong, because she can't deal with the defensiveness that comes with telling her she isn't perfect.

'I'm pregnant,' she says, in one of her biggest 'fuck it' moments of all time.

'Oh God,' says her dad, sitting down and rubbing his face with his hands. Her mother doesn't move, just stares at the cups. 'Oh,' she eventually says. Cam is surprised by her unenthusiastic reaction; she thought at least that part of the story would make her mum happy. She doesn't see much reason to hold back on the rest after that.

'I don't want to lie to you both, but you know how I feel about having children. I'm having an abortion on Thursday.'

This isn't entirely true. Cam would happily have lied to her mum, but she thought that maybe if she knew about the abortion, she would truly understand that she means it when she says she doesn't want children. And besides, she plans to write about it, so she'd better tell her first.

'Is it the twenty-eight-year-old's?' her mother asks, still staring into the middle distance.

'Yes.'

'Have you told him?'

'Yes.'

'And I suppose this is because he is too young and irresponsible to stand up to his mistakes?'

'No, Mum, this is my decision.'

With this, her mother picks up one of the cups, and smashes it in the sink. Cam's dad instantly starts picking up the broken pieces of clay.

'What happened to you to make you like this?' Cam's mum says, walking closer to her.

'Nothing, Mum. Nothing happened. It's just how I am.'

'Jeremy, come on. We're leaving,' she says, picking up her bag. 'I'm going to send one of your sisters round, maybe they can talk some sense into you.'

'Mum, they won't. I've made up my mind. I've booked the appointment.'

'Why? Why can't you even consider keeping it? We could help you, you could come and live with us. Bring your rug, if that is what you need.'

'Oh for God's sake, Patricia,' Cam's dad bursts out. 'Will you leave her alone. There is more to life than just being a mother, she isn't one of those women.'

'One of "those women"? Like me, you mean?'

'Yes!' exclaim Cam and her father, a little too enthusiastically.

'I see.'

'No, Mum, I didn't mean it like that, I . . . '

'Oh I know exactly what you meant. You think that because I dedicated my life to my family that I failed in some way, don't you? You think it wasn't real work?'

'No, Mum, I don't . . . '

'How do you think it feels, Camilla? To read your daily blogs that promote a lifestyle so opposite to the one I lived? You talk about women like me in this dismissive way, like career is everything, like choosing family over fortune is a bleak alternative to real happiness. Like women like me are brainwashed in some way. Sad, even? Feminism thinks we are a waste of space, like our choices make us weak, like we create a problem. Your blog is a daily attack on everything I stand for, do you think I don't see that?'

'Mum, no. That isn't what it is, it's not against you, or who you are. It's about me, and who *I* am.'

'But you are *my* child, Camilla. You are a piece of me, no matter how much you try to deny it. I know you hate me, but this public slaying has gone far enough. Even in the piece you wrote about the photo, the one where you said you thought I was amazing, or however it was you put it, even then, there was this tone. This "but you'd never catch me being like her" attitude that you've pushed on to me since you were a little girl. What did I do so wrong to you?'

Cam tries to speak but nothing comes out.

Her mother thinks she hates her. That's worse than being punched in the head.

'Congratulations on your success, I am very proud of you. There, I've said it. Now maybe you can quit with this crusade. You've hurt me, for years, well done. Mission accomplished. Jeremy, come on.'

She slams the door as she leaves, leaving Camilla and her dad motionless.

'That was horrible,' Camilla says after a few moments. 'That was just horrible.'

'Yes, it was,' her dad confirms.

Cam moves slowly over to her chaise longue and sits down.

'Maybe she's right,' she says, looking at her dad. 'Maybe everything I am is a huge reaction to her. I guess it's all so deep inside of me that I didn't even realise.'

'You've always challenged her, by being different. Right from when you were a little girl. She thought she had parenting down, and then you came along and threw it all up in the air. You wouldn't wear the hand-me-downs, you didn't cling onto her like the other girls did. There was this independent spirit and your mother doesn't know what to do with people like that.'

'People like you, Dad. That's who you are?'

'Yes, maybe. But I became what I needed to become to make this family work. I changed myself to be happy. It was a small sacrifice for the family that I wanted. Sounds pathetic, I suppose.'

'No, Dad. None of it is pathetic. Nothing about parenting is pathetic. Is that what you both really think I believe?'

He shrugs his shoulders a little, and Cam feels even worse.

'Dad, will you give us five minutes?' she says, putting some flip flops on and heading outside. Her dad, of course, gives her whatever she needs.

As she approaches her parents' car, Cam sees her mum sobbing in the passenger seat. Despite the tension that has always been a part of their relationship, this level of confrontation is very new.

'Mum,' she says, tapping on the window. 'Mum, can we talk?'

Her mother slowly winds the window down. Cam knows this won't be easy, but that they have to have this conversation. The sun is shining, the air is mild, it's the perfect weather for a storm.

'Look, I think you are a brilliant parent.' Her mum huffs, and turns away. 'Mum, come on, get out the car, please.'

Cam stands back and waits, making it quite clear she is not going anywhere until her mum has got out. Eventually she does as she asks, and they stand opposite each other, both wondering how this will play out.

'Mum, please believe me when I say my work is not a direct attack at you. But maybe, in some subliminal way, I have been trying to make you understand me better by writing intricate details of who I am, and how I feel, with the hope that you will read it and accept me for me.'

Cam is surprised by how easily that comes to her, but more surprised at how true it is. It's just never been a conscious thought until now. Her mother looks distraught.

'Mum, you have never, ever, just taken me for who I am. You have always tried to make me like the other girls, to mould me into what you thought a daughter should be. You made me wear their clothes, you made me do gymnastics, you made me do everything they did. I used to tell you I wanted to be alone and you would make me play with them. And the older I got, the more there was at stake. The things I wanted to do, the person I wanted to be became clearer and clearer to me but still you never just looked at me and thought,

"That's my Cam, she's different, she's unique." You just saw me as unsociable, or difficult, and so you built this chasm between us. By not accepting the little things about me, you could never accept the bigger things and now here we are, me telling you that I don't want to have children, that I am not keeping this baby because it isn't what I want, and you still think you can change me. But you can't. You can't change me, Mum, because I don't need to be changed.'

Cam stands firm, feeling guilty for making her mum cry, but determined to stand her ground.

'I just want you to be happy,' says her mum, pathetically.

'Do you though? I don't believe you. You've never ever tried to make me happy, you've just tried to shape me into what you want me to be. It's your happiness you're after, Mum, not mine.'

'Camilla, that isn't very nice.'

'Well, Mum, you've not been very nice. I'm really good. I'm focused, I'm kind, I'm clever and I am happy with my life. It's OK for me to be a little weird, no one judges you for it. You have plenty of normal daughters.'

'Bringing you girls up was my job. I wanted to be good at it. I'm sorry if you think I wasn't.'

'Mum, stop it. Stop seeing me as a failure of yours. Seriously, what is that about?'

'I just think that to not want kids you must be so angry at me for something. That you were uninspired by me, to want to be the exact opposite to who I was.'

'Mum, yes, you have been a bitch at times, and yes, you should have accepted me right from the start, but you have to see that you have four really great daughters. We are all really, really happy. Sure, Mel might moan about her varicose veins but she's OK. She loves her kids, she is a brilliant mum. Tanya and Angela are brilliant mums too. Me? I'm a loner but so, so happy in my life. How can you have been anything but a great mum when you look at the adults you have created? We're all excellent, Mum, and that's down to you and Dad. OK?'

They stand in silence for a few seconds, as what Cam says sinks in.

'You really are, aren't you? You're all really great girls?' her mum says, smiling sweetly.

'Yes, Mum, all of us.'

'Thank you, Camilla. I think I needed to hear that. You try so hard as a parent and no one ever tells you if you're doing it right. I just always presumed your life was a big reaction to my mistakes.'

'It isn't. It's a reaction to who *I* am. OK?'

'OK.' They step towards each other and hug, years of tension evaporating just like that. *If only I had found the confidence to say all of these things years ago,* Cam thinks. But then, maybe if she had, she wouldn't have had the career that she has.

'Are you sure about the baby?' her mum says, pulling away.

'I've never been more sure of anything, Mum. I need you to understand that.'

'I do. OK, I do. Maybe I can come with you? You've never liked going to the doctor?'

Cam wants to cry at the thought of this gesture, but she manages to hold it together.

'That would be great, thanks, Mum.'

'I'd like to be there for you. It's my job.' She grins, proudly.

'Well, have my two favourite women worked things out?' says Cam's dad, coming up to them. Clearly he'd been listening for a while.

'Yeah, I think we have,' Cam says.

'We have,' confirms her mum.

'Great, then we will see you on Thursday, Camilla. What time did you say your appointment was?'

'Two.'

'We will be here at one to get you. Try to get some sleep. It will be over before you know it, OK?'

'Thanks, Dad, love you.'

Cam watches her mum and dad drive away. She can't quite believe the turn that today took. After all her preaching to her readers, she's proved herself right. Speaking up can change things.

Tara

All I do these days is Google myself. I used to trawl the Internet finding dirt on my contributors, now I do it to find dirt on me. Sitting in my parents' kitchen, I am on my fourth cup of tea of the day and it's only ten a.m. I've just found a website called *DadsWhoWantTheirBabiesBack.com,* where they've found a picture of Annie off Facebook, taken away her features that look like me (not many, as embarrassingly, she doesn't look much like me at all), and created various Photofits of what her biological father could potentially look like with what is left. All with the hope he recognises himself and wants to be a part of her life. Apparently, some old cop who lost custody of his son in a divorce set this site up, and is making it his life's ambition to reunite dads with their kids. In most cases that sounds perfectly valid, but in mine, what the ACTUAL fuck?

This is the kind of thing you'd see in a movie and think *no way, no way would human beings be this ridiculous*. But here I am, looking at a number of images that look nothing like Nick, and reading words like, 'If this is you, you have the right to know your daughter.'

OH, FUCK OFF.

Just as I'm about to slam shut my computer in a fit of rage, Sophie starts calling me on Skype. I decline the call. I don't want to speak to her. She's abandoned me in my time of need and whatever she has to say can wait until I am in the mood for it. But she calls again. And then again. And the truth is, I am bored out of my mind and maybe it might actually be quite nice to have a conversation with someone other than my mum or daughter. So I answer.

'Hello?' I say in a grumpy voice as our videos fire up. I see turquoise water behind her, and an even bluer sky. She is to the right of the screen, huge bug-eye black sunglasses swamping her face, her blonde hair wet and tangled in that cool sand-and-seawater way. Her tan is fantastic and I feel disgusting and pale, sitting at the kitchen table in my M&S pyjamas.

'Hiiiii!' she says, and I wish I'd never answered the call. 'How are you?'

'Oh, so you care then?' I say back, trying to hide as much of my face as I can with my cup of tea. I can see myself in the camera and I look really ugly.

'Of course I care,' she says, acting all offended. 'It's the Internet connection here, it's really bad.'

'Where are you?'

'The Four Seasons Bora Bora. Oh hon, it's amazing. The water is like sea soup, I'm swimming every day, eating really well. Been having loads of sex too, so that's a bonus.'

'Nice. With Carl?' I ask, facetiously.

'Yes, with Carl. God, you're not still angry with me are you?'

I think about having a go at her but I really can't be bothered. Also, it would be pointless. No matter what I say, the reality is when we get off this call I will still be in the kitchen in my pyjamas, and Sophie will still be in Bora Bora. She wins, no matter how this goes.

'It's been a shit week,' I say.

'Oh, Tara, I know. I've seen all the articles. God, it's like you're Katie Price or something, they can't get enough, can they?'

I choose not to ask how she's managed to keep so up to date when she has such a terrible Internet connection. I knew she was lying.

'It's been horrible, and all the stuff about how I had Annie has really hurt me. I feel like they are going through my bins, they know everything about me. I don't understand it.'

'They've been really snooping haven't they? I couldn't believe it when I got that Facebook message from the *Mail*. And the way they worded it, all "We want to write a piece that tells the truth about who Tara is", blah blah blah. They are such fuckers!'

'Wait, what? What Facebook message? What are you talking about?'

'You didn't see it? I presumed you saw it; they sent it to everyone?'

'Everyone who? Who sent it and who is everyone?'

'All of your Facebook friends. Just after they found out your name, a journalist wrote to all your friends on Facebook and asked them for stories on you, offering money and everything. I didn't take any money, I swear!'

'God, I haven't been on Facebook since this happened. It's so horrible they contacted you all, that's so creepy. Wait—what do you mean you didn't take any money? Any money for what?'

'It's the way they worded it, babe; at first I didn't know who I was talking to and I genuinely thought they were trying to help. It wasn't until I was on the phone with her and I realised she was going to use it against you, she was all "So she never told the guy?" and I thought, uh oh . . . '

'Wait, *you* told the *Daily Mail* about how I had Annie? It was you?'

'Yeah, I mean, they would have found out about it anyway but I didn't realise they'd use it the way that they did. I genuinely thought they'd sympathise with you or something, you know, you being a single mum and everything.'

I want to smash my fist through my computer screen, grab her by the neck and pull her into this kitchen so I can stamp repeatedly on her head. What friend does that? I see Carl in the background. He's in expensive-looking swimming trunks, his tan glistening as water cascades over his handsome fifty-one-year-old body. He should know the truth about who he's married to.

'Hey, Carl,' I shout, like a crazy drunk woman trying to get the attention of an ex-boyfriend. 'Carl, want to know a few things about your wife?'

I see him try to work out what I'm saying, but he's coming over to the screen.

'Tara, what are you doing?' says Sophie, nervously. But I am not stopping and there is a commotion as he gets closer to the microphone. I raise my voice even louder.

'Hey, Carl, what about this . . . Your wife got the clap when she was twenty-three because she had a one-night stand with a barman.'

'Tara, please, no,' says Sophie, but I am like a dog with a bone, it's all coming out.

'Wanna know what else? I once found her asleep by a mountain of cocaine with two naked guys next to her and she couldn't remember which one she'd slept with – or if it was both! Classy, huh?'

'She did what?' I hear him say, just before Sophie manages to get rid of the connection. She must have shut her laptop, because the picture is suddenly gone. I hope he heard every word, and that she is forced into honesty and dealing with the consequences of who she really is. I've stood by her through so much and the way she repays me is to tell the *Daily* fucking *Mail* my story? Urgh! No more, that friendship is done. I can't wait to meet Camilla Stacey. I officially have a huge opening for a decent friend.

Stella

I keep getting the giggles at my desk. Jessica's face when I told her I was pregnant, it was priceless. People won't believe it when it happens, who would expect such good news for me? No one. I can't wait to get it out there, I'll write a Facebook post on that day for sure. How will I put it?

I am thrilled to announce that I'm having a baby. Before you ask, I have decided to do this on my own. I couldn't be happier. I know that might surprise some of you, as I was always the quiet twin. But I know you will all be happy for me, and the bundle of joy on his or her way . . .

Of course I know there will be some judgement, but when the baby comes, people will move on. I'll say it was a one-night stand. That I contacted him but he didn't want to be a part of it, that I feel strong enough to do it without him. I'm not friends with Jason on Facebook so he'll never see it, and if anyone asks too many questions I'll just say I don't want to go into it. I'll swear Jessica to secrecy and I know she'll keep it, because she's loyal.

I'm going to love being a mum, I can tell. I'll tell my baby what my mum always told me, that his dad didn't want to be involved, and that you are better off being alone than surrounded by people who don't love you.

I wonder if I'm ovulating? It makes me nervous to think that when I am, I'll have to move fast. Jason and I have been getting on so well. I've been dressing a little sexier, more make-up, tighter tops, and I'm sure he's noticed. He's more tactile than he used to be. This morning he hugged me when he came in, he's never done that before. I held onto him quite tightly when I did it, and kissed him softly on his cheek. If we'd have done that a week ago it would have been so weird, but it turns out cancer breaks down physical and emotional boundaries between colleagues. Who knew.

I check over my shoulder to see him busying away at his desk, and hide my ovulation test up my sleeve. In the toilet, I pee on it then wrap it in tissue and hide it up my sleeve again. I don't want to spend ages in the loo waiting for the result, Jason might think I'm doing a poo, and I want him to fancy me. As I come out, I nearly leap twenty feet into the air and drop the ovulation stick on the floor, because Jessica is standing right in front of me.

'Jessica, what are you doing here?' I say, panicked. 'How the fuck did you get in?'

'Gosh, what a welcome.'

'Sorry, you took me by surprise. How on earth did you get in, I didn't hear the buzzer?' I see Jason getting up from his desk. He'll be wondering who it is.

'The door was open; I think the catch might have broken.

Anyway, I wanted to give you this, I stupidly went off with Mini Stella's gift,' Jessica says, pulling the bib out of her bag and waving it in the air just as Jason walks in. I throw myself at it and hide it under my top.

'Oh, hello. What's that?' he says, quite rightly wondering what I just wedged between my breasts.

'Oh, it's a present, right Jessica, a *surprise*?' I wink at her, as if to play along.

'Oh, yes, OK, a surprise. Cute!' She giggles.

'Jessica, isn't it? How are you, I haven't seen you in ages?' Jason says, with all the charm of Hugh Grant in *Love, Actually*. I see her melt towards him as he kisses her on each cheek. I can tell Jessica is repeating, *I'm married with a baby on the way, I'm married with a baby on the way*, in her mind.

'Really well, thanks,' she replies, gathering herself, and we all stand for a minute, feeling a bit awkward. I am hoping that she will leave now that she has given me the bib.

'So, I guess congratulations are in order?' she says, suddenly.

Oh, Jesus Christ.

'Congratulations?' Jason asks, confused.

'Yes, congratulations about the b—'

'THE BOOK,' I butt in. 'Congratulations about the book. I was telling Jess all about it at lunch. The book, right, Jess?' I wink at her again, I have no idea what she thinks this game will be, but I push for her cooperation anyway. Another OTT wink from me and she realises that for whatever reason, I don't want her to mention the baby.

'Oh, yes, the book,' she says. 'Congratulations on the book?'

I move behind Jason and mouth, 'He's in a terrible mood'

to Jessica. She nods in a 'oh, men, I get it' type way. I think I covered my tracks.

'Oh, thanks. Yeah, it's been tough. Impossible in fact, but I'm nearly there.'

'Well, I hope it does really well and that you get to live off the royalties and just lounge around at home with your lovely family,' she says, unable to help herself.

'My lovely family? Ha, now there's a distant dream,' Jason says, which to Jessica will sound like rather a heartless thing to say when I am pregnant with his child. Jessica throws me a look as if to say, 'See what you mean about the mood' and I roll my eyes.

'Right, then,' she says, 'I better go. I want to go to the supermarket and get one of their three courses for £10 meals before they all sell out. That interview with the girl who . . . you know . . . on the train is on tonight and I do not want to miss that.'

My ears prick up again and more panic sets in.

'What interview is that?' Jason asks, intrigued.

'Oh, you haven't heard? Everyone's talking about her. It's the woman who,' Jess pauses again, but this time finds the confidence to say the words, 'masturbated on a train and got filmed and . . . '

'OK, weird,' I yelp. 'Can't talk about this at work. No no no, ewwwww, too much information. Brrrrrr. OK, Jess, we better crack on, it's busy busy here this afternoon, OK? Thanks for dropping off the present and I'll text you later, yeah?' I am literally pushing her towards the door. My heart is thumping at the thought of her saying Tara's name. I had totally forgotten about that show being on tonight; if Jason sees it, my plans will be ruined.

I see Jessica downstairs, moaning about Jason's mood the whole way, promising he'll get over it soon and that we can all go for a night out, then I shut the door behind her. It swings open. She was right, the catch is broken.

Back upstairs, Jason is still standing where I left him.

'Are you OK, Stella? You are acting a little strange?'

'Oh, yes, yes I'm OK. Well, you know, as fine as you can be when you are going through what I'm going through.' *Pause for sympathy.* 'I just wanted her out, I'm still annoyed with her for making my birthday all about her pregnancy, to be honest.'

'Does she know? About . . . the cancer?'

'No. Just you, I've only told you,' I say, knowing that will make him feel special. Also, Jessica doesn't even know about the BRCA gene; I couldn't handle the level of sympathy she would drown me with.

'I'm so glad you told me. If you need anything tonight, just let me know. I'll leave my phone on again, OK?'

'Cool, thanks. How's it all going, anyway? Book coming along OK?'

'Actually, yes. I'm a lot less stressed. I think seeing you cope so brilliantly with what is happening to you has given me some perspective. I'm lucky, I'm healthy. I need to focus on the positive more, and make this book really really good.'

'That's exactly right. This book is your legacy.'

'I guess it is. What is your legacy going to be?'

'Helping you with your book,' I say, smiling. 'You'll give

me a credit, won't you? *Stella Davies, the bossy bitch who made me write this*.'

'I will, although I might use stronger language than that. You've been incredibly mean about the Internet.'

'It had to be done. You feeling better about Tara now?' I ask, testing his desperation levels.

'Yeah, I guess I realised that I'm pretty easy to find online. If Tara had liked me, she'd have found me by now, you were right. She could have just texted me, and she hasn't, so I should probably just move on.' I let out a huge sigh of relief. 'Yup, I'm just going to go home, lie on the sofa, write for a bit, then I might watch that interview with the girl on the train, sounds hilarious, I could do with a laugh.'

That relief instantly turns into fear.

'Oh, um. No, don't bother. I read some reviews, apparently it's rubbish.'

'To be honest, that's what I need. Something inane and stupid that I don't have to think about. A woman masturbating on a train sounds ideal. See you tomorrow, you OK to lock up?'

He goes to leave. Again, I have to think quickly. I see a glass, should I smash that? No, tried that, didn't work last time and just resulted in some very sore knees. How can I trump shouting cancer? Nothing trumps cancer. Fuck, he's leaving. He'll watch Tara and all this will be over. That can't happen, I'll be ovulating in the next few days, I have to keep him away from her for a little bit longer. I have to stop him. How? *Think Stella, think, think. Cancer . . . treatment . . . HAIR*!

I put my hand to my head, clench my fist and pull it as hard as I can, screaming while I do it because it really, really hurts.

'Jesus, what happened?' Jason says, concerned and coming back into the room.

'My hair,' I say, with genuine pain and horror for the self-inflicted agony I just put upon myself.

'My hair, it's falling out.'

As I sit on the sofa in the studio clutching the cup of tea that Jason just made me, I try not to focus on the stinging burn on my head. Pulling your own hair out takes determination and force; I didn't know I was capable of such a high level of self-administered pain.

'I thought you just wanted to go home to watch TV?' I ask, pretending not to be thrilled that the night has turned in my favour.

'Oh, I hate TV. I'd just have sat there trying to relax while actually getting annoyed and then I wouldn't have slept and then I'd have felt guilty that I hadn't spent the night writing,' he says, turning the studio lights on and putting a tall stool in front of us.

'What are you doing?' I ask.

'Setting up the shot. I want to photograph you.'

'What? No. Jason, this is not how I want to be photographed,' I say, freaking at the thought of my lie being caught on camera.

'This is exactly how you should be photographed. Then, I think we should shave your head.'

I stand up quickly.

'No, Jason. I don't want to do that. I'll let it fall out naturally, it will be fine.'

Jason stands behind the camera, takes a shot and the bright flash makes us both blink.

'My friend had chemotherapy,' he says, concentrating. 'She said the thing she regretted was not shaving her head, because she ended up looking like Worzel Gummidge. You can own this, Stella. Or it can own you. Come on, get on the stool.'

I have seen Jason work this way multiple times. He gets so determined when he thinks of a shot that he ignores the subject's insecurities. It can seem a little rude and insensitive and the model often huffs and puffs as they are directed by him to do what he wants, not what they want. But then they see the photo and they call him a genius, and they want to do it again and again. He is famous for photographing the un-photographable. And even though I have witnessed the magic that happens when he is behind the camera, I do not want to sit on that stool and be the subject of his work.

'Jason, I can't. I'm not comfortable in front of the camera.'

'Stella, no one I ever photograph is comfortable in front of that camera, that is what I actively seek out. You're intriguing to me. You've sat here for a year running my life, being cool, calm, presenting yourself like you have your shit together. You've always been so confident, so strong. I spend five days a week with you and I'd never have guessed you had been through what you've been through, and I certainly wouldn't have guessed you were ill. You're incredible, Stella. Really incredible.'

Did he really have no idea that my life is actually the way it is? None at all? I always presumed that sadness seeped out of my pores, that people pick up on my pain instantly, and that was why they generally don't like me. I don't know how a person can feel the way I do inside and keep that truly hidden. Phil saw it, he couldn't ignore it. I thought Jason just professionally ignored my anxiety, but maybe he didn't. Maybe he really likes me. Maybe he *does* think I'm amazing.

I do as he says, I suppose he's right. If I don't like the photo, we can just delete it? I feel a little plumper than usual, due to all the cough syrup I've been drinking that is pretty much pure sugar. Not losing weight was another tip for conceiving a boy. I suck in my tummy, and try to feel beautiful.

'OK, perch on the stool,' he tells me. 'Fluff your hair up a bit. This is the "before" shot, so we need that hair as bouncy as possible.'

I do as he says, and draw my hands upwards against my scalp to raise the volume of my hair. The right side stings like I've been punched in the head, as I skim over the bald patch.

'OK, look straight into the lens.'

I straighten my back and push my chest out. Despite the pain, I scratch my head with the tips of my fingers to add as much volume to my hair as I can. I relax my face and look deeply into the lens. Jason takes photo after photo. I don't even need to see them to know I don't want them deleted.

'Stella,' says Jason after we've been lost in a blur of

something indescribable for over twenty minutes. 'You're really beautiful.'

'You sound surprised,' I say, smiling. A real smile, caused by real happiness at being called beautiful by someone who I believe means it.

'I should have taken your picture years ago,' he says, looking at one of the images on the back of his camera.

'There was no need though, was there?'

'No need? To take a photograph?'

'Maybe there was nothing to photograph before I had cancer.'

Jason slightly readjusts the lights. A little softer, a little closer. I feel like a statue. A beautiful centrepiece in a room. The pull of energy around me is like flowers reaching towards the light. Has the world just noticed me for the first time?

'OK, that's it,' he says, when his camera card is full. He looks down, like he's having a thought he shouldn't be having.

'What is it?' I ask, hoping it's about me.

'Your hair, it's so sexy.'

'Jason, please!' I say, pretending to be horrified.

'But you're going to look good without it, it won't change that look in your eye.'

'I don't want to shave it, honestly, I'll just wait. My hair, it's my thing,' I say, swishing it a little, knowing how much he loves girls with long hair and needing him to fancy me.

He walks over to me, 'But when I saw you through the lens, it's your eyes that captured me. Trust me, Stella, it's not your hair that makes you sexy.'

And with that, I say, 'Let's do it.'

Tara

I remember the night really well. It's always been important to me that I did. I met Nick in the queue to the loos in a pub when I was out celebrating a friend's birthday. We were waiting for ages; someone in the toilet was either really ill, having sex or fast asleep. We were both desperate and it made for quite a funny introduction. 'I actually think it would have been quicker for me to go home,' he said. 'I live minutes away. If you're desperate, you can come with me?'

I agreed; it was either that or peeing on the floor. Which I was becoming more and more comfortable with the idea of, but a toilet in a house was always going to win.

Back at his place, he showed me into the downstairs loo while he went to the one upstairs. I peed for ages, like two pints were coming out of me. I made it just in time. When he came down I told him I was thinking of going home anyway, and asked if he minded hanging on while I ordered a taxi. Next thing I know, we are having a whisky, and not long after that, my knickers are on his kitchen floor and we were having sex on the kitchen worktop. Twenty minutes later, I was getting into a taxi and watching him walk back to the pub. We didn't even swap numbers. It sounds absolutely terrible, but weirdly, it wasn't. It wasn't seedy, or uncomfortable or dirty, it was just a shag. Just a nice moment between two strangers who really fancied each other and acted on it. One of my best sexual encounters ever, actually. It felt really, really good. I remember thinking how cool that was on the way home, that sex like that existed between two consenting adults. No pressure, no hassle, no strings. I was cool with it; he was cool with it. I did beat myself up for not using a condom though, so a week later I went and had an STD test. It all came back negative, so I just banked the whole experience as something really fun and a bit wild and cracked on with my life. He knew no one I knew, and vice versa. We never had to see each other again. There was something really liberating about it.

Until three weeks later, when I realised I should probably have had a period but hadn't. I got a test, it was positive and I went through all the motions of how I thought I should deal with it. I immediately booked an appointment for an abortion a week later but when the day came, I just couldn't go. I was thirty-six, with no prospects of a relationship. I wanted kids and was pragmatic enough to be honest with myself that it might not happen with moonlight and roses. So I cancelled the appointment, told my mum and dad I was doing it, and kept the baby. Dad didn't speak to me for two months, but when I came home with a scan photo and told him it was a girl, he cried and has supported me ever since.

Once the decision was made, I never allowed myself to question it. It was my choice, my body, my baby. I didn't want to go into motherhood feeling like Annie was a mistake. Sure, the conception wasn't intentional, but my decision to keep her was. It was a well-thought-out, calculated decision.

I knew it was controversial not to tell Nick, but I didn't feel that it was wrong. Married people have affairs, parents abandon kids, people steal, rape, and hurt other people all the time. All I did was not give an innocent guy a big problem.

We wouldn't have fallen in love just because of the baby, because real life is not like a Jennifer Aniston movie. If I'd have told him, he would be bound to be involved, and if he wasn't, then he'd feel like an arsehole. So I never told him. And now, for the first time in six years, I am questioning if that was a massively cuntish thing to have done. It seems to be the part of my recent exposure that has upset people the most. And it has made me rethink a decision that for so many years felt so simple, and so right. It was my body, my baby. But was it my right? Maybe I should just tell him?

The pub was The Sun on Clapham High Street. To get to his house we took a right, then a left and it was about four doors up on the right. It was dark, but I'm pretty sure the front door was green. I'll find it. I'm certain he owned it, it was a bit fancy for a rental. If he's still there, I'll tell him. He might have seen the video. He could have recognised me, Googled me, read about Annie and done the maths himself. Maybe he's trying to find me. Or maybe he never wants to see me again. I guess I'm about to find out.

Wearing a beanie hat and a scarf, I get the tube across town to Clapham Common. I watch everyone on the train. Are all these people really squeaky clean? Of course not. If cameras followed them all to where they are going I bet a bunch of them would commit some lurid sexual act that would have them victimised by society like I have been. Debauchery is all around. It only matters if you're unlucky enough to get caught.

I look suspicious with my hat pulled down and my scarf

over my face on such a warm evening. People are looking at me as if I have a bomb up my shirt, but I'd rather they thought that than have them see my face and recognise me. I'm not OK with being in public yet. I'm not sure I ever will be, especially after tonight's interview goes out. Oh God, every time I think about it I get shivers.

At Clapham Common tube, I walk to The Sun pub. I take a right, then a left. This is the street. Four doors up on the right. I'm certain that's the house. Number eight. It doesn't look much different apart from a few window boxes, which may or may not have been there the night we had sex. I see myself tottering away, getting in the taxi and watching him walk back to the pub, unaware that inside me, Annie was being created.

Being here feels strange. I always felt I had no connection to this place or Nick but now I'm back, knowing it was the place that my child was created, I have an odd feeling of nostalgia, like this house matters to us. Annie's soul is here, I can't pretend this place isn't important.

But why am I here? I'm here because maybe everyone on the Internet is right, maybe I did do a terrible thing. I wonder how it would have felt to come back here three weeks later to tell Nick I was pregnant. How horrible that would have been for both of us, how weird, how awkward. And then what? What would I have been asking of him? For his money, for his time? Neither. I would have just been telling him he was having a baby I didn't want him to have anything to do with. It was my decision to keep it, it was right for me. Telling him would have been selfish, I have always fully believed that.

Until now. Until I read multiple articles and tweets calling me evil for not telling him he was having a baby. So here I am, six years later. To tell him he has a daughter.

I knock on the door. I hear footsteps and then Nick is standing in front of me, I didn't think that would happen so quickly, but of course it would, if he is home. I wasn't sure I'd recognise him from that one night, but he looks exactly the same.

'Hi,' I say, knowing he'll be shocked to see me but standing firm that this is the right thing to do. I see the kitchen at the end of the hall. That's where we did it.

'Hello?' he says back, much less awkwardly than I imagine. He has no idea who I am. Maybe I should have planned what to say, because I'm suddenly completely stuck for words.

'Remember me?' I ask, doing a big cheesy smile as if I'm a long-lost cousin who he loved as a kid.

'Um, no, I'm sorry, am I supposed to?'

Is he supposed to? I don't know.

'I'm Tara, from the pub.' As I say this, I can't even be sure I ever told him my name.

'Tara from the pub? Oh, did I leave my card?'

'No, no not the pub now. I mean the pub six years ago. We met in the pub six years ago. I came back here with you, we— I need to tell you something.'

'What is this?' he asks, looking down the street as if maybe he is being filmed or something. I am struggling to think of anything to say because he looks so much like Annie, and it's really floored me. Her eyes, her nose, they are just a mini version of his. It's too surreal. He's her flesh and blood.

'I think you've got the wrong house,' he says, going to shut the door. I put my hand out to keep it open.

'No, I haven't. You're Nick, I'm Tara, although I don't know if I ever told you my name. We had sex in your kitchen before I got a taxi home, six years ago, remember?'

'OK, you're clearly having some kind of laugh. You're turning up six years later because?'

'Because I have a six-year-old daughter and I thought you should know.'

I don't think I've ever seen someone look as terrified. His entire face grew by a few millimetres as veins and sweat popped out of him like splats from a paintball gun. I feel sick for him; this is so cruel.

And then I see a gorgeous, heavily pregnant woman appear on the stairs behind him. 'I'm only joking,' I find myself shrieking, 'totally got the wrong house.'

'Who is it, baby?' asks his pregnant wife. I see a ring glistening on her left hand.

'I'm no one,' I tell her. 'I got the wrong house. Don't mind me.'

Nick keeps looking at me. The horror in his eyes going from fear to hate to anger and back to fear. He doesn't deserve this. I should never have come.

'Sorry to bother you,' I say, all cheery and weird to protect this poor guy from having to deal with what could ruin this otherwise magical time in his life. He gives me one final look of disgust, that unequivocally tells me that he does not want to know about Annie. And I don't feel a shred of anger back, I couldn't agree with him more. And as I walk away from what was potentially a terrible, horrible and demoralising moment, I feel an odd sense of empowerment. I did the right thing back then, and no one has the right to tell me otherwise. I am an excellent mother, and my daughter will grow up understanding that her own choices are the right choices, no matter what anyone else thinks. That's the greatest lesson I can teach her.

13

Tara

I've sat on this sofa a million times watching TV with my parents. We've all squirmed uncomfortably during sex scenes and talked energetically over extreme swearing but never has the atmosphere felt as tense as it is right now. It's 9.55 p.m. and my interview on Sky is airing at ten. I dared look at Twitter to see if anyone cared, and saw that #WankWomanOnTV has been trending all afternoon.

I'm nervous about how I'll come across. They will hardly be kind because I didn't give them what they wanted, but I'm hoping that by not apologising they will realise I am not weak, and that I deserve to be edited well. Maybe people will be inspired by me.

Maybe not.

My dad is sitting in his armchair with his head in his right hand. He's wearing a knitted jumper that my mum got from a charity shop. She cut the label out and made me give it to him as a present, saying I knitted it for him. I did as she said, and felt ridiculous. He hasn't said a word to me, but I know he's coming round, because he hasn't taken the jumper off for days. He's flitting between looking at the curtains and looking at the TV. My mother told him he has to watch the interview. He said he didn't want to, but I know he's as intrigued as I am to see what happens. Mum has made us all popcorn, and she won't shut up about it. It's so surreal, like we're about to sit down and watch a Bond movie.

'Do you think it's too salty? I never know how much salt to put on,' Mum asks.

Dad and I both ignore her. The news starts and my face pops up on screen. The host speaks.

'Tonight we have an exclusive interview with the woman who has become a global sensation for being filmed pleasuring herself in public.'

My father lets out a huge groan and stares at the curtains again. I feel sick. The humiliation just washes over in waves, hot and sweaty, then sickly and cold.

'I think it's too salty,' says my mother.

'Oh shut up about the popcorn,' my dad and I bark, in our first moment of solidarity since this whole shit fest began.

'Now, in her first interview since the video of her antics became a global viral sensation, Damien Weymouth interviews Tara Thomas about life after public shame.'

'Oh, Tara,' says Mum, putting down the popcorn. 'That doesn't sound good.'

The TV cuts to Damien, sitting on Dad's chair, in this very room. He begins his introduction.

'Hello, and welcome to the special interview with me,

Damien Weymouth. Now, unless you have been living under a stone, you will have heard of my guest today. Twelve days ago Tara Thomas was living a normal life, working in television and taking care of her daughter, Annie . . . '

'I can't. I'm sorry, I can't bloody do this,' says my dad, suddenly standing up. 'I can't watch my daughter talk about that, with that man, on my chair, on our TV. I just can't bloody do it.'

He's up and out the door, stomping up the stairs too quickly for Mum or I to talk him out of it. Part of me is pissed off he isn't man enough to deal with this, the other part is delighted that he's gone.

'He finds it all very hard,' Mum confirms. I tell her to shush and turn back to the TV.

'Take me back to that night. The night on the train. Where had you been previously to that?'

'I'd been on a date and I was heading home,' I say back to him.

'You look lovely on TV darling, I always said you should be in front of the camera, not behind it.'

'Thanks, Mum, now please be quiet,' I snap.

'Did you deliberately have sex with that man with the hope of getting pregnant?' Damien asks me.

'Oh dear,' says Mum.

'No, I didn't. Now, please can we talk about me on the train?'

Oh fuck, they left that in? The bastards, I didn't think they would leave that in. I thought if I kept saying it they would have to leave it out. But no.

'I'd really like to just talk about the masturbating part, please,' I say to Damien, again.

'How does it feel to have the public judge you in this way?' he continues.

'Please can we talk about me on the train,' I say, looking more annoyed.

'Mum, no, I didn't just keep saying that. There is more about Nick, and how I didn't tell him. And I get snappy and say I don't feel sorry for him. They can't just leave that out?'

Mum passes me more popcorn; I shove it away with my hand.

'You must deeply regret what you did?' Damien asks.

And this is maybe the worst bit so far, they don't even air my answer, just the weird, creepy smile I did after I said, 'I wish I had waited until I got home.' Which I absolutely remember saying, because I thought it was quite funny.

They cut to the clip of Adam, and his squirmy, chubby stupid little face makes me want to kick the TV. He makes me sound vicious and nasty and cruel. All because I picked him up on the hidden sexuality that he seriously needs to just admit to.

'Oh, was that Adam?' Mum says. 'He's not what I imagined. He's quite handsome isn't he?'

'Shush, Mum, please!'

'Tara,' Damien says, 'is there anything you would like to say?'

Here it comes, my brilliant line about the orgasm. At least I'll end on a high note.

'I'd really like to just talk about the masturbating part, please,' I say.

Nooooooo!!!

I get up and scream at the TV and hurl a handful of popcorn at it. 'Jesus fucking Christ,' I say, forgetting who I am with.

'Language, Tara, please.'

'Oh, Mum, what does it matter? You tell kids not to swear so people don't think they are trashy; well, everyone already thinks I'm trashy, so what is the point in not fucking swearing?'

She has nothing to say to that.

I can't believe this is happening. What did I agree to go on TV for? I didn't have sex with David Beckham or the future king of England, I had a quiet wank on a grotty tube, it should never have turned into this. Why did I think anyone would improve their opinion of me by selling my soul to TV? I should know better than that! I said nothing of any value, I got slammed by my ex-boss, I looked angry, resentful, a bit crazy and now I've only seen to it that this story gets bigger and bigger. It's just a matter of time until 'Please can we talk about me masturbating' is printed on t-shirts and a bestselling ringtone. WHY did I do it? I throw myself back into the sofa and aggressively eat popcorn.

'I'm ruined. That's it. I might as well move to Spain and work in a bar. At least if everyone was speaking about me in Spanish I wouldn't understand what they were saying. I miss my life.'

'You miss *your* life, really?' says my mum, angrily, slamming a bowl onto the coffee table. 'The life you moaned about constantly? The boss you hated? The misogyny in that office? That bloody awful Sophie who you insisted on being friends with your whole life, despite her being terrible to you? You miss how little you used to see Annie? How your main social life was me and your dad? What do you really miss about that, Tara? Tell me?'

'Mum, don't shout at me, I—'

'I might not be the most forthcoming of mothers, but I did not raise you to let the world beat you down. You have fought judgement ever since the day you had Annie, and I stuck by you and we never let anyone tell us that our way was wrong. Now you're just going to allow people to make assumptions about who you are and run away with your tail between your legs because you can't be bothered to fight back? Is that what you want Annie to learn from all this? Really? Get a grip of yourself and find a way to get your life on track that doesn't involve hideous tabloid news stations and sleazy male journalists with terrible hair.' She storms off into the kitchen.

I was not expecting that. After a few moments, I follow her.

'Mum?' I say, putting my arms around her. 'Your popcorn was perfect.'

'Thank you,' she says, and I hug her. After a few minutes, my dad comes back downstairs and joins in. As the three of us cling onto each other in the kitchen, I wonder if I can cling onto any hope. My mother is right; my life wasn't perfect. And if I am honest with myself, I actually don't miss it.

Cam

Cam still feels dreadful. Only two days to go before she can have the abortion, she hopes the relief will be instant. Her body is physically rejecting being pregnant. She's heard of morning sickness, but this is twenty-four-hour. Her boobs are massive and rock hard, and she pees after the smallest sip of water. The entire thing is awful, but she feels more of a solidarity with her body than ever before. It's backing her up, confirming what she already knew; she is not mentally or physically into the idea of being a mum. After this, even the tiniest inkling of doubt will have gone.

The only thing she's managing to keep down are roast-beef-flavoured Monster Munch, so about an hour ago she managed to drag herself to the shop to get seven packets of those. She's currently on her sofa wearing a white Bella Freud t-shirt with 'close to my heart' written on it, and she's about to finish her fourth packet of crisps. Tara's interview just finished on the TV, and Cam feels genuinely sad for her friend, because it was truly awful. Her phone beeps.

Cam, please answer your phone.

It's Mark. This is his twenty-seventh text today and he's called constantly; he is desperate to talk to her but she just can't face it. She's pretty sure he wants to keep the baby, and that he will make her feel bad for not wanting it. She should never have told him. He didn't need to know. She wonders why it matters so much to him. What is it about an egg and a sperm connecting that makes people so emotional? Do they forget, in situations like these, that literally a minute before they found out about the conception they had no desire or intentions to have a child with that person? She understands the baby part, of course, but there *is* no baby yet. It's just a mass of cells, it shouldn't make people lose sight of the reality of what allowing this blob to grow into human form would mean. Yet Mark is willing to change the course of his entire life for it? That doesn't make sense. If he wants kids, doesn't he want to wait until it's with someone he loves? He's young enough not to do this. He sends another text.

OK, that's it, I'm coming over.

Cam quickly gets up and turns off all the lights and the TV. She huddles up under a cashmere blanket and waits for the doorbell to go ballistic. Taking advantage of the twenty minutes it will take him to reach her place, she emails Tara.

Hey, I saw the interview. You must feel shitty. All is not lost, I think I can help you. We can do something through my site? It will all be OK, I promise. Let's discuss tomorrow. Hopefully I won't puke on you . . . I'll explain tomorrow. Can't wait, C x

Scrolling through her emails, there are more from Stella Davies.

Camilla, the day is getting closer. I've got it all planned. Did you know you can do things to help decide the sex of your baby? I want a boy, why? So they never have to deal with the shit I've had to deal with.

My plan is pretty simple. Later this week I will seduce my boss, get pregnant with his child, and get what I want. Just as you said. You use that twenty-eight-year-old for sex, I use my boss for sperm. What is the difference?

Huge, actually.

What you are doing is worse, so don't judge me. I'm not wasting anyone's time, leading anyone on. My plan is a simple transaction. You're just a selfish, heartless bitch. If only the rest of your readers saw what I see.

I hope my child turns out to be nothing like you.

Cam tries not to let it get to her but something about this girl's tone is getting through. She can't work out if she is threatening her or not. She's seems smart, unlike other trolls whose spelling usually shows them up as stupid fools with nothing else to do. But Stella's language is so vicious, so calculated. And what she is doing to her boss, that's so wrong.

Or is it?

Maybe it's Cam that was crazy, for telling Mark about the baby? Is this Stella really hurting her boss by giving him some sex then disappearing without a trace? How can it be cruel if he never knows? By not telling him, she's not hurting him, right? That's accidentally what Tara did, and yes, it wasn't quite as calculated but it all adds up to the same thing, doesn't it?

What you are doing is worse, so don't judge me. I'm not wasting anyone's time, leading anyone on. Why is that line playing over and over in her head?

Cam knows that Mark will struggle with her decision for ages. Her terminating this pregnancy will be something he has to deal with his whole life, because he wants kids and terminations are hard for people who feel that way. If she had never told him, and just done what she knows is right, then he would probably be doing a late-night session in the gym right now, happy as usual with his simple and easy existence. Nasty as Stella seems in her emails, is what she is doing really so crazy if it's what she wants this much? Of course, there is the worrying factor of someone who is clearly this mentally unstable being a mother, but maybe she'll be good at it. Maybe it really is what she needs.

Then the doorbell rings. One continuous brrriiiiiinnggggg. Cam puts her phone on silent and lies down with a cushion over her ear. She knows she has to face Mark and be a decent person at some point, but she can't face it tonight. This is her decision, and nothing can get in the way of it.

An hour and a half later, he eventually gives up.

Stella

Looking into my bathroom mirror, I stare back at my reflection and laugh. A loud, hearty guffaw that erupts like champagne out of a shaken bottle. I have a shaved head. Holy shit.

I hadn't wanted to do it at first, for the obvious reason that I don't really have cancer, and I'm not really having chemotherapy. But then, as I realised I needed to do everything I could to pull off this lie, the idea didn't feel so stupid. And something about the photoshoot, me feeling like a piece of art, Jason looking at me like I was the most beautiful thing in the world, and my need for something to change – something dramatic, something distracting – it all made sense to go through with it. I run my hands over my head. It feels so small, so cold, so odd. I can't believe it's me.

I cut chunks off with scissors, and then Jason wet shaved my head with the razor he keeps at work. It was strange and freaky, but weirdly erotic. I wondered at one point if it might lead to something, like I could have turned it that way if I'd wanted it to. But it wasn't the right time. I have to wait for ovulation, in case it only happens once.

Alice and I used to stand in front of this mirror together and stare at our faces, trying to spot differences that the naked eye could never see. I had an extra freckle on my left cheek, Alice's chin was marginally squarer. But that was it. It was just our natures that set us apart. But now, me and Alice, we are not the same. A stranger would take a minute to identify us as sisters, let alone identical twins. For the first time in my entire life, I look back at my reflection and see myself as my own person. I like it.

I quickly strip off every item of clothing. My naked body is as bald as my head, apart from a dark, dense triangle of pubic hair. If I'm going to do this, I might as well really do this. From a drawer under the sink I retrieve some scissors and a razor. With one foot on the toilet and one on the floor, I begin to chop it away. Every chunk that falls to the ground feels like the old me falling away. I am making space, clearing the way for Jason to penetrate me, feeling like my future is just around the corner. When I'm done, I look at my bald vagina. My childhood feels like yesterday as I remember Alice and I laughing at the first sprouts of pubic hair. We were so innocent then, so unaware of the emotional chaos we were yet to endure.

I want to see that innocence in someone else. My own child. I want to preserve it and protect his heart.

I'm going to nail motherhood. I just know it.

14

Tara

I didn't know what to wear to meet Camilla. It's not a date, of course, but it feels a bit like one. I'm properly nervous. I open my work wardrobe and grab my favourite silk navy jumpsuit, nude wedges and black leather jacket. It's cool, relaxed but sexy. I don't know why I want to feel sexy meeting Cam, but I want her to find me attractive in every way. I want to impress her, for her to admire me. If I wear a good outfit, it might help distract from how nervous I am. I put on some red lipstick. My curly brown hair was so distinctive in the video, so I scrape it back as hard as I can. I look good, I think. And it feels nice to have made a bit of effort.

My experience of Internet dating is that people can present a version of themselves online that doesn't translate in person. I've seen Cam on TV once or twice, and I can't lie, she isn't great. She's a little stiff and awkward, but it's OK, she's a writer, she doesn't have to be a free-flowing, perfectly articulate TV presenter-type. But I hope she is more relaxed with me tonight, otherwise there might be an anxiety overload. She's written a lot about her social issues. I'm expecting her to be lovely, of course, but harder to talk to than write to. I keep telling myself anything is better than Sophie, who was a hot mess of over-the-top, fake love. I'm quite up for the harder-to-get attitude; I think maybe I could trust it more.

My own anxiety is taking some controlling too. I have to remind myself before I walk into the bar that the world has more important things to think about than me, that not everyone will have seen the video, and that behind every door there are not hordes of people waving placards saying 'WANK WOMAN IS IN THE HOUSE'.

When I walk in, I see her sitting in a booth. She is bigger than I imagined. Very skinny, but her shoulders are broad; she has a touch of the Amazonian about her. She sees me and stands up, then walks towards me quickly and puts her arms around me, squeezing me quite tight with her exceptionally long arms. I wasn't expecting that.

'I'm so happy to see you,' she says, holding onto me firmly. It's a really friendly gesture that feels completely impulsive, but the hesitation before she pulls away suggests she isn't quite sure how to follow it up. I help her out.

'It's strange to think this is the first time we've met.'

'I know,' she says, letting go. 'Sorry, that hug was a bit intense. I'm nervous, why is that?'

'I think it's because we really want to like each other. And also that we are both suffering with anxiety disorders. Is it just me or is everyone in here staring?' I look around, there are about seven people in the place, none of them are looking at us, but that doesn't calm me down.

'No, they're not. Come on, come to my booth, it's safe over here.' She takes me by the hand and leads me over. Her hands are big, cold and knobbly. Mine feel fat and hot in comparison. A waiter comes over to take our order.

'I'll get a ginger beer please,' Cam says, 'and what salty snacks have you got?'

'Nachos? They are excellent, they have melted cheese, salsa—'

'Great, two portions of those, please. Tara?'

'Can I get a whisky and Coke please, thanks.' The waiter walks away. 'Ha, if it wasn't you I'd think you were pregnant,' I laugh. 'I lived on ginger beer and salty snacks when I was up the duff.'

Cam opens her huge eyes wide and tilts her head. She looks at me persuasively. It's quite clear what she means by it.

'What? No, really?'

'Yup. The Face of Childless Women is pregnant. You couldn't make it up.'

I don't know what to say. I don't want to presume this is bad news.

'Right, um . . . How are you feeling?'

'Awful. Disgusting, I hate it and can't wait to get it out. I have an abortion booked for tomorrow and I just want it done.'

'Phew. I don't know what went through my head there but I think I would have felt really weird about you keeping it. Shit, sorry, that sounded terrible. Obviously if you wanted to keep it I'd have been all—'

'No, it's fine, it would have been really weird. I'm "The Face of Childless Women", having a baby would have meant that I'd been talking shit, and that would not be cool.'

She's right. I would have been disappointed.

'Can I ask the obvious next question?' I say.

'Whose is it?'

'Yup.'

'The twenty-eight-year-old I've written about.'

'Right, are you going to tell him? Welcome to my specialist subject . . . '

'I did. I told him right away and I regret it. He wants to keep it.'

'Fuck.'

'Yep, fuck. He wants kids; he doesn't seem to care about the scenario under which he has them. I wasn't expecting this reaction from him at all.'

'What's he said? That he doesn't want you to get rid of it?'

'Not exactly. I've been a total bitch since we found out and not spoken to him, it's just the impression I get. He is calling every five minutes, all "Babe, we need to talk about this." I just can't take it. I can't answer the phone.'

I think of Nick at his front door, his pregnant wife behind him, the look of terror on his face as I told him about his six-year-old child. I was right the first time. I wish Cam had asked me what to do. But every situation is different, this isn't something you can give advice about, I suppose.

'He'll be OK. It will be like a breakup; he'll feel all consumed by it then it will just suddenly stop bothering him. Especially as you're not keeping the baby.'

'Exactly. God, who knows what the right thing to do is. I think your way might be right; why does the guy have to know?'

'I guess it's more about the kid than him, maybe. I'll have some big explaining to do one day. I think about that a lot. Also, people who want kids have blinkers on. Every embryo feels like their last chance; they worry that getting rid of it will mean they won't get the opportunity again. It's why I kept Annie. I think that thought terrifies people, makes them crazy.'

'Yeah, maybe. I feel bad for him, but I just can't go there, you know?'

I nod, and our first awkward pause reminds us how bizarre this is. How we don't know each other. How much we want to like each other.

'Hey, speaking of crazy,' Cam says, changing the subject. 'This girl has been emailing me the weirdest stuff. She's so horrible, like really aggressive, mean stuff. But then she also confides in me, it's really bizarre. I'll have to forward it to you, it's fascinating reading. She's got this plan to seduce her boss so she gets pregnant, but she's not going to tell him. She'll just quit her job and he'll be none the wiser. I thought that sounded really cruel until I saw Mark's reaction and now I think, *is* she crazy? Or is she actually really together?'

'I don't know, that all sounds a bit calculated and psychopathic to me. I think getting pregnant accidentally is one thing, but actually going out to deliberately get pregnant by your boss? That's fucked up.'

'Yeah, I suppose it is. Jesus, I think my crazydar is wonky. I've been on the fence about it. Anyway. How are you?' Cam asks as the waiter brings over our drinks. She sucks the entire glass of ginger beer up through a straw and orders another one. 'I could puke on demand,' she adds, burping into her hand. 'And I literally can't stop thinking about doughnuts. Like, I could break into a Krispy Kreme shop and wipe the whole place out. But I won't, I will not give in. Anyway, sorry. How are you coping with everything?'

'I'm OK. Kind of. Not really. The interview was a disaster. It's so annoying because I actually dealt with it really well. I didn't apologise, I stood my ground, but they edited me to look like a total fruit loop. I wish I'd never done it.'

'Yeah, it's going to go one of two ways doing TV. You don't have any control; they can do what they want.'

'I should have known better. That's my world and I feel like I walked straight into a wasps' nest.'

Cam looks at her hands for a second, obviously thinking about what she's going to say next. Her nervousness pokes through sometimes; it's less obvious than I thought it would be but it's there, for sure. Online, she has such honesty and openness, it allows her to say abrasive things without coming across as too spiky. In real life, she's harder. Still kind, still gentle, but the edges are more defined. I get the impression that she has to think about what she says more than she has to think about what she writes.

'I think we can turn this around. I have an idea,' she begins hesitantly, obviously not wanting to presume I'll jump at whatever it is she is about to suggest.

'Go on.'

'My sponsors want me to have some guest bloggers. Mums, specifically. They are worried my desire not to have kids will push away the readers that do. They suggested the kinds of mummy bloggers and Vloggers that give me nightmares, so I wondered if maybe you wanted to do it?'

'Oh, wow. I'm not sure. I mean, I can't write?'

'Yes you can, of course you can. All writing is getting down what's in your head. You've been through a lot, and as a mum, I think my readers would respond really well to it.'

'Really? I'm hardly a beacon of inspirational parenting.'

'It depends how you look at it. *HowItIs.com* has always been about the alternative. My readers want to break free from the shackles of society and do their own thing. My job is to encourage them to do that. You might be controversial to some, but to others, you'll be an inspiration. Raising a kid alone because it's what you wanted? I love that story. God, being a woman can make you feel like you're in a meat factory sometimes. We're supposed to fall in love, get married, have kids. But more and more women aren't doing it that way. They are choosing not to have babies, or finding a way to do it on their own. And I think it's important to promote those alternatives positively. Women can do, and be, whoever they want, and women like you and me can help them do it. Don't follow the herd, you know? Live your life your way.'

I smile at her. That speech sounded just like the voice I

hear when I read her work. That was the Cam I've been following all these years.

'I suppose I could give it a go. You could maybe edit it a bit for me, make sure I haven't said anything stupid, or spelt my own name wrong or anything?'

'Of course, we will get it perfect. What do you think?'

'I think yes, OK, why not?'

'Great! Don't follow the herd,' Cam says, holding her half full glass up to meet mine.

'Don't follow the herd,' I repeat, letting them clink together.

'Will you be OK tomorrow? Do you have someone to pick you up, I could if not?' I ask, knowing the abortion is what she wants, but hoping she has someone to take care of her.

'Yeah, my mum and dad are going to take me. Which is lovely of them but also so weird. Thanks though.' She finishes off a plate of nachos by scooping way too much cheese and guacamole onto one chip. 'You could come over the following night though, if you like? We could discuss your piece, have pizza. I dunno, just hang out?'

'I'd love that. Sure!' I say, slipping on my leather jacket, and wishing away the next two days so I can see my friend again.

As we wait for our taxis, we swap numbers and she texts me her address. We hug as we say goodbye, this time it's much more relaxed. As my car drives away, I feel the huge gap in my life begin to fill up.

Cam

In the cab on the way home, Cam hangs her head out of the back window to stop feeling sick. When she's sure she's OK, she winds the window up a bit and gets her phone out of her bag. Scrolling through her emails, she finds the latest from Stella, the one outlining her plan to get pregnant by her boss, and forwards it to Tara with a note.

Loved tonight. It's made me realise how much I need someone like you in my life. I think maybe I am a bit lonely, although I'd never say that out loud. Sorry if that's cheesy, but it's true. Sleep well, write something for me tomorrow and let's just make this happen. Don't follow the herd . . . I love it!
Cam x
P.S see below, have forwarded email from that girl that's trolling me. I think you're right, she is just crazy!

When the cab pulls up, she rushes to the front door. She can't wait to get into bed. One more sleep until this is over.

As she puts her key in the lock, she hears the footsteps of someone running up behind her. Before she can open the door, he is so close she can hear his breath.

'GET AWAY FROM ME!' she screams, spinning around and using her key to stab him in the face, a trick her dad taught her that she never thought she'd use. The man bends down, pressing his hand into his cheek.

'Fucking hell. Fuck. Why did you do that?' he says, and Cam realises it's Mark.

'Jesus, Mark. It's you. Why did you sneak up on me like that?' she says, going to help him, but he pushes her hand away.

'Because you have been ignoring me for days. You won't answer the door, you won't answer my texts. I just want to talk to you, OK?' He wiggles his jaw from side to side and presses his hand against his cheek. He's clearly in agony. 'I've been waiting here for ages, where have you even been, you never go out?'

'I was with a friend.'

'A *friend*?' says Mark, making presumptions that irritate Cam.

'Yes, a friend,' she says stroppily, then checking herself. She brushes over his jealousy. She's really hurt him. 'I'm sorry, I thought I was being mugged or something.'

Mark checks his hand for blood, there is a little bit but nothing too awful. It could have been a lot worse. They both relax a little physically.

'Oh yeah? Which bit are you sorry about, breaking my heart or breaking my face?'

'Your face, Mark. Jesus! Don't say that.'

'Say what? Anything emotional?'

'I didn't break your heart. Be fair,' Cam says defensively. 'I know you want kids but there is no need to make this more dramatic than it is.'

'"More dramatic"? What did you think this was, Cam?' he asks, like a proper grown-up and not the kid she's always treated him as. 'What do you think happens when two people have a relationship like this, where do you think it goes?'

'I don't know where it goes, it's not about a future is it? It's about two people, getting what they need out of each other.' She realises that sounds harsh. 'In a nice way, obviously.'

'God, you can be so cold. If you don't want the baby, that's your choice, I won't make you keep it. What kind of guy do you think I am?'

'Wow, I suppose I just . . . hadn't thought this was about us, I just thought it was about the baby,' she says, guilt stabbing harder than any attacker on her doorstep could have managed. *He isn't going to try to make her keep the baby?*

'Of course it's about us. Why do you think I've been here at the drop of a hat every time you've asked me to be? You've never come into my life, or even really asked about it, but I dealt with that because I see who you are. I see that you need your space, your own life, and I respect that. But then you get pregnant and you don't ask me anything, you just tell me what you want, what is right for you, and you don't even give me the chance to tell you that I'd do whatever makes you happy. Keep it, or not keep it. Because I love you.'

'Mark, you don't love me. Stop it. We can talk about stuff without being silly.'

'No, I do. I love you. I've never met anyone like you. You live the life you want to live and even though I want to be in it more, I think that's the sexiest thing I've ever seen. I don't want you to change, or be anything you're not. I just want you to be mine, whatever that means for the baby. I just want you to be mine.'

Cam feels winded, guilty, and quite uncomfortable. These high-octane emotional outbursts are not how she works. She doesn't cope well with people putting her on the spot like this; she needs time to think about responses to statements like that. *He loves her*? Where did that even come from?

Rather than give herself a minute to think, she says the things she is preprogrammed to say.

'Mark, look, I'm sorry but that's not how I feel. I didn't realise you felt that way and if I had, maybe I'd have been more sensitive towards it. But I'm not, I don't . . . I'm not looking for a relationship out of this. I'm sorry.'

Mark looks devastated. He's losing the power to keep begging.

'I'm going to go upstairs now, because I am tired and I have a procedure tomorrow that I am nervous about. Go home, Mark. Get some sleep. I'll let you know how tomorrow goes.'

'Do you promise?'

'Yes, Mark, I promise, OK?'

She turns slowly away from him. He doesn't move. Cam puts her key in the lock, opens the door and goes inside. She stands at the bottom of the stairs, as still as she can for around thirty seconds, until she hears his footsteps disappear down the path.

He loves me? she says to herself, walking slowly up the stairs. He just called her cold, but a warm glow is burning deep inside her. *What is it?*

As she climbs up the steps to the door of her flat, that glow turns into a heat she can't ignore.

'Wait, Mark,' she shouts, a change of heart spinning her round too quickly for the narrow stairs. She loses her balance and reaches for the bannister but her grip doesn't hold. Paralysed by the shock of knowing she will fall, her body smashes onto every step. Her neck snaps as she lands heavily in a heap, squashed hard against the front door.

She is killed instantly.

15

Tara

Lying in my bed, I can barely breathe as I read the email from Cam over and over.

But it isn't *what* Stella Davies said that's making me lose control of my lineaments, it's the signature at the end of her email.

PA to Jason Scott @Jason Scott Photography.

The crazy cow has been trolling Camilla from her work email. What am I supposed to do now? I can't believe this. It's like the planets have aligned but then shoved me to the edge of a black hole.

My date with Jason feels like a different person walked into that bar, a lifetime ago. What bizarre and cosmic force is pulling me back into his world?

I want to tell him about this email, but how can I? He quite clearly told me he wanted nothing to do with me, I can hardly text him and say, 'Hey, me again. Look, this is a bit random but I think your PA is trying to steal your sperm.' I could call him, but he'd probably not answer. But I can't let this happen. I mean, this is just wrong. I know Jason wants kids; fathering a child he doesn't even know about could be really, really devastating for him, if he found out. I can't be the one to tell him. But then, how can I ignore this? Maybe I'll email him. But she's his PA; what if she reads his emails?

I have to do something, but what? Maybe it's none of my business and I should just stay away, but my gut is telling me I can't do that. I liked this guy, I don't want this to happen to him. I text Cam.

Wow, you're not going to believe this, but I know Stella Davies boss!

She doesn't reply, maybe she's already asleep. I don't text again; I don't want her waking up to my dramas when she's facing an abortion. Maybe I'll leave something for her while she's getting it done, something nice for when she gets home. I'm sure she said it's at two p.m. I'll get a box of Krispy Kreme doughnuts, she said she can't stop thinking about them. I know she was trying to resist but it might at least make her laugh after a grim day. Yes, I'll do that. I'll do something nice for my new friend.

With that thought, I turn off my light, and fall asleep.

I'll decide what to do about Jason tomorrow.

Stella

I nearly choke on my roasted vegetable and brown rice salad as I read my newspaper. I clear my throat with a glug of cough syrup. *Camilla Stacey, dead? What?*

I grab my phone, almost every news website has written about her. They start with sympathy for her death but almost all move on to lambasting her for lying about not wanting kids.

`The Face of Childless Women was pregnant. So much for the crusade . . .`

Camilla Stacey is being publicly shamed but is too dead to stick up for herself. I can't stop shaking, I feel like if I let myself, I could cry and never stop. But why am I sad? I didn't know her.

But maybe she knew *me*. Did she ever read my emails? I'll never know now. This is so surreal. I feel like a friend died, but a friend I didn't like. I don't want to write big sad messages on Facebook about it, like all Alice's friends did about her. But I feel like I've lost something. I confided in Camilla Stacey, whether she read it or not. Was I too mean? Did she die sad because of me? It's really stressing me out. But I mustn't get stressed; it's bad for fertility apparently. But this is impossible not to think about.

And she was pregnant? Trust Cam, with her perfect life, to end up having a baby too. But then, I guess her life isn't perfect, not any more. I think about that baby, dead too. How horribly unfair. And in some strange way, I feel an extra connection with Cam because today the ovulation test gave me a flashing smiley face, meaning that I have 'high fertility'. That likely means that tomorrow it will have just a smiley face, meaning my chances of getting pregnant are at the highest peak. Just one more day to go, and my plan will come together.

Tara

The smell of doughnuts fills the tube carriage. I can even smell them through the scarf that I have subtly draped over my head. I've obviously gained a little confidence, because I braved the journey with my hair down, but I couldn't bring myself not to cover my face. Especially because the smell of doughnuts was radiating from my lap and people kept looking over at the box, obviously being as tempted by the smell as me. I think about having one, but I could hardly leave eleven doughnuts on Cam's doorstep, could I? Everyone knows you buy six or twelve, I'd just look greedy. Or maybe she'd think it was funny.

NO, Tara, you cannot eat one of Camilla's Get Well Soon doughnuts!

I feel so good about this. It's three p.m., she'll be at the clinic now and I'm going to leave them for her for when she gets back. I considered if it was insensitive, seeing as she was having a pregnancy craving and by the time she gets home she won't be pregnant any more, but I think Cam is more resilient than that, and hopefully she'll treat herself to one after this pretty intense ordeal.

I follow Google Maps to her road, careful not to drop the

box and ruin my lovely surprise. This will be the first of many thoughtful gestures we do for each other, I am sure. This is what real friends do. They don't bog off to Bora Bora in your time of need, what they actually do is drop doughnuts off without stealing any for themselves. As I get to what looks like her house, I am told to step back by a policeman who is on the other side of some yellow tape. There are lots of people around. Police, paramedics, news cameras. Number 11, which I am sure is Cam's house, is completely sectioned off. I must have got the wrong road. I check the address with the policeman.

'Yup, that's it,' he confirms. 'Step back, please.'

I stare at the front door. I can't see in because there are so many people. There's a woman, around seventy years old, with her hands over her mouth, approximately ten feet from the front door, looking in, and silent from shock. A man, around the same age – her husband? – is comforting her, but he can't do it. He falls to his knees and sobs with such volume that the air fills with his grief.

What is inside that door?

A paramedic appears on one end of a stretcher. As it emerges, I see that a body is covered from head to toe under a white sheet. Then I see the second paramedic holding the bed at the head end. They both guide it towards the back of an ambulance.

Who is on that stretcher?

I look at the front door. Number 11. Where is . . .

'CAMILLA!' shouts the woman, suddenly, running hysterically towards the ambulance. The man jumps to his feet to stop her, and they both fall down again, grief overwhelming them as they realise they are helpless.

I drop the box of doughnuts on the ground.

Sitting on the sofa between my mum and my dad, I can't take my watery eyes off the TV as the news about Cam's death breaks. I watch the newsreader, in her pink blouse and perfectly straightened hair, as footage of the scene I was at this afternoon plays in a small box next to her head.

'Camilla Stacey, "The Face of Childless Women", found dead at her home' runs across the rolling news headlines at the bottom of the screen.

The small box turns to a full screen, and a journalist at the scene speaks to camera. It's now dark, but the yellow tape flickers behind him, the front door of number 11 is still open, but the ambulance has gone.

'At around one p.m. this afternoon, blogger and renowned feminist activist, Camilla Stacey, was found dead at her home. It's unknown yet what the cause of death was, but police are currently saying there is no sign of foul play. Ms Stacey was found dead at the bottom of a flight of stairs by her mother and father, who had come to pick her up to take her to lunch, they told police. Paramedics who arrived at the scene say she had been there for a number of hours, and that she would have died instantly from a fatal break of the neck, most likely late last night.'

'This isn't real,' I say, biting my thumbnail, my top lip quivering.

'I'm sorry, love,' says Mum, sitting next to me.

'But she was fine, we were just together last night. How can this happen?'

The journalist continues speaking.

'Camilla Stacey had an enormous fanbase, and although tributes are flooding her Twitter feed, there is also a lot of confusion. Ms Stacey built a lucrative career out of her child-free lifestyle, and her fans have been shocked to discover she was actually nine weeks pregnant. This has left her loyal followers torn by what some people are saying to be an "emotionally corrupt money-making scam". Ms Stacey's main sponsor, L'Oréal, have made this statement.'

A graphic appears on screen.

'We are of course devastated by the news of Camilla Stacey's passing. We were always huge supporters of her blog HowItIs.com. However, we feel it important to say that as a brand we do not endorse, support or approve of misleading our customers.

We were shocked to hear about the pregnancy, and would like to assure everyone that we were not involved in any kind of deceit. We are looking to have all branding removed from the website, and our sponsorship will end here.

Samantha Byron, Head of Sponsorship, L'Oréal.'

'Of course it ends there you retard, she's dead!' I shout, so angry my teeth grate together.

'OK, Camilla, please, watch your language, that word is not OK,' says my mother, rushing to close the living room window in case Mrs Bradley heard me use the 'R' word.

'Sorry,' I say, 'I just can't believe it. This can't be right. She was brilliant, Mum. And yes, she was pregnant but she was booked in for an abortion today. I was taking her doughnuts.'

I drop my head into my hands and they are soon full of tears. This makes no sense. She was my friend.

'I'd never met anyone like that before. She was so fearless, so through and through herself. She was everything she set out to be and more. People like Cam can't die,' I say, trying to make sense of this.

'She sounds a bit like you,' Dad says, putting his arm around me. 'I'm not surprised you got on. She's lucky that she spent the last night of her life with you, love,' he says, squeezing me tightly. He's still wearing the jumper I pretended to knit him. I smile at him as I start to cry again. He shuffles up close and I realise how much a daughter needs her dad sometimes.

Mum sits to my other side and turns off the TV, and the three of us sit in a line on the sofa. They both rub my thighs and pat my back as I bawl with devastation at the death of my friend. When my head is empty of tears and aching from the pressure of my grief, I tell them I need to go to bed.

Helping me into my room, they tuck me in and kiss my head, just as they did when I was a little girl.

'We'll get up with Annie in the morning and take her to school,' Mum says, 'You just rest.'

'Thank you,' I say as she pulls the door closed. 'I love you.'

'We love you too, love. Very very much.'

When the door is shut, I look back at our texts and emails. Cam offered me so much support, and I wanted to do the same for her. Now she's just been snatched from me. What evil twist of fate gives you a person in that way, then just takes them away? Reading through our emails I come to the last one, where Jason's name glows at me from the end of Stella Davies' email, and I wonder if maybe this isn't an act of evil at all. I had wondered what cosmic force had brought Jason back into my life, and now, feeling over-spiritual and like the universe can't just hand you a sign in this way, I wonder if Cam was sent to me for a reason?

That reason being Jason.

Stella

I pee on the stick. A smiley face appears. I am at peak fertility. Today is the day. I've drunk a full bottle of Benylin, eaten a breakfast of high-alkaline fruits, and I've not exercised in two weeks so have put on a couple of pounds.

I'm wearing a shorter skirt than usual, and a low-cut, red vest top underneath a blue cardigan that I'm leaving open. I am conscious of the extra weight, but most of it has gone to my chest so I am maximising on that with a push-up bra. I've kept relatively out of Jason's way all day, knowing that he's so close to finishing his book. I need to pick the moment carefully. He's a sensitive guy, if I get my move wrong, I'll scare him off. Patience is everything; this cannot fail.

I still feel really weird about Camilla Stacey, to think she knew about all this. But I have to focus. I push it to the back of my head.

I take a few deep breaths, go to run my hands through my hair and get the fright I keep getting when I remember that it's not there any more. My image is so much easier to maintain now though – I hadn't realised how much time I spent trying to get my hair right. I put on some lip balm, scoop my boobs up into my bra so they sit nicely on my chest, and I knock gently on his door.

'How you getting on?' I say. I cock a hip to accentuate the curve of my body, just in case he notices.

'One hour, Stella. Come back in one hour and I think I'll be done.'

'You star!' I say, closing his door. I sit back at my desk. How can I pass the time? I Google Cam Stacey again; the *Mirror* have straight up called her a liar. The *Mail* are quoting her fans.

'It's such a betrayal. She made me feel OK for not having a child and now I feel like the one person I looked up to couldn't even bear to be like me. It's made me so depressed.'

'She lied to us all for money. She was a terrible human and isn't around to be held accountable for it. It's not fair.'

'I loved her so much, I'd sent her emails, she even replied a few times. I'm struggling to understand how someone can wear the mask that she did. I really believed that she was who she said she was. I feel so stupid.

Cam replied to someone's emails? That means she definitely read the ones she received. It makes me feel bad to think that she may have died feeling hated. But my emails are nothing on the vitriol Twitter is spouting about her. But did she really lie about not wanting kids for money? I'm numb, I don't know what to think. I can only think about what I'm about to do . . .

*

Finally, an hour has passed. I get a bottle of champagne out of the fridge – the one Phil's parents gave me for my birthday – and two glasses. I tap on Jason's door again.

'Well, can we celebrate?' I ask.

'Hang on, nearly there . . . here it comes . . . OK, *The End* . . . DONE! Fucking hell, I've fucking finished it,' Jason says, exploding with laughter and running over to me, wrapping his arms around me and picking me up off the ground. 'Thank fucking fuck it's fucking over!' he shouts, getting so carried away that he forgets he is handling someone very delicate. 'Shit, Stella, I'm so sorry, did I hurt you?' he says, putting me back down and checking me over for signs of damage.

'No, no I'm totally fine. Well done! I'm proud of you,' I say, going over to his desk, putting down the glasses and opening the champagne. I turn my head away as the cork pops out, and then pour it out.

'Cheers,' we say, holding up our drinks. Jason downs his immediately. 'Fuck me, I want to get hammered,' he says, pointing the glass at me for a refill. I happily top it up, taking tiny sips of mine.

'So, what shall we do to celebrate?' I ask him.

'God, I don't know. I didn't plan anything.'

'Well, lucky I got this champagne then, isn't it?' I say. 'I thought you might need a drink.'

I walk over to his desk and sit on it. His eyes scan over the thigh that I deliberately flash a little too much of. I clock it, and he tries to pretend it didn't happen.

'I wanted to thank you for shaving my head,' I say, 'you

were right, it's way better than waiting for it all to fall out, and I really like it.'

'I like it too, it suits you. You have a lovely shaped head.'

'Thanks,' I say, seductively taking a small sip of champagne. 'Yeah, I feel more comfortable in my skin than ever.' I run a hand up my thigh, drawing attention to that skin. Jason shuffles a little uncomfortably, but his eyes lock onto my leg. I do a huge fake yawn. 'Gosh, this champagne is making me sleepy. I think I need a coffee to go with it, would you like one?' I say, knowing Jason never turns down a shot of espresso. I'll have to act pretty quickly after that, to get the full impact of it in his sperm. As I walk past him to the Nespresso machine, I wiggle my hips, just enough to make him notice.

'Here you go,' I say, coming back in and handing him a double shot. I watch him drink it like I'm murdering him with poison and I want to know he took every last drop. I pour more champagne into our glasses, then take my seat back on his desk, pulling my skirt up a little higher. The game is on.

'It really does suit you, you know,' Jason says, nervously. 'Your hair, I mean, your head.'

He's nervous. Something is in the air. We can't ignore it now.

I offer him a suggestive look and a little smile while I uncross my legs, and run my hands up my thighs. 'Thanks,' I say eventually. 'Why don't you come over here?'

'Stella, what are you doing?'

'What do you mean, "what am I doing?" I just want to congratulate you, that's all. Come over here.'

There is now no doubt what is on my mind. 'Stella, I'm not sure this is a good idea. You work here, and you . . . and your . . . '

'Go on, say it.'

'You have cancer,' he says, matter-of-factly.

'So that means I can't have sex?'

He splutters, as if he thought he knew what I was suggesting, but hoped he might be wrong.

'Jason, I still need sex.'

'I'm sorry, Stella. You're beautiful, but I don't think this is right. I'm going to leave, OK. We don't have to mention this again. Take a week off, I will too now the book is done. Let's just forget this happened.'

He turns to go and I run to him. He will not leave; I won't let him.

'Jason, no. It's OK. We can do this, it doesn't have to matter, it doesn't have to change anything. It's just fun, for two people who probably need a little fun, right?' I'm right up in his face, my chest pushing against his. 'Just a bit of fun?' I say, running my lips over his. It soon escalates into a deep, penetrative kiss where I thrust my tongue into his mouth. He resists at first, but not for long. I take his hand and lead him back to his desk. I lift my top above my head and undo my bra. Like every guy I've ever slept with has ever done, Jason buckles at the sight of my breasts. I've got him, I can tell.

I push my skirt down to the floor, and then my knickers too. My bald vagina surprises him. 'God, Stella, I never thought of you as the type of girl to shave,' he says, before checking himself. 'Fuck. Sorry, is that because of the treatment?' I push a finger against his mouth, as if to make him stop talking. 'So you've thought about my pussy then?' I say, smiling.

'No, I mean I . . . I just mean you don't seem like the kind of . . . '

'Good. Well, now you don't have to think about it. It's all yours.'

I sit back on his desk and open my legs. He has a full view of my vagina and he's looking right into it.

'Come here, Jason. It's OK. It's just sex, we can go back to how we were.' I open my legs even more, giving him the kind of view that few men could walk away from. I'm so close to getting what I need from him.

'Jason, please,' I say, desperately. 'I need this. It could be my last time.'

'Oh God, could it?' he says, grabbing my body and kissing me. For a few seconds I stay here, because it feels so good. His mouth is so soft; the kiss is perfect. But I must stay focused. I want a boy. I quickly flip myself over. 'Take me like this,' I say, pushing my bottom against his crotch. I can feel he is hard. It's seconds away from happening. I rub myself so I come too, just like I read. My orgasm will suck up the male sperm and help them get to the egg first. It's going great. Everything is going great.

Jason unzips his trousers and guides his penis towards me as I spread myself open so he can find his way. I feel the tip touch my skin and just as I'm about to push back onto it we both jump as someone shouts, 'No! Jason, don't enter her!'

'Don't enter her?' *What?* We both turn to see who said that.

'TARA?' Jason and I say in unison.

'Jason, she's trying to steal your baby. I mean, she's trying to have your baby. She wants you to make her a baby. Shit . . . I can't believe I said "don't enter her". Sorry, I wasn't expecting to walk in at exactly that moment, I—' Tara says, holding her hand over her eyes to stop having to see all of the genitals.

'OK,' says Jason, pulling up his trousers. 'What did you say?'

'Sorry, yeah, I didn't explain that very well. Um. So I presume that's Stella, right?' she asks, pointing at me, her other hand still over her eyes.

I nod. There isn't much more I can do. I also pull up my knickers.

'Yeah, that's Stella, how do you . . . and wait, Stella, how did you know this was Tara?'

Uh oh.

'Everyone knows I am Tara, because of the *video*?'

'The video?' he asks her, obviously having no idea what she is talking about.

'Yeah, the video? Of me . . . Wait, you never saw it?'

As Jason explains that he has been on a TV and Internet ban because of his book, I lean down to pick up my skirt, but he shouts and I stand bolt upright again, like a soldier, with my stupid shaved head.

'Stella, why did you— no, wait, Tara, how do you know Stella?' he asks, so confused he scratches his head like Stan Laurel.

'I know her because she's been trolling my friend Camilla Stacey from her work email. I saw the messages myself.'

Jason looks at Tara, then looks back at me. 'Are you two talking in code?'

'I was with Camilla two nights ago, just before she died, Stella,' she says, obviously determined not to cry. 'I saw your last email and where you worked. I had to tell you what she is planning, Jason. This information was given to me; I couldn't ignore it. I know you said you didn't want to see me again but . . . '

'Wait, when did I say that?' Jason says, still looking utterly bewildered.

'When I texted you last week and you replied, saying I'd misread the signs? I mean, if you say so I suppose, but I . . . '

'No I didn't, I haven't had a phone. Some guy cycled into me just as you walked off that night. My phone went down a drain, I only got it back a few days ago and I never texted you because you never texted me.'

The air goes very still as pennies begin to drop. Jason and Tara both turn to look at me. I cover myself as best as I can, but it's pointless, I'm beyond dignity at this point. I want to shut my eyes and just let whatever is about to happen happen so I can leave and hide in my house for the rest of eternity. This has all gone really, really wrong.

'Stella, did you text Tara and say I didn't want to see her even though you knew how I much I liked her?'

How do I get out of this? If I tell the truth, will it go away? I don't think I have any choice.

'Yes,' I say. 'I saw the text and I replied to it and told her you didn't want to see her again. I did that.'

'Why?' Jason asks, looking really hurt.

'Because I wanted to keep her away from you. I needed you.'

'You needed me? Why, because you have cancer? Stella, you had me; I told you I am here for you.'

'Fuck, you have cancer?' asks Tara, looking genuinely concerned, then adds, as if something's clicked, 'Ooh, is that why your . . . ' She tugs on her hair. I just stare back at her. *What am I supposed to say?* I feel my face start to sink into the floor.

'You *do* have cancer, don't you, Stella?' Jason pushes, acknowledging my expression.

I say nothing.

'Stella, do you have cancer?' Jason asks again, firmly.

'No, I don't have cancer,' I burst. 'I lied. I don't have cancer. I haven't had treatment for cancer and yes, I wanted you to get me pregnant, OK? That's it, that's the truth.'

'What the hell kind of person are you?' Jason says, picking up the nearest champagne glass and smashing it on the floor. He looks so angry. I've seen him express so many emotions but never this; I am really shocked by it. I start to cry, pathetically.

'I've been so nice to you; I took care of you. Jesus, I nearly just sympathy fucked you. Why would you make that up?'

'I want to have a baby.'

'Are you kidding me?'

'No. I really, really want a baby,' I say, sobbing heavily now, realising, as I say it out loud, how insane this all sounds. Have I actually lost my mind?

'You let me shave your hair off?' he says, shaking his head. Tara looks at me then looks at him. 'Wow,' she says, realising the extent of my lie.

'Get out. Please. I can't look at you right now. Oh my God, to think I nearly— get out!' Jason yells, pointing at the door. He looks disgusted with me, like he hates me.

I pick my clothes off the floor and edge past him, moving closer to Tara as I reach the door. I have nothing more to lose, so I turn to face him and just let the words flow out of my mouth.

'I don't have cancer, but I have the BRCA gene. It means I have an eighty-five per cent chance of getting cancer and because of how young my mother and identical twin were when they died, the best thing for me to do is have surgery to remove both of my breasts and my ovaries. The doctor told me if I wanted to have a baby naturally, I need to do it now, but I had no one to do it with.'

They are both staring at me, stunned. As the tears pour down my face, I talk quickly, because I have to get this out.

'And you say all the time how much you want kids, but how you can't find anyone either, and I thought maybe we could do it together. But I wasn't even going to tell you, because I knew you'd never love me. I didn't want to trap you, I just thought . . . When I read about how Tara did it, I realised you never even needed to know. It seemed so simple.'

'Wait, what do you mean you read about Tara, when?' Jason asks, looking blindsided again.

'Like, a few days after your date. She was all over the news, Walthamstow Wank Woman. She masturbated on the train after your date and . . . '

'You did what?' he says, looking at Tara.

'I'll explain later,' she says, and they both turn back to me.

'I knew if you saw it you'd track her down, so I kept you off the Internet so you couldn't do that. You had to finish your book.'

'Fuck my book, this has nothing to do with that. You knew how much I wanted to see Tara. Jesus. I was in bits after that date and you just left me to suffer. You could have got sperm from anyone if that's all you wanted, you selfish, selfish b—'

He stops himself.

'I'm sorry. I think maybe I'm really fucked up,' I say in a small voice.

No one says anything.

'You're fucking crazy,' Jason says, softly, as it all sinks in. 'Stella, leave my studio now and don't come back. I never want to see you here again, understood?'

'But Jason, I—'

'Stella, you're the worst person I've ever met. Get the fuck out my studio, right now.'

I do as I am told, and leave.

Tara

Jason and I stand in silence. It's hard to know exactly what to say after something like that. I'm trying not to think about what I saw. He's not my boyfriend, he didn't know this was happening. He was free to sleep with who he wants. But no, that is not how I wanted to see his penis for the first time, about to enter another woman's . . .

'Thank you,' he says, finally.

'That's OK. I wasn't quite sure what would happen if I came. I certainly didn't expect that.'

'Look, nothing happened, OK? I mean, a little bit happened but honestly, you got here just in time,' he says, shaking his head and rubbing his face, obviously really embarrassed.

'Hey, don't worry. I've had my fair share of being embarrassed too. It's not your fault, I get it,' I say, knowing that is the right reaction, and feeling like maybe it cancels out a little of my own shame.

He pours some champagne into a glass and gives it to me, then gets a mug and pours some for himself. Then he goes over to the window and gazes outside.

'Are you OK?' I ask.

'Not really,' he says, still staring out the window. 'I don't know if I feel stupid, or if I'm angry, or if I just feel really sorry for her. Maybe it's a mix of all three. She must have pulled hair out of her head. What agony must someone be in to do something like that?'

'A lot.'

He thinks for a minute, then turns to me. 'I'm sorry about your friend that died. That's really sad.'

'Thanks, I'm not sure it's hit me yet,' I say, wondering what the grief will feel like when it really does. Will it be easier because I only met her once? Or harder because I never got to know her as I should?

'It's really nice to see you again, Tara. I'd started to think it would never happen.'

'Yeah, me too. When you didn't text back I didn't know what to think. I couldn't see how I'd got it so wrong.'

'You didn't get it wrong. Literally as soon as you walked away this arsehole banged into me and I lost my phone. I wanted to text you, but when I eventually got my phone back your number wasn't there. I guess now we know why. God, she worked really hard at keeping us apart.'

'I presumed you'd seen the video and thought I was a hooker after all.'

'OK, so what is this? This is what I'm not getting. Wank Woman? Stella's friend mentioned it, I thought it was a TV show or something. It's you? Is that what you meant when you said you worked in TV?'

I can't believe he hasn't seen it. To think that all this time I have been creating a narrative where he thought I was crazy.

'OK, well my life changed that night, in every way. You got me so horny that I masturbated on the train. When I opened my eyes some creep was filming me and by the time I got to work on Monday I was a global Internet sensation. I honestly don't know how you missed it.'

'I've been on an Internet ban. Now I know why Stella was so militant. Fucking hell.' He looks sad again, but then his eyes light up and my stomach flips.

'I'm totally watching it now though.'

'No, please. We don't have to. Watch it another time, not now.'

'Look, today couldn't get any weirder. I have to watch it at some point, let's just get it over and done with,' he says, getting into Stella's computer which is still on her desk. I try to deter him but then think, *if I can sit through watching this with my mum, I can watch it with Jason*. At least then it will be done.

'OK, search "Walthamstow Wank Woman",' I tell him, cringing inside. This is worse than my dad seeing it.

When it comes up, he presses play.

'Holy shit,' he says when it ends, his eyes popping out of his head. 'Wow, nearly seven million people have seen you masturbate?'

'Yup.'

'That's made me feel better about you seeing me . . . nope, I have no idea how to word what you saw.'

'Aim your penis at your bald assistant's vagina so she could steal your sperm?'

'Yeah, that. Christ.'

'I think we're equal. OK, not equal; half the world didn't see what you did.'

'True, but hey, at least you looked hot. It's really good to see you again, Tara. I know I only met you once but I really missed you.'

Is he for real?

'I missed you too,' I say back, meaning it.

And then, despite just having watched me do what the rest of the world seems to think is the greatest act of sluttitude imaginable, he kisses me.

At eight a.m. we wake up wrapped in a huge black curtain in the middle of the studio floor. Our bodies fit together so perfectly, I wonder how it's possible I ever thought he didn't care. We drank everything there was in the studio to drink last night, and screwed on everything there was to screw on. God knows what time we fell asleep; I know we talked for hours.

'Fuck!' I shout, suddenly realising I am a mother and that I live with my parents. 'Annie!' I grab my phone and text Mum. I've got five missed calls; she must be worried sick.

Mum, I'm so sorry. I'm absolutely fine. Is Annie OK? I'll be home soon, sorry sorry xxx

She texts back right away.

Ok, love. Just dropping Annie at school. I'll tell your dad you were with Sophie, shall I? x

I don't reply. I am forty-two. All my mother and father need to know is that I am fine.

Jason gets up to make coffee and I lie back down. I look around his studio. Huge prints of his photographs adorn the walls. I know them all well; I've looked at them on his website so many times in the last couple of weeks.

'So, who was Camilla?' he asks, bringing me coffee, still putting the pieces of all this together. I sit up and rest my back against the wall, he lies down on the curtain next to me.

'Camilla Stacey. She had a blog, *HowItIs.com*. She was amazing, one of those writers who laid herself on the line. People loved her, I loved her, and she died a couple of days ago. She fell down the stairs after I'd been out with her. I still can't . . .'

I put the coffee beside me and cover my face with my hands, and tears just come. 'She became an icon for women who couldn't have or didn't want children, but she was pregnant. She was booked in for an abortion, she told me. But now she's being held up as some scam artist, a liar and it's just not true.'

'So you were good friends?'

'Actually it was the first time we'd met. But she'd written a piece sticking up for me and we'd been emailing loads. I felt like I'd known her forever and then that was that, she's gone. I just wish I could help her like she helped me. But she's dead, so I can't.'

'Maybe you *can* help her. You could write an article sticking up for her? Telling people how she wasn't going to keep the baby?'

'I can't write it. Not in a way that would do her justice, anyway. And who would publish it? If I send it to a newspaper they'll have a field day with it. I'll get edited to look like a right twat again.'

I nestle up close to him, lay my head on his shoulder and gently curl his chest hairs around my finger. I can feel his heart beating. I remember something Cam said in an email. How her dad told her to turn life in her favour. 'Don't hide, keep your head up and keep your eye out for a way to spin this in a way that works for you.'

Keep your eye out for a way to spin this in a way that works for you.

An idea strikes me. Maybe I *can* help her.

'Hey, does that camera do video?' I ask Jason, sitting up quickly and pointing at a professional-looking camera that's on top of a tripod.

'Yup, it does everything. Why? You want to make a sexy film with me?'

'No, I think I'm done doing anything sexual on camera. But there is something I'd like to record. Will you help me?'

'Of course.'

I get up, put my clothes on, and move a stool between the camera and a white backdrop that is set up in the middle of the studio. I grab my handbag, and in a mirror on the left hand side of the room, I tidy up my hair, put on some foundation, a little blusher, some mascara and some pink lip gloss.

'How do I look?' I ask him, needing a little reassurance.

'Well, you've got sex hair, but you're gorgeous. What are we filming?' he asks, turning his camera on.

'My story,' I say, as I adjust some lights and set up my scene. 'Camilla said that I could write it and that she'd publish it on her site, but that's not going to happen now. She made me feel so certain that saying something in my own words was the best way to put this all to bed, and I still think I should do it. But I'm going to do it my way, on film.'

I take a seat on the stool and ask him to take a picture so I can see the shot.

'OK, who is the photographer here?' he jokes.

'You are, and I am the documentary maker. Don't argue.'

When I see the photo I jump off the stool, drag in another light to make it perfect.

'Are you always this lively in the morning?' he asks, nervously.

'I have a child. The mornings are the liveliest part of the day. Come on, let's do this before I chicken out.'

'OK, boss.' He looks down the lens, then back at me. 'Perfect,' he says, clicking *record* and stepping back. 'Go for it, Wank Woman.'

I laugh. I mean, it *is* funny.

I straighten my face and look down the lens. Here goes.

'Hi, I'm Tara Thomas, but you probably know me as Wank Woman. It's OK, you can laugh, that's what a lot of other people have been doing at me for the last few weeks. Either that or calling me disgusting, perverted or sick in the head. The truth is, I'm none of those things.

Three weeks ago on a Friday night, I had just been on a date. It was so great that I didn't want to mess it up with a drunken one-night stand, so I went home alone. Despite my good intentions, when I was on the train I found myself feeling horny, and seeing as the carriage was completely empty except me, I decided to do something about it. If you're watching this, you know what happened next.

By 9 a.m. Monday morning I was a global Internet sensation. By Thursday I had lost my job, been arrested (they didn't charge me) and had such a severe panic attack in my local Tesco that I ended up in hospital. I then did a horrible TV interview on *Sky News* where I refused to apologise for what I had done, so I got edited to look like a sex-crazed maniac.

Now I live with my parents again, my child has called me Wank Woman numerous times, and other mums at the school gate think I'm awful. But I'm not awful. So here I am to tell you about who I really am, and what the last few weeks have been like for me.

They've been shit. Really, truly and fully shit. I've not only been judged for my actions on the train that night, but also for the way I had my little girl. I had a one-night stand, and I never told the guy I was pregnant, and there are a lot of people out there who think that's a terrible thing to do.

But I think it would have been more terrible to force that man into having a child that he hadn't intended to have. I did what was right for me, my daughter and him at the time. And until the world judged me for it, our situation was absolutely fine. I'm a very good mother, and that is the last time I'm ever going to explain myself about the way that I chose to have my daughter.

So that's my story, but there is someone else I want to talk about today too, Camilla Stacey. If you didn't know Camilla Stacey's work, then you've probably heard of her now because she just died and the media is making her out to be a liar because she wrote relentlessly about not wanting kids, and at the time of her death she was indeed pregnant.

For the record, to all those people saying that Camilla Stacey was a money-grabbing fake, she was booked in for an abortion the next day. She was everything she ever said she was. And it's not fair that what happened to me in life, should happen to her in death. She doesn't deserve to be shamed. To all her fans, be reassured, Camilla didn't lie to you. She found out she was pregnant late, and she wasn't going to keep it.

As for me, I am not taking this any more either. I will not be forced into submission by a judgmental society that is full of hypocrites. I will not apologise because I am a mother, and

I certainly won't apologise because I'm a woman. I would be more ashamed if my daughter grew up to see me destroyed by this, than by her seeing that stupid video of a snapshot of my life that does not, and will not define who I am.

Thank you for watching.'

You could hear a pin drop in the studio, as Jason lets the camera roll long enough for him to get out of whatever trance he's gone into. 'Wow,' he says, when he's ready. 'That was amazing.'

'Thanks,' I say, feeling pretty good about it.

'Shit though, isn't it, that because she'd said she didn't want kids she was held accountable. Like if she had changed her mind, and did want to have them, that would have been completely unacceptable. I'd hate to be a woman.'

He's right, I hadn't even thought of it like that. Who says a woman can't change her mind about having kids?

'I can't believe you're my girlfriend,' Jason says, coming over to me on the stool and opening my legs with his hips.

'Hey!' I say, trying to act cool. 'You can't just decide I am your girlfriend and then tell me without asking.'

'You want me to ask you? What is this, the Fifties? OK. Tara, will you be my girlfriend?'

I suddenly start laughing. The ridiculousness of all this just struck me.

'What, what's so funny?' Jason asks, a little offended.

'We have only met twice. I mean, what the hell?'

'Shit, really? I suppose we have. Weird, huh?

'Yeah, weird.' I kiss him, that doesn't feel weird at all. 'Yes,

Jason. I will, I will be your girlfriend. Now give me the camera card, I want to get that video out there before I change my mind.'

I sit at Stella's computer and log in to my Twitter account. I now have 759,000 followers. As I upload the video to YouTube, I imagine all of those people's joy when they see that Wank Woman has finally broken her cyber silence. I suppose this could go one of two ways, but what does it matter now if it goes against me? Jason isn't judging me, my parents love me, and Annie is happy and healthy. I think of Cam, unable to say these things herself, and no matter what is in store for me, I owe it to her to get this out there.

When the video is loaded, I copy and paste the link.

'OK,' I say, looking at the screen and exhaling as I type, 'I am Tara Thomas, and this is my story' into Twitter.

'Here it goes . . . '

'Do it!' says Jason.

I press SEND.

16

Ten Days Later

Tara

Wearing a black, sleeveless dress, I sit at my own kitchen table and wipe away the last of my tears. Today was rough. It was Cam's funeral, and I've never seen so many grown people cry in one room. All three of her sisters read poems, her nieces and nephews sang a song, her mother and father, whom I recognised from that horrible afternoon outside her house, held each other and sobbed the whole way through. I snuck in at the back, not wanting to make a scene, but I needed to be there to say my goodbyes to Cam.

I'm not a religious person, but despite the sadness of her death, since becoming friends with Cam my life has only gotten better. It's like she gave me something, a piece of herself, that she couldn't live without. I've felt so connected to my own existence since she died;. my perspective on everything has changed. I watched Cam's family in the church and realised that no matter how big your life is, how far you spread your wings, when it comes down to it, it's a tiny unit that really matters. As long as that is strong, so are you. I have my tiny unit, and I feel pretty indestructible right now.

It's been so confusing, knowing that I only met her once, but feeling the sadness I do. But the truth is, sometimes you just love people right away. It doesn't matter how many times you look them in the eye.

I log on to Twitter. It's such a symbol of the frivolity of society. Two weeks ago I was a hated icon of irresponsibility, now I'm a hero for standing my ground. The world flips and changes constantly; the best we can do is remain ourselves. My refusal to bow down has won me the love of a public who tried so hard to destroy me when they thought I was weak. I should hate them, but the positivity is like a drug. I can't stop reading the tweets.

The video I made has been viewed by nearly three million people. Now, rather than rape threats, I'm getting marriage proposals. And rather than being slammed as some psycho, I am being hailed as a feminist hero for not apologising for my sexuality.

But maybe the thing that I am most proud of, is that almost every newspaper that wrote negatively about Camilla has written something to the contrary since my video went live. They had to admit that they were wrong to make assumptions about Cam's pregnancy, and that she planned to keep the baby and deceive her fans for money. The whole thing has opened up conversations about abortions, cyber abuse, a woman's right to change her mind. I hope that somewhere Cam is watching it all, because she'd absolutely love the shit storm she created, especially the bit about her being proved right.

As I scroll through my tweets, allowing the compliments and support to go to my head, one in particular grabs my eye.

@TaraThomas123 hello Tara, my name is Susan and I work for L'Oréal. We sponsored Camilla Stacey's blog. Can you DM me your email so I can get in touch. Thanks.

I do it instantly. And within five minutes, an email from Susan Jeffries appears.

Dear Tara
Thanks for sending me your email address. I've been wanting to get in touch for a few days, but I'm sure the sheer volume of appreciation you are getting on Twitter means you missed my tweets.

A little about me . . . I used to be Head of Sponsorship at L'Oréal UK, until I got offered the chance to do the same job in NYC. I took it, but the person doing my job was dreadful (totally unprofessional to say that but she's gone, so who cares), and they begged me to return. I get back to London next week. One of my proudest brand partners when I was here was Camilla Stacey; I loved her writing and was so happy when she chose L'Oréal to be her primary sponsor. When I heard about her death I couldn't believe it, I still can't. We lost a legend.

I've been sitting here mulling over how L'Oréal can continue to promote such a positive attitude to being female, and since watching your video I've been trawling through your back catalogue of work. The shows you have made are fantastic, and it's given me an idea.

I find myself with a large chunk of budget now available and I'm wondering where best to place it. Tara, would you consider setting up a digital TV channel, sponsored by L'Oréal, where you would produce one-off and mini documentary series, all inspired by real women's stories?

I'm sure you are being inundated with offers, so have a think and let me know. I'll be anticipating your response.

Best wishes,

Susan.

Holy shit! I don't want to look desperate, so I give it all of thirty seconds before I respond.

Dear Susan

Thanks for getting in touch. This sounds very interesting, we should absolutely discuss. Perhaps we should schedule in a meeting?

Tara

I send it, then wonder why was I so formal? She basically just offered me my dream future and I am acting like I'm on *The*

Apprentice. I smile and look up. This is Cam again, I know it. I send another email to Susan.

Susan, excuse my previous response to your email. This is how I really feel...

FUCK, YEAH – I'D LOVE TO!!

Thanks, Tara!

Seconds later, she replies.

WONDERFUL! OK, well I really want you to lead this. It would be good to get an idea of a few stories you would like to cover, just so I can run it past the big guns here and get final sign off. So . . . any ideas?

I think for a minute. And then it hits me.

Susan, I have the perfect subject. Give me twenty-four hours x

Stella

I stand in the bathroom with thirty painkillers in my right hand, and a glass of water in the other. I am disgusted with myself. The only thing stopping me swallowing the pills is the thought of what my mother and Alice would say if they knew what I was going to do. If I kill myself and there is such a thing as an afterlife, they'd never speak to me again. I have the chance to live, something neither of them had. The faint nagging of logic is what makes me pour the pills back into the bottle for the third time today.

The last week has been my darkest. I haven't even left my front door. I even asked the Tesco delivery man to leave everything on the step, and signed the receipt by having him pass it through the letterbox. I don't want to see anyone. I'm not ready to face the world.

What did I become? I look in the bathroom mirror, and see my hair is growing back. I may look like a soldier, but I feel like a victim of war. Dismemberment, or death? Are they really my choices? What a bleak existence.

The doorbell goes and I freeze. I don't care who it is. It rings again.

I push myself into the corner of the bathroom; it feels safer here than the middle of the room. Whoever it is, they are banging now, and calling my name through the letterbox. It's a woman's voice. I recognise it. I move slowly out into the hall.

Tara

'Come on, Stella. I know you're in there,' I say, peering through her letterbox, not actually knowing if she is in there. The lights are off, but I sense her inside the flat, in that weird way you know that someone is watching you when you're asleep.

'Stella, it's Tara. Wank Woman. Come on, don't make me say that again.'

She appears at the end of a corridor, making me jump. She's wearing a white, off-the-shoulder t-shirt and black leggings. Backlit, with her shaved head, she looks really scary. She has something of the Britney Spears about her, circa 2007. But as our eyes meet I see a hint of genuine fear in her eyes; the same fear I saw in Jason's studio.

'What are you doing here?' she says nervously, about six feet from the door.

'I have your laptop. I thought you might want it back?' I say, pleased I have an excuse to talk to her. Jason wanted to keep it as evidence in case she burnt the studio down, or tried to kill him. But I assured him she'd done all the damage she intended to do.

'Come on, it can't be fun cooped up in here having to read *MailOnline* on your phone,' I say, smiling, and move my face up so that she can see my grin through the letterbox. She walks closer to the door, and eventually opens it. She squints as daylight floods over her face, making me question if she has left the house for days.

'Look, if you're here to have a go at me you don't need to, OK? I know what I did was wrong,' Stella says, calmly, but with a strength that tells me she's taken enough and will slam the door in my face if I say the wrong thing.

Up close, I can see that she's tired, her eyes are bloodshot and her skin is shining from a film of grease. That was pretty much me a few weeks ago.

'I'm not going to have a go at you, OK? I promise. Can I come in?'

She steps aside, and as I brush past her, I feel nervous about her shutting the door.

We go into the living room and she makes no effort to clear up the mess. There are coffee cups on the floor, and dirty plates with half-eaten pieces of toast on the sofa. It feels all too familiar to me. *The Jeremy Kyle Show* is on the TV.

'You have a gorgeous place,' I say, looking around. Despite the mess, it really is lovely. 'Have you left the house since last week?' I ask her, taking a seat. She stands at the door with her arms crossed, and I wish I hadn't sat down.

'No, I have nowhere to go. I saw your video. Talk about turning it around,' she says, and I think she might be warming to my visit. But then she snaps, bluntly, 'What are you doing here?' proving she isn't.

I planned to build up to this, but something tells me I might get asked to leave in any minute, so I need to just spit it out. But the smell is making me feel sick, and the lack of light is freaking me out.

'Can I open the curtains?' I ask her. She nods, shamefaced.

I get up and pull the curtains open, and also open a window. The fresh air rushes in and I feel some tension leave the room.

'Stella, I have an offer for you,' I say, confidently.

'An offer? What? You want me to leave the country or something?'

'God, no, I . . . no, I don't want you to leave the country,' I say, surprised she even suggested I would come here and demand that. 'No, I want to make a documentary about you.'

She looks instantly enraged. She uncrosses her arms and storms towards me.

'What, do you think I'm some freak show? What the fuck do you mean, a documentary about me?' Woah, the hair, the anger; I feel like we are being sucked into the TV and Jeremy Kyle's bodyguard will have to get her off me. Without asking permission, I turn it off.

'Just that. You, your story. I should hate you after what you did but when you made that little speech at Jason's studio it resonated with me. I haven't experienced the loss that you have but I understand the isolation, and I get why you wanted a baby. I used to feel the same way; it's why I had Annie the way I did. You're right, having a kid is a reason to live. I get it, I think. I mean, the way you went about it was fucking crazy, but I get it. I nearly lost my mind when that video went viral; Annie, my mum, my dad, they are the only reason I kept my shit together. If I'd have been alone, I don't know what I would have done. I'd probably still be in my flat, cooped up, watching daytime TV, like you are.'

'You don't understand what it's like to lose a twin,' she says, angrily. I persevere.

'You're right, I have no idea. I can't even begin to imagine. But I do understand what it's like to lose a part of yourself. What has happened to you over the course of your life, what you are facing now, it's a legit reason to go crazy for a bit. I understand why you lost it.' I pause before I say this again, nervous of potential violence. 'That's why I think we should document your journey from here on. The surgery, you rebuilding your life after grief.'

'"My journey from here on"? You want to document me having my breasts and ovaries removed? Oh yeah, great TV, a real feelgood watch.'

'But it's more than that, isn't it? You can talk about what you've been through.'

'On TV? Are you kidding me?'

'No, I'm not. And actually, it's not on TV, it would be through my website. We would have control over it, you can say whatever you want. Your struggle is real. I think you could really inspire people.'

'Wait,' she says, looking less hostile now. 'Since when did you have a website?'

'Since now. L'Oréal, who used to sponsor Camilla, have said they'll fund an online channel of mine. I'm going to make short films and mini-series about women who live extraordinary lives. I want to launch it with you.'

Stella puts her head down. I must have said something that's upset her.

'I didn't hate Camilla, not really,' she says, slowly. 'It just made me feel better, to make someone else hurt like I was hurting. Her life seemed perfect compared to mine. I got addicted to it, I guess. I'm not proud of it.'

'And I think we should talk about it in the film,' I say, meaning it.

'Oh yeah right. What would I be, The Face of Trolling?'

'No, because you will tell the truth as to why you did it. I got trolled so badly and I thought the people writing the messages were pure evil. But now I see it for what it is. You've changed how I feel about online abuse, it will never hurt me like it did, because now I get it. The only reason to do that to someone is because of the misery in your own life. My trolls don't really hate me, their words aren't real, and I think we can tell that story.' I walk over to her. 'I'm not looking to make a programme that vilifies you, Stella. I'm looking to make a programme that shows how life can come close to destroying you, but that anyone can get themselves out of a hole.'

'I read all of Camilla's articles about not wanting kids again. I think maybe I've got a different mindset now, but they made me feel better about it. I'm accepting it, I suppose. I should have read them properly the first time around,' she says, nervously picking off the remnants of nail polish from her fingernails. 'I guess in some ways, these programmes could be my legacy?' she says, looking at me, obviously coming round to the idea. 'Proof of my life, something to leave behind other than this mess?'

I nod. 'Exactly.'

'OK, I'll do it,' she says, showing me her smile for the first time since I met her.

'Thank you. I'll help you get your life back on track, I promise.'

I stand to leave and she walks with me to the front door. 'I'll be in touch, OK?'

'OK. In the meantime, open the curtains, clean the plates. Go for a walk. I've done this housebound thing and it's no good. You're going to be OK,' I say. 'It's all about making the right decisions, you know, like Cam said. She was right.'

Stella nods. 'How's Jason?' she asks, looking nervous to mention his name.

'He's pissed off. Understandably. Oh, and he needs the passwords for his phone and computer to unblock him from the Internet. Can you email them to him? I wouldn't hold out for a reply though, not yet, but he'll come round eventually, I think. He knows what you're going through is hard. I think you probably need to find a new job though.'

'Yeah, I guessed that. I think I need to just focus on myself for a while anyway. I'll book the surgery, and start with that.'

'Good girl. I'll get you some money for doing the filming, and you never know, it might be really successful and you end up being "The Face of Boobless Women". Who knows where that could take you!' I laugh, then feel sick at what I said. 'Jesus, I am sorry, that was *so* inappropriate.'

'No, don't. I liked it. "The Face of Boobless Women", it's got a ring to it.' She smiles, and the fear in her eyes seems to have gone, at least for a moment.

'OK, I'll leave you now. I'll be in touch soon, OK? I'll get your number from Jason, I'll call and we'll talk, yes?'

'Yes. So what's your website called?' she asks, a beam of excitement coming from her.

'Don't Follow the Herd,' I say. 'It's for women who do things their own way. Like us.'

'I like it,' she says as I walk away.

I can't wait to tell Susan we're on.

Six Months Later

Tara

I'm so excited to tell her, that I call while I'm cooking breakfast.

'Stella, it's me. I watched the footage, it's unbelievable. Honestly, the bit where you come around from the anaesthetic and say "How do they look?" is one of the sweetest things I've ever seen on screen. You're going to be so proud,' I say, meaning it.

'Oh my God, I'm nervous to see it,' she says, but I know she can't wait.

'Look, it's surgery, some bits are hard to watch but the way that doctor just whipped out your breast tissue, then slid in your new boob. I mean, it's just amazing what they can do. How are you feeling?'

'I feel good. I managed a walk today, I got my hair cut. I'm just so relieved it's done. I wish I'd done it years ago. When does this episode go out?'

'End of next week. The last one has had nearly two million

viewers, this one might break the Internet. They love you, they love your honesty. Do you need anything? I can drop in later with some food if you like?' I offer, not loving the idea of her being alone.

'No, I'm fine, thanks though. I'm going to go and see Jessica and the baby.'

'Oh yeah, how you feeling about that?' I ask, worried this could be a trigger for her.

'Honestly? She was in labour for fifty-eight hours, had seventeen stiches in her vagina and anus. I feel like I got off lightly.'

'Ha! That's the spirit. OK, call me later, love you, bye.'

I hang up and I drop the phone in the frying pan.

'Mmm, fried phone, my favourite,' Jason says, coming back from dropping Annie to school. I get my phone out of the pan with a spatula, and put it on a tea towel.

'I messed up the eggs. Toast?'

'They're not the eggs I'm after anyway,' he says, kissing me and putting his arms around my waist.

'Don't forget what the doctor said; I'm old, this could take a while.'

'I know, so let's enjoy the practising,' he lifts me onto the work surface, and lifts up my skirt. My phone rings. Still with the spatula in my left hand, I answer it. My hand and ear are now covered in grease.

'Vicky!'

'Oh, hey, boss. So I've done pretty well on pinning down that woman you read about in *Grazia*. The one who was a part of that cult for years and none of her family knew? She's running her own retreat in the Hebrides, she left the kids with her man in London. She's really something; I can't work out if I like her or not. Perfect fodder for *DontFollowTheHerd*. Thought maybe I could go up and meet her at the end of the week? Wouldn't mind getting away from the kids, to be honest.'

'Yeah, sounds great. Do it. Good work.'

'Thanks, boss!'

I offered Vicky a job as soon as L'Oréal sent me the contract. I had to give in and admit that her ideas were really good. She's actually one of the best researchers I've ever worked with. Who knew?

'Sorry, Jason, what were we saying?'

'You were saying you were old, or something really sexy like that.'

'Oh yes,' I say, as he pulls my knickers off and throws them over his shoulder.

I drop the spatula on the floor.

Acknowledgements

This wouldn't have happened had it not been for the brilliant Sarah Benton. Having worked together on my last two books, Sarah moved over to HarperCollins and told her new team about me. I then got invited in and offered a two-book deal. I love writing and I'm delighted to be published by anyone, but HarperCollins was always my dream, so thanks Sarah, I hope I did you proud!

Next up is my editor Kimberley Young. Kim pitched to me with Sarah, and there was an element of 'if you choose to go with us' about the first meeting. I may have played it cool, but it took all my efforts not to straddle her and scream 'YES' right there and then. Kimberley's patience over the past two years is something for which I am very grateful. It turns out promising a novel nine months after the birth of your first child is, in my case anyway, a little ambitious. The delivery date (the book's, not the child's) moved back and back until I got enough of my brain back to write the book we both love. Thank you Kimberley, if you had been an arsehole about it, this might never have happened. I hope I did you proud too!

Then to my agent, Adrian Sington, who as always takes great care of me and remains passionate about my work. Thank you thank you!

And to all at HarperCollins who put this together. From cover design, to PR and marketing to correcting my spelling. What a team!

OK, now for the personal ones . . . I'd like to thank every single one of my friends who dealt with me going on and on about the struggles of writing. To those who wanted to go and have fun, but who had to set aside their joy to listen to my anxiety issues. Every moan, every chat, every time I said 'I CAN'T DO THIS' got me to the point where I did it. So thank you. My friends are the best! There are many of you, but a few in particular to mention are . . . Jo Elvin, Johnny and Michelle, Mel and TJ, Mamrie, Louise, Carrie, Mary Moo and my sister Jane.

Thanks to all the women who write and think and put themselves out there, it's so important that we do. I'm not going to write a list of who you are, but I will give a shout-out to Polly Vernon, who wrote her view and then got told to shut up about it. Your book was really useful with putting Cam together, don't shut up. So on that note, can we all stop telling women to shut up? It's really great that there are lots of different ways to be a woman, and many ways to feel about being female. We should try to accept them all. Apart from a small few, but again, I won't list them either.

And now on to my heart . . .

Chris, you're the best. The best husband, the best dad, the best date, the best mate. You also, very gracefully, handled a couple of my meltdowns, and for that I say thank you. Your support is ridiculous. My love for you is ridiculous. For a big, juicy self-doubting writer, I feel immensely secure because of the life I come home to after a day of pulling my hair out and climbing up walls. Thanks for all of the love and the things and the joy. And of course, for Art . . . the little nugget that changed my life. Who came out of me so effortlessly (I'm lying) and who turned out to be the best baby ever (that bit is true). Little Art, you gave me less hours in the day to do anything else but you gave me more love than I ever imagined. My little guy. With the best cheeks. I love you so much it hurts, but stop throwing your food on the floor. That shit drives me mental.

Thanks to anyone I didn't mention who feels they should have been. These acknowledgements could have gone on for pages. That's the truth. Writing is a solitary experience in many ways, but very often it's the support around you that gets the job done. So, thanks!